I0675452

The Souls of the Fire Dragon

John Wrieden

Published in 2009 by New Generation
Publishing

Copyright © Text John Wrieden

First Edition

The author asserts the moral right under the
Copyright, Designs and Patents Act 1988 to
be identified as the author of this work.

All Rights reserved. No part of this
publication may be reproduced, stored in a
retrieval system or transmitted, in any form or
by any means without the prior consent of
the author, nor be otherwise circulated in any
form of binding or cover other than that which
it is published and without a similar condition
being imposed on the subsequent purchaser.

Prologue

". . . And now for the evening news," said the announcer from the Ordinea state television channel. He spoke with a clear Ordeanian accent as he introduced the Tuesday night broadcast. The catchy uplifting music started. Pictures of people and places came scrolling across the screen, ending in a crescendo of music and the standard shot of the Patrician looking out and down at the viewers. Janine and Aldon Avandates sat in silence as the main headlines came and went. Aldon as usual simmered with anger; like many others, he felt tyranny was killing the city. Time for change, Aldon thought, though he dare not say it to anyone, not even his wife.

"Will you listen to that, the injustice?" said Aldon, as they watched a youth being beaten by four men clothed in black. "All that for free speech."

"Careful dear, you don't know who's listening," Janine said, for the umpteenth time. "Ah, that's nice — the Patrician has opened a new wing in the Ordinea City hospital."

The screen was now displaying pictures of the city leader cutting ribbons and kissing babies.

"Yeah, he needs the space for all the people he's had beaten up."

He took off his thin wire-rim glasses and rubbed his tanned face, then ran his thin fingers though his greying brown hair. He leant over the arm of the cream leather sofa and pulled out a fresh beer from the little fridge that Janine, bless her, had bought for his forty-fifth birthday. He smiled every time he opened it; they earned a bit, but this little fridge, now that was a luxury — all his friends were just green with envy.

3

"Well," he would say to them, "be a lawyer."
Except for Akea—he was a weird bloke.

"Darling, please be quiet. There's a rumour the TV
can hear you," said Janine.

She had just put the kids to bed—Lorna, aged four,
and Cibor, aged six—and had come downstairs to
have five minutes peace and quiet. She'd had her hair
done today. Not that he noticed, she thought. Once a
month, she would splash out and have her hair
highlighted blonde. To match her blue eyes, she
would always say. Her argument to Aldon was "Well,
you don't want to be seen with and a podgy and grey-
haired woman. The podgy bit can wait, but I am
having my hair done."

Aldon always tried to appease her, but it never
worked. It seemed that men were doomed for eternity
to misunderstand the notions of women.

"Janine, sweetheart, rumours, rumours, rumours
everywhere, and not a drop to think."

"Aldon, if you don't shut up, you'll get us all
killed."

"I've had enough of this. I'm going to bed. Janine,
I do love you."

"I love you too."

Around two a.m., Aldon awoke to severe knocking
at the door. He could hear the sound of the pounding
reverberating down the street, disrupting the quiet
spring morning. He got out of bed and pulled the
curtain aside. From the upstairs window, he could
make out four men standing at the front door. There
was a crash as the door gave way to a small battering
ram. The men were now in his house. Aldon was
beside himself. Where were the children? He looked
around frantically for the cricket bat, cursing as panic
set in. His heart pounded so loud, he thought the men
could use it as a homing beacon. He could hear the

4

men crashing up the stairs, destroying everything in their pathway as they went.

Aroused from heavy sleep, Janine sat up and looked around stupidly. Aldon held up his hand, cautioning her to remain in place. Spotting the cricket bat lying against a corner in the room, he grabbed it and rushed out onto the upstairs landing outside the bedroom door, slamming the door behind him. There he stood, in his pyjamas, the cricket bat raised in both hands. He turned on the light with the end of the bat and found himself facing four large men dressed in black. They wore black helmets, and their faces were covered with reflective visors. Each held a silenced pistol and carried a silenced semiautomatic slung over his back.

"You ain't gonna take the children!" Aldon cried out, his voice shaking in terror.

The man nearest to Aldon held up his gun and pointed it at Aldon's face. Aldon heard three clicks as the others focused their guns on him and removed their safeties. "Move!" the nearest said, and motioned him away from the bedroom door with his gun. When Aldon did not move aside, the nearest man shot him in the knee. Aldon screamed in agony as he crumpled to the floor. The man opened the door, stepped in and forcibly pulled Janine out of the bedroom. He held her tightly as he looked down at Aldon.

"Avandates, you're under arrest for not paying taxes. You don't have the right to a lawyer or a phone call. And you can scream down the bloody house for all I care."

Janine, petrified with fear, just stood there as the men handcuffed and gagged her with heavy-duty tape. One of the men knelt down to Aldon and dealt with him in the same manner, while two of the men went looking for the children.

The children screamed as they awakened to the dark forms leaning over them. One of the men grabbed Lorna and put a gun to her head. Turning his head toward Cibor, he said, "If you make a sound, I will kill your sister. Stand still." The other man moved forward, grabbed Cibor and roughly dragged him out into the hall.

Out on the landing with their parents, the children's chins started to wobble, but not a sound escaped. The family and their captors moved down the stairs and out the front door, two men mercilessly half-carrying, half-dragging Aldon.

The children and Janine were half-thrown, half-shoved into the back of a waiting unmarked van. As they pushed Aldon into the van, one of the men punched him in the face with the butt of his gun, and Aldon fell unconscious onto the floor of the van. Before pulling away from the house, the men set fire to it. As they drove through the streets, Janine, tears running down her face and out of her mind with fear, looked up from her unconscious husband and out the window as they drove past a large poster near the Watchmen's headquarters. It said simply, "THE WATCHMEN ARE WATCHING YOU!"

Book One: The Technology
Chapter 1: Serendipity

It was early Friday evening, and the streets of the financial districts were heaving with people trying to get home for the weekend. Akea wandered through the crowds, in no particular hurry. As he headed for the old shopping mall near the underground station, Akea watched the clouds sail gently past and go out of view over the high-rise blocks. He longed to be up there, on his own, away from all these people. Thankfully, at this time of the evening, the mall would be reasonably quiet. Akea's tall, thin frame lumbered on. He combed his blond hair with his fingers as he entered the mall. The billboards read the retina of his green eyes and flashed his name, trying to convince him that he should have their latest product that he could not do without.

The coffee shop smelt of rich coffee and warm pastries; the soft lighting made the shop look homely in a corporate way. As he walked in, the eye scanner flashed across his eyes and provided the staff with an instant record of his identity and his usual choice. They knew his name, but they did not know him. Akea sat in his usual spot, a red leather sofa and low table located in a cubbyhole.

A tranquil picture of: a large tree by the side of an empty road and clear green fields in the distance, the sky dark and moody, hung on the wall in front of him. Akea stared at it for a while, almost forgetting his drink. He thought, more people are swinging in traitor's row. I am sure there are more random beatings today than a year ago. It seems there is no place where I am not watched or spied upon. I can't move without someone knowing about it.

The people wanted security, to be safe at night, but it seems that it has cost us our freedoms, because now we are tied up in religious and social bondage. And the populace bleat out, "Two cheers for tyranny." They can take away my human rights, but they can't take away my ability to think and dream. Ultimately, I can choose. In a way, I am free.

Akea rubbed his face and swept away the thoughts. His face showed signs of care and worries, perhaps beyond his age. At twenty-seven, he should be happily married, with two point four kids, a cat, a dog and a blue midrange estate. Not living at home with his mother. The stigma of his untimely birth wore on him. Though he was not ugly, the opposite sex would run away as soon as they met his mother. He had a sweet rogue look, but his innocence inevitably showed through.

The cubbyhole shielded Akea from the closed-circuit television cameras and billboards. Akea liked this privacy, his private little world. The embedded chip in the newspaper screen showed Akea the news he wanted to read. He sipped the froth from the coffee. The cup analysed his saliva, noted that he might have a cold coming and e-mailed Dr Norse, Akea's doctor, and booked an appointment for next week. It then updated Akea's calendar and told Akea of the appointment by e-mail.

His coffee finished, Akea left the shop and found the entrance to the underground. He strolled down the escalator to the underground platform and stood with the other people waiting to get on the train. Posters of a proud man were plastered on every available wall.

Although he was in a world of his own, Akea could not help but notice the posters of the Patrician everywhere, looking down at him and everyone else, encouraging them to work harder and be good citizens.

The train arrived, and Akea pushed his way onto it, found a seat and tried to ignore the complaints from other patrons about the conditions of the overstuffed train. The train whistled through the tunnels, and cool air drifted through the open slotted windows. He closed his eyes and dreamt.

He was standing on a rocky hillock, staring at the horizon; the wind blew, ruffling the bottom of his cloak. . . .

It was always the same dream; it haunted him.

With a slight squeal and a sudden jolt, the train entered the station and stopped. People crammed the doorways, trying to get out, tediously reliving the daily nightmare of getting home. Akea stepped off the underground train, rode up the crammed escalator and hurried through the busy ticket hall, where armed Watchmen stood and watched, eager for someone to look at them or start trouble. Random searches happened everyday. As Akea turned left onto New Street, he noticed a man standing in front of a wall with his arms spread out and guards searching his things. They looked like they wanted to find a reason to beat someone to a pulp.

It was odd, Akea thought, as he crossed the road to get out of the way. I wish I could do something about this. That poor bastard, just happening to walk past at the wrong moment. What, the Watchmen have run out of doughnuts? His thoughts ran on sarcastically. Wish I could stop the whole abuse and let the city live—like I could do anything. I'm just a lowly lonely computer programmer. I guess it's going to be like this a long time. Goddamn it, I hate my job, my life. It's all just crap. But I must be lucky—I never had to deal with the animals. Except for that one time when that rookie Watchmen came up to me and tried to search me, and the senior took one look at my face and stopped him. Bizarre.

As he continued on his way home, Akea's thoughts swam around and around. The evening was drawing in, and the light wind felt fresh. Akea enjoyed the cool breeze after a long hot day. Despite the clear blue sky and the summer warmth, the people hurried, trying to get home in time, on time and out of the way of the notorious Watchmen. Akea walked for about twenty minutes and then right into Upton Drive. I wonder if Aldon and Janine are home this weekend. I think I might go and see them. Aldon always cheers me up, Akea thought as he turned into his drive.

Akea noticed that the gardener had been here today. The flowers reflected the late afternoon light, bright reds, yellows and blues, accented by the blossom of the old cherry tree. The house stood back from the road: white, wooden, slatted walls, with blue grey slate tiles, a garage on one side and, matching in shape, a main sitting room on the other. Unlike most of the houses in the area, it was single storey, the main room big, light and airy. Akea walked up the few steps to the front door, which was situated on a short porch. As he opened the front door, Akea placed his coat on the coat rack and took off his shoes, as was the custom. He stepped into the dining area. Highly polished wood flooring added to the character of the back stone wall.

"Hi, you had a good day? Dinner is nearly ready," Cassandra, Akea's mother, called from the kitchen.

"Yeah, I guess," he said. He went about setting the old oak table for dinner. Their relationship, at best, was false. Akea really didn't understand his mother. He felt unwanted. Well, he knew that—she had told him once or twice when she got drunk and raged at him for ruining her life. She'd never said who his

10

father was. This hurt Akea badly. He tried to force the issue once, but she had fled to her room and cried for hours; after that, she wouldn't speak to him for weeks. Akea decided then that one day he would find out; or maybe not. In a way, it didn't matter. As much as their relationship was uneasy, it kind of worked. Both of them got something out of it. He got a roof over his head, in a rather nice neighbourhood; she got a fairly good supplemental income from his salary, which he shared with her. As rich as they were, the cost of living at the moment made it virtually impossible to live alone.

Sexual promiscuity was forbidden, and single mothers with bastard children were shunned. They had risen above the stigma, mainly due to the wealth and generosity shown by Cassandra to the community. Such was the power and influence Cassandra had generated through her social activities, that over the years, the neighbourhood had rallied round, and the social barriers had lessened.

When Cassandra came in, she found Akea sitting at the table, his head in his hands.

"What's the matter?"

"Not much, just been thinking, that's all," said Akea.

Cassandra placed a warm plate in front of Akea. She was a well-dressed, prim woman in her mid-fifties; her vibrant chestnut hair was now accented with grey. She once could have been mistaken for a model. She wore conservative clothes and never seemed to have any male friends. In her youth, she had been the most favoured woman on the Patrician's staff and had subsequently married the Patrician. One day it all fell to pieces. No one seemed to know why. Years of harassment and looking after a child that she did not want had slowly eaten away her debonair

11

manner and good looks. She had not had a husband or any serious relationships since the divorce. When the Patrician had found out about the last boyfriend, he had disappeared in the middle of the night, dragged kicking and screaming from her bed.

Akea noticed that her eyes were slightly puffy, as though she had been crying. "Mother, what's the matter?"

Cassandra didn't like being called "Mother." She preferred "Mum" or "Cass," but she let it slip. Collapsing into a chair at the table, she let out a deep sigh. Akea got out of his chair and embraced her shoulder. He didn't normally like doing this sort of thing, and it felt wooden, a bit stiff.

The local gossip machine of which Cassandra was the founder had produced some disturbing news. Although she knew she would be safe from the Watchmen, this news hit a bit too close to home. "The Watchmen have taken the Avandates. I wish I had known; I would have given them money, food— anything but this," she said. She began to cry softly.

Akea's first reaction was indifference. Perhaps, he thought, I am turning numb. Then the thoughts from earlier rushed into his mind, and the anger and hopelessness grabbed a hold again.

Akea returned to his chair, and they sat in silence, eating their dinner for what seemed liked days, silently sharing the thought that they could be next. Finally, Cassandra interrupted the silence.

"I saw a job going at ATD—they're looking for programmers. If you got the job, you would be down the road from me. We could go to work together."

Akea responded, "Mmm . . . sorry; oh, yes, job. Right. I'll apply."

"Oh, god, we'll be late for prayers. Leave the plates, you can do them later," Cassandra exclaimed, looking at the clock.

It was dusk. While they walked the two blocks to the temple, Cassandra wanted to talk. Akea found it annoying; he found it difficult to talk about everyday events. The temple stood out from the street houses, three storeys high, with large stained-glass windows displaying the Patrician in various poses. The massive doors opened up into the main lobby, which served as a general meeting point before the service started. Cassandra was in her element; she was the richest person in her block, and she was treated with respect and honour and known for acts of kindness. She met the usual faces, overheard whisperings about the Avandates—gossip, half-truths and hearsay. Akea did not want to listen; he was in no mood for gossip. He found a space on one of the pews near the back.

The bells rang out calling people to prayer, the minister took the dais, and the congregation sat down and waited for the signal to start. A picture of a large bird of prey, its wings spread, a hammer in one claw and a key in the other, hung above the dais. To the right of the picture hung yet another portrait of the Patrician, looking on his people in the same way one might depict a god looking down on his subjects. A slogan underneath spelled out the truth. "The Watchmen are watching you."

Akea knew the minister would spout out the same old pious rubbish, perhaps mentioning—though not by name—the Avandates: how they were careless, how they had too much pride to call out for help and not enough faith. This spiritual abuse annoyed Akea; he decided to turn off. He looked around. The architect had designed the building to be both impressive and homely, but its overall atmosphere

13

was daunting, impersonal and cold. With its high windows and vaulted ceiling, it was a three-hundred-year-old cathedral put up in a hurry. You will not find any self-respecting god here, Akea thought. There is no peace, no hope here, just more control.

As he brooded, Akea's eye caught the chandelier, high in the ceiling, puffing out the smoke of incense. The crystals glinted in the light and gently swung in the breeze, marking off segments of time. He watched the chandelier swing and imagined the chandelier stopping at the zenith, just for a moment. He was about ten when he first did it, and he wasn't sure then if the chandelier actually stopped, but he tried again and again. Slowly he became rather good at it, taking less and less concentration to arrest the swing. He loved doing this, seeing how long he could hold it. The temple warder had noticed once, last year, and had set up a committee to get the chandelier fixed. They started a fund-raiser, got the money together and repaired the chandelier. This amused Akea.

Akea never told anyone. Public execution on traitor's row awaited any trespassers of the anti-magic law.

His mother nudged him from his torpor. "Akea, damn it, you haven't been listening. Time to go, we must be quick." The meeting had gone on longer than expected, and they had to get home before the curfew.

They moved swiftly and nervously through the streets, arriving home before the curfew bells rang out. Akea went straight to his room. It was a large room, professionally decorated, but retaining signs of his formative years. Plastic models hung from the ceiling. The bookcase in the corner displayed his education in software. A large mirror stood near the double wardrobe. He stood in the doorway and called out commands, "Lights. Computer. Music, tracks 114 to 120, volume quiet." The lights came on, illuminating in soft tones. The computer screen flickered to life. Jazz music began to play quietly. He sat on his bed, turned on his lamp and read a novel. The knock on the bedroom door brought him back to reality with a slight crash. Cassandra came in and placed a cup of tea on the bedside table next to a glass of water.

"Look, Akea, I know you are troubled, but things can only get better, you'll see."

"Doesn't it seem odd that each day we lose more freedoms?"

"We live in a nice part of town. We are secure. What else do you want? If you left the city, where would you go? How would you pay for it? Even if you managed to get an exit visa, the immigration laws in Solberg are very tight. Be content, you have a good life." Cassandra smiled reassuringly and left the room quietly.

As Akea undressed, he pulled his identity card from around his neck and stared at it. He shook those damn thoughts from his mind and got ready for bed.

Akea lay on his side and tried to sleep, but he was upset. Why had the Watchmen arrested the Avandates? The more he thought about it, the angrier he became, until suddenly the glass on the bedside table shattered. This was not good. If his mother found out, he would get a beating within inches of his life. It sometimes happened when he was angry. Akea got up and paced around the room. He stopped and stared into the old full-length dress mirror that stood in the corner. He was taller than the mirror; he tilted it up slightly. A strange, light blue hue hung around him like an aura. His dark green eyes studied the blue aura. Still staring at the mirror, he ran his hands through his long, blond, wavy hair. He was thin, though not skinny. The aura faded as he regained his composure. He got back into bed, pulled the duvet up toward his head and curled up. Sleep crept over him.

*

From the west, Solberg geese approached the house, spread out, high up in a great V. They continued in flight, honking as though practicing for an audition. A lone figure watched them fly as he strolled up the meandering drive. An undulating green percussion was washed gently by the wind. The first of spring dawned, announced itself.

The sunlight danced on the leaves and on the grass like trumpets and violins. Creatures of every sort wandered though the grounds. Life at her best. Rabbits and hares bounced away like oboes announcing the next movement. And the beat went on. Over in the distance the figure could see large wildebeest and bison charging, a cacophony of basses and tubas. The figure hummed to the symphony He so enjoyed his sister's work. The gothic structure of the stately home rose up amidst the beauty of the gardens and the orchard, like a full chord from a large pipe organ in the full swing of a toccata and fugue—or perhaps more like a painting from a modern artist on mind-altering drugs. As the figure continued his stroll along the drive towards the house, he stopped occasionally to admire the particular beauty of a creature or flower. As he walked, the sun beat down, warming his skeletal body. Even under his long, ragged, hooded cloak, his milky white skin enjoyed the lavish rays. The fragrances from the garden filled his head.

His grandfather, Old Man Time, had given the estate to his parents, Fate and Chance, for a wedding present. Death approached the large oak front door that had darkened with age; it boasted ornate carvings and a large black knocker. He raised his hand to knock, but the butler opened the door before his bony finger touched the aged oak. The butler stood at the door, five feet eight inches tall, a gentleman's gentleman in a long black tail-coat. In his starched collar and charcoal grey and black pin-stripe trousers, he stood like the audience standing in ovation.

"Ah, Master; it is so good to see you," said the butler.

"Yes, Sibson. How's life?" The low, grave voice could send a shiver down the hardest of hearts.

"She is in the garden, with her mother."

"No, no—I meant, how's your life?" said Death.

"Same old, same old, sir," said Sibson. "Your father is waiting for you in the study," he continued without missing a beat.

Death entered the great hall. The grand staircase dominated the centre, surrounded by numerous doors. As Death walked down the passageway, the old clock ticked vociferously, *tick-tock, tick-tock*. His sandals clicked on the old marble mosaic. With a quick rap on the door, Death entered the study. Inside, the musty smell hit Death as hard as the flowers outside. The cool, darkened room was filled with books, many books. The old room hadn't changed in years. And why should it? Death thought. An old man sat huddled over a large desk. The old man's mane of grey hair hung towards the desk; his beard was tucked into his waistcoat.

Death coughed politely.

"Yes, what is it, Sibson? I said no disturbances," said Fate, without looking up.

"Father!" said Death, annoyed.

The old man craned his head around and peered in Death's direction. "Oh, it's you. Must apologise."

His red irises gleamed. "Won't you have a seat?"

"You summoned me," said Death, as he lowered himself into an old red leather chair. It felt soft and moulded to his bony derrière.

"Tea?" Fate said, too politely.

"We haven't seen each other in years, and you summon me for tea."

Fate ignored the retort and rang a little bell. Sibson appeared with a silver tray bearing two cups, a silver teapot, and some milk and sugar. Death poured two cups. He picked up one, sipped, and sat back and crossed his bony legs, relaxing a little. The taste of the Earl Grey reminded him of years past, when he would sit and watch his father plot the fate of all living creatures. He put his fingers together under his chin.

"The reason . . . this is not easy," said Fate. He fiddled with his quill for a few seconds. "So I will get straight to the point." He braced himself before going on. "Someone has cheated me," he growled in a low, sullen voice.

"What?" said Death. He sat up quickly and leaned forward. "This is impossible. You—cheated? This is an outrage!" He gripped the sides of the chair with rage. His dark purple eyes blazed.

"Yes, I know. Calm down." Fate turned his red gaze to a list of names lying in front of him on the desk. "Look. See here: this man does not belong." Fate's finger pointed to a name. "Why didn't I see it earlier? I must be getting old." He looked at Death and shook his head.

"It's not one of the gods playing a prank again is it?" asked Death.

"No, no, checked that." Fate went back to the book. "I thought he died, but he just moved, how bizarre," he muttered to himself as he scrutinised the pages.

"See, his line, it's smudged under this tea ring."

"We must put this right. He will pay the price," Death said, shaking his head.

Death knew his father was in trouble—otherwise he never would have contacted him. And so they sat there in Fate's office, amongst the books and musty smell, and contemplated plans. Sometimes their discussion grew heated. They argued the moral implications of getting involved with mortal affairs. They talked through scenarios where Fate did nothing. What really upset him was the fact that, somehow, someone had cheated him.

After some hours, Fate finally said, "I suppose I should get out more." He deliberated for a few more minutes. "It's agreed, then. I will get involved," he rumbled in his deep baritone voice.

"It is agreed. I will do my part," said Death in his graveyard voice.

Fate leaned back in his chair and smiled. "The right man in the wrong place can make all the difference."

Death nodded in concurrence. "Wake up, Akea, and see the truth."

*

Akea woke with a start. It was cold. He looked around and found himself in a tiny alley. The patchwork grey walls went up on either side for what must have been three storeys, a few air conditioning units protruding out like pigeons in a loft. The musty walls revealed various stages of development over the years. Old windows and doors had been bricked in, and new ones had been fitted. Akea found himself dressed in heavy cotton trousers, a plain shirt, and a duffle coat. Where am I? Who I am? He thought in bewilderment. As he pulled his coat tighter, anxiety clammed in on him like a sudden fog. Akea knew for certain he could not stay here, but where would he go?

Then a young woman, no more than twenty-two, ran past him and suddenly stopped. She did a double take and tried to run on, but slowed as though there was some internal battle going on. Finally, she turned and ran up to him. She put out her hand. Akea took it.

"You better come with me. I won't hurt you—we got to go, the Watchmen are coming!" She spoke in a local dialect, her voice tinged with desperation. Her breath condensed in the cold air as she helped Akea up from the damp alley floor. They could hear running footsteps some way off, obviously a bit too close for her liking.

A small, thin woman, the years of undernourishment showed on her. She smelt wholesome, but her clothes were tired and patched. What, why, where, who? Akea's mind was racing. He had no memory of this place and how he got here. Distant footsteps approached slowly, as though someone were searching. "We must run," she said to him in a hushed voice.

They stole through the streets, her dirty blonde hair whipping behind her. Akea had a hard time keeping up. "Look," Akea said, "We've got to—please stop. Please tell me what is going on—where am I, who am I, who are these Watchmen? I don't understand!" The girl looked back at him with surprise, but ran on. She led him down this alley, then that, Akea stumbling behind her in bewilderment. Suddenly the woman stopped and turned. Akea was so busy thinking that he ran right into her.

"What you mean, who are the Watchmen? For God's sake, where have you been? You better keep close or you'll find out soon enough, and you might not like it."

The dim yellow glow from the sodium street lighting gave no comfort; the cold air fought through Akea's coat. Their breath puffed out like clouds of steam from a train. The terraced houses looked identical to the last hundred that they had run past. Akea felt sick with anxiety, and his head was dizzy from overexertion.

"I'm gonna take you to my uncle; he'll know what to do."

They started off again; a stitch was breaking through Akea's ribs, like a red-hot poker. Akea could taste blood in his mouth. The woman stopped at a nondescript, redbrick terrace house and knocked on its blue door. The door cracked open, revealing a big man pointing a rifle at Akea's face. Despite the gun, Akea couldn't help remarking how big this man was, not only in height but also in width. He wore old trousers and a plain white shirt, and his mousy brown hair was long and shaggy and tinted with grey.

"Cruz! What the hell!" The man swore and then remembered that they were standing on the doorstep. "Get in; get in, before you're seen." He spoke in the same dialect the woman had used.

They entered and stood in the hallway.

"Who's this? What are you doing out after curfew?" said the man. He seemed to get bigger as his anger rose.

"I was—was . . . stealing bread." She breathed heavily. "He, ah—he, ah . . . I saw him. Watchmen were after us. Stopped to help! God knows why, I just did." Her words came out in gasps of air. The big man looked Akea up and down, trying to assess the threat.

"You—you better get in the kitchen," the big man said.

21

Cruz and Akea followed the man down the hallway, past a living room on the left. The carpet was old but clean. The man opened a door leading into the kitchen, which was large and homely. From the clutter, it seemed that this man spent most of his time here. The man motioned with his arm to sit.

"You better sit down, take a chair. The one by the oven is warmest." Akea sat down numbly; the warmth from the cast iron oven warmed his body. He thought, who are these people? What do I say to them? His massive intellect started to fight back. I am safe, he told himself, away from whoever was chasing us, and that will do for now.

The man looked at Akea again, for what seemed to Akea a long and uncomfortable time. He looked as if he were trying to place a face he had seen a long time ago. Finally, he said to Akea, "What's your story?"

Akea stared at him and thought, What should I say? He decided on the truth, but before he could say anything, the young woman cut in, "He's got amnesia. He asked who the Watchmen are."

Not fazed by the interruption, Akea said, "Sir, I don't know who I am, what I am doing here, how I got here or where I come from. I awoke in a dark alley. Who are the Watchmen, anyway?" He pointed to Cruz sitting opposite him and continued, "And she ran past and stopped, she insisted that I should move quickly."

The girl giggled, realising that she had not even introduced herself. "The name's Cruz."

Akea had a sudden idea. He felt a wallet in his trouser pocket and took it out. Looking inside it, he extracted his ID card. He felt some of his tension and fear drain away. He said, smiling, "My name, it seems, is Akea de Silva."

22

The man's eyes widened in surprise and then became sad, as if he were remembering something from a distant past. He shook his head and then put his hand out. With some hesitation, Akea took it. As their bare hands touched, Akea's eyes changed, flashing from green, with round irises, to bright orange, with tiger slits. He quickly pulled his hand away, and his eyes returned to normal. Cruz jerked back in the chair and put her hand to her mouth, muffling a scream.

The big man sat there staring at his hand. He muttered, "It can't be, it can't." Then he looked at his guest. "Akea? That is not a common name."

They looked deep into each other's eyes. Akea felt strange, as if he were looking into space in the rich, dark blue irises of this man. He thought, I know this man.

The man said, "Some call me Juween. With your permission I am going to look into your mind, see where your memories went to."

"You want to do what?"

"Look, I am a magician; I am the only one who stayed. We needed a magician in the city. All the others left because of the anti-magic law."

Cruz looked at Juween with wide eyes. "You, a magician?"

Akea hesitated, but Fate, who sat unseen on a spare chair in the corner, spoke to Akea's mind. "It's okay, Akea. Trust him."

A feeling of reassurance came over Akea. He nodded. Juween leant forward, took Akea's hand again and looked into Akea's eyes and past them, into the darkness beyond. Both men saw the same images: stars, galaxies, planets, moons, dragons, magicians, red and blue. Then, without warning, Akea's mind repelled Juween with such force that Juween was knocked back against the back of his chair.

Juween turned to Cruz and said rather timidly, uncharacteristically of him, "You better get us a large stiff drink. Or I'll be remembering you been stealing."

Cruz got up, went to the cupboard and got out a litre bottle with no label on it. She poured out two small drinks and handed them to Juween and Akea. She lifted the bottle again and looked inquiringly at Juween. He nodded, and she poured herself a drink.

"Normally," said Juween to Cruz, "I would not allow you to be drinking at such a young age. But tonight, 'tis different. You may be needing a drink after what I have to say."

Akea sat there thinking, taking in all that he could. What was going on? As he assessed his new friends, he could not stop staring at the lines and scars on the older man's face. He looked around the kitchen. Jars of herbs and spices sat next to an old radio on the shelf above the dresser. The blue and white wall tiles showed stories. Through an open door at the back of the kitchen, Akea could see an annexe in which flowers hung drying. The room was permeated with the smell of many home cooked meals. The table they sat at was old but scrubbed spotlessly clean. Akea took a swallow of his drink and coughed. The liquid burnt the back of his throat and left an aftertaste of smoked wheat. He sipped again, more carefully this time. The three sat and nursed their drinks silently for what seemed a long time. Ten minutes slowly passed. Juween was deep in thought. Finally, downing the dredges of his homemade whisky, he sat up straight.

"Akea, did you like the homemade juice?" he asked politely.

Akea nodded, wondering how many brain cells had died because of it.

Juween took a deep breath. "Look Akea, I know what it's like to have no memories. About thirty years ago, I woke up in a hospital ward, severely wounded. From what I managed to glean from the doctors, I had been mauled by an animal, or animals. I was brought in unconscious by a man, and he left while I was in the emergency room."

Akea shifted slightly and took another sip of the whisky.

"It certainly foxed the doctors for a while. I have retained all my knowledge, but for the life of me, I can't remember any personal experiences. The doctors could not agree whether I had dissociative fatigue or lacunar amnesia—not that it matters. I could have a wife and not know about her. That's probably why I never married." Juween smiled. "It's been a long, long time since I've bared his soul to anyone."

Akea may have lost his memories, but not his brains. He just sat there listening. Cruz, on the other hand, fidgeted a little, obviously wanting to ask questions. It was the look on Juween's face that said,

"Please, don't ask me anything."

"Akea, I am not sure, but I think you do not belong in this reality. I think you come from a place where magic is strong. But I cannot be sure. We must go to a wise, old man, in the mountains. His name is Prometheus. I met him about twenty years ago, when I first started with the resistance movement. They have a base inside an old nuclear reactor. Behind it is a large forest—the Delwiderlen Forest. He lives there. On my visits, we grew close, and he told me the whole history of the city, stuff you would never find in the history books. If I am correct, he can show you how to control your power. He might even give you back your memories. One thing is for certain: you can't stay here for long without being missed or noticed."

Akea said, "I may have lost my memories, but I doubt that I am anything other than an ordinary person, with an ordinary job. Somewhere in this city, I have a home."

"Yeah, right! Akea, earlier, you looked into my eyes; what did you see?"

Akea blushed. What sort of question is this? he thought.

Juween, sensing the young man's embarrassment, prompted, "You looked into my eyes, and you saw stars, galaxies, planets, moons, dragons, magicians. Yes?"

Akea nodded, feeling the burning redness in his cheeks.

"That's why I think you don't belong here. You have some magic, and the way you threw me out of your mind—I have no doubts."

Akea looked stunned.

"Let me explain," Juween continued. "The problem with magic, like all natural forces, is that if it is not used, then it will die. Technology sometimes replaces magic, a sad and terrible thing. There are, as far as I have worked out, ten realities. Each has its own mix of magic and technology. In one reality, technology rules and magic has almost died, while in another magic is plentiful and a glorious wonder and the technology is crude and primitive. There are no natural-born magicians, mages, fortune-tellers, or any other magical talents in this reality. Putting two and two together, either you are a phenomenon, or you were not born here. Some, more wise than me, say that it's like a race trait. Like the colour of your skin, or type of hair, or a natural ability to run or think fast."

Juween took a sip from the glass to clear his throat, and carried on. "Now to your other question: who are the Watchmen? Indeed, who are the Watchmen? Once, Ordinea was free, but two generations have passed since the revolution. This country was a prosperous country, wealthy, rivalling its neighbours. The borders were open. People came and went as they pleased. A small, unknown, but fanatical group of people wanted change, and they sought the ear of the Emperor. Overnight the pubs, inns, and whorehouses were pulled down. The borders were closed, and non-native people were displaced. And temples to the new religion went up. The Emperor of Ordeania over a short period had become a god, and the Patrician tried to mimic him."

Akea pulled a face.

Juween shrugged. "This was the way of the religion. The hysteria and riots that followed were unbelievable; the police and the army could not cope. A new force was employed—the Watchmen. They were the most ruthless and cruel beings who ever walked these lands. Many fled, many died. The Watchmen did not differentiate between the rioters and the onlookers. The death toll was high. But they stopped the riots, and the country started to get back on its feet. It became the world leader in technology."

"The Watchmen, though powerful, became even more powerful, and more and more corrupt, until one day they decided to hold Ordinea City ransom. Stealthily of course. The leader of the Watchmen, who is also the assistant to the Patrician, kept all news about the Watchmen to a minimum. If you do not pay your 'protection money'," Juween raised his hands and made inverted commas in the air, "your 'dues', you and maybe your family will disappear and never be seen again." Juween brushed his thick, brown,

27

greying hair with his hands.

Akea shifted slightly. Juween was a good storyteller.

"The current Patrician does not allow magic. You are a magician—a powerful one, I imagine. But for some reason, you are not safe here. You must leave. I will take you. We have to find Prometheus. If I am correct about you, we can train you. We were going to smuggle a family to the rebel base. The Watchmen got to 'em first." Juween swore again; there was sadness in his eyes. "I hate losing people to those bastards.

"We are going to take their place. I'll a get a word to my man, and he'll know what to do."

Juween went off to make a phone call. He returned a few minutes later. "We are leaving tomorrow, first thing. We need a photo of you. And Cruz, you better come with us. It'll be better if we look and act like a family just enjoying a day trip. You must understand that an exit visa is unheard of. The movement is running a great risk in doing this, with such a short notice. But they owe me a great deal. Someone will be here shortly to take photos and forge documents."

Juween lapsed into silence, while Cruz bubbled with excitement; she finally was going to be leaving this hell. For his part, Akea felt the need to be with his own thoughts for a while. "Juween, would you mind if I went out and sat in the garden for a bit?"

"Yeah, sure, get some fresh air."

Akea got up and walked to the back door. Cruz jumped up to follow, but Juween put his hand out and shook his head. "Give the guy a break."

"Look, Cruz, this is not going to be easy. It's not a holiday. You will never be able to come back here. I know you, but you got to, for once in your life, not break the rules. I want you to promise me that tomorrow you will do exactly as I say, no ifs, no buts—just do it. Consider it a reality check, 'cuz when you get to the rebel base, you will have to join the rebel army, and they will not put up with your shit!"

Cruz nodded. She had lost some of her bubble. "I know, Uncle. I promise. But I've waited so long to get out and do something."

"Cruz, you are my niece, almost my daughter. I will not let those bastards take you."

"Uncle, I know I'm a pain in the ass, but I also know you love me and that you have never allowed any harm come to me."

Chance stood behind her husband Fate, her face full of bemusement and interest. She bore the same distant attitude she always did, amusing herself at the agonisings of these humans. She wore a summer floral dress and a bright pink cardigan and little black dress shoes. She stroked Fate's long white hair. Rousing himself from his torpor, the old man stood up and kissed his wife absently on the cheek, deep in thought, wondering whether he had done right. They had so far to go.

Chance spoke with a soft clear voice. "Darling, what are you up to? What are you doing?"

Fate turned to his lovely wife. "My dear Chance, I am doing my job, the same job I always do. The right people in the right time and the proper place," he intoned in a most serious voice, deep baritone and old as the years.

"Okay, if that's the way you want it," she quipped, and disappeared.

*

Akea came in from the garden. "There's a man out the back, I heard him."

Juween got up. "Okay. It's all right Akea, it'll be Pablo. He's doing the forging tonight."

29

The man came in. He was short, bald and overweight, and was breathing rather heavily.

"Juween, this better be important. Sod the Watchmen. I left the car three blocks from here. I had to run the rest. Do you know when was the last time I ran three yards, let alone three blocks? And carrying this stuff." Pablo pointed to the suitcase that he had tucked under his arm. "I could feel my heart pumping from my arse. Get us a drink—water and then some home brew—coffee and some food. Cheers."

The man sat at the table recovering his breath while Juween busied himself around the kitchen. It had been a while since anyone had eaten, and it was going to be a long night. Everyone should have ample food and coffee. He put a big lump of cheese, a loaf of bread and a pot of coffee on the table. "Help yourself. Here's a shot glass, Pab."

Pablo took the glass with a smile and a hearty laugh. He poured himself some whisky and knocked it back, coughing slightly. "God's sake, I swear this gets stronger every time I see you." He cleared his throat and breathed in heavily, slapped his chest. "That's the job.

"Right then, we're going to have to do this quickly. I knew this day would come, but who'd a thought it; Juween you are going to be sorely missed. Who's the bloke?"

"I ain't dead yet. The bloke is Akea de Silva, don't ask dumb questions," Juween said.

"If I can't get it right, you will be," Pablo retorted. "Enough of the dramatics society." He pulled a small laptop out of the suitcase and booted it up. He got out a piece of blue cloth, about eighteen inches by two feet, and hung it on the wall in front of the computer. "Cruz, please sit here," he said. He pulled a chair to face the little camera in the lid of the laptop. "Look straight ahead, and don't smile."

Cruz got up and sat in the chair.

"I said don't smile. . . . That's it. Okay, all done. Akea, please, would you mind?"

Akea sat in the chair. He didn't need to try and not smile.

"Juween, we got yours done already; we just need to fill in the blanks."

Akea sat at the table and watched Pablo do his thing. Every few minutes there was a "tut" or "No, no that's not right." After about half an hour, Pablo got out some blank ID cards, passports and official-looking documents, and filled them in. Then he got out a portable printer and ran the documents through the device to give them a fake seal of approval.

"Okay, almost finished. I've given you all a new name. Juween, you are Armadas; Cruz, you are Lorna; Akea, you are Cloud. Your family name is Ehrlichmann, got that? Right, I need you all to sign the documents with an authentic-looking signature. You could practice a while, but it's got to look natural." They practiced on scratch paper for about five minutes, and then signed their new signatures on the papers.

"Okay, all finished. I will put them in the usual place by 7:30 a.m. You should pick them up around 8." Pablo turned to Cruz and Akea. "If you ever see me again, please remember you don't know me." He left out the back the way he'd come in.

"Look, we better get some sleep. Akea, you can sleep on the sofa."

Cruz made a bed for Akea on the sofa in the living room, and everyone went to bed.

Akea didn't want to sleep, he had so many questions, but as soon as he lay down he was asleep.

31

Chapter 2: Flight through the City

It was in the garden where she lay, prone on the grass, under the sky, under the sun, her subtle, supple mind drifting with the clouds. Chance was daydreaming; she remembered about the day that she had met Fate. Her father, Old Man Time, had held a getting-to-know-our-new-neighbour party. She and her twin sister Luck and her older sister Destiny had been busy all day cleaning the house, getting ready. In the evening there was a knock on the door, and Fate walked in. He was stunning, a tall, dark, handsome, striking figure.

The three girls had giggled. Destiny had horsy features and was surly in nature, with a shrewd disposition. The twins, Luck and Chance, were completely opposite to their elder sister. Luck had long blonde hair and a perfect figure, and owned an uncanny way to subdue any heart. Although physically identical to her twin, Chance was considered by many as the oddball of the family, always off in her own world. She was so fickle, it was hard to know what she would do next.

Over the fish course, their eyes met, Fate transfixed by the beauty of Chance. She had flowers braided in her light brown hair and wore an odd mixture of clothes: summer dress with combat boots. In that moment Fate and Chance knew they were meant for each other. Old Man Time was euphoric. After a short and steamy relationship, Chance became pregnant; it had been more a fumble in the dark than a big bang.

Chance sighed. Her children were so different from each other. Chance loved the way that Life was in everything, and Chance understood Death and embraced him. She could not love Death, but she

32

cared for him all the same.

Now, as Chance lay dreamily on the lawn, a dangerous thought fluttered through the chasms of her cranium; a plan was forming. She knew that Fate was meddling, which was unusual for him. He may have altered the book for a god or two, but never this much. She decided she was going to help, whether Fate wanted it or not. She had learned a trick or two from her sisters, and she wasn't the daughter of Old Man Time for nothing.

*

The Patrician's palace was as grand as it was large. It was ornate in every detail, covered in gold, marble, and carved cedar wood. On the surface it looked equally as impressive and ornate as the surrounding temples, but like them had been erected in a hurry. Despite all the wealth displayed, it lacked the character that comes with age. In the main hall stood the throne, on a marble dais. The high-backed, carved seat was decorated with patterns of creatures and swirling images hammered in gold, their details highlighted with gems. To one side of the hall a door led to the Patrician's office. Bodyguards stood around like badly dressed figurines.

Inside the office, the Patrician sat in his purple morning gown, his black hair combed straight back, eating his breakfast noisily and looking over last night's reports. He was old, though it did not show — he kept his long, thin body trim. When he glanced up over his half-moon glasses, the clock on the wall showed 7:00 a.m.

The office door burst open. A wailing woman came running in and fell prostrate on the floor.

The Patrician recognised her immediately, though he did not show it. He stared down at her for an overly long time. "What do you want?" he asked. He felt disgusted by the presence of this woman. The love they had once shared had died long ago. Her weakness, her frailty, but even more—much more— her willingness to do his bidding made nausea rise inside him.

She made no sense through her babbling. "AK— AK—Akea, he's gone, gone." The words came through crying gulps of air.

The Patrician felt mixed emotions, first pity and then annoyance. He requested one of the guards to provide the woman with a drink. The guard came back and gave the wreck a glass of water. She gulped the water, wiped her eyes, and sniffed, with all the composure that she could muster.

In clear, deliberate words, Cassandra spoke. "Akea: He has gone, his clothes are missing, his bed made."

The Patrician went white. "Guards, leave us," he said in a voice of sheer deadliness.

The guards obeyed in an instant.

"Oh, is that all?" the Patrician said, apparently nonplussed. Then it happened. He narrowed his dark blue eyes, and like a slowly exploding bomb he released his fury. An orange aura formed around him; objects on the table shook. The pictures rattled, the papers on the desk started to smoulder. Cassandra wet herself out of sheer terror and then sat on the cold marble floor in her own effluence.

"What did I pay you for?" the Patrician raged. "Why did I put Akea through college? Why did I get Akea off those charges of magic? You were supposed to make sure he was blind to the truth. I even bound him up with spells and enchantments, so he could not perform magic. Now he has gone. As I explained before, rebellion is not born from contentment. You have made a fool of me, and now you will suffer."

Calming down, his voice became gentler though just as deadly. "Why do you think he left? Was he upset?"

Cassandra still sat on the floor. She was wrecked, destroyed; she finally understood that she had been a pawn all her life. Her need and her greed had allowed her to become an object of pity. The smell of urine started to make her feel ill, but it was nothing compared to the depression that now gripped her. What had she become, a pitiful wreck now consigned to oblivion, now brought to her knees? What could she do now? She had nothing left. She had given up the best years of her life for a lie, for a silver lining. She had destroyed herself. She knew that she would die, but not yet; she would be used again and again to bring Akea down. She did not ask for forgiveness, as she spoke in a monotone.

"He was upset about the Avandates. He was quiet, he didn't say much. But I know he broke a glass again; I heard it shatter. And when I went to find out I saw a blue hue coming from under his door."

"Please my dear, wipe your tears, I know they are not for Akea's sake. Show some dignity."

The Patrician called the guards back in. He produced a photograph of Akea. "Guards, find this man." Then he turned to the head of the guards. "Put this wretched woman in prison, and give her some clean clothing. Now leave."

Alone with his thoughts, the Patrician pointed a finger in the air in front of him and said, *"Os ultra os."* Mist like steam flowed and swirled, and a small rectangle slowly grew in size and form, wobbling like jelly. It bounced as it became hard, and the Patrician grabbed hold of it, muttering to himself, and stared into the screen before him. An image shrouded in mist came into view. He looked closely at the figure. *Juween*. His eyes burned bright with malice as the realisation hit him that his worst fear had come to pass. He must find Akea before he got out of the city.

*

Akea awoke to find himself on a sofa. It seemed like an age since last night's conversations. He leaned back, hands over his face, and rubbed. "This can't be real," he muttered sleepily.

Dawn was breaking. As sleep scurried away, Akea sat up on the sofa and looked around the living room. The décor was clean, but tired, as if it had been up for along time. There were no flowers or any sign of a woman living here. This was definitely a man's house. There were many books, but no television. Though with his amnesia Akea did not realize it, this was unusual. The religion had banned most books. At the start of the revolution, the whole country had gone on a book-burning crusade. It is a good way to kill a culture, to burn the books. History is splattered with such obscenities as this. Akea heard voices in the kitchen; he dressed quickly and went to see if he could help.

"Hi," said Akea as he walked into the kitchen, rubbing his hair and trying to clean his teeth with his tongue.

"Hey, sorry we don't have any spare toothbrushes. You want bacon? How do you like your eggs? Toast?" said Cruz.

"I don't know, how *do* I want my eggs?" said Akea, smiling groggily.

"Well aren't you the ray of sunshine this morning?" said Juween.

Cruz leant in close to whisper in Akea's ear,

36

"Ignore him. He gets like that, you know, the morning after the night before."

"Oi, I may be hung over, but I ain't deaf."

On the table were bacon, eggs, and homemade bread, and a large pot of coffee. The aroma permeated the rest of the house. Both Cruz and Juween wore outdoors clothes and looked ready for a couple of days roughing it.

Birdsong emanated through the windows. The radio was on. Juween sat listening to the forecasts for that day. He looked a little tense.

"Good morning, city! It's 7 o'clock in the a.m., and it's going to be a bright and sunny day, with a high of around 24°C. Tomorrow will be much the same, with the highs around 25°C," squeaked the weather forecaster.

Akea didn't know if this was good or bad. Juween turned down the radio, muttering to himself about people who were bright and cheery in the morning.

They finished their breakfast. Juween poured out some more coffee.

"Right," he said. "Listen up: The plan is, we're gonna take this car to the launderette on Mornington Crescent. It's about fifteen minutes' drive. The attendant is gonna give us some clothes. The keys to another car are gonna be inside. We drive westbound on the A432 for half an hour, turn right into Weatherington, find Pablo's shop—it's called Harpers Hardware. Buy some nails. In the bag will be the keys for the third car. We have to get to a bus station locker, in which are the keys for the fourth car and false papers. From there, we drive to the north gate border. We've got official permission to leave the city. I'll brief you later. Take no possessions. Leave all identifying items here. I'll burn them."

Akea's back ached with tension as they sat around the open fire burning their papers, licences, credit cards, and debit cards. Akea felt a lump in the pit of his stomach as he watched the photo on his ID card burn. What happens if they catch us? he wondered.

Juween came into the living room and, noticing Akea's tenseness, patted him on the shoulder.

"Look, Akea, we're all a little tense. We can do this; we just got to hold our nerve. Remember: it ain't the bollocks you got; it's the bollocks you show."

"Yeah, I guess. No point in brooding. When do we leave?"

"About ten minutes."

Ten minutes later, they got into the small, cheap, blue car. It was about ten years old, but it was acceptable. The 1.3 litre diesel fired up, and they were off. They got to the launderette double-quick smart. The air was light, and the feeling was easygoing. They changed to the next car, a green estate, roomy and comfortable.

With stage one completed, they drove off listening to the radio. There was no traffic on the roads in the early Saturday morning. The early sun rose through fingers of pink and orange; there were high winds in the troposphere. The clouds formed ripples, accented with colour. On another day, Akea would have stopped to look at nature's little marvel. The car pulled up outside the hardware store, and Juween got out and stepped up to the building.

The Patrician watched the image with mild perplexity; he wasn't sure about what he saw. He watched Akea and Juween cross the city. It looked like they were on a shopping spree. Did he need to tell his guards, thus revealing to them that he was a magician, or should he allow his men to do their job? The questions bounced around his head like overexcited tennis balls in a steel box. It was unusual for the Patrician to think like this; he was normally clear in every detail.

Chance stood next to the Patrician, stroking his hair and whispering suggestions in his mind, just as she had seen her sister Luck do with many a hapless soul.

The hardware store stood third in on a row of shops, with an alley on each side for easy access to the back. Cruz noticed that each of the shops had flat roofs; she imagined what it would be like to have a flat roof, a roof garden, a tiny piece of freedom. Juween came out of the hardware store with a bag of nails and smiled; it was going well. They walked down two streets and got into a brown family saloon, about fifteen years old. The odd dents added character—a stubborn mule having a bad day. It smelt odd, old, and musty.

Juween sat in the driving seat of the beaten-up saloon. Cruz sat in the front passenger seat. Akea sat in the back. They made their way through town, trying to look inconspicuous. The traffic lights at the end of the road turned red. Juween looked round. A clean, new saloon car, one of the palace cars, sat at the opposite junction waiting for the green light.

"Ah, crap, palace guards," Juween said to Cruz.

He watched the patrol cop put the mike to his mouth. Probably requesting back up.

Juween carried on as if he had not a care in the world. Still looking at the road ahead, he said to the others, "Remember we have legitimate reasons to go to the border; they are not looking for three people, just Akea. They don't know about us. Akea, for God's sake don't look at them."

The Patrician woke up from his torpor like a clamshell snapping. He grabbed the radio and called the captain of the guard. "There's a brown saloon on Gothering Road, headed for the border. Seize them, but do not kill. And get some Watchmen out there," he bellowed.

In a disused area of an industrial estate, a patrol of Watchmen dressed in black and eating fast food out of paper containers sat in their beaten-up, super-charged, black sports car. To relieve the boredom that happens between beatings and to release their post-homicidal depression, they scanned the radio. They heard the Patrician's order and decided to investigate. They radioed their buddies; this could be interesting.

Two minutes later the brown saloon turned left on to Victory Way. Two unmarked palace cars followed. As they crossed a junction, another police car joined in. Juween wondered why they hadn't tried to stop them. Perhaps they wanted a closer look, or waited for more guards to turn up. His thoughts churned. At the third junction the Watchmen joined in the fray. It looked like a cadaverous funeral procession travelling at 30 mph through the streets. Finally, they joined the road to the north gate border, which was mostly empty at this time of day. Juween said, "We're nearly there."

Suddenly the Watchmen's sports car sped up and passed them, speeding on toward the border. The palace guards phoned the palace to let the Patrician know about the Watchmen. The Patrician stood at the image, said a few words in Latin and watched. It was like some obscure CCTV.

Juween knew this was going to get nasty. He turned to Akea. "When I say to, I want you to hold out your hand like this." He held out his hand as though to stop someone, fingers together and pointing to the sky. "Concentrate on the engine of the lead car and say *incendia tactim*. Got that?"

Akea nodded. He looked nervous. He asked, "What's the word for shield?"

Juween looked worried. *"Contego.* Wh—"

"Get down!" Akea shouted.

At that moment a hail of bullets erupted from the car behind and smashed through the back window. Akea closed his eyes. He imagined the car he was sitting in and put a mental shield around it. He whispered, *"Contego."* The bullets bounced off the magic shield. Then he turned and knelt on the back seat, looking out of the now broken back window and focusing intently on the car behind. He held out his hand and said, *"Incendia tactim."* Fingers of flame exploded out of his hand, like a locomotive on a mission. They hit the first car and lifted it clean into the air. A ball of flaming, molten metal, glass and bodies, it flipped over and landed on top of the car following. The third car crashed right into the inferno. The fire licked at stray branches of trees and bushes that lined the road, consuming the dry foliage till the highway became a burning gauntlet.

The tarmac melted, and the remaining cars careered into the crisis the fingers of fire had caused. The final car skidded to a stop and blocked the road. The smell of burning tarmac, rubber, plastic and flesh filled the air. The smoke could be seen for miles, almost blocking out the sun. Just as immense was the heat; none could go near it.

Fate sat invisibly in the back seat of the brown saloon, looking back at the wreckage. Beneath the roar of chaos, he heard his son ushering the souls of the dead to the next world.

"Can we block their radio?" asked Akea.

"Try *clausus radio,* that should work," Juween said.

The fugitive car raced on down the road toward the northern border. Akea was scared, but not as half as scared as Cruz. The ferocity of their first battle had overwhelmed her, and she started crying out of sheer terror. Akea concentrated and said, *"Clausus radio."*

The captain of the guard, who had been following the procession at a safe distance, tried to radio for help, but all he got was static. He turned his car around and limped back to the palace for further orders. He walked straight into the Patrician's office without knocking, too excited to observe the niceties.

"They got away. They destroyed three cars. God knows what happened," said the captain.

The Patrician was white with fury; an orange glow hung over him. His anger filled the room and became stifling. "Captain; this fugitive is a magician. He has broken the law. He must be stopped."

The captain whispered under his breath, "Magician. Yeah, right."

The Patrician heard and said a few choice words. The captain gripped his chest and fell to his knees and died. The Patrician stepped over the body as if it were not there and called for a lieutenant. The lieutenant came in and looked at the body of his former captain. Slightly shaken, he slowly looked up to the Patrician.

"Clear this mess up. And FIND ME THAT FUGITIVE," the Patrician bellowed.

"Yes sir," the lieutenant said. He turned crisply, strode from the room and radioed a request for backup at the border from all available palace, Watchman, and police cars.

Akea was punch-drunk. The encounter had taken a lot out of him, and he felt beaten up but victorious. As the car skidded to a stop about fifty yards from the border, the Watchmen in the guard house trained their specially modified semiautomatic light assault rifles with under-slung grenade launchers and armour-piercing rounds on the fugitives. Behind them, hounding palace cars had managed to get past the wreckage and were hot on their heels.

Juween turned to Cruz and said, "Whatever happens, hide in the car, under the foot well. We're gonna protect you. If we fail, you'll be better off dead."

Akea looked around. He noticed the clear blue sky, except for a few light clouds, the smell of the fresh air, the warm sun on the car roof, the little things that mean so much. Akea wondered if he would see another day. What was it like to die?

Just inside the border, thirty Watchmen cars spanned the road. Lights flashed, and sirens wailed. The only exit was blocked by an articulated lorry, which the Watchmen had commandeered. The driver and co-driver lay dead on the floor. The border patrol guards sat in their chairs, half-eaten doughnuts in their mouths and cups of hot tea on the table. They stared blankly at the images flashing on the CCTV. Only the bullet holes in their foreheads betrayed their status.

Inside the saloon, Akea and Juween looked at each other. Fear shone from the eyes of both.

Juween told Akea, "You need to control yourself, or you'll kill us all."

Akea looked at Juween helplessly. "What do I do?"

"We meld minds. I'll try to help you control your power. But there are risks—you could kill us both."

Akea smiled. "I think we are already dead."

"Look me in the eyes and say with me, *iungo ut unus*," Juween ordered.

They stared into each other's eyes, not for the first time in twenty-four hours, but perhaps for the last.

43

Akea's eyes turned orange and elongated, like a tiger's eyes, and a faint blue haze began to form around him. Together they said, *"Iungo ut unus."* It hit each of them like a head rush.

Akea and Juween got out of the car and stood next to it, back-to-back, one staring down the Watchmen and the other staring at the police. Two dogs of war in perfect harmony, they had a 360-degree view of the situation. They steeled themselves for the worst. A call from a megaphone broke through the tension like a hot knife through frozen butter. A stern voice ordered the two to lay down their weapons and give themselves up. Time slowed down. There was electricity in the air. Many of the pursuers and police looked disconcerted and worried; a gold watch and a pension were hardly worth this. Hot, sticky air pressed on all sides, and the morning sun beat down relentlessly. No one moved. It was like a macabre stand off. More than seventy well-armed men stood in the way of freedom. The only trouble was that Akea and Juween had no physical weapons, and they had to protect Cruz.

Juween produced a shield that encapsulated them and the car. The power from Akea was hurting Juween badly, but he held on for all he was worth. Blood trickled from the corners of his eyes. At some unseen signal, the police, the guards, and in particular the Watchmen unleashed their weapons, but the bullets and grenades sprayed at the two fugitives just zinged off the shield. The ferocity stunned Akea as through his mind he felt the bullets hit the shield. The noise was horrific. Smoke billowed into the air. Juween transferred a spell through their mind meld: *lux lucis telum.* Akea spoke the spell, unleashing his power. Small arrows of silver shot out of his fingers, like rounds from a high-powered machine-gun.

He sprayed indiscriminately at the enemy, seeing nothing but red wrath. Bits of cars, bodies, glass and metal flew into the air. The screams of the enemy elated Akea. Godlike feelings rose within him. Drunk on power, he began to enjoy himself. He laughed insanely. The dark feelings behind his eyes had reared their heads.

Juween fell to the ground; the power of Akea flowing through him was too much to bear. The shield fell, and bullets smashed into both of them. Blood was pouring out of Juween; his body represented a grotesque colander.

"AHHH—IS THAT ALL YOU GOT?" Akea screamed.

Akea, the enraged animal, tried to regain control, throwing out a shield around the car and Juween once more, but Juween was dying. He whispered to Akea, *"Vigoratus."* Akea repeated the word, and the blood stopped, but Juween lay as though dead. Akea chanced a look at the bullet-riddled car. He saw Cruz, with her head at an odd angle; she was dead, a bullet hole in her forehead. The clouds slowly drifted on, the sun still beat down and a light wind blew from the south.

Akea was alone, no one to stop or control him. The fury that he had released seemed limitless. He reached out with his mind and crushed all those who opposed him. The wave of energy rolled over the Watchmen, like the energy from an atom bomb rolled up into a small white ribbon, destroying everything in its wake, a wave of instant death. None survived. The wave atomised most of the men. The white energy of all that Akea could muster hit everything in a half-mile radius. The blue hue that had formed around him became as bright as the sun and as deep as the ocean. The bonds of the Patrician's spells had broken; the

45

magic and the power were free at last. It rushed up in Akea like a suppressed spring being released.

In the grand palace of the Patrician, the power of Akea was too great for the image, and it exploded. The force threw the Patrician across the room. He picked himself up. "Damn."

Three minutes had passed. Akea sat on the ground; he looked at his body for the first time and noticed his wounds. He felt the bullets in his body with his mind and pushed them out. With the incantation *vigoratus,* the holes quickly healed up, but he had lost much blood. He was spent; if more Watchmen came now he would not be able to stop them. But they did not come. Instead, a small green saloon car came hurtling through the wreckage of mangled cars and bodies. It screeched to a halt, and a bald, podgy man jumped out. It was Pablo, not at the moment sporting his habitual broad smile. The hardware store owner and forger had been tracking the events on his police scanner. He could see smoke from miles away, and at Fate's prompting, he got in his car and drove towards it. Now, witnessing the carnage, he didn't know what to do. He had to do something, anything. He was scared out of his wits.

He ran over and pulled the lump of dead weight that was Juween into his car and then turned to Akea. "Can you walk?"

Akea nodded. He rose gingerly to his feet and staggered to the car.

"We will have to leave the girl," the hardware store owner said.

Akea didn't hear the words. He got into the car and fell unconscious.

As Pablo was turning to get into the saloon, a car came hurtling towards them. He jumped in and drove as fast as he could down the road and across the border. The chasing black saloon started to gain on them. Watchmen in the back leant out of the window and started to shoot at them.

"Wake up, DO something!" Pablo screamed at Akea.

Akea looked around groggily and realised what was going on. He tried to stop the Watchmen, but he was too weak; all he could manage was a shield around the car. The Watchmen's bullets zinging off the shield hurt Akea, but he held on. A fight ensued between the cars, as the Watchmen tried to push Pablo into the barriers. But Pablo managed to stay on course. After a few miles, Pablo took the next junction. The minor road was empty. Mile after mile Pablo drove, his foot to the floor, the Watchmen right on their tail. Akea kept falling into unconsciousness, but the shield held. Pablo nearly missed the turn off that led to the mountains. He slammed on the brakes and skidded to a stop. The car fishtailed and smoke from the tyres hung in the air. The Watchmen carried on past and did a U-turn. Pablo turned down the pot-holed, dirt road and drove as fast as he dared, with the Watchmen close behind. Half-concentrating on the road, he grabbed the transmitter for the short-wave radio and called for help.

"Home Run, come in, Home Run. For God's sake, where are you?" Pablo's voice was pitched a bit higher than usual, almost hysterical.

"This is Home Run; state your name and purpose."

"This is Lone Wolf; I have two unwanted presents, coming in fast. Visitors, I repeat visitors, code 15, 46. I repeat, code 15, 46. Be at the right place, now."

"Got that, see you there," said a bored voice, which brought no comfort to Pablo.

Would they be there? His thoughts bounced around as much as the car.

A cloud of dust betrayed the position of the fleeing car and its pursuer. The sun beat down; it was getting hot. The smell of blood and sweat was nauseating Pablo. He had a hard time keeping hold of his breakfast. The hot, arid air streaming through the windows did not ease the discomfort.

The mountains in front of them towered above the wastelands. Forests grew on their slopes. The road suddenly turned right and started to climb, becoming even narrower. The car struggled to climb the steep ascent. Two cars waited in a lay-by. Pablo streaked past them, followed closely by the Watchmen's car. The two cars gave chase. A rebel leant out of the back window holding a rocket-propelled grenade launcher, aimed at the Watchmen and fired. The Watchmen's car leapt off the road and rolled down the mountainside, engulfed in flames. Eventually Pablo realised what was going on. He stopped the car, got out and collapsed on the ground. His heart had not beaten so fast in years; his body had forgotten what adrenaline tasted like.

The rebel cars pulled up, and five men got out of the cars and ran over to Pablo.

"I thought you guys were never going to turn up. Oh God, I feel sick. We got two severely wounded in the back. We had to leave one dead at the border," Pablo told them. He stood up shakily. "You better move." He pushed one of the rebels out of the way, stumbled to the side of the road and sprayed his stomach contents off the edge of the cliff.

Three of the rebel patrolmen hauled Juween and Akea into their car. When Pablo returned, one of the rebels spoke. "We'll introduce ourselves in the car. Get in." The car drove off as fast as the road allowed up the mountain, to the waiting arms of the rebel base. The two remaining rebels set fire to the brown saloon

48

and pushed it off the mountain. It tumbled down the mountainside end over end and finally settled on the ground below.

Both the rebel cars drove several more miles along the dirt road before they turned off at the site of a disused nuclear reactor.

Chapter 3: Caranthir Tinúviel

The University of Magician Excellence sat between two hills, in a valley of southern Merid. Merid was a small country similar to Ordeania, but whereas Ordeania existed in the first reality, Merid occupied the sixth reality. On a particularly cool summer's morning a teenager named Vaxihimler wandered among the stacks of the university library looking for books on his favourite subjects. He was a tall, thin boy with no particular friends, the loner's loner. The library boasted that it held a copy of every book ever published in any of the known realities. Vaxihimler's hand fell on a book. It had an interesting title: *Seeing the Future from Caranthir's Eyes*. He grabbed it and placed it on the pile with the others. He went and sat at an empty table in the corner, away from prying eyes.

He enjoyed the sun that streamed through the high, vaulted windows. The ancient crystals in the chandelier twinkled in the sunlight like stars. He coughed slightly at the tickly musty smell one associates with old books. Settling into his seat, he tucked his coat around him. The sun might be warm, but the library wasn't.

Vaxihimler picked up the book with the intriguing title. "Hello, what have we here? I don't think you belong in this section." He often talked to his books. It seemed natural. The more he met people, the more he liked his books.

He opened *Seeing the Future from Caranthir's Eyes* and began to leaf through it. Feeling a pleasant sense of distraction, he read the first few pages. It seemed mindless nonsense. However, he read on. He enjoyed the imaginary places the book described.

He imagined what it would be like for those people. The book described the banished one. Vaxihimler read on. . . .

Seeing the Future from Caranthir's Eyes
by
T. Poluth

Page 337: Ripped from his home of forest green and magic plenty, the enemy will be found crying in a cradle seeking the attention of his dead mother.

Page 338: A young magician will seek out the banished one. He will rule with an iron rod. The tears of suffering will reach out to one who can change fate. The magician, the ruler will seek his equal and pamper him. Only then can the magician have total rule.

Page 344: He will smite his enemy into the ground.

*

The ten-year-old boy sat in the study of the mansion as his governess tried to teach the intricacies of basic algebra. Caranthir Tinúviel played with his blond hair, half listening, and wondered what adventures lay in the grounds outside. Unlike most, he could read and write. To the manor born, he suffered a privileged upbringing. The knock on the door echoed throughout the mansion, jogging him out of his stupor. He ran from the study to the front door to see who it was. Lord Tinúviel stood next to the butler. The messenger at the door gasped for air.

"My lord, I have some bad news," said the messenger.

"Timpson, get this man a drink of water," said Lord Tinúviel.

"Much obliged, your honour."

"Well, what is it, man? Speak up."

"The plague has hit the northern end of town, your honour."

"What!"

For Caranthir's tenth birthday, a terrible disease swept across the land and wiped out two-thirds of the populace. Caranthir's parents died trying to save as many as they could and tending to the sick. Delirious with fever, hunger and grief, Caranthir wandered into the forest. There Ikarius the tormentor discovered Caranthir and ushered the boy to a cave, where he was to remain, away from civilisation, until his dying day.

Ikarius the imp was almost cute, except for his cruel smile; he came across as a short man. He always smoked a crooked cigar. He had been sent by the lords of the three hells to torment souls. He enjoyed his work, giving hope to those who had none and then ripping it away just at the right time. Caranthir was different. He had no hope, but neither did he seek it. He was a soul waiting to greet Death. The cave Ikarius led Caranthir to was warm and dry. The imp taught Caranthir how to look after himself.

"Caranthir, do you have enough food? Are you warm enough?" Ikarius spoke with a gravely voice sweetened with a hint of cruelty.

"Yes to both, thank you for your kindness."

"Soon I must leave you, but I want to leave you with a gift. If I could grant you a wish, one wish, what would you wish for?"

"I'd wish for the gift of second sight. Then I could warn others of impending doom," said the ten-year-old.

Caranthir was granted his wish, and Ikarius left for other pastures. As time went on Caranthir could no longer distinguish between his present reality and the futures he saw. Townsfolk would seek him out for two reasons: to seek their future or to mock him. None trusted him nor loved him. He resembled a pitiful animal. He lived off locusts and wore sackcloth clothes. His hair was wild and matted, a world away from the once beautiful golden locks, and his eyes shone wild and mad. Many believed that he was either insane or a babbling idiot.

Then, in Caranthir's thirtieth year, Trisha, a young, beautiful maiden, full of life, hope and joy, took pity on him. She visited his cave daily, fed him with proper food and sat listening to his visions. She cut his hair and provided him with decent clothes. Caranthir gained weight and, over time, his hair grew out once again blond and curly. But when Trisha's father found out about her visits to Caranthir, he assumed the worst and banished her from the family home. From then on she lived with Caranthir in the cave. When she discovered that Caranthir could write, she encouraged him to write down his prophecies, and he did so, laboriously listing out over three hundred of them.

Many years later, long after the death of Caranthir and Trisha, a traveller was caught in a storm. Spying the long-deserted cave, Mathew ducked into it for shelter. As he huddled in the cave and waited out the storm, he looked around. Clearly someone had once abided here in relative comfort. There were chairs and tables and a bed, all in a state of neglect and decay. Spying a trunk sitting against one wall of the cave, Mathew pried it open and discovered inside a

53

carefully bundled stack of papers. It was Caranthir's prophecies. Fascinated with the cryptic lettering, he took the bundle with him.

Later, Mathew shared the papers with his friend Theodor over tea.

Theodor had some command of the old language. He studied the writing intently as he sipped his tea. Finally he looked up at Mathew. "They appear to be predictions or prophecies of some kind. But I am afraid that they meld, one into another. I am not sure where one starts and the other stops," he said.

"I have a proposition for you: translate the prophecies the best you can. We can put them in a book and sell it," said Mathew.

"But this may be heresy. It may turn everything upside-down. We could get in trouble."

"Most people will read it for vanity's sake. And ignore the rest."

"What do you mean, 'vanity's sake'?"

"People will read it hoping for a glimpse of their future."

"You mean sell the book, and let people make up their own mind."

So after a year of translating and writing, the book was published, and was met with scorn in some quarters and praise in others. The controversy ensured its immediate success, and Theodor and Mathew toured the world presenting the prophecies. Many people jumped on board, providing their own commentaries on what the prophecies were supposed to mean. A religion was started, but it provided no basis for moral judgment and soon failed. The traveller Mathew and the wise old Theodor died rich men.

The books, the conspiracy theorists, all had their day. In time they fell out of fashion. The prophecies were widely considered mystic dribble, forgotten by many, ignored by the rest, shelved forgotten in a dusty library in a remote reality.

*

First fascinated, and then obsessed, Vaxihimler's life quest became to find the banished one. His obsession consumed his every waking moment. When he graduated from the University of Magician Excellence, Vaxihimler began his voyage to find his fate.

Chapter 4: Rebellion and Retribution

Fate sat in his cool, dark office, writing away. There was a knock, and Chance walked in and stood next to her husband, bemusement on her face. He looked up from his work and smiled. It was nice to see her tranquil face in a sea of frustration.

"That's right, the big man can handle anything," she muttered.

"Morning dear, it's nice to see you too." After a pause Fate continued, "You don't normally get involved with my work. Why now?"

"You don't normally get this involved in the affairs of mortals."

"Dear, I have made a mistake. Someone cheated me—an oversight on my behalf. I am trying to correct it. The right people, in the right place, at the right time. That is the way of the universes."

Chance had watched the proceedings at the border that day. "Don't you dare try to fob me off with that 'That is the way of the universe' rubbish. What do you mean, a mistake? You don't make mistakes," she chided her husband.

For the first time in her life, she realised how old he was. The fire had not left him, though. She leant over and kissed him on the cheek.

"Dear, it's not like you to get het up about anything," Fate retorted. He sighed deeply. "I found an entity that I thought had died, but it hadn't—it was moved. Now I have to correct it. More importantly I have to find how it happened. Senility: it's a bitch."

"You are not senile. Old, but not senile. I may flutter around, but that does not mean I don't know what's going on."

Fate pushed himself from the desk and got up from the chair. He gently put his arms around Chance and held her, whispering, "I love you" in her ear.

Still holding her, he continued to voice his dismay. "I am too involved now. I have set things in motion which cannot be stopped. Chance, for the first time in history, I am in too deep; I have feelings for this human and am angry with another human. I—I . . . don't know what to do. I feel lost."

Chance was not ready for this kind of admission. She just held him for a few seconds. Then she combed her fingers through his white hair. "Dearest, love of my eternity, I think we are all changing. I have never been so focused."

They stood there for a pseudo-eternity.

Chance finally spoke. "I want my husband back. So I am going to help you. Maybe the kids can help, too."

Fate felt moved to argue, but he knew better. "I doubt that Life will help; she doesn't like fighting or killing. Death is already in on it. He helped with the plans. All he knows is war and, well, death."

"You big, silly oaf, you don't have to stand alone. Are we not a family? We will sort this out together."

Fate smiled and held Chance close, closer than he could remember.

*

The knowledge of the fight for freedom could not be contained. The rebel resistance had the CCTV footage of two men, unarmed, facing down seventy fully armed guards, police, and Watchmen. They planned to use it to their best advantage. Soon it would be common knowledge. They had already broadcast the first half of the battle right up to the point where the shield collapsed on unofficial secure

57

Web sites, and now the media had gotten hold of it. They of course could not mention it outright, but mention it they did. The names Akea and Juween were rapidly becoming the most secret household names in the history of mankind. It went without saying many critics and sceptics portrayed the event as a sick hoax. But like the seeds of mistletoe on an old oak tree, change was stirring. Like the embers of an old fire blown back into life, people started to remember what the notion of freedom actually meant.

*

The Patrician sat in a dimly lit office in the depths of the palace. The office was plain, without the usual grandeur of the palace. The fewer people who knew about this meeting the better. The Patrician sat and waited at the head of a long, hundred-year-old oak table. It was plainly decorated and proudly bore the markings of age.

There was a knock on the door, and two men entered and sat down. To the Patrician's right now sat the leader of the Watchmen, Morguhis. His name meant nothing to almost everyone. He was the silent power behind the vicious men under his command, and like Juween he was much older than he seemed. He had a thin face, smooth and somehow evil. Light, cornflower blue eyes gazed from a narrow head and thin, fit body. His hands, swift and adept, rested on the table. Opposite to him in more than one way sat the leader of the religion, Obegetho, a balding man with warm eyes and a hearty laugh. He came across as the giver of presents. He was known for much charity work and spent most of his time ministering to the parishioners at large, gaining their confidence, learning their secrets and feeding them lies. His favourite lie, because it was the hardest to prove, was

58

"You do not have enough faith."

The Patrician began the meeting. He spoke in a cool, soothing voice. "Gentlemen, we are here today to discuss—"

"We know why we are here. We are going discuss the fight at the border and find out what you intend to do about it," hissed Morguhis.

"If you will allow me to continue," said the Patrician, even more smoothly. "We have put a trace on the leaked footage. It came from the rebel resistance in their damn base, which of course we can't attack and gain control of. As always we are in a stalemate, they not strong enough to attack, but too secure in their base to be attacked. We can, however, fight back in other ways. We need to stop the rot. We need to show force to those who oppose us. We, gentlemen, are going to beat, hang, shoot, whisper and refute the name of Akea and the fight at the border. Morguhis, anyone found mentioning the name Akea will be shot for treason, or hanged. I want you to beat up random people, put them in prison, hang them from lampposts—I leave it to your vast imagination. In short, I want to put the fear of God into the people.

"Obegetho, I want you to condemn these actions, urging the people that their god is angry because of what happened at the border. Tell them what happened, but put a spin on it. Work together. Obegetho, you give Morguhis names, people and places. Obegetho, make this out as a holy war. Feed them lies, exaggerate.

"By the end of the week, if Akea shows his face, people will either be too afraid to help him or so angry they'll chase him to the city limits."

"Who is this Akea?" Morguhis asked.

"Hang on, I know an Akea—Akea de Silva, is that him?" Obegetho butted in.

"Yes, that's him. He is a magician of inordinate power. If the rebels have him, then we need to prepare for war, or at least an attack."

"Why did you allow him to live?" Morguhis asked.

"He of course, up until yesterday, had no idea. I blinded him from his identity," the Patrician said coolly. "But somehow his powers have become evident to him."

"Ah, great. Not only did your plan fail, but we have a real enemy that we cannot contain. Oh, well done," said Morguhis.

An orange glow had begun to form around the Patrician. The water jug on the table started to rattle as the water inside began to simmer. The Patrician reached out for Morguhis neck with his mind and squeezed. "How dare you speak to me in this manner? Do not forget who it is you are talking to, and who gave you incredible licence to roam the streets. If you are not careful, all that can disappear."

Gasping for air, Morguhis groaned, "Okay. I'll get it done."

*

It had been three days since the flight from the city. Pablo was given a new car and false papers. He sneaked back into the city by the south gate and acted as if nothing had happened. The road had been shut for "essential repairs", and rumours of the battle circulated the city like wildfire.

*

The peaks of the high mountain range stuck out like a smile of broken teeth. . . .

Akea woke up. That dream again. It haunted all of his sleeping moments.

He moved his eyes inside his aching head to see that he was in a hospital wing without windows. The walls were painted white; it seemed the paint had been up for some time. The high ceiling bore florescent lights that illuminated the wing with clinical sterility. He turned his head to see Juween in the bed next to him, awake and talking to a nurse. He turned his head the other way and saw that the large ward was full of people, patients and nurses. The mixture of cleanliness and patients being patients annoyed Akea's nose.

"Where are we? Where—where is Cruz?" Akea said groggily.

The smartly dressed nurse who was tending to Juween turned and bit her lower lip. Then it hit him, like a tsunami of emotion. The bullet-riddled car, and Cruz's head at a strange angle. His memory focused on the bloodstained face of Cruz. Tears welled in his eyes and rolled down his face. How did I let this happen, where did all that power come from, why can't I control it? To have all this power and no control—what use am I? Akea's thoughts raged on. "Cruz, Cruz," he called out, not realising that his thoughts were vocal.

Juween turned to him. "We are at the rebel base, my lad. You destroyed everything after she died. You did not kill her. Mourn for her, but don't you blame yourself." Juween started to cry. "She was the nearest thing to a daughter."

Akea collapsed in pain and turmoil as he recalled the events over and over again. Worst of all was the memory of his insane, self-imposed, godlike megalomania. I want to be free, but I want to free the city, if I can. I want to make the Watchmen pay for what they have done to Cruz, but how can I, if I can't control my anger?

Hours later Juween got out of bed. He sat on the chair beside Akea's bed and softly spoke a few words in Latin. The words were like a mother's embrace. Akea began to feel more like his former self.

A nurse walked by.

"Nurse, nurse," Juween called out, trying to get her attention.

"Yes, can I help you?"

"When can we be discharged? We would like to see the leader of the rebel army."

"I'll go and see the doctor, and arrange an escort, if the doctor says you can go."

The nurse went to check with a doctor and was back soon with an armload of clothing. "Your old clothes were covered in blood and full of holes. You'll have to wear these."

Juween took the clothes and thanked her for her trouble. The clothes looked like street clothes: two pairs of heavy cotton trousers, one blue shirt, one light green shirt, and two pairs of shoes.

"We've got to see the leader and ask him for food and supplies for a three-day hike. We're gonna go on a walk," Juween said as Akea and he dressed. Akea took the light green shirt as it fitted him better.

A guard came up to them and stood to attention. "We are here to escort you to the captain."

"Thank you, soldier. Would you mind if we went to the canteen? If that prick—I mean, if your commanding officer gives you trouble, just blame me. He will readily accept that," said Juween.

"Yes. Right sir, and canteen it is."

Akea spoke softly to Juween, "What do you want to gain by calling his boss a prick?"

Juween whispered back, "I'll tell you later, but before we meet Nalik the prick. Tell you the truth; I

62

don't think he likes me."

A guard showed them the way; they were guests, after all, and one couldn't have them wandering around unattended. They walked through what seemed miles of large, well-lit tunnels, homely in a bizarre way. The base had stood as a home for two generations of nonbelievers and dissidents. There seemed to be lots of people coming and going; none gave them a second look. It was not unusual to see new faces here. It seemed well organised. The sounds of the operations were like a ticking clock without the ticking. The rebel guard explained in a conversational manner that they had a good system, if a bit bizarre.

They walked down this tunnel and then that. Akea tried to keep track, but he had to admit he was thoroughly lost. Finally they entered the canteen, where a group of guards huddled around a table. One of the men, apparently the leader, looked up at them and gestured to a nearby table. He said, "I am corporal thevenin, though it is of no consequence. Please sit down at that table. I was just going to have some food brought. It's a limited menu. Would you like tea or coffee?"

Juween replied, "Hello, Corporal Thevenin. We will have two coffees, and whatever you normally have. We're starving and not picky."

Corporal Thevenin ordered a couple of the guards to bring coffee and food and then said to Juween, "Sir, I will give you some space." He ordered his men and the guard who had brought them to move three tables away, and then joined his men. Close enough to see them, far enough not to overhear. The corporal was not stupid. This Juween knew stuff about Nalik, and he did not want to know; more importantly, he should not let his men overhear.

The guards returned with trays of coffee and food, which they distributed to the two tables. After several hungry bites, Juween said to Akea, "I knew Nalik when he was a platoon leader. One night we were on a sortie. All magicians in the rebel army are either officers or advisers; since I didn't have any military experience; I was an adviser, placed where I could use magic for covert surveillance. Well, anyway, we were on the sortie, and the Watchmen jumped the platoon. Nalik and I were the only ones who survived. He blamed me for incompetent surveillance. The fight we just had will be another piece of evidence that I am incompetent. We have to tread carefully; don't expect any grace from him."

Akea just shook his head when Juween said "incompetent".

Their guard had finished his dinner and waited for Juween and Akea to finish theirs. They got up and walked down to the operations room.

The well-lit room had computers and operators along the back wall. Maps hung on the adjacent wall, and in the corner there sat what appeared to be a radar screen.

An average-looking man in mid forties turned his head and looked up from his work. He got up and faced his guests. He nodded to Juween, and an arrogant smile appeared on his face as he said to Akea, "My name is Nalik. How do you like our home? It was once a nuclear power plant, built deep underground, long before the revolution. Most people had forgotten about it. But as soon as the revolution started the people who were displaced or exiled ran for shelter here. It was built to withstand a nuclear strike, and only one official entrance exists. No army in their right mind would attack us from the front. We are perfectly safe here. In any case, I can see that you

64

are well and ready to leave."

Juween looked at him with incomprehension on his face. He had not discussed his plans with anyone.

Nalik continued, "Seemingly, between the two of you, you destroyed thirty cars, seventy-five men, three hundred yards of road and two hundred trees. I expect the Watchmen will execute people for this." He paused for effect. "Therefore you are not welcome here—you just made our job a hundred times harder. People want you to leave in a hurry, so forgive me if I don't take time to hand out any medals."

Juween and Akea still stood in the doorway where the guard had presented them.

Juween said, "Well, we all have bad days. Give us food for three days, and we'll be on our way."

Nalik laughed. "You've got a nerve. Give you food!"

Juween retorted, "You sanctimonious, lily-livered, liberal-minded, chicken-headed, short-sighted son of a slum bitch."

"How dare you talk to me in that manner! Get out!"

Akea whispered to Juween, "Calm down a bit. This is not like you."

Juween whispered back rather coarsely, "You know shit about me," and then he took a deep breath and sighed. "Are you going to give us food or not? For old times' sake."

"Did you not hear me? I said get out." Nalik's anger rose even higher.

A light blue aura had begun to form around Akea. Worriedly, Juween told him to calm down.

"Guards, take these two freaks out of my sight," Nalik said. He turned back to Juween and said, "Your faith in your bugger boy will be your downfall."

Akea moved to rush Nalik, but Juween put a hand on Akea's shoulder.

Akea stopped and said, "And the award for the asshole of the year goes to . . ."

Juween cottoned on and did a drum role on his thighs.

"General Nalik," Akea. He put his thumb out as a pretend microphone. "How does it feel to be a complete prick?" He and Juween then did a crisp about face and walked out, followed hastily by three guards.

The second in command, Bavlin, approached Nalik.

"Sir, they'll freeze at night," said Bavlin.

"Tough. Hopefully the wolves will finish them off," Nalik replied, and then demanded, "Are you questioning my authority?"

"No, sir, but he is right about one thing," Bavlin said to Nalik.

"And what's that?"

"You are an asshole." With that Bavlin walked out.

"That could have gone better," Akea said to Juween, as the guards led them away from the operations room. They showed Akea and Juween a hidden passage that led to the mountains. The tunnel opened into a loading bay, where at one end stood two massive reinforced concrete doors. To one side was a small control room, about six feet by eight feet, with a large window on the leading wall, under which sat a bank of controls. One of the guards went into the control room and spoke to one of his colleagues. The door creaked and groaned as it started to open. Akea and Juween glimpsed a slight slope outside, with vehicles parked neatly on one side. They heard running footsteps behind them and turned to see Bavlin approaching.

A second later, Bavlin had caught up with them. He turned to the escorting guards and said, "Right, you three, you can leave. I'll take it from here."

The guards turned, saluted and marched off. Bavlin waited until the guards were out of sight.

"All I could get for you are these two coats. They're not much, I'm afraid."

Juween faced him and said, "Thanks, sorry you had to see that."

"Not a problem. Good luck, it gets cold at night."

He handed over two grey trench-coats. Juween and Akea tried them on. Finding he was too big for either of them, Juween held one out in front of him and applied an engrossment charm to it. The coat fluttered in his hands as though in a breeze, expanding across the shoulders and along the arms. When the coat stopped fluttering, Juween smiled with satisfaction and donned it. Bavlin gave them a map showing the rough area where the old man had last been seen. They thanked him and went out through the fifteen-foot doors. The doors creaked shut behind them, nestling into a high cliff face at the foot of the slope. They set out on their way.

The cool, fresh air was slightly overwhelming compared to the stuffiness of the old nuclear reactor.

Chapter 5: Higher Authority

The Patrician sat at his desk and stared into middle space; he had his elbows on the desk and rested his head on his interlocked fingers. He knew what he must do. But the prospect worried him. He picked up the phone from its plain cradle and dialled a secret number. The Emperor's personal assistant answered, and the Patrician asked to see the Emperor as soon as it was convenient. He didn't want to talk over the phone. He must see the Emperor in person. The Patrician walked out of his office and out of the palace, where a black stretched luxury car with blacked-out windows waited. He ignored the four heavily armed bodyguards stationed around it and got into the back of the limousine. The Patrician often had this car driven around the city, to see if anyone would try and attack it, but so far no one had.

The Patrician told the driver to drive as fast as he could to Mevelin, the capital city. He was not looking forward to meeting with the Emperor. His mind raced and pondered on how Akea had managed to disappear. He would have to explain that his plans had failed, and a great enemy was gaining power.

As the car raced though the city, the Patrician looked out onto the streets and wondered how many people he truly controlled. How many were starting to wake up to the truth? The car sped on. At the city border, the Patrician, lost in thought, paid no attention as the guard opened the gate. Out on the motorway the car hurtled along. The Patrician gazed out on the sparse landscape and the mountains in the distance and breathed deeply. It was nice to get out of the city once in a while.

On the motorway the car raced though the Ordeanian countryside. They passed small villages surrounded by green fields and farmland. The car stopped for fuel at a small village and then continued on. All too soon, they neared the outskirts of the capital city. The four-hundred-mile journey had taken less time than the Patrician had hoped.

The car entered Mevelin and wound through the streets of the suburbs. Finally the roads straightened out to face the massive wall-lined square and palaces. In front of the square stood a large, ornately carved granite gate. No matter how many times he saw it, it always took the Patrician's breath away. The car stopped outside the gate; no vehicle was allowed past the sacred gate.

Beyond the gate was a square, which led to the main palace and opened at the sides into a fine park with beautiful trees bearing a variety of fruits. In the park roamed beasts of many kinds, white stags and fallow deer, gazelles and roe-bucks. Squirrels of various sorts scampered about freely. There were numbers also of the animal that gives musk, and all manner of other beautiful creatures. The whole place was full of them, and no spot remained void except where there was the traffic of people going and coming. The ground was covered with abundant grass, and the roads through it were all paved and raised two feet above the surface, so they never become muddy, nor did the rain lodge on them, but flowed off into the meadows, quickening the soil and producing an abundance of herbage.

From that corner of the enclosure that was towards the northwest there extended a fine lake, containing fish of different kinds that the Emperor had caused to be put in there, so that whenever he desired any, he could have them at his pleasure. A river entered this lake and issued from it, but there was a grating of iron or brass at its mouth so that the fish couldn't escape.

The park was enclosed all round by a great wall forming a square, each side a mile in length. It was very thick and a good twelve feet in height, brightly painted in tasteful colours and loop-holed all round. At each angle of the wall there was a small palace, richly decorated, and midway between every two of these corner palaces was another: one palace for each major point of the compass. They were stored with the Emperor's readiness for war, each palace dedicated to one article of war, such as ammunition or guns.

Inside the outer wall there was a second, enclosing a space somewhat greater in length than in breadth. This enclosure also had eight palaces, corresponding to those of the outer wall, and stored, like them, with the Emperor's readiness of war. This wall had five gates on the southern face, corresponding to five gates in the outer wall, and one gate on each of the other faces.

Inside the inner wall stood the main palace, whose great hall was so large that in it could easily dine seven thousand people. It was quite a marvel to see how many rooms there were besides. The building was altogether so vast, so rich and so beautiful that no man on the planet could design anything superior to it. The roof was coloured with vermilion and yellow and green and blue and other hues, which were fixed with a varnish so fine and exquisite that they shone like crystal and lent a resplendent luster to the palace that could be seen for a great way round. This roof was constructed with such strength and solidity that it was fit to last forever.

On the far side of the palace were large buildings with halls and chambers, where the Emperor's private property was placed, such as his treasures of gold, silver, gems, pearls and gold plate, and in which resided the ladies and concubines. There he occupied himself at his own convenience, and no one else had access.

The Patrician walked through the square towards the palace. On certain days tourists were allowed to marvel at the mosaics on the walls and wonder at the monuments, but only a privileged few saw the park beyond. Royal blue flags fluttered in the breeze on one wall, and on another wall hung a twenty-foot-tall portrait of the Emperor looking down on his people. His kindly looking face held just a tinge of sternness as it gazed across the square. The Patrician walked up the main steps to the palace entrance and was greeted by the captain of the palace guards, who told him the Emperor was expecting him. The guard escorted him to the Emperor's private gardens.

The Patrician followed the guard through the palace, trying not to look impressed. As they entered the gardens, the fresh air and the sounds and smells of nature invigorated the Patrician and gave him a sense of being alive. He found the Emperor sitting on a chair in the shade, meditating. He wore a bright-coloured silk gown. He had white hair down to his knees, and a beard just as long. The eyes in his old wrinkled face were closed. The Patrician bowed low and waited for the signal to raise his head.

The Emperor opened his eyes slowly and said, "Ah, Vaxihimler. Welcome, welcome. Please sit." The Emperor clicked a finger, and a chair appeared from nowhere.

The Emperor continued, "What brings you here — not idle chit-chat, I trust?"

"My lord, mentor and wise counsel, I bring ill news. My — my . . . plan for Akea has failed, my lord.

71

He is free and gaining strength."

"When you first approached me with your plan, I seem to remember saying that it would fail. You cannot crush rebellion through kindness or chance. You should have killed him when he was a baby."

"Yes, my lord, your counsel is always wise."

"So you have come here looking for help and guidance, I suppose."

"Yes, my lord."

The Emperor continued to gaze out over the garden, deep in thought. Vaxihimler, if he had not known better, would have suspected the Emperor was asleep. After a full five minutes, the Emperor spoke.

"When you first freed me, you were so eager to learn everything. I nursed you and gave you power beyond your imagination. Yet you are still foolish. Did I not show you how to use the gates between realities without a Gatekeeper? Did I not give you Morguhis, the most evil man alive? Did I not reward you for your unyielding belief in me? You were so young and naive. Yet you remain foolish."

"Yes, my lord."

"I have no doubt that you tried to find your counterparts in other realities and ask for help. But they will not come."

"No, my lord."

"You have come to me, expecting me to wave a magic hand and save you from your stupidity. This is what we shall do: You will go to the alternate realities and find your counterparts. You will raise an army of the most dark and terrible creatures. Do whatever it takes to get them on your side. When you are ready, you will send word to me. I will bring a large force from here, and we will meet this problem head on. In the end, there will not be much left of your precious city. I shall take control of what is left of it, until such time as I find you fit for rule again."

The Emperor paused for a few minutes to let the rebuke set in. Then he continued.

"I shall give you one more chance, but if you fail, you better hope that Akea kills you before I do. Now the Latin to change form: *Extraho vir*. Use it well. You will need arms; I will supply them, and although I don't think the dark creatures are accustomed to such things, I will supply you with the blueprints for ancient war machines."

"Yes, my lord, thank you, lord."

"One last thing, Vaxihimler: you have disappointed me and embarrassed me in front of the whole world. I am giving you a chance to redeem yourself. Now take your leave. I've had enough of your folly."

The Patrician bowed low and walked away slowly. He was surprised to find the Emperor so helpful. And it was the Emperor's helpfulness that worried him the most.

The journey home was not quick enough for the Patrician, although the driver spent most of the time with his foot on the floor. They had to stop twice for fuel, which infuriated the Patrician something chronic. When they arrived back at the palace, the Patrician went directly to his office.

Some time ago he'd had a tailor make a simple garment of rough white cotton with hidden pockets and high-density polymer plates for armour. He sat in the office examining the garments for a while, and then donned them. He grabbed his long, dark green travelling cloak and a bundle of clothes and all the resources he would need. He stuffed everything into a large knapsack and then used a simple spell to make it small and light.

He picked up the phone and called his secretary. "Elizabeth, I am going away for about five days—I might be a bit longer. I don't want anyone to know, so please take all calls; I will deal with them when I get back. Oh, and I will need a car, nothing too elaborate."

"Yes sir, I will get the limo out. Will you need a driver?"

"What did I just say? *No one* is to know. What car do you drive?"

"A ten-year-old estate, sir."

"I will use your car, and no, I will not need a driver. Please make the arrangements."

"Sir, what will I use?"

He sighed, "To be honest I don't give a toss what you use. You can use one of the limos. Bring me a requisition form, and I'll sign it."

Having exchanged the limo requisition form for the keys to Elizabeth's car, the Patrician got into the ten-year-old vehicle and drove out of the south gate of the city and a further fifty miles into the countryside. The open fields lifted his heart. Finally, in the distance he spotted the dilapidated farm. As he pulled into the drive leading to the abandoned house, he recalled all those years ago, when he had made that fateful mistake. I should have killed Akea when I had the chance, he thought. Now I have to fight him as a man and possibly the most powerful magician known for a hundred years. Damn the compassion of Cassandra.

He parked and entered the house. Finding the old iron stove still functional, he dusted off the rusty kettle sitting on it, pumped some water to fill it and made a cup of the tea he had packed in his knapsack. He sat there in an old dust-covered chair and pondered how the hell he was going to do this. He sighed and got up, and stood in the centre of the kitchen. He drew an oblong in the air with his first finger and said the chant; blue light followed his finger, and light blue smoke emanated from the light. He told the oblong where he wanted to go. The image in the centre simmered and faded to show a glen with bright sunlight dancing on the grass.

There was a slight pop, and the Patrician stood in the woods near a group of high hills that from the air would look like a horseshoe. He walked for five miles through the woods to the edge of the Everlon Woods. He rather enjoyed it. At the edge of the woods, a road ran past, east to west. He stopped and waited there for ten minutes. A coach bolted past and stopped suddenly. The driver got out and walked back to the Patrician. A fat young man of about twenty-five, his dark black hair matched his skin colour; he was tall, almost the same height as the Patrician.

The man bowed low, "My lord."

Caught out by this, the Patrician retorted, "Please don't bow to me, I am not your lord."

Perplexed, the man held his bow. "My lord, are you not my Lord Vandavor?"

A smile broke across the Patrician's face. "I am not Vandavor. My name is Vaxihimler. I am a lord of a city. I have come a long way, and I wish to speak with your lord. Take me to him."

Bemused, the driver escorted Vaxihimler to the coach and then climbed up and drove on. As they crested a steep rise, there appeared before them in the distance a castle with a gate of brilliant gold and bronze. The tall castle stood as imposing as his grand palace back home. The battlements could be seen for miles. From a distance they looked like soldiers standing, watching. They pulled up at the gate, and Vaxihimler got out. He banged on the massive doors.

"I am Vaxihimler; I wish to see your lord. Take me to him!" he shouted.

A guard came out and did a double take. "The lord does like to have his little joke." He opened the door and made a bow.

Vaxihimler walked through the door and told the incessantly bowing guard to take him to the lord. Firelight from torches bounced off the walls, marking off segments of time and space. Vaxihimler had to admit he was impressed by the size and grandeur of the main hall. Banners and tapestries hung on the wall, and at the back in the centre stood the throne. When he saw the man sitting in it, he blinked. So it was true, there really were doubles. No wonder people had a hard time. He walked up to the throne and bowed slightly. "I am Vaxihimler, and I have come a long way to see you . . . my lord."

"I know who you are; I think we should have a private meeting. I said *private*," replied Vandavor, slowly raising his voice.

They moved to a private chamber. A servant brought in some refreshments.

"So it's true, we are doubles," said Vandavor. "But I bet you did not break your left hand when you were three."

"No I did not. But I did fall down some stairs at that age."

"What was it like growing up in the first reality? I understand that magic has almost died. And that you use technology as a substitute. Exactly what is a 'car'?"

"My lord, I am originally from the sixth reality, where I studied magic at a university. My travels brought me to the first. The car is a form of transport, like your carts, but without horses. It uses refined oil, and the engine causes a controlled explosion to push pistons, a bit like a steam engine."

"What's a steam engine?"

Vandavor's questions went on and on. Vaxihimler tried to be patient and answer each question in turn politely but, not being a very patient man, he eventually said, "Vandavor. May I call you Vandavor?"

Vandavor nodded. He was in awe of anyone who had travelled between the realities.

"I imagine that we could sit here for a long time discussing our lives and their differences, in some sort of ego masturbation. But I am in need of some help.

"My city has been under attack from a rebel force for a hundred years. I am determined to finish it once and for all. The rebels now have a new saviour. And I mean to smash him before he becomes too powerful."

"Who is the saviour? What does he look like? I will have to kill his counterpart."

"His name is Akea, but I doubt that you have to worry about his counterpart."

"Why is that, exactly?"

"When he was a baby, a foolish woman from the first reality took pity on him. She found him 'crying in a cradle seeking the attention of his dead mother'," Vaxihimler said, quoting from Caranthir's prophecies. He felt pang of pain as he said "mother". That damn book, I wish I had never read it, he thought, trying to keep his face deadpan.

"How do you know all of this?"

"The foolish woman came to me when he went missing. He exhibited signs of magic, which is forbidden in my country."

"Okay. . . . Would you like tea or coffee?"

"I will take tea—milk, no sugar."

"Really? I like it black, with a touch of sugar. Do your eat meat?"

77

"Of course I bloody well do."

"There is no need for that kind of language. It seems that we are very different you and I. We may look identical. But we are not the same."

"When I was young, my master and teacher told me that we are the sum of our experiences and the product of our decisions. I didn't really believe it until today," said Vaxihimler, trying his best to hide his annoyance and appease his counterpart.

"Who was your master? What did he look like?" Vandavor was still curious.

"He was—is Limath. He is very old. I doubt that any of his counterparts are alive today. Most of them were killed by Gelamen."

"The Gelamen! That makes him three thousand years old."

Vaxihimler again struggled to cover his impatience. "Sorry to push the point, but I need help; I would like you to loan me any troops you can spare, and I would like you to be my liaison to the elves and dwarfs."

"Yes, yes, of course. The elves will be easy to persuade, but it's the dwarfs and men that will be the hardest. I think it will cost a lot. Perhaps you could give them new weapons or some of your technology."

"Thank you. Yes, that can be arranged. What about you, what will be your fee?"

"I want to see this other reality and bring back some of this technology for myself."

"I can give you that, and as a bonus for raising a very large army, I will give you a copy of the most powerful spell book in existence, the *Nacrotave*."

"Really, you got one of those? I will definitely get you an army to be proud of."

Vandavor smiled as he thought, the *Nacrotave*, wow.

78

Book Two: The Magic

Chapter 6: Delwiderlen Forest

Long ago, there was a group of magicians known as the Gelamen. These magicians were a powerful force among the known realities. They wandered freely through the ten realities, but twice a year they gathered at the stone circle in the most magical reality, where they spoke of their travels, made laws, swapped spells and generally showed off.

As they grew in numbers and strength, a council was formed, and it was the council that decided that controls must be put in place. By council decree, magicians now were the only ones permitted to travel through the gates between the realities. This necessitated a keeper to control each gate, and so the council elected gatekeepers from their number. Over time a sect of magicians formed known as the Gatekeepers. Each generation sought new Gatekeepers.

To each reality there were three gates. They could be moved around if the threat of war loomed, and the Gatekeepers had often closed down all gates leading from a warlike reality until things had simmered down and the next generation of Gatekeepers had arisen. It had been decided long since that only the most trustworthy of magicians could be a Gatekeeper. They trained long and hard, and not until their mid-twenties were they allowed the control of a gate. It was common for the counterparts of the same person in each reality to be Gatekeepers.

On one particular summer solstice a powerful mage brought with him an army of elves, dwarfs and trolls to destroy the Gelamen council. The coup failed, and the leader, Limath, was banished from the ten realities to a prison, where he was to stay for all time.

Fact fell into legend, legend into myth, and for several millennia Limath stayed imprisoned, until a power-hungry young magician, after years of study and searching, found the mythical gaol and set Limath free. In return, Limath spent many years teaching Vaxihimler the ways of the Gatekeeper. Vaxihimler was an excellent student and in time became a powerful magician worthy of Limath's teachings. By stealth and subterfuge, Limath became Emperor of Ordinea, and Vaxihimler became the Patrician. And after some time Limath introduced a fanatical religion to control the masses.

*

The old, round cottage had sat in a clearing in the Delwiderlen Forest. It looked peculiar, with its odd-shaped windows and brightly coloured runes and symbols covering it from foundation to roof. The roof had once been thatched, but a menagerie of growth had formed its own ecosystem over the years.

Inside the cottage, Prometheus had tucked his long beard into his purple and black coat and tied his long hair back. He had just celebrated his seventy-second birthday. He sat quietly at his chair in front of the large fireplace that took up most of the kitchen and prepared his breakfast over the cooking fire. Suddenly the medallion on his chest grew warm and started to glow. Someone wanted to come through the gate. Prometheus took the food from the fire and went outside to see who it was. He approached a circle of stones about ten feet in diameter. Ancient runes covered each stone from top to bottom. In the centre was a large, flat, stone dais.

A man who bore a remarkable resemblance to Prometheus appeared on the dais, stepped off and greeted Prometheus like a long-lost brother. After a hearty embrace, they went into the cottage. Amalthea was Prometheus's counterpart from another reality, and they looked very much alike, except Prometheus had a broken nose. Both had bright yellow eyes that appeared to see through to the truth.

"Dear Amalthea!" said Prometheus. "Would you like some breakfast? Eggs, bacon, sausages—locally made, you know, absolutely exquisite—tea?"

"Oh, if you're offering, I'll have what you're eating. Shall we sit outside, Bunny?" Prometheus had never worked out why Amalthea called him "Bunny".

Prometheus conjured two red leather chairs with big ears. They sat outside enjoying the view, the tall trees, the blue sky and birdsong. They talked for ages about this and that. When all things had been said, they sat silently, just watching the world go by.

Finally Amalthea broke the hypnotic silence. "Bunny, it was our birthday last week, and I have brought you a present. I found this egg. The parents must have been killed. I think it's a blue thorn-crown. I know you like dragons—would you like to raise one?" From the deep pocket of his knapsack he produced a large egg. It was blue and yellow and approximately thirty inches in diameter.

Prometheus's yellow eyes lit up like a six-year-old's on his birthday. "Yes, definitely. . . ."

That had been sixty years ago. Now Prometheus sat in his favourite chair by the evening campfire, enjoying a smoke. He remembered with pleasure that fate-filled day when Argonath walked—well, was carried—into his life. His reminiscences continued. . .
.

After Amalthea had left, Prometheus had stoked the fire in the grate and laid the egg carefully on the embers. After some days, early one morning, there came a cracking sound from the grate. The egg was about to hatch. Prometheus took the egg out of fire and put it on the stone floor. A little, bluish grey snout popped out of the crack and sniffed the air. The tiny creature strained to push her little neck out, and the egg burst open. The baby dragon collapsed on the floor and squeaked. Her soft, warm, blue grey skin seemed too big for her. Her stubby wings stuck out slightly. She wobbled as she tried to stand up for the first time. Prometheus cut small chunks of raw meat and gently offered them to the miniature dragon. Her eyes flashed orange, and her sharp beak nipped as she lunged at the meat. Prometheus leaped back, sucking his finger.

He had named her Argonath, and a life-long friendship was born. The first few days took up all of Prometheus's time as he fed her and kept her warm. The little dragon had grown quickly, and soon she was filling the house and consuming massive amounts of food. Prometheus realised his folly: he could not teach Argonath how to hunt properly, and he could not catch enough food. After much deliberation, he ventured with Argonath to the second reality, the reality of Amalthea and where Amalthea had discovered the clutch of dragon eggs, to find his old friend Lord Adrigonidd. It took him two weeks to find him, and by this time Argonath was demonstrating her hunting instinct. He found the lordly dragon with several others, one summer's morning in a glen. He approached with caution and bowed, as dragons are noble creatures and have the unfortunate trait of being easily offended.

"Sir," Prometheus said, "I bring you a young dragon for your care, until such time as both age and wisdom show that she is ready to leave."

"Indeed," said Adrigonidd. "And how came you by this child?"

"My counterpart Amalthea discovered her egg, abandoned, and brought it to me."

"Well, then, I must thank you for your consideration in caring for her. We will adopt her into our clan and watch after her until she is mature enough to mingle with humans. Meet us here in ten years' time, on the evening of summer solstice. You will have her care from then onwards, young magician, if she and you so choose."

With a sad heart and a lump in his throat, Prometheus kissed Argonath gently on the nose, bowed again and left. Ten long years later, at the end of a warm summer afternoon, he re-entered the glen. He was rather apprehensive about meeting his Argonath again after so many years. Would she recognise him? Would she want to go with him? Up in the dusky sky he made out several large black objects approaching. Four dragons landed and ambled towards him. One was significantly smaller that the others. Prometheus bowed.

"Greetings, young magician," said Lord Adrigonidd. "Your adopted daughter has been trained in our ways. Although we have little familiarity with human ways, we have sought not to turn her against your kind. If she wishes she is free to go with you."

Argonath casually moved towards Prometheus and sniffed. Perhaps she remembered his smell. Could she once again feel his kiss on her cheek from long ago? She looked at the human and stared into those bright yellow eyes. Her own eyes glowed orange, with elongated slots, like tiger eyes. Then she bowed her head and tried to speak human for the first time. *"Dyta?"* she roared gently. She remembered. Tears welled up in Prometheus's eyes. . . .

Tonight, all these many years later, the evening was cool but not cold. Prometheus had set up camp with Argonath near her cave in the forest. He wanted to spend time with his daughter. She could not fit into his cottage, and he was reticent to go to her cave. A gentleman would never impose on a dragon, unless it was absolutely vital.

As Prometheus sat staring into the fire, an old man dressed in black, with white hair and dark red eyes, walked into the camp. He politely hitched his cloak up and gave a slight bow.

"May I join your party, good sir? I bring some mead to help the evening pass."

Prometheus looked at the stranger. He was old— really old—and thin. He looked both wise and harmless, but his eyes seemed strange, although friendly enough.

"Sure, please take a chair," said Prometheus. He conjured another chair and two goblets out of thin air. He waved at the dragon, who lay comfortably on the ground several feet behind him. "This is Argonath, my adopted daughter." She looked up at the guest and sniffed the air. She uncurled and got to her feet and wandered in a bit closer, partly out of curiosity, but mainly wanting to be closer to Prometheus to protect him.

Prometheus handed the goblets to the old man, who extracted a jug from somewhere in his garments and poured two drinks. He handed one to Prometheus.

Prometheus accepted the goblet and raised it slightly toward the old man. "Would you like some food with that mead?" he asked.

"No, no, just the mead would be fine."

"It is certainly a nice evening. I love sitting watching the event of the sky going from blue, to pink, to red. I never bore of it."

"Where I come from, I don't get to see the sunset. It is always like a spring day there, a perpetual spring morning."

"'Tis a pity. Well, enjoy it with me." Prometheus tasted the mead that his guest had poured for him. "Damn, this is a good drop. Oh—where are my manners? I got so caught up in our conversation, I forgot to introduce myself. My name is Prometheus." He offered his hand.

Fate smiled as he shook Prometheus's hand. "My name is Fate. I am a being not from these realities, nor this time. Some call us gods, but I loathe such labels; gods are lazy creatures."

"Well, I must say this is a turn-up for the books. This drink must be strong; I thought you said you were Fate."

Argonath cut in, with a low growling voice, "He did. How can we help you?"

"I must task you with a small job. In a few days time, you will meet up with Juween. A young man will accompany him. You must help them. Teach them. The young man, Akea, is powerful, but dangerous. He is naive and for the most part unaware of his magical capabilities. He should meet Argonath. Make plans to overthrow the Patrician and free the city. Everything has its time and place. Please give them this." He gave Prometheus a large, bulging, brown, leather knapsack. Accepting it, Prometheus was surprised at its weight.

Fate sat down opposite Prometheus and gazed into the fire for a few seconds, talking almost to himself. "The right man in the wrong place can make all the difference," he muttered. Then he looked at Prometheus. "The bag contains clothes for Juween, Akea and Argonath. It has some extras, including Akea's new insignia and birthright. There is an ancient spell that allows people to become dragons, and vice versa; I think you are aware of it. Normally they would have to be naked for it to work, but these clothes will not have to come off. Oh, one last thing: teach the young man how to fight in the sky, even the spells you fear."

Prometheus was taken aback, but in his heart he knew, somehow, that this man was telling the truth. You didn't celebrate your one hundred and thirty-second birthday unless you knew about truth and lies, and those who spoke them. Quickly recovering, he said, "Oh, I see. Yes, indeed I shall. Which direction are they coming from? I take it they are coming from the base. Would you like some more mead?"

Fate laughed. "You were always the one who never got perplexed—well, not for long, anyway. Yes, they are coming from the base, and they will be cold and tired. Oh, and yes, why not? Let's have another drop. It seems like a millennium since I sat and talked to friends—well, actually, come to think on it . . ."

*

The night was cold. The forest took Akea's breath away, the beauty of the rich greens and browns, the fresh air, the apparent freedom. But the cold was eating away at his urbanity.

"We better find some shelter, Akea. It's getting late. Since we didn't have time to catch food, I am afraid it's going to be vegetables. We might be lucky and find a potato. See if you can find some food."

Akea looked at Juween as if to say, "What are you playing at? I don't know what anything looks like. I can't remember a damn thing."

Juween's eyes lit with realisation. "Oh, crap, sorry—pick us out a tree with long overhanging branches and gather some dry wood, while I find us some food."

Juween returned shortly to find Akea sitting under a tree with thick, low-lying branches. Juween gently weaved them in a bit to give better cover and allow smoke from a fire to escape through an opening. He spoke a charm to the leaves to keep the rain out. He smiled; Akea had picked a good tree. They had about five square feet of room. In the centre Akea made a ring of stones and neatly stacked some dead twigs in the middle and to one side.

"I think it's time for your first lesson. Don't say anything, just listen. We don't know how powerful you are. If you repeat the names of things, you could put us in danger," Juween said gently.

Akea nodded.

Juween continued. "The language of power; Latin was one of the original languages, and there is a power in calling everything by its proper name. We have to say thank you to the tree for giving us shelter; then we can start a fire." With that, Juween spoke to the tree. It seemed to Akea that the tree might have nodded in recognition—or was it the wind? Juween sat down and spoke to the twigs; they smouldered at first, and then burst into flames. Juween had found some carrots, onions, and two large potatoes; he placed them near the fire.

"We can change things, but remember that we can not make something do anything which by nature it cannot do, or change something into something else that can not be fashioned by tools."

Akea looked perplexed.

"We, for example, can not make this twig . . ." Juween picked up a twig from the neat pile of spare firewood ". . . into a metal knife, or turn it into gold. It would be like asking a fish to hunt deer."

Akea nodded in response.

Juween continued, "We, however, can make a wooden knife or spoon, or whatever."

"But a wooden knife would not be much use, would it?" said Akea.

"Good point. On our travels tomorrow, we should be on the look-out for a good-sized flint stone or piece of iron ore."

Juween started to peel back the bark from a piece of ash. "Please, Akea, don't repeat this." When the branch was free from the bark, Juween muttered something in Latin and gently ran his fingers over the wood, outlining the shape he wanted. The twig responded, conforming to the shape Juween had traced. In no time at all, a spoon appeared out of the twig. He picked another twig; it seemed to have listened to Juween's previous attempt on the other twig and was eager to accommodate by also producing a spoon.

Juween explained, "Different words can do different things. It's not only nouns. Verbs also have power. If I requested a tree to fling you out of the way, I would have to say in Latin, which I am not going to do, 'Please, tree, see that man over there? He is my enemy. Would you protect me by throwing him somewhere?' or if I were in a hurry, I could say, 'Tree—Man' and point to you and say, 'Throw.' But it is considered rude to be so abrupt. If you have time later you can say thanks."

"What about the magic I did at the border?"

"Ah, yes. I am sorry, Akea, I should have explained. They are different kinds of magic. Earth lore: that is what we have been speaking about. There's also dragon lore, which some call the lore of the air, and human lore, which is what you performed at the border."

"Is there lore for water?"

"Yep, there is, it's bit of an odd art. I don't know anything about it, but I know a man who does."

Juween carried on late into the night. They stopped only to eat their baked potatoes with their new spoons. Juween would not string sentences together in Latin, but rather he said each word separately and explained in Ordeanian how to string them together. Finally realising the late hour from the position of the moon, Juween cursed and said, "We better get some sleep." He enchanted their coats to help keep the cold out and set an intruder spell to keep watch over them as they slept close to the fire.

The dawn sun rose precariously over the horizon. Amber light broke through the tops of the trees. Mist hung on the floor. Akea got out from under their temporary shelter and started munching on a carrot. Juween rose from the shelter a few moments later. He turned to the tree and said thank you to it and released it from the charms and spells. It sprang back to its original shape and bowed gently in the wind as if to say, "That's okay. Thank you for not hurting me."

Now that it was daylight Akea could see the forest clearly. He wondered in delight as he gazed at the deep blues, reds and yellows of the flowers on the forest floor. He realised that they must be deep in the forest; he could not see the sky, just the tall trees straining to touch the sky in their everlasting conquest to get more sunlight. The early morning mist in the sunlight showed up as patches of ghostly white ballet dancers performing a tragic scene of jumping into a lake. It was so peaceful, so tranquil, accented by the songs of birds of all kinds announcing the day's break, like the fanfare of a royal gala.

"It's so peaceful, I don't want to leave," Akea said to Juween.

"I know, I wish I never left. But leave we must. Our track leads us to about halfway up the mountain, just above the tree line. If you think this is beautiful, you just wait."

Their path led through a gulley with dense tree growth on either side. Ferns grew right up to the edge of the brown path. The air was cool, but not uncomfortable. Juween loved being in the forest. The trees seemed so green and tall. They must be three or four hundred years old. This was freedom. Breathing the fresh, invigorating air, he regretted staying in the city for so long. He missed hearing the birds, talking to the trees, resting his eyes on the leaves of greenest green, feeling the sun beat down, its heat filtered through the canopy. Ah, peace, he thought. They hiked for miles. The effort was tiring, but if Akea was tired he didn't complain. As they went Juween called out the true names of the fauna. They found a stream. Nearby were flint stones and granite rocks. Juween sat down on a rock next to the stream, and Akea joined him; they took off their shoes and soaked their feet in the cool waters, watching the late afternoon sun whisk through the clouds. Juween grabbed a large flint stone and spoke to it in Latin while outlining the shape of a knife blade. The stone slowly became a knife-edge. Juween ran his finger over the edge until it became keen.

"We better make camp here; I don't want a repeat of last night's hasty camp. We do it properly this time," Juween said. He got up and began looking around for a particular tree.

"Right lad, time for some food. Try and encourage that cherry tree to bear fruit."

"Alo nemus commodo gero fructus," Akea said in the faintest of whispers. The tree burst into flames.

Juween laughed heartily and put out the fire. "That's okay, Akea, I'll get the food."

"Can we catch animals with magic?"

"No, no, we cannot do that; magic should be used for growth. However, we are men. We will catch rabbits with traps and snares," said Juween.

They set up camp in a small clearing about seventy-five yards the fast-flowing stream of fresh cool water. Birds sang nearby in the bright green, healthy foliage of the trees. Akea made a crude shelter from low-lying branches. Juween encouraged the foliage to grow, to give more shelter. He caught a brace of rabbits using a crude snare fashioned from some ivy twine and three branches. They had them for dinner. Akea was useless; he could neither hunt nor grow fruit. As Juween started a cooking fire he smiled to himself. Poor Akea could not even start a fire. After their meal they relaxed. Then, without warning, Juween started weeping. Akea moved close to him and put his arm around him.

Juween spoke through his tears. "She wasn't my niece. She—I adopted her, about five years ago. Now I feel so alone."

Akea sat listening to Juween for some time as he talked about Cruz; it seemed the tranquillity of this place brought back memories of a better time long since past. Juween shook his head and rubbed the tears away. He used magic to fashion a needle from a small rabbit bone and sewed the rabbit skins into a crude water container. He filled it with water from the nearby stream.

"Red or white?" said Juween.

"I don't know," said Akea.

"Okay, I decide: red it is. *Unda in ut vinum.*"

The water turned to a rich, dark red wine. Each man took a sip from the bag. The wine had a slight fruity aftertaste.

"This will ease my mood. Cheeky Cruz, she always liked her drink. She thought I didn't know. I just made sure she never got out of hand."

"To Cruz. Your antics are over now, may you rest in peace," Akea said with tears in his eyes. He really liked Cruz. He remembered the sense of godlike power he'd felt at the border. And yet he could not save her. A surge of pain stung him.

The wine flowed, and they got very drunk. When they awoke late the next morning, the birds were singing, and the forest seemed noisier than ever.

They walked over to the stream and dunked their heads in the cold refreshing water. Juween combed his hair back into place, while Akea shook his hair like a dog. *"Grrrr,"* he said, as droplets of water zinged off his head. They ate the remains of the night's dinner and then started onwards, continuing on a northwest course. At one point Juween, altered their course slightly, and they walked to a viewpoint at the edge of the forest. Akea stood there, completely bewildered by the beauty. Through the overhanging branches he could see the southwest valley covered in dense foliage. The magnificent colours of greens, browns and yellows glistened in the daylight. Mists and low-lying clouds hung just above the treetops. In the distance Akea could see other mountains in the range. Their snow-capped tips were in stark contrast to the vivid brightness of the trees below. The cool breeze cut through the warm air. Akea and Juween stopped and sat looking at the view for some time.

It was mid-afternoon on the fourth day, when Juween put out his arm and stopped Akea mid step and crouched down. Akea copied him.

"We are being watched," Juween whispered to Akea. Then with his mind Juween called out for Prometheus. No one answered.

"I know he's out there. We better stay here for the night. You know the drill."

"Right, I make the shelter. I don't suppose there is any chance of something other than rabbit, is there?" Akea replied.

"Hmm. I will see what I can do," Juween said. He wandered off.

The afternoon became dull, and the weather turned from sunny to drizzly, making a vain effort to penetrate their clothing. Wisps of steam emanated from their coats. Akea spent time setting up the camp and constructing a makeshift shelter, while Juween caught a wild boar and foraged for root vegetables.

Juween built a fire and then gutted and cleaned the boar using the flint knife that Juween had fashioned with magic. Akea dug a hole with the crude knife and placed embers at the bottom and over them a layer of moist grass, then the vegetables and meat, then some more grass, and finally covered the hole with dirt. Steam gently rose from the warm mound. The smell of a hearty meal lifted their hearts and took their minds off the steady drizzle. Halfway through a conversation about animal husbandry, Akea changed the subject completely.

"I feel so useless—I can't even start a fire, and all I can do is destroy. I don't want to be like this."

"I don't know why you are so powerful and yet can't control it, but we will find a way," said Juween.

Akea continued, "What really gets me, if I think

93

about it, is if the Patrician knew about my powers, he would have sent for the Watchmen, and I would be dead. Ergo, I must not have shown any real threat."

"Yeah, I don't get that either; one thing did cross my mind, though. Wherever you came from, it must have been a particularly magical place. Whoever moved you must have put some sort of spell on you to stop you from your powers. It must have been broken at the border. One thing is for sure: whoever it did is in for a bit of a surprise, when they find out."

"I guess."

"Look, Prometheus is a wise man. He will figure out a way of channelling your energy. I know lots, but I know nothing compared to him. He has travelled far and met many peoples. He will have an answer. Just have patience." Juween shifted slightly. "Look, I promise not to take the piss anymore."

"Got any wine left?"

The wine flowed again. Finally, the rain let up, and the stars came out. Akea lay on his back looking at the stars and fell into a restless sleep.

*

The peaks of the high mountain range stuck out like a smile of broken teeth. Three outcrops stood apart from the others. Heather and grasses clung to the sides of the outcrops, covering the mountains' modesty. The sun beat down from the clear blue sky. Autumn was in the air, and the trees sang their seasonal symphony. Akea stood defiantly against the wind. His cloak fluttered in the breeze. He was searching, scanning the horizon. He spied a big black shape circling in the sky. . . .

Akea woke up. It was about ten in the morning. Juween was already up, rekindling the fire. They ate some pork. Akea didn't mention his dream to Juween.

When an old man suddenly appeared by the fireside, Akea fell backwards in surprise. The old man laughed.

"Can I have some coffee, stranger?" the old man asked.

"There are no strangers here, old man—no coffee, either," Juween retorted. Both men laughed heartily. Akea looked on in confusion.

The old man turned to Akea. "For all your power, you did not see me, and you didn't even hear me." The old man put out a hand. "My name is Prometheus."

Akea's mouth dropped; he had been expecting someone, well, a little different.

The old man had a long beard, bright yellow eyes, and a long, grey mane of hair. He had a slight hunch in his back. His beard came down to his navel, covering most of his lacy white shirt, over which he wore a full-length purple and black coat covered with gold and silver symbols. Although the coat clearly had seen many years of wear, somehow it looked as new as the day it was created.

Prometheus looked with amusement at Akea. "Old?" he said. "Old? I am only 132."

Prometheus laughed. "We have lots to discuss, and a little to decide; but first, Akea, forgive me."

Akea looked at him with confusion on his face. Prometheus said, *"Ostendo mihi vestri animus."*

Akea's eyes briefly flashed orange, with elongated slits, like tiger eyes. He sat deep in thought, working out what Prometheus had said. After a long pause, he said, *"Show me your soul?"*

Prometheus laughed again. "You have come a long way." He sat down by the fire, letting the warmth fill his lean frame, and began to search through innumerable pockets. Shortly, spices, herbs and infusions lay on the ground. Finally he found some coffee beans, a small kettle, three small cups and his pipe. As he filled the pipe, he spoke.

"Oh, we Gatekeepers are all alike; my counterpart, for instance, carries an infusion of willow bark. Be a good chap, put the kettle on."

Juween took the kettle and filled it with some water that they had been carrying. Prometheus sat on the ground and spoke gently to the tobacco. It soon started to smoulder.

He put the pipe between his teeth and tugged on it as he spoke. "Five days ago, an old man came to me and sat at my fire, and he said that a man whom I knew and a young man would come looking for me, and I must teach them dragon lore, earth lore, Latin — everything. 'The young man is powerful,' he told me. 'He must meet Argonath.'"

"He told me I would recognise the young man by saying, *'Ostendo mihi vestri animus.'* He said the young man would show me Argonath's eyes. 'Give him back his memories,' he said. 'Tell him where he is from and why he is unique.'"

Akea and Juween stared at the old man, thunderstruck. "Err . . ." Akea said, trying to unstick his tongue. Juween busied himself with the coffee.

Once the coffee had brewed, Juween poured it into the three cups. He handed cups to the others and took a sip from the third.

"Ah, that's better. I can't remember the last time I had coffee. It must be a week," said Juween.

"It's rather good, isn't it?" said Prometheus.

"Can I ask you a personal question?" Akea said to Prometheus.

"Sure, ask away."

"How can you be one hundred and thirty-two?

When, if you don't mind me saying so, you look about seventy."

"Odd, that, isn't it? More odd is that you didn't ask all the other questions that you must be dying to ask."

"I know that I will find out in due course, but I think I will start with something you may be more inclined to answer freely."

"My, you are a shrewd one. No doubt Juween has told you that you are either born with magical tendencies or not. It's something to do with genes and race. If you are magical, the aging process slows down. But—now this is the odd bit—it doesn't happen to everyone, and it doesn't start at the same time, like the onset of puberty. More curiously, if someone spends a lot of time in a non-magic place the phenomenon slows down. They age slower, but not as slowly as someone who lived in a magical place all of their life. I have two examples, one my counterpart, Amalthea—"

Akea butted in, "Who is Amalthea? What do you mean by counterpart?"

"Ah, yes, I see. He is a Gatekeeper like me. We are, if you like, twins, born in different realities. But we will get to that later. Anyway, where was I? Oh yes, Amalthea, bless 'im, has a heart condition and has to ingest that confounded willow bark everyday to thin his blood. As far as we can work out, we were born on the same day, obviously—well, not to you. But his aging slow-down didn't happen until ten years after mine. I don't know why. The other example of course is Juween here; he lost his memories about twenty-five to thirty years ago. We tried to get them back, but we couldn't; the spell was too strong. I think Juween is around a hundred and twenty, give or take a decade. He looks sixtyish now, and he looked about fifty when we met, so if the aging phenomenon kicked in around twenty, you see he could have been around eighty when he lost his marbles, so to speak." He paused and looked at Juween. "Sorry, I have spoken for too long."

"Yes, you bloody well have," retorted Juween.

"Sorry old bean, I meant no offence," said Prometheus, rather sheepishly.

"None taken, you old rascal, but I believe you are as old as you feel. Well, right now after being out in the open for four days, without proper food or shelter, I think you could be right about my age."

"So, if someone lived in a magical place all their life they would live for hundreds of years?" asked Akea.

"Good heavens, no. As far as we can work out, its slows the age down by half; so you look forty when you're eighty, fifty when you're a hundred. But as you approach the end of your life, the magic has to do more to compensate for all the niggles and diseases. If you're one hundred and thirty, you look around seventy to eighty."

They sat for some time enjoying the remainder of the coffee.

When Prometheus spoke again his joviality had wavered slightly. "Akea, you are not from this reality. Each reality has a version of us, which by nature is slightly different; after all, we are the sum of our experiences and product of our decisions. I cannot give you your memories back just yet, and you are too powerful for me. We must seek help. We will go and see Argonath. Oh yes—this, I think belongs to you: a gift from a friend." He handed Akea the bulky knapsack Fate had entrusted him with.

Akea opened the bag and took out six sets of clothes: two each for Juween, Akea and Argonath. All were similar in size and style—thigh-length black boots, trousers and tunics, but the colours of the trousers and tunics differed. In addition, there were three long, heavy traveller's cloaks, embroidered on the back with the outline of a dragon, its wings outstretched and its tail curving out behind it. Akea's trousers and cloak were black, and the tunic was black with embroidered purple swirls. He tried on the trousers. At first he thought they must be for Juween, they were so loose, but as soon as he did up the double buckle on the trousers, they shrank to fit his body. He donned the rest of the clothing, which also adjusted to his size.

"Wow, it feels so warm and light. Juween, try yours on—and who are the other clothes for?" said Akea. His eyes were bright with delight.

"Here, this I think is your insignia and birthright," Prometheus said, handing him a brooch. "The other set of clothes are for Argonath, I guess—we will see eventually."

The brooch contained a similar design to the cloak; the dragon depicted on it seemed to want to growl.

Juween tried his clothes on: black boots, fawn trousers, dark brown tunic and a fawn traveller's cloak. Akea looked into the knapsack and found hunting knives, water canteens, fishing hooks, cooking utensils, coffee, whisky, dried meats and herbs.

With Prometheus taking the lead, the three set out. They walked for some time in silence. A certain something hung in the air of the forest now. It didn't seem so green anymore, nor did it smell so fresh.

Prometheus stopped. "A word to the wise. Dragons are noble and proud. They can be graceful creatures, but unfortunately, they have one rather unpleasant trait: they consider themselves above humans, and some don't even like us. It is very easy to upset their sense of pride, so don't."

They climbed out of the forest and into the mountains. They came across a stream, and as they followed it up, the green trees thinned to reveal granite rock and moor land spotted with tufted grasses and speckled with heather. Akea saw a mountain peak to the left. On the other side of the stream a ways up perched what Akea at first took to be a house-sized boulder. On closer inspection, he decided it was the most beautiful thing he had ever seen.

Argonath sat watching the three men approach with her bright orange eyes, her long slender tail swishing behind her, her light, blue grey scales shimmering in the daylight. Two main horns swept back from her head about three feet, curving up slightly at their tips. Her mane consisted of three soft horns that moved like hair, and stiffer horns ran all the way down her back. Her snout was about eighteen inches long and covered in scales. Her face bore a soft expression that would change to hard and fierce the instant anyone commented on it. The orange eyes seemed to soften her countenance even more. Her entire body was covered in grey blue scales, strong enough to provide protection, small enough to show extreme muscle definition. She sat so still it was hard to see her sometimes. A voice popped into Akea's head.

"Hello, Akea, I am Argonath." Her voice in his mind was gentle, soft, almost erotic.

"This sounds silly, but can you hear me?"

Argonath snorted. *"Obviously you need training."*

"I never met a dragon before; well, at least I don't think so."

"I have not met many humans, and I know so."

100

"Yes indeed, I suppose I am foolish, so naive about so many things."

"Yes, you are, but you will learn."

"Look, if I offend you out of ignorance, then please forgive me," said Akea.

"As I said, you will learn," Argonath retorted with a slight smile in her eye. She liked him. His smile, his openness. She could feel the raw power emanating from him and wondered to herself, Should he be worried about offending me? What happens if I offend him?

"Please tell me everything about you—your race, if I may use that term, your history and your lore," Akea asked rather nervously.

As the four hiked toward Argonath's cave, Akea and Argonath conversed about Argonath, history and dragon lore. Argonath carried the conversation serenely. It was early evening when they arrived at Argonath's cave. Argonath had to fly each of them the final distance to the mouth of the cave. It was situated high up, inaccessible by foot and protected by an overhanging cliff. The cave mouth opened into a large cavern. Light from a small opening in the roof shone on the smooth walls. Left of centre sat Argonath's bed; the pile of gold and jewels glistened in the cave light. A large pool fed by a spring took up most of the back. Stalactites hung above the pool, and stalagmites stood around it like soldiers at attention.

At the entrance to the cave Prometheus stopped and said, "Gents, we must ask permission to enter Argonath's cave."

He turned to Argonath. "My dearest daughter, tomorrow we will set up camp nearby, but for tonight, please, may we find refuge in your cave? We may have to cook some food, if you don't mind."

"Yes, of course, please set up on the right-hand side. I will find some food. Deer okay?" she said, smiling.

After she left, Juween asked Prometheus, "What was all that about? She brought us here—she obviously agreed."

"Yes, funny isn't it? But the niceties have to be respected. Remember what I said about dragon pride. If I had not, and she was another dragon, she may have thrown us off the cliff face, and rightly, too."

Argonath returned with a roe deer. She ate the head, front legs and intestines. Juween and Prometheus cooked the rest. Argonath sat talking to them.

As the three men enjoyed the deer, Akea asked Prometheus, "Can you explain what you meant by counterpart?"

"There are, as I believe Juween has told you, ten different realities, each one slightly different. In the early days wizards and magicians could move from reality to reality. After a few years it was decided that controls should be put in place to stop cross-contamination. A group of the best magicians would look after the gates, which were set to control the movements. Generation after generation of these Gatekeepers held the gates. In each reality, there is a Gatekeeper, normally the same person, but from a different reality. Odd that, isn't it? I am the Gatekeeper of this reality, and Amalthea, who is me but not—if you see what I mean—is the Gatekeeper of the second reality. Each reality is numbered according to when it was found. It started here. Therefore this is known as the first reality; Amalthea's was next, the second, and so on."

Prometheus paused for a few seconds. "Akea, look, be patient. When you have your memories back we can go through the whole thing, but I don't want to do it now. The spell I have to perform may cause your old memories to overwrite the new ones; sorry old bean."

Akea nodded, and the conversation went back to other matters of state. Akea had no idea what they were talking about. After listening to the conversation for a while, and trying to be patient, he decided to fight his nerves of Argonath and talk to her. The dragon was sitting on her bed away from the main group. He got up and approached her.

"Is it okay, if I—sit by you?" He conversed through thought.

"Yes, of course. I won't bite."

Akea gave a nervous laugh.

"You are going to have to trust me, I have spent most of my life with humans, and I am not as arrogant as other dragons. Look, I'll prove it. Please stroke my flank."

Ever since she had met Akea just a short few hours ago, she had been looking forward to Akea stroking her flank. If she had been a human, she would have said that she fancied him.

Akea got up and walked round to her side. She was scarily beautiful. When he stroked her flank, her warm scales scintillated with his touch.

Almost absent-mindedly he said out loud, *"You are the most beautiful being I have ever seen."*

Argonath didn't know what to make of this. If he had lost his memories, he would not have seen very many beings, but she took it as a compliment anyway.

The conversation between Prometheus and Juween seemed to have tailed off. "It's getting late; I think we need to get to sleep," Prometheus announced to the group. Noticing Akea and Argonath sitting near each other seemly talking without words, Prometheus smiled. He hoped that they would get on. It was critical to his plans.

As they settled for the night, the taste of the fine deer still in their mouths, Prometheus explained their plans.

"Tomorrow we will try the seemly impossible: we will hold a group meld, sharing our experiences and knowledge with each other. If this proves successful, we will hold three sessions. We will all have the benefit of shared knowledge. Akea will be the power that will hold the group up, Argonath will temper the control. Let's hope we don't end up lobotomised."

Chapter 7: Togetherness

The firelight danced around the walls, taking the edge off the cool, fresh, night air. Akea went to move away from Argonath to give her room to go to sleep.

"It's okay—you can sleep here, if you like. I am sure that I am more comfortable than the floor."

Argonath moved her front leg and Akea sat in the crook of the elbow. Their silent conversation continued. They talked for hours. Slowly the exchange died down. Akea sat musing. Suddenly he felt Argonath in his thoughts.

"So I am in your dreams; mmm . . . am I perhaps the woman of your dreams?"

Akea smiled. *"You are truly beautiful."*

She put her tail around him, and he fell asleep.

The peaks of the high mountain range stuck out like a smile of broken teeth. Three outcrops stood apart from the others. Heather and grasses clung to the sides of the outcrops, covering the mountains' modesty. The sun beat down from the clear blue sky. Autumn was in the air, and the trees sang their seasonal symphony. Akea stood defiantly against the wind. His cloak fluttered in the breeze. He was searching, scanning the horizon. He spied a big black shape circling in the sky. Soon it came into sharper relief. It was a dragon. Akea's heart leapt with excitement, recognition and love. Argonath landed and settled by his side and nuzzled him. He turned to her with tears streaming down his face. "I love you," he said. . . .

Akea woke with a start.

Argonath growled in his mind, *"What was that you were dreaming?"*

Embarrassed, he spoke aloud. "Err; I have this dream every night. But this is the first time I dreamt that last part."

Argonath looked embarrassed too, going slightly pink in her muzzle. As they pondered the dream together, Akea yawned. He could not keep his eyes open. Soon they were both asleep again.

About midmorning, after breakfast, the men set up a temporary camp in a clearing a short distance from Argonath's cave. They could not stay at Prometheus's cottage; the location was known. This camp would do until they could find a good location for a more permanent camp. Everyone settled down in a circle on the soft grass. Argonath joined them, sitting with her body away from the group and her tail wrapped round her legs. The men all felt relaxed after the previous few days of roughing it followed by a good night's sleep. They enjoyed the warm sun peering through the clouds and the birds telling the world what they were doing. The coffee tasted good. Prometheus said to Argonath, "Control his mind." Then to Akea, he said, "I am going to release your memories."

Gently Argonath grabbed hold of Akea's mind as a mother would nestle a baby. Then Prometheus spoke *"Memor, memor"* into Akea's mind. Akea watched images flash into and out of view, like a high-speed videotape of Akea's life, as his memory came flooding back.

Argonath smiled. *"That wasn't bad at all."*

Worried, Juween said to Akea, "Can you remember anything about what happened in the last week?"

Akea shook his head, "No, I can't. Who are you? What am I doing here?"

"Ah, odd isn't it? Akea, my name is Prometheus. I want you to listen carefully."

"You are in the forest outside of the city. You are safe and with friends. You lost all your memories; I have just said a spell and given them back to you."

They sat there for a few seconds. Then Akea said, "Prometheus, if you tried the spell again would it release the rest of my memories?"

"To be honest, you might not want them back," said Juween, rather gloomily.

"Why? What happened?" Akea said.

"What happened!" said Juween loudly.

"Right, that does it; I am going to do it. Prometheus?"

"All right, but there is a risk you could become a vegetable at the end. This time, however, you must invoke the spell yourself."

"I will hold your mind and temper the power," said Argonath gently to Akea. Something flickered in the back of his mind. He knew this voice.

"If you can!" he thought.

"What do you mean if I can? My mind is a lot more complex and powerful than yours. Just do it. I won't let you down! Besides, if we fail who would stroke my flank? Look into your mind for the blank area, and when you are ready say, 'Memor, memor'."

Akea concentrated on looking for the missing pieces in his mind. Argonath pointed them out to him. Once he had a picture of where they were, he said, *"Memor, memor."*

All the memories came charging back like a stampede of bison: the chase through the streets, the fight through the border, the death of Cruz. Then the head rush. Akea was knocked unconscious. Argonath growled with pain as Akea's true power showed itself again for the second time. This time it stayed, simmering like a thunderstorm caught in a glass jar. The feelings: rage, anger, grief and pain rose in their heads like humpbacked whales coming up for air in the deep sea and disappearing again.

Juween and Prometheus spoke soft words of healing in Latin. Ten minutes later Akea regained consciousness.

"How do you feel? Who am I? What do I call Nalik?" Juween said, deeply concerned.

Akea lifted his head from the ground and rubbed it with his hands.

"I'm fine. But I have got one mother of a headache. You are Juween, uncle to the deceased Cruz. You were responsible for saving my life on numerous occasions over the last week. You called Nalik a slum bitch, and rightly, too."

Juween laughed and clapped his hands. Akea dropped his head back to the ground and lay there, thoughts swimming through his mind. "I know how I got here, I know all these people, I remember the previous life, but it seems so bizarre. I am so confused."

Argonath sat nearby. She could read Akea's thoughts; they were so clear, it was like someone shouting at her. *"Akea, let me help. Tell me how you think the story went, and let me put it in the right order."*

Prometheus interrupted their thoughts. "As I said before, you are not from this reality. The man who gave you those gifts also charged me to tell you why you are unique. There are, as I said, ten realities, and in each there is a counterpart of the same person. Sometimes the same or similar events can happen to some or all of the counterparts. Rarely do all ten counterparts die at the same time. . . . Odd, isn't it?" Prometheus sat there mulling things over for a few

108

seconds, and then he continued, "The oddest thing is that all your counterparts died when you were a baby, but you were removed from your own reality and saved. In a way you cheated Fate, or at least someone cheated Fate for you. This of course is not why you are unique, but it seems that the magical tendencies prevalent in all your counterparts were distilled in you; hence the power."

Akea just nodded. They sat there for half an hour as Akea tried to make sense of what had happened to him. Prometheus looked across and sensed that Akea and Argonath had again begun conversing privately. At first he was jealous, but then he saw the wisdom. Argonath was his daughter. Parents and children should never really understand each other. He got up and rummaged through his knapsack for his pipe, some more coffee and the remains of last night's dinner, which they had wrapped in tanned deerskin.

"It's time for a spot of lunch. We got a lot to do this afternoon, and we should get some food."

"Prometheus, I will see you in about an hour. I am hungry. I might even bring back tonight's dinner, but don't get used to being waited on," Argonath said in her deep growly voice.

Prometheus could swear there was a glint in her eye. She flew off hunting for food. One hour later she came back with another deer. She had eaten what she wanted and then cleaned it as best she could. She dropped it near the group, but far enough away so as not to put Akea off her. They all sat in the circle again. Prometheus said, "We need to say *iungo ut unus* together. Argonath, you must concentrate on keeping things slow, one at a time. At my prompting, say the words *meus scientia, meus sapientia.*"

Together, the four chanted, *"Iungo ut unus."* They closed their eyes and listened for each other's thoughts. Prometheus went first. *"Meus scientia, meus sapientia,"* he intoned, and his wisdom and knowledge flowed from him and through the group like water flowing through a dry riverbed. Argonath used Akea's power to push Prometheus's thoughts round. In five minutes, everyone had learned a lifetime's worth of knowledge. Juween prepared to go next. But Akea was getting tired, and Argonath was exhausted.

"Please stop," she said. "I can't control it any more."

They paused and rested for an hour. Prometheus made some more coffee and everyone sat with their own thoughts. Refreshed, they once again faced each other and closed their eyes. Juween said, *"Meus scientia, meus sapientia,"* and again the group absorbed in five minutes another lifetime of knowledge. Akea spoke the incantation, *"Meus scientia, meus sapientia,"* and in thirty seconds, there sat four highly skilled computer programmers, only one of whom had ever even seen a computer and one of whom in her current embodiment could not even use a keyboard. The hardest challenge now faced them: it was Argonath's turn to say the incantation. She had to continue to hold control while she showed them all her wisdom.

Akea offered to make her task a little easier. He said, "I'll sit this one out. I'd rather learn the hard — and perhaps more exciting — way."

Argonath thought to Akea, *"Thank you; you are truly beautiful."*

Akea sat outside the circle. Watching intently, he received flashes of information, but nothing coherent. The three-way meld was completed, and everyone took some time to rest and ponder their new wisdom.

Akea, too, wanted to be alone with his thoughts. So much had happened today. He got his memories back; he gained enough knowledge to fill two lifetimes. Most of the knowledge was the same, but so much was different at the same time. He could understand most of it; there was more than one way to do things and cast different spells. Then there was the fight at the border. He remembered it again for the first time, and it hurt badly. He sat crying to himself. His mind ached, his heart ached, and his soul ached. He replayed some memories from the earlier days; he decided to call them pre-alley memories. The time in the coffee shop, wondering what it would be like to be free. Here I am free. And I am not free. Perhaps for the first time in my life, I am not free. I know I have to go and fight. Is this what this is all about? Why me? I am no one.

Argonath sat there trying desperately not to listen. Her heart went out to Akea. He has to cope with so much at once. How can I help him? she wondered.

"*I can hear you as clear as bird song. Why is that?*" she thought to him.

"*Odd, isn't it?*" Akea mimicked Prometheus.

"*Hmmm . . . indeed. Sorry—no offence, old bean,*" she returned. "*I didn't want to listen to your thoughts, but I felt your pain. I want to soothe it. The thing that really narks me is I am not this nice to anyone.*"

Akea smiled.

"*Look, Akea, you won't go into battle until we are ready. I know Prometheus. He has a plan, and it involves both of us. I imagine that we won't be ready for at least a year. We may have acquired vast amounts of knowledge, but we don't know how to use it. Now we have power in you, control in me and the knowledge of those two. From there, it's just a simple task of figuring out how to use it.*"

111

Akea got up and walked to her as though he saw her for the first time. He had been so wrapped up in his own worries and fears that it never occurred to him that she might be worried, too. He kissed her muzzle. She blushed. Then he stroked her flank, and her tail thumped gently with delight.

"*I don't feel the same; I remember what I was like before the alley: I was quite the analyst, quite the thinker. Now I don't feel that way, I feel extrovert. I feel like a revolutionary. The last time I felt like this was just before I passed out at the border after I unleashed the nuclear wave. Argonath, I am scared. What happens if I can't control it again?*"

She tried to be sympathetic. "*You are here to help, and I am here to help. Let's learn how to control the power, train as hard as we can. You will be a good magician. I know it. We could take over the city and free it.*"

*

The dungeons of the Watchmen's headquarters stank of blood, fear and urine. The walls were dark and covered in stains, and the dim lighting was no help either. In one particular cell, a man named Headen was strapped to a rack. He was naked. His face was beyond recognition, covered in deep welts and bruises, his left eye gouged out, the right swollen shut. Blood trickled down his face into his matted blond beard. Severe burns covered his armpits and upper torso. His testicles had been burnt away. His knees, ankles and feet were broken. The cell stank of blood, burned flesh, urine and terror. The man fell in and out of consciousness. Fate had made sure the man couldn't remember anything about Akea's former life. Morguhis had tried for three days to get information out of this guy. He loved it—the smell, the screams,

112

the blood and pain. Next to raping the women and burning people's balls off, pulling teeth was his favourite form of torture.

Life could not stand it. She wanted to leave, but her compassion for Headen kept her there. She stroked his mind and took some of the pain away. Fate checked his book and nodded to his son. Death walked up to the man and cut his soul from this world and set it free. Morguhis stubbed out the remains of his cigar on the cold, dead body.

*

In the city, people who worked with Akea had been questioned, tortured and hung on lampposts; not many could remember him. They collectively thought of him as that quiet guy who sat in cubicle nineteen. Fate made sure that people died at the appropriate time, and Life helped those that should live. Death carefully consulted the book before cutting the souls from their bodies. Chance flittered around, rusting the guns of the guards, making the hangman's rope rot, getting things lost. The Watchmen might try to flay the city to within inches of its life, but Fate was not going to make it easy.

*

In a dark dungeon cell, curled against the cold dampness of the wall, sat Cassandra. She had not spoken to any one except the odd guard in nearly a week. She was on the edge of insanity. She cursed the day the Patrician had first come to her with a proposal.

The guard Kythus entered the cell with food. He looked skittish and kept looking over his shoulder. He bent low to Cassandra's ear and whispered quickly, "Your son has been spotted; he is with the old man of

113

the mountains. We are going to try and rescue you—
just hold on."

She smiled back and whispered in a hoarse voice,
"Thank you."

"You will be safe soon. I must go. I will try and get
some more food, clothing and blankets," Kythus
whispered again.

*

Akea's group found a small clearing in the forest
where the trees thinned a bit. It had taken a week to
locate a suitable clearing that was close to Argonath's
cave. The brown of leaves covering the floor was
accented by new growth in the centre of the coppice.
The trees were about fifteen feet apart. The ground
sloped gently to the south, and in the middle was a
small stream running east to west. Fallen logs covered
in moss served as a makeshift boundary. The canopy
from the dense high trees at the edges of the clearing
helped to disperse the smoke from the camp-fire. The
new knives from the knapsack Prometheus had
brought made short work of cutting down the
branches and logs that were needed. It took some
convincing on Juween and Prometheus's part to get
four trees to fall over. Fortunately the sixty-foot tall
trees were old and full of wisdom. They considered
the arguments for three days. Their wisdom showed.
The trees would not last another winter. They
considered that being used for the protection of others
was a decent sacrifice indeed. Juween promised that
he would encourage the growth of the fated trees'
offspring. Prometheus and Juween used magic to
fashion the wood into a small hut about seven feet
high. Grasses and moss served as the roof. It was
somewhere to store firewood and food, somewhere to
sleep. Argonath flew in some provisions from

Prometheus's cottage.

The sun shone brightly through the trees as Prometheus found an acorn and then buried it. He said, *"Auctus,"* the incantation for growth.

A small sapling appeared.

"Right, my boy. Try and get this to grow. Argonath, hold on to his mind," said Prometheus.

Akea looked at the sapling intently and whispered the incantation. The tree shone brightly and burst into flames.

"It's all right, lad, I'll put it out," said Juween. He smothered the fire.

Akea thought, I got to get this right. I feel so helpless—every time I try and do something, I just blow it up or set fire to it. Soon as I think about doing magic, this furious storm wells up behind my eyes, and I can't stop it or temper it. The sooner I can control it, the sooner I can do some good.

"Akea, don't put so much pressure on yourself, you're just making it worse. Please try and relax. I can help you, but you have to help yourself," thought Argonath, sensing Akea's thoughts. She felt desperate and frustrated, but determined as ever.

"I just don't know how," he thought back.

Prometheus bent down to the ground and whispered, *"Vigoratus."* The ground shivered as a new sapling appeared. They tried again. Argonath tried to help by holding on to Akea's mind. This time, the sapling grew about four inches, shone brightly and then died.

Argonath growled in agitation. *"We might as well call it the phoenix tree. Akea, it's not hard. Do not try, just do,"* she said.

Akea's frustration took over, and he gave her a funny look, as if to say, "I am trying, damn it. Get lost."

Prometheus intervened. "My dearest Argonath, I think we may try another approach. Please, if you would be so kind as to find us some food?"

"Akea, don't you ever look at me like that again," she snapped, and took off.

Prometheus turned to Akea. "Dragons are a proud race and easily offended."

Akea nodded and looked downcast. I should not be easy to anger, she is trying to help me. I hope I can make it up, he thought.

"We are going to meditate. Sit down on the ground cross-legged facing those flowers."

Akea sat on the grass and looked at the pansies enjoying the warm sun. Prometheus sat down next to him.

"The idea is to concentrate on a single object, say a flower petal. You and the flower are the only thing in the universe. Nothing else exists. Breathe slowly and deeply, and then say this mantra."

As he repeated the mantra, Akea could feel Argonath reaching toward him from her hunting ground, trying to help him, soothing his ragged power. After some time he felt quiet in his mind. He felt what it was like to be the petal in the wind. The sun warmed his body, and he felt good about himself, finally at peace. He must do this every day before training. He stood up and faced the sapling, concentrating on the sapling growing and budding into life. He whispered, *"Auctus."* The sapling gently resonated; its young branches thickened and grew slowly. The lightest blue hue hung in the air around Akea and the sapling. The young oak creaked as it grew in strength and vigour.

"That's it, old bean! Now try and get it to bud."

Akea tried to feel the tree from the tree's point of view. In his own arms, he could feel the branches as they grew. He extended his fingers, and the first signs

116

of buds appeared.

"That'll do, lad. Stop there. I think we can call it a day. Our phoenix tree has finally budded," said Juween with a big grin on his face.

The day's lesson had been a sort of success. Akea felt elated, although he knew in his heart that Argonath had done most of the work.

Argonath came into view over the treetops and circled the clearing. Suddenly Akea felt down. She had not deserved that look. The dragon landed and dropped the remains of a boar by Juween. Akea slowly moved towards her, but she snarled at him. He paused and then approached again, slowly and gently.

"I am sorry, it's just you were not helping."

"I am a dragon and should be treated as such."

Akea bowed low and walked away. Juween watched the young man as he left the clearing, and then busied himself with dinner and some coffee. Prometheus offered to help, but Juween declined his offer, and so he sat on the grass and watched the world go past. The smell of roasting pork brought Akea back to his senses and to the camp. After dinner the three men sat around talking about the different incantations and how to use them correctly. Argonath sat there listening to them. After a while she got up and stretched all four legs and moved towards Akea.

"I am sorry, too. Please . . . please forgive me," said Argonath.

Akea got up and turned to her. He gingerly put his hand to her cheek and stroked it. She shuddered as he touched her, and at first he took this the wrong way; but then he noticed the glint in her eyes and smile on her face.

For the next three days, after his morning meditation, Akea practiced growing the oak tree. Argonath found that she needed to control him less

117

and less every day. In the afternoon, bored, Argonath would fly off for a hunt and to stretch her wings. Each time, Akea managed to grow the tree without her being there, and when she got back she looked impressed.

"Okay, old bean," Prometheus announced to Akea the next day, "I think we are ready to move on to another spell: camouflaging. This is a helpful one if you wish to lay in wait and ambush or merely hide from your enemy. First, I will demonstrate for you." The magician stepped next to a large bush, observed it carefully and intoned, *"Velieris mihi."* The colour of Prometheus's skin and clothes began to change subtly into greens and browns, and within a minute, he had disappeared, blending into the foliage.

Akea stepped forward and swiped at the location where Prometheus had disappeared. His open hand met with resistance, and there was a pained grunt.

"Ooof! Watch it, I'm still here," came Prometheus's disembodied voice.

"Sorry," said Akea.

Behind him Argonath rolled her eyes. *"You work on your little disappearing thing. I'm off to hunt."*

Akea turned and looked at her with dismay. *"But I need you—I mean, what if I overdo it?"*

Argonath gave him an exasperated look. *"How could you possibly overdo a simple camouflage spell? You'll be okay. I'm off."* She took to the sky, soaring up and over the trees.

"Manifestum mihi" came Prometheus's voice from the shrubbery, and he reappeared, rubbing his stomach gently. "Really, old bean, I believe you're in little danger of overdoing this one. The key to this one is to really feel and be the surroundings. When you've got that, repeat *'Velieris mihi.'"*

118

Akea stood for a few minutes observing and drinking in the vegetation, and then repeated the spell. He slowly faded into the background.

"Excellent!" proclaimed Prometheus. "Now, do you recall the reappearance spell?" . . .

*

It was another mild, sunny day. It had been nearly three months now, and Argonath, increasingly impatient with the slow pace of the training, had gone off to fly around and enjoy the beautiful weather. Juween leaned lazily against a tree as Prometheus taught Akea a new spell.

"This spell will help to lighten a load. It can be applied to quite large objects, but we will start with something relatively small," said Prometheus. He looked around the clearing and pointed to a large rock lying on the ground nearby. "Akea, if you wouldn't mind, would you go lift that rock?"

Akea went over to the rock and crouched down and put his arms around it. It was roughly spherical in shape with a diameter of about two feet. Akea's hands barely met on the other side. With a soft grunt, he picked the rock up. It weighed about twenty kilograms.

Prometheus looked at the rock and said, "*Gravis elucido sarcina.*"

Akea's arms bounced upward, and he smiled with surprise as the rock lost most of its weight.

Prometheus had Akea return the rock to the ground and then reversed the spell. "Juween, would you come over and lift up this rock? It's a bit heavy for an old man."

Juween obligingly rose from his position against the tree and came over to the rock. He picked it up easily and held it against his stomach and chest, facing

Akea.

"Now you try it, Akea. Remember, the words are important, but it is your intention, your will, that makes them effective."

Akea stared at the rock and repeated the incantation. "*Gravis elucido sarcina.*"

"Nope," said Juween. "Try again."

Akea frowned and looked at the rock intently. He spoke more forcefully this time. "*Gravis elucido sarcina.*"

The rock flew upwards out of Juween's grasp and then fell lightly to the ground.

"Damn!" Akea swore. A faint, light blue hue began to form around him.

Prometheus looked at Akea uneasily. "Stay calm," he said.

But Akea ignored him. "*Gravis elucido sarcina!*" he shouted angrily.

The rock shot into the air and exploded, sending little pieces of shrapnel everywhere.

When Argonath returned a few hours later, everyone was sitting glumly around the camp. Juween had a small bandage on one arm, and Prometheus was forming a bruise on his right cheek.

"That must have been some training session," Argonath remarked cheerfully.

Akea glared at her. "I need you!" he said. "I can't control myself. I could have killed everyone."

Argonath responded with equal force. "It's not my fault, you juvenile little twerp. Don't come crying to mummy every time you can't have your way. Grow up!" She raised her tail stiffly and stomped off into the forest.

Prometheus and Akea exchanged glances.

"Oops," said Akea.

When Argonath had not returned by nightfall,

Akea went in search of her. He found her at her cave, and humbly requested permission to enter.

Inside, Akea stood and faced Argonath, who lay curled in her golden nest. His face bore a sheepish expression. *"I'm sorry, I was out of line. I guess I just scared myself. But I shouldn't have taken it out on you. Yes, I need to learn to control myself. I can't expect you to be there to stop me whenever I have a hissy fit."*

Argonath nodded regally. *"I forgive you. I, too, can be impatient. Sometimes I forget that you are, after all, only human. If you like, tomorrow I will stay and help."*

Chapter 8: Falling

Six months passed, and then a year. With each new skill, Akea had gained confidence. Argonath continued to join in on most of the training sessions. Inevitably, being different species and having different standards caused some friction, but each made an effort to compromise where he or she could, and gradually over the months their relationship grew from uneasy allies to true friendship. Once Akea and Argonath found the right mix of power and control their training became enjoyable, and the days, weeks and months flew past. At one point about six months into the training, Akea realised that most of what he had learned from Juween and Prometheus now made sense. He could perceive the structure of magic. Since that day they had stormed through their training. It scared Prometheus and Juween sometimes just how powerful Akea could be.

Prometheus's plan became clear: they were to train as hard as they could, and when the time was right, they would overthrow the Patrician and free the city from tyranny.

The night-time air was cool after the hot day. It was a welcome relief for Prometheus. Two days before he had suffered from heat stroke and had to lay down in the hut while Juween took over the training for that day. The after-dinner cooking fire glowed red as the embers dwindled away.

"How are you feeling tonight? Want some wine?" Juween asked as Prometheus came back from cleaning duties.

"I'm okay. Tomorrow I should be fine. Yes, why not? I could do with a tipple," said Prometheus. He sat down by the fire and gazed at the glowing embers. Juween sat down near him and passed him a cup of water and spoke the incantation. Prometheus tasted the wine. It seemed to soothe him from some of his ails.

Juween sensed something wrong with Prometheus's tone. "What's up?"

"I am worried about Akea."

"Why? He's coming along so well. Soon we will be able to leave."

"It's . . . it's his state of mind that concerns me. When he gets angry, he seems to lose control. I fear for his sanity."

"What do you mean?"

"Take last week. When he tried to make that cloning potion, it had taken him three weeks to get it to the final stages, and then he didn't mix it well enough, and it blew up. Do you remember?"

Juween chuckled. "Yes, I remember. It was quite funny, seeing great clouds of multi-coloured smoke billowing in the wind. He got up and stormed off, and Argonath chased after him."

"I followed him and found him crying, Argonath trying to comfort him. Then all of a sudden he jumped up. He acted like a scared animal, trying to fight unseen attackers, screaming and shouting. I could not believe it. He told Argonath to take off quickly. Then he shot silver arrows and lightning from his fingers. He spun all around like he was looking for some ghost or something."

"We have put him under a lot for a long time. He was probably just venting."

"You could be right, but I think he has an unseen enemy. Maybe he is haunted by rage, anger, frustration, loss, grief."

"What, like unseen darkness?"

"My dear chap, you really can be thick sometimes."

"Yes, he has not mentioned his mother once. I'm sure she is in a cell somewhere. Though I doubt she is his real mother."

Some distance away, out of sight of the two older men, Akea and Argonath dwindled the evening away talking. Akea still had a lot of learning to do about dragons. Akea blissfully lay against Argonath with her tail curling around him. They had moved off from the clearing and relaxed on a grassy spot near a large rock that had retained some heat from the sun. He felt hypnotised by the slow beat of her massive heart. He didn't want to be anywhere but right here, right now.

Argonath thought to him, *"What do you know about dragon mating?"*

"Nothing."

"A dragon chooses his or her mate for life. If one partner dies, the other will die—the turmoil is too great. They meld minds permanently; their thoughts are one, their hearts are one, they are one. Their eyes become the same—normally the weaker will take on the eyes of the stronger, and normally females will take the male's eye colour. I have chosen my mate. If you wish, I would like you to choose me as your mate."

Akea sat there for what seemed like ten seconds. Then he thought, with all the openness and honesty he could muster, *"I love you."*

He touched her scales with his hand; his eyes turned orange, and the irises elongated into slits. This time the change was permanent.

"What do we do now?" he asked her.

"We meld. Normally dragons ascend to the sky to do this, but I am quite content to sit here. Say after me, 'Ut unus iam quod pro infiniti'—but I would prefer it if you said it in my tongue as well: 'Thi dwosghat enurhf.' We will open up completely; there

124

will be no hiding from each other. This is the true meaning of love: to be in love with someone's mind is so much more than to love someone's body."

Akea stood up and stared straight into Argonath's gorgeous orange eyes. He spoke the sacred words in Latin and in Argonath's mother tongue.

Their minds first touched each other gently, as though they were uncertain of each other. Then walls and defences came off like layers of clothing. Mental shirts and blouses lay strewn over the lounge floor of the collective mind, trousers lay crumpled in the hallway of the joined psyches. Socks lay discarded on the floor of inhibition. The undergarments of apprehension fell on the bedroom floor. Akea had never experienced anything like this. He felt like he had come home. He saw the world through her eyes, and she saw the world through his.

Akea ejaculated. He suddenly felt self-conscious. *"Sorry."*

"Not to worry, I felt the same."

Akea lay down in her arms. Their hearts were in sync; they were complete.

When the morning came, Akea woke and smiled at his love; she smiled back. They went to find the others.

Prometheus took one look in Akea's eyes and smiled. "About time! Between the two of you, you can accomplish the impossible. By the way," he continued, "If Argonath is willing, she can become human by saying the words *extraho mulier,* and change back by saying *mulier extraho,* and you can become a dragon by saying *extraho vir* and back by reversing the words."

"I wish I had known that last night."

Prometheus laughed. "If you had, you would have killed us all; with your lack of control, you would

125

have unleashed forces a hundred times more terrible than that at the border. Now that you and Argonath are one, you can come to know each other safely, both as dragons and as humans. We must give Argonath her clothes if she going to transform into a human; I wonder what she will look like. I think that you may not have to take your clothes off to transform; try it and see."

Argonath snorted. "Humans are always the same!"

They sat down to eat breakfast. It seemed strange that though the food was the same, the sky was the same, the grass, the trees of the nearby forest, somehow to Akea and Argonath everything seemed more real.

"*Do you want to see what I look like as a woman?*"

Akea smiled wickedly, and they went to a secluded spot, taking the knapsack containing Argonath's clothing with them.

The two faced each other, and Argonath spoke the incantation *extraho mulier*. A wind blew around her body, hiding her from view, and a light blue hue formed around Akea as he watched with awe. The wind died down, and Argonath stood before Akea, naked. He stared at her. She was the most beautiful creature on the planet. The goddess Venus would have been jealous. Her fine, silky brown hair hung over the top of her body and down to her navel, covering some of her modesty. Even so, Akea could work out her breasts, perfect in shape and size. He knew he was staring, but he could not help it. He kicked out his libido, and his conscience came marching back in. In his mind, he knelt on the ground and thanked any god who was listening for making him hers. Finally breaking his eyes away, Akea opened the knapsack and presented Argonath's clothes to her. She tried them on, and again she looked stunning: thigh-length black boots, black trousers, a black tunic with embroidered purple swirls and long, wide sleeves. Her black traveller's cloak, like the others, displayed the outline of a dragon.

"Can we see what you look like as a dragon?" Argonath asked, and then said, *"Mulier extraho."* She changed back into a dragon, her newly donned clothing seeming to blur and absorb into her skin as the transformation was made.

Akea muttered, *"Extraho vir."* He felt a strange sensation. The air went from clear to translucent, blurring his view, and the wind picked up and whirled around him and then died down again.

"Is that how it felt for you?" Akea thought.

Argonath nodded dumbly; she stood there with her mouth open. The creature that stood before her was thirty feet long, with a long, slender tail. His spines ran all the way down his body. His dark red armour plates faded into burnt orange where they covered his muscular belly. His nose was longer and fuller than that of Argonath. Two horns, which would sweep back in flight, stood like a crown on his head. He was the dragon of her dreams.

"Let's see you fly," she thought to him.

"Not so loud—you're shouting."

"No I'm not, it's you. You can hear me more clearly now. Try to catch me." She took off into the sky.

Akea felt his wings and unfurled them. He turned his head on his long, slender, sinewy neck and sniffed at them. They looked like bizarre bat wings, incredibly fragile and unable to support his weight. He tried flapping them, and great swirls of dust stirred up. When he looked down he was ten feet from the ground. He could see his love, floating lazily in the sky, doing a breaststroke. Right, he thought, I can do

127

this. He flapped and flapped, tumbling about in the air. It was as though a vindictive god had given a cow wings but had not told it how to fly. Finally gaining control, Akea soared several hundred feet into the sky. He let out a roar that echoed through the mountains and caused a small avalanche. Fire exploded from his mouth, tongues of searing hot flame leaping out almost as far as he was long. He flew toward Argonath, who increased her speed, climbing higher.

"I'll give you knowledge and experience, so you can catch me."

Without warning, she shot off like a rocket. Vapours of air hung behind her. Akea closed his eyes and felt for Argonath with his mind. Then he shot after her, shrieking across the sky, his wings a blur. Every time he got near she would speed up. Steadily they climbed higher and higher. Frost and ice were forming on their extremities and began to slow them down. Akea observed Argonath letting out a small flame to melt the ice on her limbs and wings, and did the same. He concentrated again on going as fast and high as he could. The air was getting thinner; the acids were doing their best in Akea's muscles. He could almost touch the stars. They flew as fast as possible, swooping this way and that. Argonath threatened him that she was not going to mate with him until he could out fly her. A sonic boom echoed around the mountain like a cannon shot, and a streak of burnt orange and dark red passed Argonath as though she were standing still. Now it was her turn to give chase.

Akea slowed down a little so she could catch up. They rolled together in an aerial pirouette, climbing higher still. Their tails entwined in a corkscrew. Akea's wings encapsulated Argonath, and their necks wrapped around each other in a lovers' embrace. Still climbing, they grabbed at each other with their claws, pulling themselves as close together as possible. Facing each other, they stared into each other's eyes. Akea closed his mouth and concentrated, baring all his soul to Argonath. He entered her body, and she entered his soul. Then, as though in slow motion, they began to fall. They were three or four miles from the ground, plummeting faster and faster. Oblivious to their speed, they screeched down like a monstrous great peregrine falcon, their hearts as one, beating faster and faster. A mile from the ground, their bodies had become covered in ice. Like an elongated water droplet, the comet kept falling. The orgasm was beyond ecstasy. Until now, Akea thought, surely no human had ever come near to this.

Three hundred yards from the ground, they began to pull away from each other. It was hard. Akea wanted to fall to his death and stay here in this place beyond the stars. One hundred and fifty yards from the ground, the instinct for survival took over, and he broke off. They arced round and met again in the sky and then flew lazily back to their secluded spot, where they both changed into human form and lay on the grassy meadow floor, entwined. Time had stopped for them; there was a place beyond the stars where Akea called home. Sometime later, they wandered down to find the others.

Prometheus smiled. "Was that you making that booming sound and the fire?"

Akea went red with embarrassment. "She's the most beautiful thing I've ever seen," he stammered.

"No matter; it is not my business what two lovers get up to." Prometheus continued, "When Argonath changes into a human, she takes on the image that you give her. Her form, for all intents and purposes, is a mental projection—your mental projection. Beauty is truly in the eye of the beholder. When you change to a dragon, you take on the form she envisions for you."

Chapter 9: A Sunlit Hollow

In the early afternoon, Akea and Argonath sat talking to each other and watching the world go by. Training had ended for the day, and everyone needed a rest. Akea was resting on Argonath's flank. Argonath stopped talking, and sat there for a while silent, as though she were trying to make up her mind.

"Akea, I know that there is a human custom to wed, or marry, or elope or something. Giving of rings, having a party, then getting a mortgage, whatever that is."

Akea laughed. A big smile broke across his sweet rogue face.

"Don't laugh at me. I am being serious. Dragons don't have the need to give rings—we know who is married to whom. But we do have a custom: the lord of the tribe has to give his permission for the . . . what's the word—I guess it would be 'intended'—to be together. Normally fighting is involved, especially if the male is an outsider. The outcome determines the status of the couple."

"And you say that dragons are more civilised."

She started to tickle him with the very tip of her tail.

Akea laughed. *"Okay, okay. I'll get Juween and Prometheus."*

"No, no—you have to do it properly," she said.

"What do you mean?"

"Get on one knee or something. Stop teasing me."

Akea got up and walked round to her front and stood about five feet from her face. He sank to one knee and spoke aloud. "Will you marry me?"

"Oh, it's such a shock. What's a young innocent dragon to say?" she said mockingly, turning her head coyly away. Then she turned her head back and looked into Akea's eyes. *"Yes, my love, I will marry you."*

"In addition to the one who performs the ceremony, it's normal to have guests, bridesmaids, the best man, ushers, flowers, music and a wedding cake."

"Well, Prometheus can marry us, and Juween can be the best man," she thought.

"I take it that I will have to face Lord Adrigonidd, if we ever get home."

The face of Argonath lit up. *"Yes, home, home!"* Suddenly she became very quiet and solemn. *"Akea, are you serious? I thought that you had never considered it. Do you want to go to the second reality? Akea, I want to go home."*

"Of course I want to go to the second reality. I was born there. Argonath, I want to go home, too! But enough of this. It should be a happy moment. It's not every day I get to marry the dragon of my dreams."

The pair got up and went to find Prometheus and Juween. After about five minutes, they found them discussing a sycamore tree that was showing signs of disease.

"Hi, what's going on?" Akea said.

"Oh, we're looking at the bark of this tree. No matter, we will come back to it another time," said Prometheus.

"What's up, lad?" said Juween.

" . . . I have asked Argonath to marry me, and she said yes," said Akea rather sheepishly.

"More like, Argonath brought it up, and you asked her, hmm, old bean?" Prometheus said, and winked at Argonath.

Akea just nodded. "We would like to hold a ceremony here. Prometheus, would you mind conducting the service, and Juween to be the witness and best man."

"Well, well, congratulations. That means we can have a stag night," said Juween.

"Not really, Juween, it wouldn't be fair on Argonath," Prometheus said. Then a thought struck him. "Oh dear; I just realised you're going to have to face the Lord Adrigonidd sometime."

"Yeah, I know, but I am going to have to face him at some point, if Argonath and I are going to be together."

"Right, then. We will spend the rest of today getting everything ready, and tomorrow at 2 p.m. you will be married. Juween, you can deal with the food and drink. I will deal with the dress. Akea, you can deal with the flowers. Does anyone know any songs?" said Prometheus excitedly.

"Yeah, I know a couple," said Juween.

"Appropriate songs, Juween," said Prometheus.

"Yes, I know a couple."

"I am not wearing a dress, but I might wear flowers in my hair," said Argonath.

"Okay, then. I'll help Juween, if you two can find the spot that you want," said Prometheus.

"I know just the spot," said Argonath. She and Akea wandered off.

The afternoon was spent making preparations. Juween caught a stag and grouse, and now they were slowly roasting on the cooking fire. Prometheus found some vegetables and fruit. Juween tried to make champagne out of water, but after several unsuccessful attempts decided that white wine would have to do. Akea and Argonath had walked for hours looking for the spot before they finally found it. It was in a sunlit hollow, at the base of the mountain. An old tree there had knotted together like an archway, with moss and grasses growing along the long, thick branches. It was early evening, but Akea and

Argonath could see the hollow would be filled with bright sunshine in the afternoon. On the way back, they walked through a meadow brimming with flowers. In the morning Akea would cut them and bring them to the hollow.

That evening the men sat together and ate the remains of the last night's dinner. Argonath was out hunting.

Juween was determined to have a stag night. "Look, lad, it's your last night of freedom, so drink up." He passed the skin of 'home-made' wine to Akea and Prometheus.

"Yes, freedom," said Akea. Suddenly he looked sad.

"Come on, lad, don't get like that. Now drink up and be merry."

Prometheus had the sudden urge that comes with old age. He walked off. On his way back he noticed someone walking toward him. He stopped and waited.

Fate walked up to him. "Prometheus, I see that you have done well."

"Thanks, old bean. Well, well. I didn't think you would be here," said Prometheus.

"After all the effort I have put in to get those two together, I wanted to see the wedding. I know they don't have any guests, so the family and I will attend. I don't think they would mind. You will not be able to see us or hear us. Remember, it's imperative that Akea does not know that I am helping him. It will go to his head, and then we will be . . . what's the human word? Ah, yes . . . screwed. Please give them these rings; it's a wedding present, so to speak." Fate handed him a small box. "It contains two rings. Like the clothes, they change size to fit the wearer," said Fate and left.

When Prometheus got back to the camp, he poured

himself a large cup of wine and drank it in one.

"Are you okay?" said Akea.

"Yes, old bean, I am fine. Let's get drunk. I see Juween has already started."

"Shhh, you better be quiet. His missus has got a bit of a fiery temper," said the less than sober Juween.

The three of them laughed and laughed.

"Been waiting ages to say that," said Juween.

Argonath had come back; she turned into her human form. "What's happening?"

"Well, it's a stag night, see," Juween started, but Prometheus cut in, "Yes, of course, you are an unusual couple, an impromptu wedding, and why not an unusual and impromptu stag night?"

Soon the inappropriate songs started. Everyone enjoyed the night immensely. The morning, however, was different. It was around 9 a.m. when they woke, moaning about the bright light and noise. Juween, who had drunk the most, struggled to get the coffee on. Still drunk, he kept putting his hand in the remains of the fire, rather than on the coffee pot. "Damn it, why do we have two fires anyways?"

Akea woke up, rolled over, and grabbed the pot. He whispered to it, and the pot boiled away. He rolled back and covered his head. Argonath had assumed human form and went into the meadow to braid her hair with flowers, humming to herself. She had never experienced human emotions before. Compared to humans, dragons had so few emotions. "I guess I am happy," she thought, half-speaking out loud.

At two o'clock in the afternoon, the sun shone brightly in the hollow, and the canopy of branches moved gently in the wind. Prometheus thought that Akea had done a fantastic job with the flowers. He had weaved the flowers over the archway. Prometheus got a long, straight branch and placed in within easy reach. He stood next to the archway and waited for Akea and Argonath.

Fate and his family had gathered unseen at the back of the hollow. Chance wore a pink bridesmaid's dress and green dress shoes. Life wore a floral dress. Death complained, "They can't see us, why dress up?" Fate shook his head and stood to attention as Akea and the human form of Argonath walked into the hollow. Juween stood near the archway, looking pensive. Akea and Argonath joined him and Prometheus. All four humans stood in a circle.

Prometheus took Akea's left and Argonath's right hand, and started the ceremony. "We have come together here in celebration of the joining together of Argonath and Akea. . . ."

Akea and Argonath listened to Prometheus and took it in turns to say their vows and commitments, expressing how much they loved each other and how death would not stop them. From now unto the ending of all time, they would love each other unconditionally. Chance had a tear in her eye. Life just giggled.

Prometheus patted his pockets and found what he was looking for; he pulled out a small, light brown, leather-covered wooden box. He opened it to reveal the small, soft velvet cushion on which sat two rings, simple bands of purest gold. He handed one to Akea. "Say after me, 'With this ring I pledge my love and my life, yours for all eternity.'"

Akea placed his ring over Argonath's ring finger and proclaimed his love again.

"Now you, Argonath," said Prometheus.

Argonath placed her ring over Akea's finger and proclaimed her love. Both rings altered their size to fit.

They sang a few songs. Juween took the lead as he knew all the words.

"Juween, please step forth and hold onto this end of the branch," said Prometheus.

Juween picked up one end of the branch and Prometheus held the other end so that the branch extended horizontally about a foot off the ground.

"Please step over the branch as a sign that you have left your old life and have started a new life together," Prometheus prompted. The couple stepped over the branch. Fate clapped, and Life cheered and wiped her eyes.

"I now pronounce you husband and wife. May your love so endure that its flame remains a guiding light unto you. Akea, you may kiss the bride."

Fate moved behind Akea, Argonath and Juween, so that only Prometheus faced him. Fate faded in slightly, just enough to look like a ghost, and winked at Prometheus, who in turn winked back. Then Fate, along with his family, disappeared.

Prometheus declared that the arch should be called the wedding arch, and spoke strengthening spells to the arch and the surrounding trees. They wandered from the hollow to the camp. They ate the stag and grouse and had fruit for dessert; even Argonath ate some cooked meat. She didn't notice, she was so happy. Soon the wine flowed, and the jokes, songs and general misbehaviour started.

Chapter 10: The Two Spells

And so the training went on. Each day Akea would meditate and then practice, gaining personal experience to enhance the knowledge he had received from Juween and Prometheus. Argonath taught him dragon lore.

On one particular morning, Prometheus and Juween sat huddled together talking to each other. It seemed that they were having an argument, or at least a discussion. Akea and Argonath sat a ways away from them, both in human form, silently waiting and enjoying the early summer sun and watching the trees in the wind. Ah, peace, Akea thought. They heard excerpts such as "He is not ready," "He can do it" and "He has Argonath." The discussion finished, and Juween turned and addressed them both.

"Prometheus wants to teach you two fighting spells, but to be honest I don't think you are ready. However; we will try the easiest one and see how you get on."

Prometheus took over. "Please, could both of you change form and get into the air? When you have reached a safe height, Akea, I want you to concentrate on an imaginary enemy and say the words *sanus offensus* and then roar. What should happen is you should be able to produce a sonic wave to knock your opponent out of the sky. Argonath, please temper him."

Argonath was aghast; only the most powerful dragon would attempt such a thing.

"Juween, I understand your concern. I will stop Akea from any real damage," said Argonath.

In no time at all Akea was in the sky, circling

higher and higher. Argonath flew lazily to him. Just below the clouds, Akea concentrated on an imaginary enemy. He imagined facing the Patrician and said the words and then roared. It took everything for Argonath to control him. Her flight path faltered slightly, and small blue circles erupted from Akea's mouth. It was too much for him; he plummeted toward the ground, unconscious. Argonath screeched down and grabbed him in her loving claws. She glided down and gently dropped him a few feet from the ground, and then landed next to him. Juween came running up and spoke softly to Akea. He opened one eye and shook his head to clear it.

"It seems, my dear Argonath, that you have controlled him too much. It looks like you may be taking his power as well," Juween said.

Argonath looked upset. It is such a fine balance, controlling Akea, and yet letting him wield the power. Again they tried. Up in the air, Akea conjured a clear picture of his enemy. He said the words and roared. This time Argonath did not control him. Clear blue shockwaves emanated from Akea in ever-increasing concentric circles. The sound reverberated around the mountains and shook the ground like an earthquake.

Prometheus looked up and smiled. "That's it, my boy, that's it."

Akea and Argonath moved away from the camp so as not to disturb Prometheus and Juween, and they practiced all day, trying different combinations of control and power. Eventually Akea could knock someone out and not kill them.

Finally, exhausted, Akea and Argonath returned to camp. They resumed human form, ate the remains of last night's dinner and settled down for the night. Akea lay in Argonath's arms and fell asleep smiling.

The peaks of the high mountain range stuck out like a smile of broken teeth. . . .

The next day brought a new sun and the most difficult challenge yet. After breakfast and meditation, everyone sat around the fire talking and drinking coffee.

"We want you to attempt the spell *putus odium, putus vox*. It is very difficult and could be disastrous if you do not control it," said Prometheus.

"No, you can't. I will not let you," said Argonath.

"Why not?" asked Akea.

"Because it's . . . it's an apparition of your soul, and if it is destroyed before it has a chance to form its own soul, it will rip your soul in two. Dragons know about it but are not stupid enough to try it," said Argonath bitterly. "There is a legend amongst my race about one who tried it. He fell to the ground like the living dead, and our lord and king killed him like a rabid dog. Akea, I love you. You are precious to me."

"Would it be safer if we did it on the ground, instead of in the sky?" asked Akea.

"If you tried it on the ground, the under formed apparition would hit the ground and explode, causing a small crater and killing you and Argonath," Prometheus said.

"What do I have to do? I want every weapon I can get my hands on," said Akea.

Argonath shook her head. "Damn humans."

"Please, Argonath, hear me out," said Prometheus. "The old man who gave you the clothes and supplies told me to teach Akea this. We will meld together and use our magic to temper his soul. I have no doubt that you will do your best to hold on to him." He turned to Akea. "What you have to do, old bean, is to discharge all your hate, anger and frustration onto the enemy that you want to kill. Yes, kill. Then say the words *putus odium, putus vox*, and guide the new soul away from trouble. Let it find itself. You will feel empty at first, but when it is ready to be freed, you will feel that, too."

Reluctantly Argonath got up, assumed her dragon form and jumped into the air. Akea changed quickly and joined her in the sky.

Below them, they heard Prometheus call out, "We are ready."

Akea and Argonath flew higher.

Akea took a deep breath, concentrated on his mental image of the Patrician and poured out all the rage, anger and hatred he could muster. *"Putus odium, putus vox,"* he roared.

Instantly, a small, underdeveloped creature—more like a chicken than a dragon—burst forth. Its small, fiery wings flapped helplessly. Completely stunned by the ferociousness of the spell, Akea fell toward the ground.

Argonath shouted to the men below, "Grab him, I'll go for the apparition."

Prometheus and Juween used their collective mental power to arrest Akea's fall. Argonath chased after the baby fire dragon, flipped over and caught it. It burned her, but she held on and spoke a spell and poured her will into it. It exploded into flames, and a loud boom echoed around the mountains as a large, fully-fledged fire dragon erupted from the flames. It screamed through the sky looking for the enemy. Akea hung in the air several feet off the ground. Juween and Prometheus struggled to hold on; the holding spell broke, and Akea crashed to the ground and lay there barely breathing, followed by Argonath, who hit the ground and slid into Akea. Her claws, legs and belly were badly burnt from the explosion.

Juween and Prometheus ran to them, Prometheus shouting Latin phrases at Akea. The fire dragon hovered over Akea and Argonath, landed and dissolved.

Akea's breathing became better, and he eventually opened his eyes. "Where's Argonath? Is she okay?"

Juween had healed Argonath's burns. He stroked her unconscious head. "Sorry, Argonath," he murmured, as tears rolled down his face.

Akea struggled to put his wings around her as Juween gently roused her from her unconsciousness. They sat quietly. Prometheus watched intently, like a nurse over a dying patient, saying the odd Latin word. Akea slid back into unconsciousness.

Hours later, Akea sat up and asked, "What happened?"

"You said the spell and produced a small underdeveloped dragon, you fell, we tried to arrest your fall," said Juween.

Argonath opened a weary eye and said, "I caught it, it burnt me, I held on, it was dying, you were dying, I poured myself into it, it exploded into a proper dragon. It took everything I had. I could not land — my legs were too burnt — so I rolled up and crashed into you."

"Argonath, I am sorry. Please forgive me. We will not try that again," said Akea. "Why did it not work?"

"Because there was not enough hatred and anger, it took your soul instead," Argonath murmured.

Prometheus set up a fire and cooked what little food they had left. In her state Argonath could not hunt. Juween went into the forest and returned with a small boar. He bowed and offered it to Argonath. She was angry that they had tried such folly and that she had agreed to help. But they had survived. She bowed her head and said, "Apology accepted. Don't ask us to

142

do that again."

Juween stroked her flank and said, "Yes, my lady."

After they had eaten, Prometheus sat staring into the fire. The others, sensing something momentous, sat and watched him from the corners of their eyes. Prometheus got up from the fire and paced around for a while, and then finally he spoke.

"We have prepared enough. Tomorrow we will pack up our stuff. We are leaving. We must return to the rebel base."

As they packed the next morning, Juween asked Argonath if she wouldn't mind carrying them. "It will quicken the journey," he said.

Argonath agreed reluctantly, grumbling, "Do I look like a packhorse?" She went off to her cave to ready it for her prolonged absence.

After Argonath had left, Prometheus pulled Juween to one side. "You must always pay the utmost respect to dragons. They are not animals, nor beasts of burden. They are graceful and majestic. They are more intelligent than us and in many ways more powerful."

Chapter 11: Plans

By early afternoon the group had almost finished the preparations for their trek back to the rebel base, when Prometheus suddenly stopped what he was doing and stood still; one of the innumerable amulets around his old neck felt warm to the touch, and when he glanced down at it, it was glowing purple. He called out mentally, and a figure stepped into the clearing.

"Bunny!" the man exclaimed, and wrapped Prometheus in a big hug. Akea did a double take; the man could have been Prometheus's twin. The two men broke their embrace, and the visitor moved to shake hands with Juween and Akea and bowed politely to Argonath.

"My name is Amalthea. I am one of the Gatekeepers between the realities."

The two Gatekeepers broke into Latin. As they conversed, flowers started to grow around their feet.

Amalthea looked similar to Prometheus, except Prometheus's nose had been broken. They both had long beards, a slight hunch and stunning yellow eyes that pierced through to the truth.

Amalthea and Prometheus finished their conversation.

"With your permission, I will join your party for a few days, until you reach the rebel base," Amalthea said.

The group at large nodded.

"That means we are walking," said Prometheus.

They finished packing. As they set out, both Akea and Argonath felt exhausted but invigorated; they marched back through the forest, leaving the tranquil mountains where the impossible had happened.

Akea pulled Juween to one side as they walked. "I thought that Amalthea and Prometheus would be identical."

Prometheus overheard and replied, "Odd, isn't it? But you must remember that we are the sum of our experiences and the product of our decisions."

After only a few hours of journeying, they arrived at a little glen. Sensing that Akea and Argonath were exhausted, still drained from yesterday's events, Juween asked the troop if they would mind stopping for the night.

After they had settled in to their new spot, Prometheus said, "Akea, please change into a dragon and help Argonath find us some food."

Amalthea put up his hand. "Allow me."

He transformed into a large, bear-sized wolf, howled and ran off deep into the woods, sniffing loudly.

The evening was warm. The trees around the little glen provided cover. Akea found some dead wood and started a fire, and then lay down against Argonath with her head gently resting over him as though protecting a baby. They had both drifted off to sleep when Amalthea returned with four rabbits. Juween had found some root vegetables, and Prometheus set about making a rabbit stew. He encouraged herbs to grow quickly nearby and added them to the pot.

Prometheus gently woke Akea and Argonath. "Dinner is ready." Akea stood up and sat with the others. Argonath stood and took flight.

"What's the matter?" Akea called to her in his mind.

"I don't fancy cooked human food. I need to hunt. I will see you in a few hours."

Akea sat with the other men and listened to their conversation, relaying it to Argonath so she did not

145

miss out. Distance does not matter when you are in love.

"Vaxihimler has visited my reality several times over the last year," Amalthea began.

"Who is Vaxihimler?" Akea interjected.

"He is the Patrician."

It had never occurred to Akea that the Patrician had a name.

"I followed him as soon as he entered my reality; I felt a tremor in the framework between the realities and went to investigate. I was walking in the woods. Bunny, he knows how to move between realities without the gates."

Prometheus said, "Oh shit!"

Amalthea said, "Yes, exactly."

"Why, what's that matter, exactly?" said Akea.

"If someone keeps moving between realities without a gate it interferes with the walls, slowly breaking down the connections holding them together." Amalthea answered.

Argonath asked a question through Akea. "What are you going on about?"

"Each reality connects to each other. Like soap bubbles, and it's just as fragile. We built gateways between realities that do not damage the walls, so the 'bubbles' don't burst or merge," said Amalthea.

"I doubt he knows how to move other people between realities without a gate; this gives us an advantage, because we know where he is going to come from," said Prometheus.

"But we can't just close the gates; once closed, they will remain so for a generation. We have to find out what he is doing." Amalthea paused and then continued, "I imagine he was talking to his counterpart. He is trying to get an army together; I bet it is proving harder than he anticipated. He miscalculated how alike his other selves would be. One could say that we are the sum of our experiences; however, we are also the product of our decisions, and that means that there are things in this multi verse that cannot be changed."

"*If you're a bastard in one reality, there is a distinct possibility that you're a bastard in other realities, too,*" Argonath thought to Akea.

Akea snickered, and shared the joke with the others.

Amalthea said, "Mmm, that's about right. Please convey to your lovely wife my congratulations on her incisiveness and power of deduction."

Akea thought to Argonath, "*He thinks you're clever.*"

"*Cleverer than you,*" responded Argonath in a jocular tone.

Amalthea continued, "In my reality, where Akea and Argonath are from, magic is strong, and there is no need for technology. Vaxihimler is magically weaker than his counterpart in the second reality, and Vandavor is reluctant to help anyone whom he deems inferior. In fact, he may decide to take Vaxihimler's place, but this must not happen—he would be worse than Vaxihimler."

"How many gates are there? Are they manned?" asked Akea.

"There are three gates between each pair of realities. Vandavor could go between realities on a convoluted course, jumping between various realities and coming in, say, at the gate for the tenth. But that would be extremely difficult. He is more than likely to come in on the second reality," said Amalthea.

The goddess of Night, in her chariot, galloped across the sky, flinging stars into place. Argonath returned, and they all greeted her. She sidled up to

Akea and nudged him. He absently stroked her flank. They settled down for the night, Akea once again resting in the arms of his lover, and the others settled around the fire.

Morning came too soon. The early dew lay on the grass. A young deer with more courage than sense came strolling into the camp, swishing its tail, eating the grass. Argonath watched it for about five minutes. She lay perfectly still.

She woke up Akea with her mind. *"Darling, breakfast has arrived. When I say, jump out of the way."*

The deer moved ever closer. Argonath thought, *"Now."* At the same time Akea moved, and Argonath leapt. The deer didn't have a chance. *"Back shortly,"* Argonath thought as she took flight with the deceased deer in her mouth. Ten minutes later, when she returned, the fire was going and the remains of the rabbit stew were bubbling. She dropped the carcass on the ground. The internal organs were gone, along with the head, shoulders and front legs.

Argonath said to Prometheus, "Tonight's supper, I think. Please prepare it."

Prometheus smiled and bowed to her. "Thank you. You are truly kind." He stretched up and kissed her lightly on the cheek. Argonath blushed.

After breakfast, while they sat finishing off the coffee, Prometheus spoke.

"Juween, I assume you have a plan?"

Juween nodded. "We cannot go into the city, kick out the Watchmen and the Patrician, and then take over. No, no—this will not do. The city is a wounded, scared animal. We need to persuade it into fighting for itself. This is best done with stealth. We will not kill any of the Watchmen, but we will imprison them. When the time is right we will confront the temple leaders, the Watchmen and the Patrician. We must have systems in place, so that when the Patrician falls, the society will not fall into chaos. We must start resistance cells, find good, honourable people who will form a government. We cannot rely on Nalik to help. We must make our way back to the rebel base post-haste to talk to the council, get provisions and organise a secure route to the city."

Akea turned to Argonath. *"Darling, I don't mind carrying them, if you don't mind me doing it."*

Argonath replied, *"I'm not a mule, but I will help."* Akea lovingly stroked her flank.

Akea spoke the incantation *extraho vir,* and shortly there stood, where Akea had been, a great and mighty dragon. He said in a deep and rumbling voice, like lead being dragged across the pavement, "Get our stuff together. We will carry you."

Prometheus had been dubious about flying, but there he sat on the back of Akea. He felt the mighty wings beating up and down. They had been flying west for no more than an hour, when they landed five miles from the rebel base. As they swooped down, Prometheus tried hard to hold down his breakfast. They landed, and Prometheus slid off and kissed the ground, muttering something about not doing that again.

Juween said to Argonath and Akea, "Please, could you change into your human form? From here on in we will be watched."

The dragons nodded. *"Extraho mulier,"* said Argonath, at the same time as Akea uttered, *"Vir extraho."* The thick wind blew about them, hiding them from view, and then died down.

Amalthea was the first to speak. "My dear," he said to Argonath, "You are easy on the eyes. However, with respect, I fear that your name may give away your true identity. Please consider an alternative — something a bit more human."

Argonath stood there for a few minutes thinking; "I shall call myself Amanda."

Amalthea nodded and smiled. He turned to Prometheus. "Well, Bunny, I fear this is as far as we two may go. You must return to your cottage and prepare, and I must return to my reality."

Prometheus shook hands with Juween and Akea. He lifted two of the medallions from his neck and handed them to Juween. "You can use these to communicate with each other and to contact me when you are ready to meet again. I bid you farewell."

"I'll use your gate, if I may. It will be a nice walk to your cottage," said Amalthea to Prometheus.

"By all means, old bean. But it's a six-day hike from here; I think we could cover more ground if we were wolves," said Prometheus. They spoke some Latin, and soon two large, bear-sized wolves sniffed the air, sniffed the ground, and then sniffed each other. Akea could have sworn those two wolves were having fun. Two loud howls signalled the charge, and the two wolves bounded off into the distance.

Amanda, Akea and Juween continued west. The five-mile march took them two hours, the uneven ground and dense patches of woods making it slightly slow going.

Finally they stood on the top part of the slope leading down to the rebel base; they knew the entrance was somewhere near here. Amanda still had some of her dragon sense of smell. "Human — I smell human, this way." She growled slightly.

Akea shivered.

"Sorry, I got confused. Do you know how many feelings . . ." she put her fingers in the air and made quotation marks, " . . .and 'human qualities' I have to deal with?"

Soon they found the trail and followed it to the fifteen-foot-tall concrete doors under the long, overhanging cliff. To one side of the doors, Akea saw a small panel and a camera.

"Juween did they give you the access code?"

Juween shook his head.

"Should I enter some codes and when we can't get in, it will call out the guards? They can see us through the camera."

"Why don't you talk to the panel and see if it will let us in?" Juween said sarcastically.

"Oh, I am sorry; I haven't done my electronics and magic integration course yet."

"You're the geek. Hack the damn thing."

"What's the matter, Juween?" said Amanda.

"I am not looking forward to meeting king dickhead again."

They didn't have time to discuss it further, because the right door opened, just a tad. Guards came out and circled them with their guns trained on Akea and the others' faces.

"Who are you? What do you want?" said one the of rebel guards.

"We are unarmed. We would like to say thanks to Nalik for providing all the equipment he gave us, the last time we were here," said Juween. He was not in a good mood.

"Juween!" Amanda said and then turned to the rebels. "I am Amanda. This is Akea, and Juween," she said, pointing to each as she named them. "We would like to speak to the elders."

Two of the men moved forward and searched them, but for some inexplicable reason, they didn't want to touch Amanda.

"I will take you to see General Nalik," said the

leader of the patrol.

"Oh good, General Nalik. I would prefer to see Commander Bavlin, if it is all the same," said Juween.

Amanda moved in closer and whispered to Juween, "Juween, get a grip, will you? It's hard enough dealing with these human feelings. I don't need your bull as well." She'd had her first experience of the notion of being overly mothering.

Chapter 12: Opposing Force

The rebels' central command room was about the same size as a large hall. Small cubicles defined administration departments. On the left hand were glassed off offices. The original strip lighting had been replaced some time ago with the softer light bulbs, which helped make the long days inside more bearable. The rebels had strong links to other countries. It was possible to get almost anything. In the second office from the right, there sat, in his green uniform, the leader of the rebellion army, listening to the reports.

"Twenty-one people were hung on traitor's row last week. That's double from the week before. Fourteen families have been reported missing; we managed to get four families out. The strange thing is that if you correlate these people with relevance to Akea, they all have something to do with him. Either knew him, worked with him or knew the family. The mother is also still in the Patrician's cell; we are still trying to get her out," said an attendant.

A polite knock interrupted their conversation. A guard walked in. "We caught three people trying to get in. They are unarmed. We are holding them in the great hall. They seem to think that you will allow them to stay, and one said that he wanted to thank you for all the equipment that you lent to them, the last time they were here."

"Who are they?" said General Nalik.

"Two men, Akea and Juween, and a woman, Amanda," the guard said.

"It's okay, I know who they are. I had hoped they had died, but we can't have everything. Bring them here."

When the guards had escorted the three in, Nalik

smiled derisively. He scorned these feigns, these fakes, these conjurers, these tricksters. What did they have to do with the rebellion? He spat on the ground near their feet. Amanda's eyes flashed dangerously.

"So we send you away, hoping that you will find your fate in the woods, and yet you have come back, and you have brought more with you. Do you wish for more food?"

Juween grabbed Akea's arm to stop him from doing any thing stupid. Anger rose in Amanda, and she answered with scorn.

"Excuse me, I am new here. Who are you? Why do you speak to my husband in this fashion?"

Nalik replied imperiously, "My name is Nalik, General Nalik. Your what?" He stood there for a second, and then a big smile came over his face. His moustache became a fat black line. "Allow me to show you the destruction wrought by your loving husband and the terrible retribution that followed. The man whom you have jumped into bed with overnight is more than dangerous, he is genocide waiting to happen."

Nalik turned to an assistant and grabbed his laptop computer; he found the CCTV file of the incident at the border.

"You stupid little man, there is no need to show the CCTV footage. I know all about what happened. And I did not jump into bed. We fell from the sky." The anger continued to slowly rise in Amanda, but she remained outwardly cool and collected.

"Has Akea disillusioned you that much? He is not a saviour, a messiah or an apparition, he is a loser, and a second-rate one at that," retorted Nalik.

"What is your problem? What have I done to you?" said Akea.

154

"Shall I draw you a picture? Thanks to you and that disgrace of yours," he pointed to Juween, "innocent people have died at the hands of the Watchmen." Nalik picked up the reports and threw them at Akea. "Read it and weep, asshole."

"What do you mean, disgrace? That's a bit harsh," said Juween.

"Oh, didn't Juween tell you about how he killed fifteen men through his incompetence?" Nalik said, hoping that Juween would be too ashamed to tell anybody.

Juween shifted slightly. He knew where this was going. He ignored the guards and sat down on the nearest chair, mainly to stop himself from beating the life out of Nalik.

"About twelve years ago, we were out on an exercise. We were sent to pick up a family," Juween started. "Nalik here told me to hang back to make sure we were not followed—"

"That's General Nalik, you insubordinate arse, and I told you to stay out of the way, because you had countermanded my orders," Nalik interrupted.

Juween continued, "We saw the very patrol of Watchmen we were trying to save the family from. *General* Nalik decided to set up an ambush in a large alley. He split his men to into two groups, opposite each other. When the Watchmen came through the alley a fire fight started; most of our men were killed by friendly fire. I was too far away to help, and even if I had gotten there in time, I could not really use effective magic because our men were in the way— most of whom, I might add, were dying, I tried to save them, but there were too many injuries. The blood was everywhere." Nalik tried to interrupt, but Juween just talked over him. He had waited a long time for this moment. *"General* Nalik was a real rock, a man of steel. Oh—hang on. No, he wasn't. He sat in the corner, staring into middle space and calling for his mummy."

"That is not what was said in the court, I suppose," said Akea. He put his hands on Juween's shoulder. Juween had begun to weep softly. Amanda knelt down in front of Juween and wiped the tears seeping from his eyes.

Juween just shook his head.

"The court revealed the truth. I was acquitted, and Juween here was sent back to the city in disgrace and no longer an adviser," Nalik said.

"The only reason you got away with your stupidity was the fact that your father was one of the judges on the panel," said Juween. "And if I remember he was struck off for corruption."

"What's the old saying, 'Time will tell'? Well, time has told. I am the captain of the rebel army, and you are, well . . ." Nalik moved his hand up and down, with distaste in his eyes. "If that was not bad enough, you took a minor in battle, that wayward, out of control bitch, Cruz. How is she? Oh, wait—she is dead, by your hands. Case in point."

"How dare you talk to Juween like that! Who the hell do you think you are? He is and always will be twice the man you are. If you want to know the truth, I killed Cruz," said Akea.

"Let's see now: Juween took an inexperienced and useless magician and a minor with no battle experience into a fire fight with the Watchmen, guards and police. Therefore the blame is his, even though you were the one who, by your failure to control yourself, killed her."

"You really have no idea, do you? If you don't stop insulting me, I will eat you for dinner," Amanda bit in. She stood up and walked closer to Nalik.

"My dear woman, I am not insulting you," said Nalik. He put his hands patronisingly on her shoulders.

"You insult my friends, you insult me. I would rather not eat you. It could get very messy. I don't like cooked food, but with you, I might lower my standards. If you don't stop, I will burn you to a cinder and rip off your head," she said.

"You may look good in bikini, but I doubt you could do anything other than stand there as a beautiful distraction, while Akea fumbles about trying to pull a rabbit from a hat."

"Enough. Please, for your own sake, stop your male chauvinistic remarks. There are things here that are not what they seem. If you can grasp this notion, do not insult a dragon, it's rude and very fatal. Argonath does not make idle threats!" Akea warned Nalik.

"Who's Argonath? You dumb arse, there are no dragons here!" Nalik looked perplexed.

Amanda sighed. This wasn't going very well. "My draconian name is Argonath." Then she spoke more clearly, as though she were trying to teach a three-year-old how to do complex algebra.

"My human name is Amanda. I am a dragon and have sworn allegiance to Akea. You insult him, you insult me. As I said, he is also my husband, so it's best if you do as Akea says, or I will bite your head off, literally."

"You brought a dragon into the base—an unstable one at that? You are dumber than I thought," said Nalik. He could not believe his ears or his eyes.

Akea and Juween looked pensive.

"Mulier extr— " Amanda started to say.

Akea jumped in the way between Nalik and Amanda. *"NO, stop this at once. Amanda, please back down. I am sorry he has insulted you, but this is not the time nor the place,"* thought Akea.

"Akea, he has insulted me for the last time," said Amanda.

"What is that mad woman drivelling on about?" said Nalik.

"Please Amanda, don't, please. I know he has, but killing him will not help our cause," Akea thought.

"I will not kill you today, but one day you will pay for your insults with your blood." Amanda spoke and breathed heavily; she was really trying to control herself.

"Look, this is going nowhere," said Juween.

"We want to see the council. We are not here to have a pissing contest with you. So be a good a chap and get the council, would you, old bean?" Akea said, mimicking Prometheus. He wished Prometheus were here; he would sort this out.

Nalik turned to the guards. "These people are dangerous. Take the safeties off. If they move, shoot them." Then he turned to his assistant, who stood there utterly bewildered by the whole thing. "Get the council, then we can get rid of the filth."

Amanda growled in her best dragon-sounding human voice, "Give me strength. Somewhere there is a village missing an idiot. Have you not listened to anything I said? I am a dragon, and I really *am* going to kill you. Have you not seen the videos? No bullet can harm the others or me. I am in the company of magicians, and we can create shields to stop bullets. So, little man, let me draw *you* a picture: if your men shoot, they will hit themselves—or worse, others. Put your testosterone away, along with your toy guns. And do us all a favour, and shut up."

"How are you humans supposed to intimidate people with a pathetic growl like that?" she thought to

158

Akea.

"Yeah, it was pretty pathetic, but I think it worked. You even gave me the shivers. I love you," he thought back.

As they were thinking this, Nalik moved his left hand downwards to disarm the guards. Amanda and Akea smiled at each other like two kids sharing a secret.

Completely ignoring the guards, Akea and his friends sat down in the nearest chairs and waited. Soon the council of elders arrived. Of the six elders four wore black robes with white trim. The eldest and his second wore red robes with yellow trim. Akea and the others got up as a sign of respect.

The eldest and most wise spoke for the council. "Good afternoon. My name is Iral. My second is Athel." He pointed to the other elder in red, and then he pointed to the other four in order of status. "Samond, Jisi, Hans and Sisama."

Iral turned to face his guests and continued, "I hear we have the privilege to have a dragon in our presence." He looked Akea, Amanda and Juween each in the eyes. "Ah, yes; please, madam, what's your real name and tribe?" he said as he stroked his short white beard and then put his hands behind his back.

"My name is Argonath, and I am from Lord Adrigonidd's tribe; he sends his regards," she replied, looking a bit sheepish.

"He worked it out; he knows dragon lore," Akea said quietly to Juween.

The eldest turned to Akea and Juween. "Yes, I know the lore of dragons. We are not all idiots here. I met Lord Adrigonidd once, when I was young, about sixty years ago. He was teaching a young dragon then, and I helped him out with some human laws he was not certain about."

159

"You! I remember you. It has been a long time."

"You are not the only magicians in this facility," the elder said. He looked from Akea to Amanda. "Oh—congratulations on your marriage. Unusual, but none the less, congratulations."

I must be taking stupidity pills or something. How does he know? Akea wondered.

"Darling, it's the eyes: Your eyes match mine, remember?" Amanda answered Akea's thoughts.

"Well, it's been a while since I last saw a mirror."

"Hopefully your marriage will bring humans and dragons closer together, something that should have happened a long time ago," Iral sighed.

The elder thought for a minute and then spoke again. "Back to more urgent and pressing problems. Please, could everyone leave the council with the guests now—orderly and quietly; we do not want to offend this magnificent being." He winked at Amanda. The guards looked at each other and murmured. They must obey the elders. One by one, they left. Nalik walked out with as much pride as he could muster. Soon only Akea, Juween, Amanda and the elders stood in the large office.

Athel smiled at Amanda. "Perhaps you and your companions would join us in our chambers."

They proceeded down the well-lit tunnels, the elders in front, talking amongst themselves, Akea, Juween and Amanda walking quietly a few respectable steps behind. They convened in a lavishly decorated room, perhaps the same size as a small flat. The walls were covered in pictures and paintings, which were banned in the city. Although they were hung on walls like discarded family photos, soft up lighting displayed the magnificence of the mostly priceless pieces. The elders filed in and sat in chintz chairs. In the back corner was a door where servants came and went with tea, coffee and sundries. On the opposite side was another door.

"Please be seated. Would you like tea, coffee or pastries, perhaps? They are very good," said Hans to their guests.

Juween relaxed a little; he needed a cup of strong, hot tea. Akea was stiff and cool towards the elders, though not unfriendly. Amanda smiled serenely; she had taken a liking to these old councillors. It was not common for humans to address a dragon correctly. She had often wondered about that nice human who visited her when she was young. She looked around at the things humans collected and considered treasures. She marvelled at the intricate work of an antique coffee table that Juween had put his cup on. Humans, she thought. What weird and wonderful creatures. The pleasant temperature smoothed any tension, and the smell of the pastries permeated the air. Corner lamps shone and gave the room soft tones of light.

Juween began the discussion. "Sirs, elders, distinguished gentlemen, I have for many days been formulating a plan. I have discussed it at length with Prometheus; he agrees that it could be conceived as the best way forward."

"Yes, how is that old rascal, anyway? I haven't seen him in years. I do miss our little chats," said Jisi. The others nodded and agreed. They gazed at Juween serenely, waiting for the great plan.

Juween continued, "I believe that the city is like a wounded, frightened animal. We cannot just storm in and take over; the citizens will not see any difference between the current regime and us. Therefore, it is my intent to wage a three-pronged attack, always in stealth, until such time as the city can stand up for itself."

"Firstly, Akea, Amanda and myself will become a

161

vigilante force, stopping the Watchmen's terror, saving people from these men by capturing or thwarting — but not killing — the Watchmen. Secondly, we will create more safe houses and infrastructure for refugees. Build on what is already there, and find good, upstanding people to form a government, so when the Patrician is removed there will not be any rioting. We will set up envoys to other cities and other rebellion strongholds and build links. We can then start the freeing of the whole country. Thirdly, when we know we have earned the people's trust, we will publicly denounce the Patrician and lead the revolution."

The group sat around and discussed the details of the plans; an aide sat in the corner and took notes. Finally, Iral again addressed the travellers. "Please remain here while my fellows discuss this. Enjoy the pastries and tea."

The octogenarians wandered out of the room and through the door not used by the servants into an anteroom.

An hour later they returned from their debate and sat down again in their favourite chairs, pleased to find some of the pastries gone, but not all of them.

Iral spoke for the elders. "We will give you thirty men, food, clothing and all the weapons that we think you will need. We will also give you a captain to lead your men, as we feel that you do not possess all the skills that you need to pull this off. Captain Nellis has many years of experience; he will suit your needs. Clearly, you have demonstrated that you do not understand the meaning of strategy."

Akea answered, "You are wise in your council, and we but have one more request."

Iral nodded.

"Please keep Nalik away from us. I do not trust him."

"Funny you should say that. That is what he said about you," responded Samond. "We also want you to train here; you will endure a month's course as humans, and you will not be allowed to do magic. You shall get to know your men in this time. Of course, as our guests, you may come and go as you please, but I encourage you to remain here and devote the next few weeks to your training."

"Of course, whatever it takes," responded Akea.

"All right, then," said Iral. "Tomorrow morning at 0800 you will muster outside the rear exit with the men who will be assigned to you."

When Akea, Amanda and Juween reported for training the next morning at eight, they found thirty troops—mostly men, but a few women—at attention, facing Captain Nellis. The captain was a stocky man, as many military men go, with shoulders that you could land aircraft on. Very short grey hair tinged with silver capped a weatherworn face that encapsulated keen, dark eyes.

"Good morning," he greeted them. "Fall in behind me, and we will proceed to our training ground."

The training ground was in a clearing about a quarter of a mile from the base. When they arrived, the captain again addressed them.

"For the next few days we will be learning the ancient and noble art of wrestling. Wrestling tests your balance, a vital skill for any soldier, who must be able to quickly regain his feet if he falls. In addition to improving your stamina and strength, it will also give you increased pushing power, gripping strength and manual dexterity. Not to mention that it's great fun. Juween, you're an old hand at this. Come on up and help me demonstrate the first position we will be

163

learning."

Juween stepped up, and the captain demonstrated with a basic wrestling position. The two men faced each other, each putting his chin on the other's right shoulder, and grasping each other with both arms, his right arm above the other's left. They broke apart, and the captain again faced the troops. "Simple enough, eh? Now, each of you pick a partner of comparable size and strength and try it."

Akea turned to Amanda and smiled. He put his arms tightly around her.

"Men with men and women with women, please," continued the captain.

Akea's smile turned to a frown, and he let go of Amanda looked around for a male partner. Amanda found a woman of about her height.

"Okay, everyone in position?" asked Captain Nellis.

The pairs of soldiers nodded.

"Now, your object is to get your opponent onto the ground. Anything goes short of kicking and biting. . ."

The troops spent the rest of the day learning basic holds and strategies, stopping only to return to the canteen for a short lunch break.

At the end of the day, Amanda and Akea collapsed on their bed in their quarters.

"That was fun, but I'm exhausted," said Akea.

"Yes, it was interesting to work so closely with humans," commented Amanda. "But it's been less than twenty-four hours since I switched to human form, and already I'm itching to be a dragon again. I don't know how long I can take this."

"You'll be fine," said Akea.

*

164

The Patrician sat in his office. The light from the large windows warmed the room. He went over the weekly reports, clearing the dead weeds from his garden that was the city. He heard a knock on the closed door. He looked up from his work, took a sip of coffee and said, "Enter." The captain of the prison guards walked in and handed the Patrician another weekly report.

"Captain Nordstrom, please see to it that Cassandra is taken to the Watchmen. Make sure they understand she is not to be killed, but other than that, they are to show her no mercy."

"Yes sir."

After a few seconds of report reading, the Patrician spoke again. "Make preparation for war. I think that the rebels might attack again."

"Yes sir. Do you think that it will be an all-out attack, or stealth?" said the captain.

"I am not sure. Our enemy is stronger than before; we must prepare for both."

"Should we prepare plans to evacuate the populace, if there is an all-out war?" asked the captain.

"Don't be an idiot. We will use them as a human shield. Use your brains for once," said the Patrician.

"But sir, people will get killed."

"That is all, Captain Nordstrom. Close the door on your way out."

*

Dogs barked, people mowed their lawns and washed their cars. They did lunch. Yet slowly but surely something was changing. No one could put a finger on it, but something was growing, like a seed of mistletoe buried deep in the bark of an old oak tree, germinating. Things were stirring. People were

165

beginning to wake up; there was something wrong with the way things were. Quiet whispers grew into murmurs. The very thing that the religion tried to stop was happening under its nose.

*

At home, Fate sat at the dinner table and enjoyed the evening supper. Chance sat on his right in an evening gown. Fate turned to his wife.

"Have you left those banned books and reports for the police chief to find?" he asked.

"No, dear, I have been so busy at the moment. But I will. I did confuse the Watchmen's reports so they will arrest the wrong people."

Fate touched his wife's hand and kissed her on the cheek. "Thank you," he whispered.

*

At the rebel base, Akea and Amanda had continued to train daily with the troops. Juween, already well trained in combat skills, helped Captain Nellis with the instruction. In only two weeks, they had become remarkably proficient wrestlers and had moved on to hand-to-hand combat. The feeling of camaraderie within their troop of soldiers grew.

Amanda enjoyed learning to use her human body, but each day her urge to fly free as a dragon became stronger and stronger. When she complained to Akea, he reminded her of their promise to the elders.

Two weeks into the course, Amanda broke. She felt like an alcoholic in a beer festival, or an anorexic at a wedding feast. One morning Amanda got out of bed and staggered unsteadily to the bathroom; she threw up. When she had cleaned up the mess, she looked in the mirror. Her porcelain white skin was tinged with grey blue. She leant in closer. She could

166

see her scales reappearing as dark grey lines. Perhaps she was dreaming, but she could have sworn that the scale lines were moving around slowly. She put her hand out to turn the hot water tap, and leapt back in shock. Her hands—her beautiful, soft, white hands—were grey, and her long slender fingers ended in great black claws. She ran into the bedroom and clawed at Akea.

"You have to get me out of here!" she screamed.

Akea jumped out of a dream and into reality. He could not believe what he was seeing. They got dressed and ran through the corridors, looking for the elders' chamber. They ran past a guard. Akea stopped and turned back.

"Please, please tell me where the elders' chambers are. It's an emergency," said Amanda, trying to keep her cool.

"Do you need a doctor?" the guard asked.

"No, I don't need a doctor, just take me to the elders *now*," Amanda screamed, her voice becoming husky and dragonesque.

The guard nearly crapped himself. "Yes, yes, certainly, this way."

They ran down three flights of stairs, and then left twice, and then right. Akea's heart was pounding, not out of exhaustion, but fear. The guard knocked on the elders' door and left.

The door opened, and a servant showed them in.

Iral was seated in a large, comfortable chair across the room. He rose as the pair entered. "Ah, Akea. Oh, Amanda. So it's happened. Just as I expected it to," he said.

He studied Amanda's face and hands. "Don't worry. There won't be any lasting effects. Were you sick this morning?"

Amanda nodded.

Iral moved forward and grabbed her hand. "It will be okay, I promise, but your stomach will turn at the sight of raw meat, and your eyesight and hearing won't be as good for at least a day. Thomas!"

A servant came into the room and bowed slightly.

"Please take Amanda to the nearest exit, and do hurry."

Amanda turned to Akea with fire in her eyes. "*I stayed in human form out of love and honour.*"

The servant escorted her to the hidden exit at the top of the base. From there a road led to the forest. Amanda walked up the slope until she reached an open, grassy patch of land. She stepped into the centre of the small clearing and whispered the incantation. The wind picked up around her. Then, there she stood, a twenty-foot-long dragon, her slender, blue grey scales shimmering in the bright sunlight. She took off. Up, up, up in the sky, where she belonged.

Back in the elders' chambers, Iral spoke to Akea.

"You have taken a dragon as a bride. You must know what this means, don't you?" said Iral.

Akea stared at the man.

"She *is* a dragon. She can't remain a human. She belongs in the sky, she belongs outside, and she *is not* human. She must be free. She loves you with all that she can muster, and she has lasted longer than we expected. However, the fact remains that you have not understood the subtlety of your wife. You did not object to putting her through a month of being human. You have disgraced her. Let's hope she does not eat you for dinner. In the future she may remain in the forest and retain her dragon form. The troops will train with her there."

Akea sat shell shocked. How could he have been so stupid? Iral was right: all that mattered was his wife, the dragon of the sky.

Akea asked the returning servant if he would not mind showing him to the exit. As they made their way through the maze of tunnels, Akea became more and more anxious, and by the time they arrived at the small control room next to the exit he was almost running. The guards activated the door release, and Akea sprinted forward and scraped through the opening gap. As the doors creaked shut behind him, he scanned the sky and finally spotted her, a dark speck in the distance. He stood and watched, and his heart broke. He had misunderstood her; she was still a dragon and could not remain a human indefinitely. It was his fault that she was here now, searching the sky like a half-starved sparrow hawk. He started walking up the slope in her direction. As he reached the edge of the wood, she finally spoke to him in thought.

"Akea, I love you; perhaps you do not understand what that means. I will do all that I can to help you. But sometimes, I need to be free. I can hardly see anything or hear anything. And these human emotions better leave soon. It's going to take me awhile to find some food. Please go away; I want to be alone. Don't come looking for me, or it will be the first divorce in dragon history. As punishment, I am going to release my control of you."

Akea felt Argonath's presence leave him; he grabbed his head and fell to his knees. For so long he had relied on her to hold him back. Then it happened. The frustration, the grief, the broken heartedness, the low self-esteem, his negligence of Argonath's needs— the darkness behind his eyes rumbled, his memories blazed with images like a fast-forward video, Cruz sitting in the driver's seat, splattered in blood, Juween by his side, dying.

Suddenly she was back in his mind, a faint trickle of thought. *"Don't you dare,"* she growled. *"Don't you dare!"*

"*What can I do?*" he cried to her. "*I can't . . . can't do it; I can't fight the Patrician and keep myself under control. Argonath! I know you're angry. But for god's sake, please help me, I can't stop them, I am going mad.*" The images in his mind went super-nova.

Argonath floated among the clouds, searching for a deer or boar, almost indifferent to Akea's pain. She spoke softly to her love. "*You can save us, but you can't do it alone. If we die in the process, that is our decision. Cruz disobeyed a direct order from Juween; she would have survived if she had obeyed. Don't you think on it! Give me your grief; I will take control of your emotions. Don't think for one second that I have forgiven you—yet!*"

Feelings swirled in Akea's head. Darkness ran around his vast mind like jack rabbits on a dark moor. It was hard for him to concentrate. "*Iungo ut unus, iungo ut unus,*" he whispered. Argonath's full presence re-entered Akea's head, like soothing, cool water on a second-degree burn. The insane darkness retreated as Argonath's logical light came in.

"*Oh, god, I'm sorry Akea. We are so tangled up, you can't live without me,*" she thought to him.

She cornered and grabbed the darkness, roaring so loudly that the ground shook. She fell slightly under the weight of Akea's confusion. Then she let out a roar of fire, and it was over. The darkness was shackled up, imprisoned in a rubber-walled room.

She circled in the air above and looked down at him. "*I must be alone for a while. Please go back to the base. I will find you.*"

Akea felt like a rejected child. As he wandered back down the slope toward the base, his thoughts whirled. Argonath, Cruz, Juween, the godlike feelings, Cruz, Nalik, insanity, Argonath, Amanda,

Argonath, I was so stupid, why couldn't I see it? The pride, oh Argonath. He didn't notice the trees or birdsong. He didn't feel the hot sun streaming down on his head. He felt cold, as if someone had sucked all the life out of him.

Just inside the concrete doors, he was blocked by Nalik and some guards.

"So, where's the bitch? Not so big now, are we? I have a right to put you in prison and throw away the key, for compromising our base."

Akea just looked at him. "Why don't I give you a reason to put me in prison?" He hauled back and landed a good-sized right hook across Nalik's face.

Nalik fell down. His look of surprise turned to rage. "Put him in irons," he ordered the guards. He glared at Akea, rubbing his chin. "You are going to the dungeons to rot, you piece of filth."

Akea didn't resist. He was too sad with the grief; his soul was missing from his heart. As the men dragged him down to the dungeons, the sounds of their boots echoed off the hard, flat walls. The paint on the walls was peeling, and the light from the fluorescent lamps was hard and cold. The guards threw Akea into a cell, where he sat on the paper-thin mattress that served for a bed. He leant back against the wall, feeling the bricks through his back. The evening sky lit the dank cell. Slowly night came on, and the cell became dark and cold. Akea did not notice.

In one corner sat Fate, listening, waiting and watching. He could not quite understand what had moved him to come here. He had felt compelled. He examined this new feeling of compassion that Life was always going on about.

Akea closed his eyes and tried to feel Argonath, but she had retreated beyond his consciousness.

He lay back on the bed and finally fell into a fitful sleep.

He was standing on a hillock; he could feel the winds wrap around his arms and legs. His long, blond hair enjoyed the feeling of being combed by the wind. The sun was warm; its rays fell on his worried face as his keen eyes scanned the horizon. Then he saw it in the distance: a black object, circling, looking for food. It flew nearer, and suddenly it came into sharp relief; it was Argonath. Akea's heart leapt for joy. . . .

The sound of the door clanging woke Akea up. A guard brought in some breakfast, and Akea sat on the cot for a while trying to eat the cold, overcooked eggs and soggy toast, thinking deep thoughts. How can I do this, how can I become something better than myself? I want to be free. Why do I feel so bad, so useless? Why do I hate myself, when all around people love me? I guess they can't see the darkness that lurks behind my eyes.

Fate intervened. "Argonath? How can she love you, after what you did to her? But she does, and unconditionally, I might add. You forced her to be something she is not. Yet all she ever does is encourage you to be you. Patience, Akea, you have such a long way to go, and not much time to do it in. Face your demons, face your darkness, unleash the true Akea, both good and bad, both powerful and weak. Violence and compassion, the rage and the calm . . ."

Akea rubbed his hands over his eyes to banish his jumbled thoughts. With a look of determination, he started to eat the rubbery eggs. Breakfast finished, he got up, walked to the door, and spoke to it. *"Commodo benigne solvo mihi."*

The metal in the lock listened to the Latin, and the bolts slid back. It had not had such a request before,

172

but it was happy to accommodate. Akea stepped through the door and spoke again. *"Gratias ago vos."* He retraced his path to the upper levels. When a guard approached, he muttered the shielding spell and continued on, ignoring his cries and others as they attempted to seize him and bounced off. At the exit, he entered the control room, pushed the release for the gate, and walked out. Soon he was standing on the very patch of rough grassy land where Argonath had transformed yesterday. He spoke the incantation, *"Extraho vir."* The wind picked up, and he felt himself changing He felt his wings again and took off searching. Where would she be? She could be anywhere.

His search took him hours. He had no idea which direction she had gone. He flew across the sky in increasing circles. Then he spotted it, about two hundred miles from the base—the place in his dream. So it is a real place. I suppose it's a good place to stop and rest, he thought. As he flew nearer, he spotted a deer running on the grassy plain. He swept back his wings, and in one fell swoop he grabbed the deer with his claws and squeezed the life out of it.

The peaks of the high mountain range stuck out like a smile of broken teeth. Three outcrops stood apart from the others. Heather and grasses clung to the sides of the outcrops, covering the mountains' modesty. The sun beat down from the clear blue sky. Autumn was in the air, and the trees sang their seasonal symphony. He landed on the top of the third peak, and rested and ate some of the deer. Then he transformed once again into human form.

Akea stood defiantly against the wind. His cloak fluttered in the breeze. He was searching, scanning the horizon. He stood there for ages, looking, staring, searching, and he could feel the wind in his hair, the sun on his back.

Finally, there in the far distance, was a black shape, circling in the sky, looking for food. He watched for some time, not calling to her, trying to hide his mental projection. Then the form came into sharp relief. Akea's heart jumped, but he still tried to hide his power from her, so that she could be alone with her thoughts.

Evening was approaching, and the sun started its daily descent, changing the colours of the sky to warm oranges and pinks. She had felt his presence ages ago, but ignored him. She was still furious with Akea; she wanted to teach him a lesson. That thick oaf must learn. The stupid idiot could have got me killed. She stewed in her own furious juices.

Finally she contacted him. "*You agreed to make me stay human for a month! That was really selfish, and stupid. You humiliated me.*"

Akea sat on the ground; he had not seen this bit of the dream. "*My love, I am truly sorry. I have been an idiot. Please give me another chance.*"

"*You must think more like a dragon. You must consider others before your own stupid pride.*"

"*Teach me more. Show me patience, give me wisdom. Please, please forgive me.*"

"*Have you not learned anything over the last year?*" scolded Argonath.

"*I guess it took something like this to really show me the subtleties of your nature. I will not do it again. Next time, if there is a next time, please tell me that I am being an unfeeling, selfish bastard.*"

Argonath circled a bit more as though she were making up her mind. Then she spiralled down and landed next to Akea. She nuzzled him. "*Oh, I do love you.*"

"*Human feelings haven't left yet, I take it?*" he

thought.

"Nope, you are going to have to put up with my soppiness for a bit longer."

"Its suits you, makes you softer," he thought, with a smile on his face.

"Don't you dare take the piss; it's your fault that I am flapping around like a school girl with a crush."

"Argonath, I do love you. Thank you for saving me."

He turned to her and cuddled her with all his might, tears in his eyes.

This was the day that the child Akea died; he knew for the first time what it meant to be a man. The darkness had started to disappear.

*

The moon shone brightly in the cloudless cool night as the Watchmen broke into 21 Bret Street with a battering ram.

"Jones, you are under arrest for violating curfew. Come quietly, or we will shoot you in your beds," shouted the leader of the Watchmen through his megaphone. A man dressed in his undergarments appeared at the top of the stairs. "We are not the Jones family; I am the brother-in-law of the captain of the guards. What the hell is the meaning of this?"

The Watchmen leader moved to the well of the staircase. From there he could see the man at the top staring him down. The leader looked at him in the half-light, and then looked at the photo of the man they were supposed to get.

"Get out," the man shouted.

Oh, this is too much, thought the leader; he pulled his gun up and shot the man dead. The rest of the family was quickly executed, and soon the house burned brightly.

*

Police Chief Wellings had always considered himself lucky to have such privilege. He sat in his executive chair staring at the walls of his office. The light wood panel with dark wood trim brought a soft, welcoming feel to the room. He loved the smell of the unfinished wood. He went to the bottom drawer to get his midmorning snack. As he pulled out the drawer and reached into it to extract his whisky bottle, he spied some books and papers lying inside. The hairs on the back of his neck stood up. Most books had been banned at the start of the revolution. How did these get here? He quickly slid the drawer shut, pressed a button on his intercom and told his secretary not to let anyone disturb him for the next two hours.

He sat for a minute drumming his fingers on the desk, and then opened the drawer and pulled out one of the books and took a closer look at it. He paged through it and read the first few pages. It definitely one of the banned books; he quickly shoved it back into the drawer. His mind was racing. What the hell I am going to do with these? I've got to hide them or get rid of them. Then curiosity crept into his mind like a skulking cat. He pulled the book back out of the drawer and read on. Three hours later he still could not believe it. The lies and the deceit—it was all here. The secret history of the city shone like the breaking dawn into a freshly opened crypt.

His phone rang, pulling him back to the present. *Ring, ring* went the phone. Wellings was hesitant. Then he thought, I must act normal. He picked up the phone.

"Wellings," he said.

"Hi, Tom, it's been awhile."

Wellings recognized the voice of George

Nordstrom, the captain of the palace guards. "What can I do for you, George?"

"Can we meet? I don't want to talk over the phone."

"Actually, I have something I'd like you to see, too. Do you want to meet here?"

"No. You remember when we were kids, you picked a fight with a foreman? You remember the place. Don't say it; just be there in half an hour," said Nordstrom and hung up.

It took Tom Wellings twenty minutes to find the old factory in the disused industrial estate. The sight of the Bigots building brought back so many memories. Bigots had once been the epicentre for all things fashionable in metal. When he was young, he and Nordstrom had left school together and got their first job there, a summer job before going to university. That foreman was a dick, he thought, as he drove his family saloon into the car park. He recognized Nordstrom's estate car and pulled into a parking space next to it. He looked at the papers and books under the passenger seat just to make sure they hadn't slid out of their hiding place. Inside the estate car he could see a man waiting. His hands gripped the steering wheel, and his head rested on them.

Wellings got out and tapped on the passenger window. The man jumped, instantly pulling out a gun and pointing it at the window.

Wellings put up his hands. "George, it's me. George, what the hell is going on?"

Nordstrom put the gun down and motioned Wellings to get in. Tom opened the passenger door and slid in. He noticed his old friend had been crying.

Nordstrom wiped his puffy eyes and tear-stained cheeks. "They killed my sis—" He started to cry again.

177

"No—not Sally." Tom was thunderstruck; he put a hand on George's shoulder.

"Sorry, Tom." George wiped his eyes again and tried to control himself. "I found out this morning. They killed the whole family. What I am going to do? They killed my kid sister."

Chance floated down though the roof and settled in the back of the car, unseen, unheard. She had to make sure this meeting went well.

George spoke softly, his voice breaking. "Tom, we have known each other since we were kids. I trust you. That's why I phoned. I need to get something off my chest. I'm frightened to talk to anyone else."

"Did they or you do anything out of the ordinary, to warrant such an attack?" asked Wellings.

Nordstrom shook his head.

"I have doubts about the Patrician. He wanted me to prepare for war, and when I asked him about the civilians, he said to use them as a human shield. I questioned his orders, and now my . . . my sister is dead."

"I don't believe it, I really don't. This morning I found some books and papers about the true history of the city. The Patrician has betrayed us all. He used magic to influence the previous emperor, who was then assassinated by the current emperor. I got the books in the car, if you want to read them."

This was trust. They sat there in George's car for half an hour going through the histories and telling each other things—inconsistencies, lies and cover ups they'd had to put up with. For the first time in a long time, Tom felt free. They both knew that if this conversation was ever relayed to anyone, they were dead—not a quick death, but one that would last for days. The Watchmen would ring every detail out, just for the hellish pleasure of it.

"Look, George, make your plans, but don't act on them. Get your forces ready. When the time is right we will side with the rebels. Then you can exact your revenge. Don't go off half-cocked. If we can do it right we could all be free. There will be no more killings."

"Yeah, you're right. I am so sick of the killings, traitor's row. If we live through this I'm going to cut down every last one and give them a proper burial, an honourable burial."

"I will prepare some plans of my own, hide stashes of weapons; there is one guy I can trust to help. I promise that I will never speak your name. I'll trick this guy into thinking that it is for an exercise. Armed response or some bull like that."

"I will get what I can. I'll call when we're ready to move," said George. The thought of revenge and freedom would push him on.

"Just say 'butter' and the place to meet. Then put the phone down." Wellings squeezed Nordstrom on the shoulder and left the car.

In the back, Chance smiled. Hubby will be pleased, she thought.

Book Three: The Power and the Justice

Chapter 13: Unexpected Plans

For the most part, Argonath remained outside. She was happy, happier then she had been in a long time. She met Akea everyday. He took the men into the forest to train, and they soon became used to working with a dragon. In the evenings Argonath usually would change to human form come in, often leaving late at night to revert to dragon form and sleep in the forest, and Akea would accompany her. One night, when Akea was too exhausted to leave the base, Argonath stayed with him all night. He awoke the next morning with a serene smile.

The training was hard and intense; they practiced urban warfare, terrorism and first aid, hacking and electronics intrusion techniques. The days were long and hard. In the evenings the men relaxed in their dormitories, which contained little else beyond a TV and books. Each member of the team was given a set of clothes for urban fighting, clothes with concealed pockets and special boots. The heel of the left boot had a small hollow, where a small, sealed bag containing one small suicide pill was held in place by a clip. The pill took two hours to work, so that it could be vomited up in case it was swallowed by accident.

Everyone ate in the canteen. Each man, woman and child who lived in the base was given a ration book. Getting food into the base was hard at the best of times, and it was by the grace of friends in neighbouring countries that they had any food at all.

One evening, Akea and Amanda and Juween were sitting in the canteen, relaxing after another hard day of training. During the six months they had been here,

Akea had started growing a beard to help with his disguise when eventually he would have to re-enter the city. Now he pulled absently at it as the three chatted over their finished meal.

Juween had been looking idly around the room. Suddenly his eyes focused in recognition. Akea followed his gaze and saw Pablo and a guard approaching them. The two men came over and stood at their table.

"Hello Pablo, how's things?" said Akea.

"What the hell are you doing here?" said Juween.

"What do you mean, what am I doing here? Why aren't you ready?" retorted Pablo.

"What do you mean, why aren't we ready? We didn't know you were coming," said Juween.

"I got word from General Nalik that you were ready. Do you know what I had to go through to get here? I'm sure the border guards recognised me. I told them that I have a common face. I got a meeting set up for you in four days' time. Now why aren't you ready?"

"That non compos mentis, I would eat him for dinner, but I think I might get a stomach ulcer. That guy has got the mental age of a baby and the IQ of diseased plankton," said Amanda.

"Who, Nalik?" said Juween.

"Yes, dummy, him. He's set us up. He made sure we didn't know that Pablo was coming. So now we have to run around like idiots getting our stuff together. I wouldn't put it past him to phone the border and rat on us."

"Okay, so we make new plans. He won't beat us," said Akea.

"New plans—we didn't have any old plans," said Juween.

"Pablo, how ready are you?" said Akea.

"Not bad. I have cleared out the basement. It took me ages. I had to do it stealthily. The city is in a terrible mess. It's been hard to find people. People are too scared, but they are out there, somewhere. We have to strike soon anyway, Juween."

"Oh, this is Amanda," said Juween, suddenly remembering that Pablo and Amanda had never met.

"How do?" said Pablo.

"So you're the one who saved my husband. I can't thank you enough. If it wasn't for you I would not have met him, and that would have been a tragedy."

"Bloody hell, Akea, you have been busy. Congratulations. How long have you been married? Why wasn't I invited?"

"We were married about ten months ago, in the forest. Prometheus performed the ceremony," said Amanda.

"Prometheus! How is the old rascal?"

"Pablo, mate, you better sit down. There's a lot you need to know," said Juween.

Pablo placed his enormous bulk on a chair. "Got any home brew? Don't tell me you ain't had time to make some. Come on, mate, if you are going to give this old man a heart attack, you might as well give him a drink."

"I'll get some water," said Amanda.

"Water? Give me a break."

Amanda returned with a cup of water and handed it to Juween. "I thought you were getting me a drink?" said Pablo.

"Hang on; it will be worth it. *Unda in ut vinum*," said Juween. He handed the cup to Pablo.

Pablo tasted it. "Red wine: not bad. Cheers and good health." He knocked back about half the cup. "Ah, that's better. So what's the news?"

"First of all, you should know that I am a dragon,

not a human. I use my magic to assume my human form," Amanda said.

"What!" said Pablo, spraying some of his drink.

"Yep, she's a dragon, so don't piss her off," said Juween.

"How does that work, anyway, you know?" He winked at Juween.

Akea and Amanda looked at each other, and Amanda blushed.

"You would have to ask them, and if I were you I wouldn't," said Juween.

"Look, it's quite simple, really. We are in love with each other's mind. Being in love with someone's mind is much, much more than being in love with some body. Don't you think?" said Amanda, the blush fading.

"Yeah, I suppose. But how is this going to work? My basement is not that big," said Pablo.

"Pablo, stop being an arse. As you can see, Amanda in human form is quite slender. We will need one double bed and three single beds, perhaps a twin room or something, a living room, kitchen and bathroom. Can you fit all that in the basement?" said Juween.

"Yeah, sure. The basement is completely gutted, you can do what you want with it," said Pablo, staring at Amanda.

"Will you stop it? I know what you are thinking, it's written all over your face. What Akea and I get up to is none of your business, so get over it. Or it will be the last thing you will think about. Do I make myself clear?" growled Amanda. She was getting better at growling at people.

"Yeah, err, sorry. I have to apologise. It won't happen again," said Pablo, looking rather embarrassed.

"Argonath, what's the matter?" thought Akea.

"He was looking at me in a creepy way, like he was trying to work out what I was wearing underneath. Probably trying to work out if I have skin or scales, or how we have sex. He is creepy, Akea," thought Amanda.

"He won't try anything; I think you scared his libido out for life."

"I can give you all the building materials you need. What about the dust and noise?" said Pablo.

"We will use magic to hide everything. You will not know we are there," said Akea.

"I have a plan. When the basement is finished, I will put my old furniture in the basement, and then I will buy new furniture bit by bit. As it comes, we can swap stuff around. Delivery people get suspicious if you order too much furniture at once. They want to make some money on the side like everyone else, and are quite happy to shop people to the Watchmen. We have to tread carefully," said Pablo.

He continued, "The word on the street is the Watchmen will pay handsomely for reports on any signs of unusual behaviour."

"Pablo, this is going to be a dangerous mission. We will need to go on sorties and contact people, and you will have to get us any equipment that we can't get. You will be protected, but you know the risks. If you want to back out, now is the time," Juween said.

"No, no, I will do it," Pablo sighed. "What else do you need?"

"I have a list, but basically, we need a video game console, a TV, a computer and sundries, and something to put it all on. Oh, and we need you to contact a group of hackers called the Elite," said Akea.

"Oh, is that all?" said Pablo sarcastically. He

paused. "Yeah, sure, I can get them."

"Look, Pablo, as Juween said, you don't have to do it," said Amanda; she was starting to get really irritated by this guy.

"*I thought you said he was good. I thought you said he was willing to help,*" thought Amanda to Akea.

"*Yeah, I know. He was. Perhaps something has happened,*" Akea thought back.

"Pablo, can I ask you a personal question?" said Amanda.

"Yeah, sure. Why the hell not?" said Pablo.

"Has any of your family been taken by the Watchmen?"

"How the hell do you know about that? Can you read my mind?" Pablo said. His face reflected sadness, and he bowed his head.

"Well, I can, but I am not reading your mind. It's your body language. Juween and Akea told me about how bravely you helped the last time. But now— forgive me for saying this, but you seem as timid as a mouse," said Amanda.

"*'Forgive me for saying this'? Since when?*" Akea thought to Amanda, trying to work out why she was being polite.

"*Oh shut up, I am trying out the notion of tact. Perhaps you should try it,*" she thought back.

"It was my cousin. We were close. He was taken three months ago, and since then I have been looking over my shoulder. He knew about my . . . efforts. I am just hoping that the secrets died with him."

"Oh. Sorry, mate," said Juween.

Pablo seemed to have found some new strength. "If you are as good as you say you are, then get the bastards, and make 'em pay."

"When do we go?" said Akea.

"Now, if you like. But I am not sure about this—I

have made too many trips lately, and I think they are starting to recognise me. The border only deals with two or three people a day. They are lazy, but not stupid," said Pablo.

"Can you get another car, once we are in the city?"

"No, my car is known. If I change it as well as getting lots of furniture, it will raise too many suspicions," said Pablo.

They sat thinking for a few minutes.

"I got it," said Akea. "Where's your car now?"

"It's parked up in the car pool, just inside the base. Why?"

"Just hear me out, okay?" said Akea.

"We will get one over Nalik, if he has shopped us. We get your car and spray it with water-based paint. Change the plates. Captain Nellis has to get into the city as well. He drives your car to the border and times it so he arrives there when the curfew is just about to end, say around 5 a.m. He makes his way to the old industrial estate first thing in the morning and washes off the paint and changes the plates back. We meet him there to cover his back, so to speak, and then he parks the car in your usual spot. That way we kill two birds with one stone."

"That's not bad, not bad at all, but you're forgetting something: how the hell do we get in?" said Pablo.

"You're not scared of heights, are you?" Akea said to Pablo.

"No, why?" said Pablo.

"What sort of roof do you have? Do you have an alley, how big?"

"Akea, what are you up to?" asked Juween.

"Pablo," said Akea.

"It's a flat roof. You must have seen it. It's where Juween got the bag of nails with the car keys in it. I

186

have an alley about six feet wide that leads to a backyard about twenty-five feet long by twenty feet wide, about five hundred square feet. And before you ask, it's mostly empty."

"That's right, you own Harpers Hardware. How strong is the roof?"

"Yes, I own it, but what do you mean—how strong is the roof?"

"Is it a tin roof, or concrete?"

"It's concrete, for god's sake. Enough already."

"Yes, Akea, what the hell are you up to? Spill the beans," said Juween.

"It's quite simple, really—if Argonath doesn't mind. You can fly in on our backs. We don't really have that much equipment. We could, in fact, bring in some of the kit that we need, like the PC and video console ready prepared. I think we could use a spell to lighten the load. But the real problem is that if we carry too much, we start to become noticeable."

"I don't mind. If you take Pablo, he could wear a rucksack with some of the essentials. And Juween can fly with me with the other bits," said Amanda. To Akea, she thought, *"That's a really good plan. I love you!"*

"I love you, too!" Akea thought.

"I suppose we better let the council know. What's the time now?" said Juween, looking at this watch. "1830. It's going to take a couple of hours to get the kit ready. I think we should leave around midnight.

"Akea, give me a list of what you need, stuff that will be hard to get in the city, then go and find Captain Nellis and fill him in. I will go and see the council. Amanda, would you mind getting what kit we have already got together?" said Juween.

Akea found Captain Nellis in his little office, three floors up. The frosted glass walls trimmed with light brown wood gave some privacy, but people could hear conversations, especially if the occupants were arguing. He was about to knock on the door, when he heard voices. One of them sounded like Nalik. His voice was muffled, but the words were distinguishable.

"Nellis, you are not serious about going through with this, are you? He is a maniac."

"General, yes, I am. I have seen him training with the others. He is good," said Nellis.

"He is not the saviour of the city. He cannot be trusted. Watch your back, is all I am saying," said Nalik.

"Nalik is here. He is trying to poison Nellis against us," Akea thought to Amanda, who was on the other side of the base, packing what little possessions they had.

"I know. I heard through your ears. I swear I am going to eat his heart out. In the meantime, behave yourself," replied Amanda.

Akea had heard enough. "Akea is dang—" Nalik was saying as Akea knocked and went in without waiting. The office was not large, twelve by fifteen feet square. Captain Nellis sat, facing the door, behind a large desk with a green leather top. The green desk lamp illuminated various papers and reports on the desk. General Nalik sat with his back to the door on the other side of the desk, and he had shifted in his chair to see who was coming in. He looked embarrassed, like a kid who has just been caught trying to steal a magazine from the top shelf.

"Finish the end of the sentence," said Akea calmly.

Nalik stared at him with annoyance.

"Let's have it out, Nalik, so Captain Nellis can make up his own mind," said Akea more assertively.

"You are dangerous. That silly bitch of yours can't

control you," said Nalik, growing enraged.

"Oh, would it not be lovely if you could make me mad enough to lose control and kill you right here, right now? But I will not. What have I told you about insulting dragons?"

"That bitch can't hear me," said Nalik.

"Oh yes she can. You see—well, maybe you don't—Argonath and I are one, unlike humans, who only think they are one with their life partners. We *are* one; we are the same creature, the power and the control. She can hear and see everything I hear and see. I roam through her mind as free as the breeze on a meadow, and vice versa."

There was a pause, and then Akea continued, "Don't go into the firing range—you have less IQ than the dummy, and they might shoot you. No, wait—go into the shooting range, and they might shoot you. She can hear you, and she wants to kill you. That is not a threat: that is a promise."

Nalik looked nervous and started to finger his pistol on his hip.

Akea said, "I have always wondered why you hate me so much, and I finally figured it out. You saw me stand up to the Watchmen, unarmed, and win—not just win, but beat them into the ground. This in a perverted way shows up how much of a coward you are. And talking of cowardice, you see Juween and me together, a constant reminder that you failed to save fifteen men, then hid behind your daddy's back, while Juween took the blame."

Nalik stood up from the chair that he was sitting on, and faced Akea, his gun in his hand and pointed at Akea. Akea moved forward so that the end of the gun was right in his chest.

"If you pull that trigger, you will never see daylight again," shouted Nellis.

"It's okay, captain. I've got it under control," said Akea.

"You arrogant piece of shit," spat Nalik.

Akea spoke to the weapon. "Amitto of vestri vires, commodo curvo."

The weapon curved out of the way. The barrel melted as if it were warm toffee; black metal started to drip on the floor. "I'd leave now, if I were you. I would hide until we have left. Argonath wants to see you about why you didn't tell us about Pablo coming here today," said Akea.

"*No I don't. He will get his. I am a bit busy now. Have you seen the jar of coffee beans?*" thought Amanda.

"*But he doesn't know that. It was in the cupboard on the right, behind the spare pair of trousers*," Akea thought back.

Nalik stared at the melting gun, and then at Akea, and then at the gun. "This is not over, do you hear?" he spat. He strode past Akea, banging his shoulder into Akea as he went by. His back straight, his head held high, he stalked out of the office.

Akea sat down in the warm chair; he did not laugh or make a joke.

Captain Nellis looked slightly embarrassed. "Akea, not all of us share his views. I personally think it's an honour to work with you, and so do my men, for that matter. He tried all sorts of things to stop my men from volunteering for this duty, but they just laughed behind his back. Now, Akea, what can I do for you?"

Akea was humbled by this admission. "Err, yes, well . . . hmm. How ready are you to leave—just you, not your men?"

"I am pretty much prepared. I saw Pablo some hours ago, and I guessed this was it. How come you didn't warn me?" asked the captain.

"We didn't know. We were as surprised as you. General Nalik felt that that little piece of information was not worth his time, or something. But we have a plan; get your kit together now. We want you to be at the border by 5 a.m." Akea went on to explain the plan.

"General Nalik has some powerful friends. That is why he has stayed in charge for so long. What about my men and my kit?" said Captain Nellis.

"When Argonath has finished with the city, I think she would like to have Nalik over for dinner to celebrate. We are not ready for your men. They will need to remain here for a while. We will take your kit with us. Shall we meet at the old industrial estate, say around 6 a.m.? We can cover you while you wash the paint off," said Akea.

"I think General Nalik is up to something. He is not very good at hiding information. I will be safe. They will be looking for Pablo and three others in Pablo's car; luckily, it's a common car. I will get the tech boys to hack into the border computer to show I am due to arrive tomorrow morning. I will assume the identity of someone we have just evacuated. Our documents section can do up the paperwork."

"Oh, one last thing, Akea: I was there, you know. I was just a young recruit. I saw it all, and I tried to stand up for Juween at the court-martial, but some jumped-up lawyer shot me down in flames. I was only just nineteen. The lawyer is an elder now."

"Err, thanks. If you would not mind, please tell that to Juween. He would like to know that someone is on his side."

Meanwhile Juween had gone to see the council. He sat in their chambers.

"Juween, why have you come to us at this late hour? You should have been packed days ago," said

Jisi.

"Sir, I did not know about this until Pablo came walking into the canteen," said Juween.

"You were informed, weren't you?" said Jisi.

"Sir, with respect, no. We spoke to Pablo, and he said that he got word from Nalik a week ago, but as I said, we did not receive that message."

"It's *General* Nalik, Juween. Don't blame our leader for your laziness."

"Come, come, Jisi, your friendship with Nalik is showing. If you continue with this line of thought, I will remove you from this meeting. Do I make myself clear?" said Iral.

"Yes, but I am unsure that Nalik would do such a thing. Therefore I conclude that Juween is making excuses. We all know the history between them. He is trying to undermine General Nalik's authority," said Jisi.

"Yes, we all know the history, and if my memory serves, you defended Nalik in the trial, and if my memory still serves, we have a great chance of winning this war. Need I remind you again that we have a dragon and the most powerful magician of all time on our side? Once again, the fight is out there and not in here. It seems that your prejudices will taint the discussions, and forgive me for saying it, but I don't think Juween would want Nalik to know the full extent of his plans. Jisi, your presence is no longer required at this meeting," said Iral.

Jisi bowed stiffly and stalked from the room.

Juween was unsure about what had just happened, but he went ahead and outlined the plan, after which the elders retired to their private chamber for discussions. Juween sat in the chair, half bored, half trying to remember where he had left his stuff, and then amused himself for an hour making plans, deciding how best to set up the basement.

The elders came back in and sat down.

"Ah, Juween, would you like some more coffee?" said Iral, noticing that Juween had finished the last one.

"Thank you, sir, but I am fine."

"I didn't realise we took so long, must apologise. I'll make it brief: your plan is a good one as long as you fly under the radar. We checked the weather reports, it should be cloudy."

The weather reports. I didn't even think about that, Juween thought.

Iral continued, "I have sent Thomas, my servant, to get someone to deal with Pablo's car and the computer and the other items on this list. How will Captain Nellis get his kit into the city, if he is taking the car?"

"I will carry it on my back, and if it doesn't fit in a rucksack then we will strap it on Akea like saddle-bags."

"Yes, saddle-bags," Iral said. He picked up a small silver bell and rang it. As it tingled, a servant came in. "Rupert, go and find the store quartermaster, will you?" The servant bowed slightly and left.

"We will get the quartermaster to cobble two tent bags together, with some straps between them. All this depends on Akea letting us treat him like a pack-horse," said Iral.

"Akea probably won't mind, and please don't ask Argonath," Juween said.

"As a parting gift we have allocated some funds for you, equivalent to three months joint income. That will get you started, but I'm afraid we can't give you much more," said Iral.

"Thank you sir. I don't think we need to worry. I think Akea has a plan."

193

Iral got up, and Juween rose to his feet. Iral walked forward to Juween and shook him by the hand. Each one of the remaining elders shook Juween's hand and wished good luck. Juween's heart felt light. The council were behind him, and Akea, and Argonath, too.

Chapter 14: The Border

Juween wandered back down to the barracks. He found Akea, Pablo and Amanda sitting on the bed, all packed up.

"Hi. How did it go?" said Amanda. She looked agitated.

"I've some good news and some bad," said Juween. "We can go. The elders have given us some money—not a lot, and we got all the equipment on your list." Juween told them what happened in the elders' chambers. "Really, Jisi was Nalik's lawyer? Nellis said that Nalik was up to something, but he thought our plan was sound enough."

"I am carrying saddle-bags now, am I?" said Amanda.

"*I thought you were getting heavier,*" Akea thought to Amanda.

"Shut your face, you, it's bad enough having to pack up Juween's stuff, without putting up with cheeky remarks from you," said Amanda.

Juween looked confused. "I wish you two would talk to each other orally, not half and half," he said.

"Sorry Juween, sorry Amanda. I was only joking," said Akea.

"What did you say, lad?" said Juween.

"Don't you dare tell him," Amanda barked.

"I knew you wouldn't have the saddle-bags, so Akea is carrying them. You can carry me and Pablo. You can take the piss all the way there, if you like," said Juween, trying to appease Amanda.

"Look, let's get an hour of sleep, and meet in the canteen at eleven," said Pablo. He got up and went off to the room provided for him.

Akea got up and looked at the clock. It read 10:30 p.m. He gently woke Amanda. They got dressed and went to the canteen; there they met Juween and Pablo.

"Want some coffee?" Juween said as he poured coffee into two mugs. "I had the equipment moved to the main exit area, near Pablo's car."

"Didn't you sleep?" asked Akea, sipping the coffee.

"No, not really. I wanted to be ready. I can sleep when we get there," said Juween.

They finished their much-needed coffee and walked to the exit. The main car pool and exit was about the same size and shape as a large aircraft hangar. The hard industrial lights shone down on the light grey concrete walls.

Pablo's compact, normally a distinct shade of silvery blue, glowed wetly orange with fresh paint. The group met up with Captain Nellis, who was inspecting two very large bags. The elders, including Jisi, came into the hangar to see their guests off. Iral secretly wanted to see the magnificent dragons close up.

"Ready for the off?" he said to the group in general.

Amanda and Juween nodded. Akea said yes. "I like what you have done to my car. I take it that the paint is still wet," said Pablo. A young mechanic came up to Pablo. "It's nearly ready, sir—about five minutes."

"Right. There's no point standing on ceremony, I want to leave soonest. I want Nalik to keep second-guessing us," said Juween. "You two better change."

Less than a minute later, in the pseudo hangar stood two magnificent dragons, a twenty-foot long, blue grey female and a thirty-foot long, dark red and orange, regal male. They nuzzled each other as to say it's good to be back. The onlookers gaped with astonishment at the sight.

Pablo just stood there with his mouth open. "Err . .

. I am supposed to fly on that."

"Careful Pablo. They are dragons now, so watch your mouth," said Iral. He walked up to Argonath. "My lady, would you be so kind as to allow this old fool the opportunity to stroke your flank? It would be a great honour, since I have not seen nor touched you for sixty years."

"Yes, of course. And you are no fool—at least, you have manners," said Argonath.

Iral gingerly walked up to the side of Argonath and lightly touched her side. She thumped her tail in delight. Akea growled in disapproval.

"My apologies, my lord. May I touch your scales, too?" said Iral.

"You may not. This is not a petting zoo," said Akea.

"You are wise in your counsel. I meant no offence," said Iral, and stepped out of the way. Jisi tried hard not to show any pleasure in Iral's apparent humiliation.

Akea noticed the smirk on Jisi's face and said to him, "You mock at what you don't understand. Iral spoke according to dragon etiquette. You are now humiliated by your ignorance." Jisi's face turned sullen and thoughtful.

"Akea, may we place these bags on your body?" said Juween.

Akea sat down and then lowered the front part of his body to the ground, folding his legs under him. Juween timidly moved forward. He beckoned Thomas to help place the heavy bags on Akea's back. Thomas just stood there and shook his head.

"Come on, he won't bite," Juween reassured him.

Thomas got hold of himself and one end of the bags. They placed the bags, one on each side, across Akea's long neck, just in front of the wing joint. As

Juween did up the canvas belts, Akea growled in pain.

"Okay, okay, sorry mate." Juween adjusted the belts. "Is this better?"

Akea nodded. He tried sitting up. He growled as he lifted the enormous weight.

"Okay, I'll lighten the load. *Gravis elucido sarcina.*"

Akea was not expecting the sudden change in weight, and his head shot up like a spring.

Argonath laughed as she watched him do a nodding dog impression. He turned to her and growled. Akea was beginning to enjoy the feelings that came with being a dragon, most of all the over-evolved sense of pride. Just as Pablo tried to climb onto Akea's back, Argonath saw General Nalik and a complement of six guards entering the hangar. She leapt forward, knocking the guards out of the way, and pinned Nalik to the ground. Almost all of Nalik's body was under her paws.

"I warned you, but you would not listen." Her left front claws started to dig into Nalik. She brought her face in close, inches from Nalik, and snarled. A hard and menacing expression had replaced her usual softer features. She sniffed. "Is that urine I can smell?" she growled loudly.

Nalik's men scrambled back and pulled their guns and pointed them at Argonath and Akea. Nellis's men aimed their guns at Nalik's men. Akea sighed. He produced shields around everyone except Nalik and his men. It took a lot of concentration, but the shields held. An aura of light blue hung around the different groups of people, and a deeper blue around Akea.

"My lady, it will not do to kill our army leader. Please explain this outburst," said Iral.

"He has insulted me on no less than ten different occasions, each one of which holds the penalty of death. He neglected to inform us that we should be leaving today. We had to run around and make last-minute plans. And to top it all, I have no doubt he has informed the border patrol that we are coming. " Argonath lifted her right paw and straightened out one claw. The sharp talon glistened in the artificial light. "Call me a bitch!" Quick as a flash, she lashed out and caught Nalik across the chest. Blood gushed out from the wound; it started at the right shoulder and extended to the left lower back near his kidney. Then she was off him, as though nothing had happened.

"I love you," thought Akea, not daring to say anything else. He jumped in front of the six guards and growled, "Stand down, or you will be next." The guards replaced their weapons, and Nellis's men relaxed. Iral just shook his head and walked out, followed by the other elders.

Pablo stared at Nalik, who was being attended to by four guards. A medic came hurrying in, stopped in shock at the sight of the two dragons and then bent over Nalik.

"Get on," Argonath growled to Pablo. Juween helped him up and then scrambled up behind him. They would have to fly bareback. Soon the two dragons waddled through the exit doors and out into the night air.

The cloudy sky gave excellent cover. They flew high above the low-lying clouds, only dipping down to get their bearings. "We are forty miles from the city; we better come in low, maybe a hundred feet. Start your descent. Pablo, hold on, but not too tight," shouted Juween. The two dragons tipped forward. This was almost too much for Pablo, and he closed his eyes and prayed to any god who was listening to get him off this thing.

Argonath could sense Pablo's fear. She craned her

neck back to him, and spoke as gently as she could. "I will go as slow and as gentle as I can."

As Akea didn't carry any passengers, he banked steeply and headed for the ground like a rocket, curving round to level off at a hundred feet, and scrubbed off speed with a great clap of his wings.

"That would be nice and quiet, would it? Maybe that dog collar around you neck has cut off the circulation to your head," said Argonath. More than anything she was irritated that she couldn't do the same. She decided to do a more regal decent, three thousand feet over five miles.

They flew low over the city walls. Pablo lost his bearings at first; he had never seen the city from above. He directed the dragons this way and that, trying to find a landmark to orient himself by.

After five minutes, Argonath was getting impatient.

"There—there it is—there's my back yard," said Pablo. "What a mess."

Argonath touched down in the yard. There was just room for her. Akea had to land on the roof. He crouched down as low as he could, toward the back of the roof. *"Hurry, I am exposed up here,"* he thought to Argonath. Those thirty seconds for Pablo to dismount and Amanda to transform seemed like an hour for Akea, who all was too aware that someone walking past the front of the hardware store could easily spotted him.

"All clear," Argonath called to Akea. She and Pablo disappeared into the back of the hardware store.

Akea came down, and Juween unstrapped the saddle-bags and pulled them off. He switched back to human form, and he and Juween entered the back of the hardware store to find Pablo in the little kitchen behind the store. He was shaking like a leaf. "Where's that fucking whisky?" he was saying to no one in particular.

Amanda, Akea and Juween stood before Pablo. Amanda went to touch him; his eyes went wide with fear, and as she touched him he jumped back. "I am not being rude, or pissing on your pride, but please just give me a minute. Look, I mean no offence. Here, have some liquor. It's just that I watched you maul a man within inches of his life, then flew two hundred miles on your back. I got culture shock."

Amanda said nothing. She took the whisky and walked back out into the yard. Akea followed her and sat next to her, with his arm around her shoulder. Twenty minutes later, at half past three, Pablo came out, all smiles; he walked into the yard and faced Amanda. He put his hand out as an offer of apology. She got up and took a step towards him and hugged him gently. It was her way of saying sorry, too.

"Right, then," Pablo said. "Until we get the bedding sorted, you can sleep where you can find it, and I suggest you get some sleep. We got to get my car back in a couple of hours."

"I have been thinking about that. Amanda, would you mind taking Juween to the site? I'll circle the border to make sure Nellis is okay," said Akea.

Fifty miles from the border, Captain Nellis hummed along in the orange compact, listening to the radio. "It is four thirty in the morning. Today will be cloudy with patches of sun. You are listening to city radio." Nellis had put the radio on to try and calm his nerves; he kept repeating his story over and over. Then he saw it, a big black shadow hovering over the front of the car, and then a red and orange object streaked past and flew over him and back up into the clouds. Nellis sighed with relief; at least Akea had his back.

Akea followed the car from above the clouds. He reached out with his mind and could sense what was happening below. The little car reached the border and stopped. Two armed border patrolmen tapped on the window "Name, papers, where have you been, where do you live," said the sleepy looking senior border patrolman.

"Travis—Fred Travis. Here are my papers. I was given permission to visit an old friend dying of cancer, and I live at 13 City Road." The patrolmen went inside and checked with the computer records. Nellis sat there and tried not to show the fear flowing in his blood. It was a tense few moments before the patrolman came back.

"You are not due until later."

"I know, officer, I am sorry, but I have to attend a meeting this afternoon, and I wanted to get some rest."

"Please get out of the car."

"Is there a problem, officer?" Nellis asked.

"Stand there. We are going to search your car."

One patrolman searched the car, while the other trained his pistol at Nellis's face.

In the clouds, Akea was of two minds. *"What do I do? I think Nellis is in trouble,"* he thought to Argonath.

"Hold tight, be ready."

The patrolman walked around the car, looking under the car in every conceivable place, and then he called to the other patrolman, "There's no one here. Just him let him go."

With as much calm as Nellis could muster, he got back into the car, tried to start it, stalled it, took a deep breath and tried again. The car jumped into life. He drove away as smoothly as he could.

Nellis had been looking for the industrial site for

fifteen minutes. As he tried to remember the way, his attention was not on the road. Suddenly a big orange object came into full view of the windshield. Nellis slammed on the brakes and skidded to a halt. Akea leapt in the air to avoid being hit.

"For god's sake Akea," said Nellis, after Akea had landed, changed into human form and gotten into the car.

"What? I got your attention, didn't I?"

"I have been bricking it since the border. I nearly shit myself when you jumped in the way. For god's sake, Akea!" said Nellis, almost shouting. His heart was pounding like a thrash metal drummer on speed.

"Calm down. I am sorry, but you are going the wrong way. You should have turned left, not right, three miles ago," said Akea.

Akea directed Nellis to the industrial site. The car turned into the parking lot, crept slowly behind a large disused warehouse and pulled up to a set of wide doors. Amanda and Juween came out of hiding from behind a tree. Akea got out of the car and tried the warehouse doors, and then spoke to the locks and hinges. The doors creaked and shuddered as the big rusted locks broke free. He and Juween pulled the doors open, and Akea motioned Nellis to drive in.

"It's my turn to be lookout," said Amanda. She transformed into Argonath and took off.

The men pushed the doors shut. Akea searched around for a source of water and found a tap at the other end of the big empty space. He signalled Nellis to bring the car down there, while Juween lugged over the petrol-powered jet sprayer that he had brought. Akea tried the tap, and a trickle came out.

"Find the stopcock, it's got to be around here somewhere," said Juween. Two minutes later the trickle turned into a torrent.

Juween started the little petrol engine. The unmuffled engine kicked and spluttered.

"For god's sake, it's too loud," said Nellis.

"Silens sanus," said Akea. The engine continued to rattle away, but no sound could be heard.

They were three quarters through the wash when Argonath sounded the alarm. *"There is a Watchmen patrol about a mile away. You should have just enough time to finish and then hide. I will let you know if they come closer."*

Akea relayed the alarm to Juween.

He cursed. "Right, leave the plates, just get the paint washed off."

Akea ran to the doors and closed them. He spoke to the doors, and the locks slid back into place.

"They're here. They're trying every door; hide."

Akea could hear muffled voices. "I am telling you it's in there. Look at the tire tracks in the dirt; that silver compact has got to be here somewhere."

Akea closed his eyes and tried to remain calm. The doors rattled as the Watchmen tried them. The locks didn't budge. Akea silently asked the door to remain steadfast.

"Look, the door is rusted shut. It ain't fucking here. Let's go and get some breakfast. I am hungry."

Akea sighed as he heard the car pull away. He ran to the other end of the warehouse. "Let's get this finished and go," said Nellis.

Chapter 15: The Rebel Insertion

Arriving back at Pablo's hardware store, they set about establishing their headquarters in the basement. On the outside of the back of the shop, a door led down a flight of stairs to another a door that opened into where the kitchenette would be situated. Now it was just a dust hole. Juween put a spell on the doors so they could not be seen or opened by anyone except Pablo, Juween, Akea, Nellis, Prometheus or Amanda. The basement was quite large; it ran under the whole shop. The ceiling was eight feet high, with small dirty windows running along the top of the west wall. The room itself was dark and musty; it needed some serious renovation.

They spent the first few days cleaning and making rooms out of dry wall and two-by-fours, trying to incorporate as much use of the available light as possible. The kitchenette was the hardest to build. They used magic to deaden the noise of the building work. It was amazing what could be done on a modest budget. They painted the walls with bright tasteful colours, pastel light blue and green in the kitchen, terracotta in the bedrooms and sitting room. In one bedroom there were two single beds and in another a small double bed. A third room with a single bed was reserved for Prometheus.

Amanda never had the opportunity to explore the notion of decorating. There were no pictures, no personal effects. Apart from the fact that no one had any, a picture could compromise a friend or family member if the Watchman ever broke into the cellar. In the modest-sized living room, chairs were arranged in a semicircle. To one side sat a small computer desk.

At 2 a.m. on the morning of the third day, Prometheus stood on his doorstep waiting for

Argonath to pick him up. In his disguise and wide brim hat, he looked like a tramp from thirty years ago. Juween had sent the signal via the medallions. For the last three months Prometheus had tried to contact as many of the hundred or so Gatekeepers as he could. He had failed to contact the ones who lived thousands of miles away, but he hoped that the others would reply to him via the medallion system. The rest of his time he spent with Amalthea. They tried to assess the size and species of Vaxihimler's new army. He sat there musing about whether he had done enough, when he spotted Argonath coming in from the clouds. She landed next to him. Prometheus bowed and stroked her flank.

"Ah, daughter, it has been too long since it was just you and me."

Argonath nodded. "One day, Father, we will sit here and talk. Just like old times. Are you ready? Do you have a change of street clothing?"

He nodded and climbed onto Argonath. "Gently, old bean. Remember, I don't like flying."

They arrived on top of one of the high-rise blocks of the ATD building in the financial district in the predawn light. Prometheus climbed down unsteadily. Argonath sniggered, then wished him luck and took off.

He walked across the roof and found the roof exit and spoke to the locks. The door gently swung open, and Prometheus carefully walked down the thirty or so flights of stairs. It was hard work for an old man, he thought, as he rested on the eleventh floor stairwell, sweating slightly. He made it down to the lobby; he kept his head down as he crossed it to make sure that the CCTV did not get a clear picture of his face. At the other end of the vast lobby, he noticed a doorman sleeping behind his desk. Prometheus crept

206

past the doorman; he did not move. Prometheus whispered to the locks on the front door. As the main door opened a siren began to wail. But it was too late for the doorman, who just stared at the freely swinging door. Prometheus ran down the street and into a side alley. He waited there for five minutes, mainly to catch his breath. He had a day to make the ten-mile journey by foot to the hardware store.

The third night heralded the first meeting of the people Pablo had gleaned. Pablo had told them to come to the store in dribs and drabs. Now, having trickled in over the course of half an hour, ten men sat together quietly. No one volunteered his name, and no one asked for it. It had taken Pablo a month to arrange this meeting. He'd kept his store open late for the last few weeks so people stopping in at this hour wouldn't draw attention. He had sent coded messages to these trusted men by dropping notes in a public rubbish bin outside a chemist's shop in Mornington Road. The intended receiver would throw something in the bin and pick up the note. Finally, despite many missed opportunities, the meeting was happening.

Prometheus was there, too. The old man's disguise was so convincing that when he had entered the hardware store, Pablo had said to him, "I am sorry, old man, but you can't stay in here. I am trying to run a business, not a drop-in centre."

"Oh, I see, old bean, has it been that long?" retorted Prometheus.

"What the hell do you mean? You be careful with that meths. That stuff fucks up your mind. And before you ask, no, I ain't gonna sell you any."

"My, my, Pablo, you have such a big heart."

"What are you talking about, for god's sake? How do you know my name?" said Pablo. He was in no mood for some tramp's antics.

"You really don't understand. I was sent here to see a friend with a sharp temper and a fiery tongue."

Pablo stared for a long moment at the old man. "Prometheus! You old rascal. Why didn't you say?"

"Sorry, old bean, but you were doing so well."

In a hushed whisper, Pablo said, "Round the back, you can't miss it." He continued in a loud voice, "Now get out, you fucking lunatic, I am not selling you meths. Go get some fucking help, for god's sake."

Prometheus made his way round to the back of the shop. He saw the door; the outline glowed with a gentle orange aura. Juween has done well, I nearly missed it, he thought as he entered. He found a seat and sat amongst the others, a picture of serenity against a backdrop of nervous chickens.

Juween started the discussion.

"Thank you gentlemen for coming; I know that you have taken great personal risks to come here. Please accept our thanks and gratitude. We are here to discuss freedom and change."

"Yeah, right, freedom—that's a bold statement from a guy who killed seventy-five men in one afternoon!" said the bravest.

Juween turned to him, and then turned to Prometheus. "Prometheus, please, could you access the secure file in the Watchmen's mainframe?"

Prometheus walked over to the computer desk, booted up the computer and accessed the mainframe. Akea thought to himself, Not bad, considering it's probably the first time he's seen a computer in his life. The main CCTV window came up, and Prometheus hacked away at it. Soon a CCTV video began to run. Amanda had to steady Akea's thoughts as he watched. The men watching gasped as the image showed Watchmen opening fire on two unarmed men. The two stood defiant as round after round, bullet after

208

bullet tried to destroy everything. The enemy tried to rip them into shreds. They watched as the CCTV showed Akea's retaliation. When the clip finished tears were rolling down the faces of all those present. Amanda got up crying, and knelt down in front of her husband. "I love you," she spoke clearly.

Juween took over. "Amanda met Akea after this happened. She knew about this event before she married him. She believes in him. I believe in him, I believe in us."

Juween told the audience of the events of the past few months, taking care not to reveal Amanda's true identity. This may have been too much for the people to take in one go.

"Gentlemen, we have the means to set the country free from tyranny, from the Watchmen, but we cannot do it alone. We need your help. We are going to bring in a small battalion of men, and they will need hiding, feeding and patching up. Initially, we will need refuge for thirty men. If you agree, you each will be assigned three people to hide," said Juween.

"I have a family and three children. I cannot do as you ask," said the bravest of the men.

"Akea will escort you to your home, but first you must take a vow of silence," said Juween.

"I don't want Akea to escort me anywhere. If the Watchmen see me with him and discover who he is, I will be dead."

Juween escorted the man to the kitchen. He spoke quietly to him and wiped his memory of any association with this meeting. Then Pablo came in, put a blindfold around the man's eyes, and escorted him away. After taking the long way round to the main street, Pablo took off the blindfold, led the man into a pub, sat him down and ordered him two very stiff drinks.

Back at the meeting room, Captain Nellis spoke. "These men who come from the rebel camp will be the first prong of our attack, instigating the rebellion."

The nine remaining men listened to all that Juween and Captain Nellis had to say. When Juween had finished, the men deliberated for just over a minute. Then one of them spoke for the group. The others nodded as he spoke.

"We will do as you ask. Since one of our number has left, three of us must accommodate four soldiers, while the rest take in three. I think that those who genuinely have enough room should volunteer." Three hands went up. Each one described how they would fit another in. Two had lofts; the third's basement was large enough to accommodate four.

"The men who come to you for shelter will ask you a question: 'Does the colour purple excite you?' You will answer, 'Only but for myself.' After they have arrived, I will visit you to seal the door to your hiding place so that only you and the three men can enter," said Juween.

"You will hide these men, you will feed these men. If interrogated, you will deny these actions unto death—and I mean *unto death*. It is imperative that this conversation never happened. If the Watchmen detain you, you must be nothing of interest," Juween continued.

Prometheus passed out three or four medallions to each man. He instructed them, "Wear one of these around your neck at all times, and give one to each soldier you take in. If you think you are about to be compromised then please do the following: if you have time, inform your men. But whatever happens, you must rub this medallion three times in a circle like this. It will contact the men that are attached to you, and me."

210

He held his medallion out in front of him and rubbed it in a clockwise circle three times. The medallions glowed red and became warm to the touch. "If you get into trouble we will be at your house in less than three minutes, and the soldiers will help you escape. If the men are not there to help you, you must drink this potion." He handed a small vial to each man. "Don't worry, it's not poison. It will wipe selected parts of your memory, and if we get hold of you before the Watchmen, we can reverse the effect. We will also be issuing you each a pair of shoes. If we have completely failed you, and you find yourself in the Watchmen's headquarters, there is a suicide pill in the heel of the left shoe; the potion will let you remember that piece of information."

In the back of the room, Fate looked at Akea and then Amanda and turned to Chance. He kissed his wife. "Thank you for making this happen."

Chance smiled. "It was not me, but Life."

Prometheus spoke again. "Gentlemen, I beg you to consider the implications. You have an opportunity to take your leave now. However, if you do so, your memory of this meeting will be wiped, for your sake more than ours."

These were real men, and each one answered the call of duty. The meeting was over. The men donned their medallions. Each man was asked for his shoe size. Their quiet, brooding hearts shouted hallelujah.

Over the next few weeks, thirty men, hard men, strolled into the city by stealth, stolen papers and false IDs. Argonath became most perturbed after the fifth soldier came in by dragon. She told Prometheus that she was not a taxi service and he should consider some other mode of transportation for the remaining men.

Captain Nellis had been overseeing the operation with Juween. Nellis was very happy with the arrangements. He inspected each hiding place, at times asking the host to reconsider a hiding place or improve on the sound-proofing, all of which came out of the monies that the council had given Akea.

Nellis met with Akea and Juween in the kitchen. The three sat at the table and enjoyed a nice cup of tea and pored over plans and maps. Argonath was in the forest doing dragon things.

"Captain," Juween said, "we need to organise the men in such a way that we can have a fighting force and a recruiting force. We also need to have men to do the running of refugees out of the city. We can't get them out by using dragon power all the time; it's too obvious. Any suggestions?"

"Gents, we will divide the men accordingly. I will lead the recruiting and running teams. You will take five men to help you fight. I feel any more and the group would lose its capability for stealth. As the main objective is to get people on our side and to freedom, the main force should concentrate on those tasks."

To one side sat a computer, which had Internet access via Akea's old work place. The link was bounced around the world a few times so that it would be hard to trace. A decent firewall and a little-known operating system running on a video console also masked their identity, as this video console did not use conventional IP, or Internet protocol. The Media Access Control address, or MAC, a hardware address that uniquely identifies each node of a network, changed at every new Internet page it visited, and was also masked; this console was protected to the hilt and virtually impossible to detect. If it were compromised, it would set off a large electromagnet to destroy the hard drive; spare hard drives were in place, ready to take over. Others had safe IP addresses and viruses, ready to hit any intruders. The government eggheads wouldn't notice it amongst the millions of other consoles looking for games servers. It was flawless in its simplicity. The best place to hide a book is in a library.

*

It was 2 a.m. The sitting room was infused with the smell of coffee, and the dim glow from a computer screen illuminated the room. Akea and Amanda sat at the small computer desk. To their left was a shelf containing books on hacking techniques and intrusion principles, and a couple of popular programming books. These books were priceless to Akea. They served as the bible and bedrock of a decent hack. It had been really hard to get them. Akea was nervous and excited. Amanda sat quietly enjoying herself, ready with the books and coffee; she felt a tinge of butterflies, mainly because she was reflecting Akea's emotions. This endeavour was a joint one. Akea's hands shook with excitement as he pulled the DVD from its sleeve. If the books had been hard to acquire, they were nothing compared to this DVD. It contained all the software he had downloaded from the hackers' website.

Pablo had spared no pains in obtaining entry to the site. He had used public access computers, libraries and Internet cafés. His mission was to contact an underground group of hackers and software crackers. They were as elusive as deer and cunning as foxes, and rightly so, many wannabes tried to join their ranks; some faked membership.

All this had made it harder for Pablo, but finally he had contacted Dr Drake. "Dr Drake" was the handle of the leader of the "Elite." He lived in Solberg, a pleasant socialist country situated north and west of Ordinea. The two-hour time difference played havoc on their communications, but Dr Drake had doubtless figured out that Pablo was using public access computers and was never in the same place for consecutive meetings.

On the night Pablo first broke through to the Elite, he sat waiting at a computer in the corner of a small café on Albion Street, enjoying a coffee. He noticed a man who sat five desks down from him. Pablo could not see his face, but he felt he was being watched. He shook it off as paranoia. The café was small and insignificant by all accounts, but it did have an enterprising owner, who had found there was money to be made in letting people have access to the Internet. People who use computers drink copious amounts of coffee. Only the hardcore sat at the computers on this rainy Sunday afternoon.

The computer screen in front of Pablo showed a bulletin board service site, a popular way to contact anonymously. Letters began to scroll across the BBS window:

> nightlark
> nightlark here
> what's the password?
> 6d792067656e697573206973
> the second password?

Some people can be so childish, thought Pablo, but he carried on regardless. He needed the services of the Elite and he was going to get it. Suffering a little indignation was nothing compared to what he had already been through. He typed in the second password.

> this is Dr Drake what do you want?
> how do I know this is Dr Drake

> my password is 6f6e6c792069

> I represent a small group of freedom fighters in Ordinea and we need some software to help our cause

> who will be using it?

> the leader, an ex software programmer from CSD

> then why do you need our stuff?

> lets just say that he is in hiding and he left in a hurry. go to the CCTV site for Ordinea City's north gate, there will be some nice footage

> back soon. wait here, don't answer to anyone, I will give the password "wine me dine me"

Ten whole minutes passed; Pablo noticed as he got his third coffee that the café would be closing soon. This guy better hurry up.

> nightlark?

> password.

> wine me dine me. cool video. sorry about the girl. I will give you what you need, I assume that you are after banks and stuff. I will email a list of books and an url, your man will know what to do with the books. from your home pc, go to the url for the software, it will be there for 24 hours only. after that, do not contact me directly. post a bbs asking about 8916 graphics driver on the unisoft help page. I will help you only if you cannot get in. I will be watching. bye. hack in peace.

It was late Wednesday night. Juween had gone to bed ages ago, telling Akea to wake him if there was a problem. Akea read the e-mail over and over; Dr Drake had sent specific instructions. Akea disconnected the PC from the network and installed all the software, closed all the open ports, and set up the firewall that Dr Drake had given him. The IP masking program was running in the background.

The system was ready. Dr Drake had told them to hack into a specific site as practice. The site had the necessary passwords for some of the programs Akea would need if he broke into the bank. Dr Drake had recommended bouncing off at least twenty servers, thus making the trace back to Akea harder. As the trace was followed, the trace alarm would ping like a sonar and also display the time left before the trace was complete. Akea and Amanda stared at the screen, looking at the main program. It was graphically simple, showing a map of the world; the major servers were highlighted as dots with their names. At the bottom left was a tool bar that showed links to other programs and services. They had written a plan, gleaned information from the net and obtained passwords from the Elite.

The deal was that Akea would put 10 percent of whatever he stole into a numbered account of the First Bank of Ordinea. Unlike other banks, the First Bank of Ordinea operated on numbers, using no personal details. Akea typed in the IP address and ran the password breaker. They needed a new numbered account. This was relatively easy, acting just like any other customer.

It was four o'clock on Thursday morning by the time they were ready to break into the Solberg Savings and Loan main server. This time they bounced off all the servers they could find, more than seventy in total.

Dr Drake was uncannily kind. He said if they could trust him, then let him know when they were planning to attack the Solberg main server. He would watch and step in if they needed. His reasoning was "Everything to screw the system."

One of the computer screens showed the BBS. Dr Drake was there. Passwords were exchanged, dignities were bruised.

"*Childish arse,*" Amanda thought.

"*Mm-hm, we geeks are all alike.*"

The message from Nightlark was scrolling across the screen.

> I dropped a logic bomb in the email yesterday. it should be going off in 5 minutes, when it does, it will open a back door. Then I will overload the email server. Denial of service. When that happens it will insert a worm which will give a fake login. The DoS will last for 3 minutes. crack the password.

The other screen showed the main page from the Solberg main server.

Welcome to the Solberg Savings and Loan Main Server

The logic bomb went off; all hell broke loose in the main server room. The plan was simple: look for companies that had large accounts with millions of credits. As each account was found, they had to make two withdrawals, one to Akea and the other to Dr Drake; the key was not to steal too much—small enough not to be missed, but big enough to make it worthwhile.

Akea located an account and completed the transactions. He found another. Another. Another. His fingers flew. Money changed accounts.

Ping went the alarm. 142 seconds left. *Ping*. Akea and Amanda were tingly with nerves. Akea accessed another account. Almost there.

"*Leave the last; just modify the system logs,*" Amanda thought.

Ping. 87 seconds.

Ping. 54 seconds.

A lot of logs needed to be changed or deleted.

Ping. *Ping*. 15 seconds. The trace was three bounces away.

"*That's the last,*" thought Akea.

"*Get out, get out.*"

217

As Akea left the site, Amanda unplugged the main power plug from the PC. Their hearts were beating fast. Nerves, caffeine and adrenaline had made them high and a bit dizzy.

They sat staring at the blank, dead screen. They had accessed over sixty accounts, and transferred sufficient funds to keep a young professional happily employed for a year. But the job was not over, not yet. They had to modify the system logs of the first bounce, thereby cutting the trail. It was fortunate they had chosen a server that was seldom checked, and no one had bothered to change the password. The lazy administrator had left the IP addresses of other servers in the company unprotected. This allowed Akea to bounce off more servers. Akea turned the computer back on and went to the BBS. Dr Drake was still there.

> so are your hearts pumping?

Nightlark had been following their movements.

> I'm impressed. I suggest that you move hideouts, that was too close, the internet gurus will find you if you try to hack again

Akea replied:

> you could say the fear was flowing. we need to put a feed from the Watchmen's headquarters. we need to know what they know

> sweet, no problems, but you are going to have to move your base. there is a trace on you now. when you delete the system logs, don't delete them. put this address 143.647.784.08 instead

> not a problem

> break in, create an account with administrator rights. write a script that emails the daily reports and stuff to you@me.com. change the logs. oh could you leave a Trojan worm in the email server?

"This needs thinking about, planning," thought

Akea.

"*We need to probe their server to see what's there, what updates they've got. Check if there are any special services in the in e-mail server.*"

"*We could e-mail ourselves, using that account.*"

"*Like, to: happy.sadist@Watchmen.com. From: happy.sadist@Watchmen.com.*"

"*Exactly that.*" Akea smiled.

"*We better tell Juween what happened,*" thought Akea.

Akea shut down the computer, and they went to bed.

It was eight o'clock in the morning, and the sun was shining through the small windows when Juween walked into the kitchen and started to make breakfast. Akea and Amanda soon joined him. They looked tired.

"Did you sleep well?" Juween asked.

"Not really. I've been worrying all night about our new problem," said Akea.

"What happened?" asked Juween. "I thought you were going to wake me up if there was a problem." He looked a bit annoyed.

"We got the money, but we took too long doing it. Our contact was there. He helped, but he said that we should move locations because we took so long. We need another place or places to hack from. I need to get into the Watchmen's server," said Akea.

"We should not do any more until we have a new hideout," said Amanda.

"In the meantime I could write a program to hack the Watchmen," said Akea.

"Okay, I'll talk to Pablo. You make a start on the program," said Juween.

Juween took hold of his medallion and signalled Pablo to come down. Pablo felt the heat of the

219

medallion against his chest, made his excuses, left the store to one of his assistants, and went out the back and down the stairs to the cellar. He walked into the kitchen and inhaled deeply the smell of eggs, bacon and coffee wafting in the air. He grabbed a plate and helped himself. Then he sat his ample frame on a chair and broke the silence.

"Right then, what can I do for you?"

Juween said to him, "We broke into a bank and stole lots of money. We think we got away with it. But if we try to hack again from here they might find us."

"Bloody hell, Akea. For god's sake, I thought you said that it was undetectable, foolproof," said Pablo.

Akea bowed his head. "Yeah, I know. We didn't plan it well enough. But now we need to get into the Watchmen's server to see what they are doing."

"You mean you were invisible, except for the big neon sign saying 'Here be hackers'?" Pablo said sarcastically.

"Can you find us a place, or at least point us in the right direction?" said Amanda rather impatiently, ignoring the gibe.

"Yeah, sure, why not? I'll take the rest of the day off and look around. But you will have to do the rest. I shouldn't leave the shop for too long, or else people will get suspicious," said Pablo. "I'll try to find a place and show it to you on a map. You can do the rest. I wish I could do more, but I'm sure the Watchmen have an eye on me."

That morning Pablo went out and looked for a place. He had a rough idea of where to go. He drove his hardware store van to a disused industrial site. The boarded-up buildings stood eerily dark and silent; even the warm sun did not want to know them anymore. Pablo drove the van some distance away from the site, parked and walked back to the old metal works. Since the revolution, Bigots had stood still, waiting, wanting to be used.

Pablo went round the back and broke in through the ladies' toilets. He clicked on his penlight torch and wandered around. The building was huge. The main floor boasted lathes, milling machines and all sorts of metal fabrication machinery. The offices were on the top level. To one end of the building was an inner office with no windows; it looked like the chairman's office. He opened the door and found a huge table in the middle of the room. He pointed the light at the skirting board that ran along the wall and spotted a telephone socket and an electricity outlet. He carefully wandered about the room. Big pictures of its former glory hung on the walls. Near the main desk he found an old telephone. He picked up the receiver, but there was no ring tone. He tried a lamp and found that at least there was electricity.

He got out of the building as carefully as he could, and drove back to the store. He went straight to Akea to tell him what he had found.

He sat down at the small kitchen table, and Akea gave him a cup of coffee. Amanda slid into a chair at the small table.

"Well, lad, you're in luck. I found a large building with an inner office with no windows. It has electricity but no phone—there's a socket, but the phone is dead."

"I'll go to the base tonight and ask if we have an ex–telephone engineer who could help us," said Akea.

Amanda looked Pablo in the eyes. "Thank you for all your help."

*

It was around six in the evening. A man walked out of his office into the car lot and got into his car; he put the key in the ignition. A large, black, supercharged sports car with bull bars came out of nowhere, and slammed into the passenger side of the stationary car. A second black car slammed into the driver's rear side. Five Watchmen got out and trained their semiautomatics on the driver, who remained sitting, stunned, in his car.

The driver suffered from severe whiplash and compression of the chest. However, he did have enough wits about him to grope for the medallion inside his shirt and rub it three times. Then he grabbed the potion vial from his trouser pocket, smashed the top off on the steering wheel, and prayed like mad that Akea would save him as he gulped the light blue, fluorescent liquid. It was cool on the tongue and tasted of strawberries. In his house, the three soldiers felt the warm glow, jumped up, grabbed their kits and warned the driver's wife. All four were out of the door in under three minutes. They were in their street clothes and carried a small holdall each.

Prometheus came running into the kitchen. "We've been compromised. It happened on New Road. Akea, get in the air. And Amanda, please, could you take me there?"

Akea ran out through the back yard and down the street. He checked to see if anyone was watching and then muttered the incantation. A wind blew up, and moments later a thirty-foot dragon rose into the air, heading west. In the back yard, Argonath crouched down and Prometheus climbed on as quickly as he could. Fifteen seconds later, she was three hundred feet in the air, heading west.

222

Akea could see the car wreck on New Road. He saw four Watchmen had trained their guns on the crumpled car, while a fifth yanked at the driver's-side door. Unable to open the door, the Watchman broke the window with the stock of his gun, reached in and started to haul the now-unconscious driver out of the car by his collar. Akea went into a steep dive, like a flattened S-shape. He said *"Contego"* and put a shield around the driver and himself. As he flew low to the ground for the last fifteen meters, he shouted *"Vir extraho."* The wind created by the transformation helped to scrub off speed. In human form he slammed into two of the Watchmen and knocked them down. The force of the blow rendered them unconscious.

The Watchman had the driver halfway out of the window when the shield formed. He let go of the man, who dropped to the ground, and was in the middle of trying to get his gun out when another man appeared from nowhere and knocked down two of his buddies. The two remaining Watchmen started to fire at the driver, but the bullets bounced off the shield and hit the fifth Watchman. He collapsed on the floor, seeping from no fewer than half a dozen bullet holes. Akea turned on the two Watchmen still standing, shouted, *"Lux lucis telum,"* and shot each in the gun arm with silver arrows from his fingertips. Argonath landed nearby, and Prometheus ran toward the driver and the Watchman lying next to him. Prometheus shouted, *"Vigoratus,"* and both the driver and the Watchman came to and looked around in confusion. "Quick drink this," Prometheus said to the driver. The driver took the small vial Prometheus handed him, drank it and fainted again. Akea ran around to each of the Watchmen and healed their wounds.

223

Akea and Amanda placed all the Watchmen in their cars, two in the first one and three in the second. One at a time, Amanda roughly opened each Watchman's mouth and poured the fluorescent light blue potion down his throat, clamping his mouth shut and pinching his nose until he swallowed. Then she punched each of the Watchmen across the chin, causing their necks to whip back, pinching the nerves at the base of the neck and knocking them unconscious. Amanda changed to Argonath and grabbed the driver carefully in her front right claws. Prometheus climbed on Akea's back, and they were away. Prometheus hung on for dear life as they climbed almost vertically to fifteen hundred feet. He held on so tight that he nearly pulled off one of Akea's scales. Akea winced in pain. The cold, thin air went right through Prometheus's clothes. He whispered, *"Contego, tepidus meus bones."* The shield kept the cold out, and he could feel a warm sensation as the Latin spell warmed him from within.

They landed near the rear entrance of the rebel base. Argonath gently put the driver down. Akea landed, and Prometheus climbed off and went to the driver and spoke gentle words of healing. The big concrete doors swung open, and Commander Bavlin stepped out.

"Akea, what are you doing here?"

"One of our civilians was ambushed by the Watchmen. He took the memory loss potion and Prometheus gave him the antidote. He has to stay here now. We'll bring his wife as soon as we can. I assume the soldiers got out and are making their way to the hardware store."

"You better stay here in this control room. Iral took pity on Nalik and healed him, and now he is on the war path." He turned to Argonath. "You really humiliated him. The whole base knows about it."

Argonath growled, "When will people learn I am a dragon and should be treated as such?"

Bavlin backed away. "I meant no offence, my lady."

Argonath was amused by this. "I am not angry at you. But that does not give you licence."

"*You horrible, mean-tempered, cantankerous beast, you*," Akea smiled as he thought to love.

"*Shut your face, or you will have to sleep on the sofa*," she returned. Her expression softened. Bavlin looked confused.

"Bavlin, it's okay, the Lady Argonath is not angry with you. In fact, she likes you. You have nothing to fear. But a word to the wise: this favour is soon rescinded if you take the piss."

"With the utmost respect, my lady, it is hard to work out what doesn't offend you."

Prometheus spoke up before Argonath could react. "Treat her with respect, old bean, the same way you would talk to the elders. Nalik didn't understand this, and kept insulting her and calling her a bitch. Argonath was actually pretty lenient with him. Anyway, could you please get this man to the hospital wing and, please, could you fix some food for us, old bean?"

"I need a telecoms engineer. Do you know of any?" Akea asked Bavlin.

"Yeah, sure." Bavlin picked up a short-wave radio, called in some help and ordered some food. He asked if the records showed of any telecoms engineers, and if so could they come to the back entrance immediately. Argonath went outside and took off, headed for her favourite hunting ground. Two medics came in and took the injured driver away. Three

225

kitchen porters brought in trays bearing steaks, chips, salad and a coffee pot. Akea, Bavlin and Prometheus sat in the little control room and ate. It was good to have food, decent food, and Akea was starving. They were about halfway through the coffee, Akea regaling Bavlin with all that had happened since he had left the base, when a thin, middle-aged man with mousy brown hair and glasses—rather short, Akea thought, timidly knocked on the open door.

"You wanted to see me, sir."

At first Bavlin didn't recognise him. "Who are you?"

"Oh, sorry. My name is George Andrews. You wanted a telecoms engineer. Apparently I am the most qualified."

"Well, Mr. Andrews, please take a seat. This is Akea and Prometheus."

"I know who you are—well at least I have heard of you. What you did to General Nalik—well, you got a quiet round of applause. How can I help?"

Akea was warming to this guy—a bit timid, but he was okay. "Don't you like the General, then?"

"I . . . I better not say," replied Mr. Andrews. He looked at Bavlin sheepishly.

"It's okay, George. Between you and me, he's not my favourite person either," said Bavlin.

"Thank you, sir. When I was rescued from the city five years ago, I found I had fled from the clutches of one egoistical megalomaniac into the arms of another. At least Nalik is incompetent and has a short leash," said Mr. Andrews.

"Well said. Don't worry, this conversation has ended, and we will not speak of it again," said Prometheus. Despite Nalik's flaws, he thought it was not good to encourage insurrection inside the base.

"Okay, down to business," said Akea. "We need

226

you to patch in a telephone into an exchange. It has to cope with a high-speed data transfer, and it must an unusable number—we don't want to be traced."

"Yeah, I can do it, if I can have some tools."

"What do you need? I will have them here in five minutes," said Bavlin.

Mr. Andrews told him what he needed. Bavlin picked up the short-wave radio and told the person on the other end to bring the tools and some fur-lined coats.

Mr. Andrews looked at Bavlin curiously when he mentioned the coats.

"Don't worry, old bean, it gets rather cold at two thousand feet," said Prometheus.

"Where are we going?" said Mr. Andrews. He started to look worried and timid again.

"We are going to an old industrial site, the Bigots building to be precise. But we are flying on Argonath's and my backs, and as Prometheus said, it gets cold at two thousand feet. There is no need to worry if you hold on tight, but not too tight"—Akea looked accusingly at Prometheus, who raised his shoulders in apology—"then you will be fine."

Akea called Argonath back from her hunting. She arrived with a sated expression on her face, and they all left as soon as the kit arrived.

Mr. Andrews enjoyed his flight by dragon immensely. Akea landed him near the Bigots building. Argonath landed a moment later, and Prometheus climbed off. Mr. Andrews soon found the exchange hub around the back of the building and set to work. Prometheus and Akea posted themselves at each end of the street, while Argonath took flight and circled the sky high above them.

"There's a black car moving slowly this way, hide," thought Argonath.

Akea ran back to the building and tapped Mr. Andrews on the shoulder. He jumped nervously.

"We gotta move. Hide your things," Akea whispered.

They tidied up and moved into the overgrown bushes around the building. A minute later, a car pulled up outside the exchange hub and a torchlight shone on it. Akea could hear two voices arguing about why they were here looking at some damn hub. Akea stepped out of the bush and walked towards them.

"Hey, hey, look—that's that guy we been looking for," said one.

"No, no, I got the mike," said the other. A small fight ensued in the car.

It was ended as a twenty-foot blue grey dragon landed on the car roof and crumpled it. The long talons made a screeching sound as they scraped on the metalwork of the flattened vehicle. She bent her head between her legs and let out a small flame. "Ooops. Didn't mean to squish them. Shall I torch it so no one can identify it?"

"I have a better idea," Akea said.

Just then Prometheus caught up with them. He asked, "What's going on?"

Akea said, "They were looking at the exchange hub. Argonath came down on them. Prometheus, if I put a shield around the car, could you disintegrate it?"

Akea put a shield around the car and Prometheus spoke the spell. *"Disintartum."* The car burst with a flash and was gone.

Akea called to Mr. Andrews, who emerged from his hiding place in the bushes.

"What did you do with the hub? Those men had been told to investigate it."

"Err, I don't know. They must have been watching," replied Mr. Andrews.

"Look, please finish it. Just make sure we are invisible," said Akea.

Mr. Andrews finished the reconnection and disappeared into the night on the back of Argonath. Prometheus and Akea snuck into Bigots. They entered the inner office. It was hard to see in the dark; they waited a moment for their night vision. They put a small laptop on the table and connected to the Internet. They placed a notice on the hackers' BBS and asked for Dr Drake to hack into the Watchmen server and complete the report on the exchange hub as "No abnormal events".

They went back to the hardware store.

Later, as they all relaxed in the kitchen, there was a clang of rubbish bins being knocked over. Amanda jumped to her feet, ready to fight. Prometheus steadied her with his arm on hers. He said *"Os ultra os."* A small square of swirling mist appeared in front of him and grew in size. The swirling stopped and four very apprehensive looking people were displayed on the screen.

Bavlin looked into the image. "That's my men, get them in."

Juween went up the small flight of steps and opened the door. Three men and a woman came in. Juween ushered them into the small living room and invited them to sit down. The woman looked about thirty-five. Her brown hair would normally be styled in a modern fashion, but was unkempt and wind-swept. She was not overly large, but she could do with some weight loss. In a bizarre way the bloodshot whites of her eyes set off her grey irises.

"Report, soldier," said Bavlin, who clearly was pleased to see them.

"We felt the medallions and got the woman out. We did not take the spare car as it would have been compromised. We split up; I took the woman shopping in the mall. Sir, I'd like to recommend the woman for a medal. She showed immense courage to act normally; she must have been out of her mind with worry. We explained to her that her husband would be okay. The second group moved slowly through the city, stopping off in different coffee shops and restaurants to see if they were being followed. We rendezvoused at the temple just before the curfew bells; we waited in a back alley for an hour and made our way here, using the back streets and alleys. It took two hours to cover six miles. There are no injuries, but my men are tired, and we have no supplies other than what we are carrying sir."

"I'll put the kettle on," said Juween. He went into the kitchen and came back out a few minutes later with two small glasses of light brown liquid in each hand.

"Here, have some whisky," he said, handing each of the four a glass.

The lead soldier looked at Nellis. "Sir, may we?"

Nellis nodded.

They relaxed a bit. The tension of finding the hideout was over, and it felt safe and warm in the cosy basement.

The woman started to cry. Through her tears she asked, "Where's my husband? Is he okay? When can I see him?"

Akea replied, "Madam, your husband is safe. He showed strength of mind. He was ambushed by two Watchmen patrols."

The woman gasped, "Is he okay? Is he hurt?"

Akea reassured her, "No, he's fine. He is at the base. He took the memory-loss potion, but Prometheus gave him the antidote. We put him in the base hospital as a precaution."

"I thought you said he wasn't hurt. I want to see him," said the woman.

"We will leave as soon as you are ready," said Prometheus.

"What? How? When?" said the woman.

"You're not scared of heights, are you?"

"Akea, I wish you would stop saying that. It's not funny," said Amanda.

"What do you mean, heights?" said the woman.

"We are going to fly you out by dragon. Nellis, tell me what you need from the base. I'll get the supplies. And Mr. Andrews's work is done here, so we may as well return him to the base, too."

"What do you mean, by dragon?"

"Well, a twenty- or thirty-foot-long, fire-breathing, two-tonne, reptilian, flying dragon," said Juween.

"How dare you call me reptilian," said Amanda.

The woman was completely confused. "Okay, please, could someone tell me in plain English what happened to my husband and what you mean by dragon?"

"Your husband was hit by two patrols of Watchmen. When we got there they were trying to pull him out of the driver's window. The Watchmen tried to shoot your husband, but the shield I put around him meant they shot their own instead; we disabled the remaining Watchmen and gave them a potion to make them lose their memories. We then healed your unconscious husband and flew him to the base."

"You're still not making any sense, but thank you," the woman said.

"I am a dragon in human form," said Amanda.

"Oh, okay," said the woman. She shifted in her seat, as though she were afraid of contracting a disease.

"Please, can we go now?" she said. She got up and turned to the group. "Who are you, anyway?"

"I am Prometheus, this is Akea, and Amanda—sometimes known as Argonath, this is Captain Nellis, Mr. Andrews, and this is Juween."

Nellis introduced his valiant men. "This is Yansey, Para and Zip."

Yansey, a tall, heavyset man, looked like he had just come from a weightlifting competition. He emanated confidence. Zip was smaller; almost ferret like; he had the air of a wiry little sod. Para seemed quiet and reluctant to talk. Akea thought he must be the brains of the group.

"Pablo has arranged for another place for you three to stay," Nellis informed his men.

Akea got up and escorted the woman and Mr. Andrews to the yard. Amanda followed. A wind came up, and when it died down, Argonath sat in the yard.

"Oh, my! What a fantastic beast."

Argonath swung her head round to growl at the woman, but Akea quickly intervened. "It is considered rude to call a dragon a beast—in fact, it is often fatal. We address Argonath as 'my lady'."

"Oh, sorry, I must apologise, my lady."

The night-time air was cold. The woman lacked adrenaline and shivered inside her warm coat. Akea spoke Latin at her, and she sighed with the warmth suddenly coursing through her.

"Please climb on. Put your left foot on the elbow joint, and Argonath will lift you up. Good. Now swing your right leg over. Okay. Don't worry about falling off—just hang on tight," said Akea.

Akea then transformed himself and knelt down for Mr. Andrews to clamber on. Mr. Andrews looked over at the woman and smiled. "It's actually quite a jolly ride," he told her.

Mr. Andrews again enjoyed his flight, as did the woman. She felt free. She wanted to stay up here amongst the clouds forever, and the flight was far too short in her view.

At the base Akea picked up the equipment Nellis had asked him to get.

Akea and Argonath flew home chasing each other.

*

The next day, Akea went shopping for computer equipment. He needed to replace all the old kit. As did Amanda when either of them went out in public, he wore sunglasses to hide his tiger eyes.

Over the next few weeks, at irregular intervals, Akea and Amanda visited the Bigots site and broke into the Watchmen's main server, first to create an account and then to check the system details, always careful to remove the logs. They were not in the server for long—maybe for a few moments—at a time. It was getting tedious, so Akea wrote a program that randomly probed the servers, looking for key information. This program would be the skeleton for their main program. They inserted it in their new account main directory and left it to run.

Chapter 16: The Innocent

It was about 9 p.m. when Akea checked the latest reports. As he scanned them, his heart sank—there were so many people on the hit list. He had to pick one out of maybe a dozen to save. Tears fell freely from his eyes as he tried to decide the fate of one family or person. Was it fair to judge a persons worth by their social status? Out of despair, he closed his eyes and pointed to a name. Right, the Dorrents it is.

He gave the list to Nellis, who was sitting in the kitchen, and told him which family he was going for. Prometheus had been sitting there talking to Nellis, and noticed the sadness on Akea's face.

"What's the matter, old bean?"

"There are so many people we need to rescue. For each person we save there are twenty more we can't. It breaks my heart having to decide each night which one family we will save. I tell you, Prometheus, I am sick of it—sick of this, sick of the sneaking about," said Akea.

"We can't look at it like that. Over the last few months, we have saved ninety families who otherwise would have been taken to the concentration camps," said Nellis.

"Look at it this way, old bean: the last few times we went out, the surrounding neighbours came out on the streets, armed—and, I must add, ready to defend you if necessary. Have you noticed the little pencil drawings of your insignia, the one on the back of your cloak? They are cropping up everywhere."

"Akea, people are starting to realise that there is hope; you are their hope," said Nellis.

"*Darling, we are going after the Dorrents, in Mornington Crescent. They are due to be picked up and taken to concentration camp 9 at 11 p.m,*" thought

Akea.

"*That gives us less than two hours. What do you want to do?*" thought Argonath.

"*We better get going,*" thought Akea.

In the quiet street, night had fallen. The streetlights had come on, people had eaten their suppers and argued with the kids, and everywhere children had gone to bed. Their parents sat down and watched the news, read the paper and had five minutes' peace.

A van parked right in front of the house. There was a knock on the door. Mrs. Dorrent looked at her husband. "Who could this be?" said her worried face. Mrs. Dorrent went toward the front door. As she reached the hallway, the door burst open. There stood four big men with scars on their faces, chips on their shoulders and large guns in their hands.

"You are under arrest. Come out quietly," said the lead Watchman.

Mrs. Dorrent put her hands up. "Move," the leader said. As the other Watchmen raced into the house, Mrs. Dorrent started to scream, but a bullet from a silenced pistol soon shut her up. She slumped onto the floor. In the house, the Watchmen found four children playing in the back bedroom. The men came out, the leader dragging Mr. Dorrent, and the others each holding one or more struggling, shrieking children. People from across the street came out shouting and screaming. Some had cricket bats, others knives or axes.

"That's my child!" cried a hysterical woman.

One of the Watchmen turned round and shot her, too.

The screams and shouts became louder.

The Watchman waiting in the van could see this was going to get ugly. The lead Watchman put a gun to Mr. Dorrrent's temple. The Watchmen in the van

235

got out and faced down the neighbours with silenced semiautomatics.

The first of the Watchmen to reach the van slung the child he was carrying into the back off the van and climbed in.

There was a soft thud as a twenty-foot dragon landed in between the neighbours and the Watchmen. Akea thought, There's got to be twenty people out here. I can't protect them all. He climbed off Argonath. *Bang!* The lead Watchman shot Mr. Dorrent in the head.

Akea saw it in slow motion—the bullet hitting the temple and milliseconds later exploding out of the other side. Argonath jumped on the lead Watchman and tore him into pieces. Akea surveyed the area; there were two more Watchmen just outside of the house holding three children and two in the van. Mr. and Mrs. Dorrent and another woman were on the floor dead. The screams and shouts of the neighbours started to call to the darkness behind Akea's eyes. He had chosen to set the Dorrents free, from over a dozen others, and now they were dead because he was too late.

"No, Akea no," Argonath screamed as her control over his mind weakened. She swayed slightly. Akea held out his hands and screamed, *"Lux lucis telum."* Twelve-inch silver arrows shot from his outstretched hands and shredded the van and anything in or near it to pieces. The screams and shouts got louder. One of the Watchmen held a gun to the head of a child that he was carrying; Akea fired a single arrow at the watchman. As the arrow sliced through the Watchman's forebrain, the involuntary reflex squeezed the trigger of the gun and shot six-year-old Tommy in the head.

236

The final Watchman dropped the two children he was carrying and ran for Akea. He was about fifteen feet away when Argonath, barely able to control herself, let out a fierce flame. The Watchman stopped dead in his tracks and fell screaming to the ground, clutching his face.

The neighbours ran to Akea, shouting and screaming. They screamed about children being in the van. What had he done?

Akea screamed. He fell to his knees, crying his heart out. Argonath recovered her control, changed to human form and ran to him. The onlooker gawked—where a moment ago had stood a twenty-foot dragon there was now a slender woman in a sexy uniform.

Amanda held Akea tight. The most astute people, the natural leaders, stopped the others from coming in close. Most were too afraid to approach too close anyway. They had just witnessed one of the worst moments in Akea's life; he had lost control and killed a six-year-old in cold blood. The darkness behind Akea's eyes swam along the high seas.

"Akea! Akea! Can you hear me, Akea?" The gentle voice of Amanda permeated Akea's sorrow.

Akea raised his head. "Innocence—I killed an innocent. Now I have condemned twelve families to death. Innocence, innocence."

Amanda slapped him across the face. He didn't react or register the pain. "Get up now, or so help me I will beat you to a pulp, right here, right now. I said get up. Now move."

She lifted him bodily from the floor. "Transform, damn you, Akea. God damn it, Akea, I can't do it for you. Now transform, you fucking bastard."

Akea just sat there on the road like a limp doll.

Amanda changed to Argonath and grabbed Akea roughly in her front claw.

She landed in the back yard of the hardware store and laid Akea on the floor, switched back into Amanda and raced into the basement.

"Prometheus, Prometheus, you better come quick. It's Akea, he's hurt," she said with as much calm as she could muster.

Prometheus shot out of the basement to find Akea slumped on the ground, mumbling about innocence and twelve families.

As Prometheus stepped lightly forward, he felt something stab his mind—blackness, a darkness, and it emanated from Akea. Prometheus spoke soothing words in Latin, and then he turned to Amanda. "Get Juween and Nellis. I am going to need help"

Juween and Nellis came running out. "Grab his arms, Juween. Nellis, you grab his feet."

The men carried Akea into the sitting room. All the time Prometheus spoke Latin to Akea.

After the men had laid Akea on the sofa, Prometheus turned to Amanda. "Now, calmly tell me what happened. Juween, get some whisky."

"We arrived too late. Mrs. Dorrent was already dead, and a neighbour was dead, too. When we arrived, one of the Watchmen killed Mr. Dorrent. I killed that Watchman. There were a lot of neighbours about, screaming and shouting. He must have seen the dead people and lost it. I felt a terrible pain, like someone had sliced my mind in half and poured hot black liquid into it. He . . . I . . . we lost control; Akea unleashed a good sixty foot-long arrows at the van. A Watchman had a child in his arm. Akea shot the Watchman, but the Watchman shot the boy. The last remaining Watchman dropped the children he was holding and ran for Akea; I burnt him to a cinder. The neighbours kept shouting about children in the van. I think some of our links have been broken. I can't feel

238

him the way I did before."

"That explains the innocents. I think he was pissed off about how many families were due to be taken by the Watchmen. I counted thirteen on the list," said Prometheus. "Odd, isn't it, the thing I have been worried about and hoped would never happen has, unfortunately, happened. I have always feared for Akea's mind, all that power in such a fragile vessel—rage, frustration, guilt, sorrow, the darkness behind all our eyes. "Juween, Argonath, we are going to have to force a mind meld, see if we can help."

"What can I do?" said Nellis.

"Nothing, I am afraid, old chap. Just keep us warm," said Prometheus.

Amanda, Juween and Prometheus held each other's and Akea's limp hands. They said together, *"Touts mens unus mens, touts mens unus mens."*

In Akea's mind, they found themselves in a little boat on an ocean stretching from horizon to horizon. The calm ocean unnerved Juween. In the distance he could see a brilliant white figure standing on a boat fighting with a mass of darkness and cloud.

"The white figure must be self-worth, self-esteem, compassion, logic and, I guess, sheer bloody mindedness," said Prometheus in a ghostly still voice.

They rowed to the figure. They heard it shouting unintelligible things to the dark thunderstorm. The roiling mass kept shifting as though being punched. The waves rose up and became choppy. Prometheus was cautious, but Amanda wasn't. She grabbed the oars, rowed to Akea and hugged him. The dark, stormy mass screamed in pain. Amanda shouted to the mass, "I love you, Akea, the whole of you, the good and the bad. Don't let go." The dark clouds screamed again. Under the surface Juween could see a black shadow swimming, circling the little boats.

239

The thunderstorm deep within shouted at Akea, in a series of thunderclaps. "You are not worthy, you have killed too many people, you are a bastard child, and no one loves you. You are scum."

Akea shouted back, "I am loved, I am worthy. I may not know who my father is, but Juween is as close to a father as any — perhaps more so, because he chose to love me." He put out his hands and let off a volley of lightning strikes.

Juween got the idea. "Akea," he shouted, "you are the closest thing I have to a son. You are not without worth. You are the greatest magician of all time. Now fight, son."

The white figure grew in power and stature. "That's my boy. Fight the fear," said Prometheus.

The white figure spoke loud and clear, "I am who I am. You cannot take that away from me. I can think, I can dream. You will not control me. I have reason and logic, love and compassion."

The darkness moved away. It shifted somehow and shrunk in size as it moved. The black shadow beneath the surface no longer rode under the open waves, but went deep for cover.

Juween and Prometheus broke off, leaving Akea and Amanda alone together. The scene changed to a long corridor with many doors without signs or handles. Akea became scared, but Amanda was resilient and steadfast. She knew which door it was; she couldn't explain it, but she knew. She held his hand as she pushed the door open.

Akea opened his eyes; he was lying on the sofa in the sitting room. Amanda knelt down beside him and stroked his hair.

"Welcome back, old bean. Here, drink this," said Prometheus. He handed Akea a glass with a few ounces of liquid in it. "This is a mild sleeping potion.

240

You need to sleep tonight."

Akea sat up and downed the drink. He made a face.

"Can you feel Argonath?" asked Prometheus.

Akea shook his head. "No, I can't. She is . . . well, she is here, but it seems like a distant whisper of an echo."

"How bizarre; still, you're the first human and dragon to have ever melded, we have no experience to draw from. I think we should go to the second reality tomorrow. You will have to perform the meld rites again. Odd that the meld didn't hold in this reality. Perhaps there wasn't enough power, or you weren't ready. Who knows?"

"Treat me like a dumb ass, but what the hell are you talking about?" said Nellis.

"With respect, it's none of your business," said Juween.

"It's okay, tell him. He's seen us together, he might as well know," said Amanda.

"But it's a private matter," said Juween.

"It doesn't matter," said Nellis.

"If I understand Prometheus correctly," said Akea, "when dragons mate, they perform a rite that melds their minds together; we performed that rite, but—how can I put this?" He paused for a second. "If you weld two pieces of metal together, but it is done wrong—not enough temperature, or there was dirt or oxidation, then the joint will be poor and break. I think that's what happened. There was not enough magic, or one or both of us weren't ready."

Prometheus nodded. "That's it, old boy, just like that."

"Then why go to this second reality?" said Nellis.

"We need more 'heat'—in this case, magic," said Akea. He explained to Nellis the theory of the realities and the differing strengths of technology and magic in

241

each.

That night, even with the sleeping potion, Akea had vivid dreams; he kept replaying the scene of the boy being shot in the head. The darkness and the storm were not going to let Akea's sense of worth get away that easily. Amanda slept next to him. She also had bad dreams. The sense of loss, the quietness and emptiness haunted her. She hadn't realised how badly the links were broken. She missed Akea's quiet thoughts roaming freely through her mind.

The next morning Amanda woke first and cuddled Akea as he slept. She held him like a mother holding a baby, stroking his head and whispering notions of love. She wouldn't let go. She could not stand the feeling of loss. She was determined to get Akea back inside her head. When Akea woke up, he lay there and enjoyed the affection.

They walked into the light blue and green kitchenette.

"Want some breakfast? How do you like your eggs?" Prometheus greeted them.

"Since you're cooking breakfast," said Amanda, "I'll have some eggs well done, raw bacon, sausages and raw black pudding."

"Where's the coffee?" said Juween, wandering in. He looked blurry eyed. "That God damned whisky."

They sat in silence for while.

Prometheus thought Akea did not look happy. "Did the potion work, old bean?"

"Not really. I dreamt of that boy being shot in the head, over and over again," said Akea. "It was odd; I kept thinking that something was missing."

Amanda injected, "I had the same feelings, too. It was like half of me wasn't there."

"Right. Juween, I want you and Nellis to plan the next stage of our little adventure," said Prometheus.

Chapter 17: The Birth of Diligo

It was an early Wednesday morning, and the dull overcast reflected everyone's mood. Pablo drove Akea, Amanda and Prometheus to the old industrial site where months ago they had cleaned Pablo's car. Pablo stopped the car and turned to the front passenger seat. "Do I need to pick you up, and if so, what time?"

"No, we will come in late tonight. I think these two are going to be all day. We all could do with a rest. Please pass on this message to Juween and Nellis: If they want to make a start with the plans that would be great, but if they just want to get some time out, that's okay also," said Prometheus.

Akea, Amanda and Prometheus got out of the little compact and wandered off. Two small gusts of wind came up, and Prometheus climbed onto Argonath's back. He much preferred Argonath's flying to Akea's; his was too aggressive for an old man. They climbed up above the clouds. Prometheus was glad he had his thick coat on. Some time later they touched down near Prometheus's cottage. Prometheus sighed; it had been ages since he had seen his beloved cottage. The ecology on the roof seemed to be getting out of hand. Oh well, he thought.

The three stood on the dais inside the ancient circle of stones. Akea and Amanda had reverted to human form to make the passage easier. Prometheus spoke the words *patefacio mihi, patefacio mihi* to the stones. The stones shuddered and moved into place, and a soft light hung around the flat dais. The three human forms blurred and then became translucent and then transparent, and finally disappeared altogether. Stepping from one reality to another was not a pleasant experience. It was like stepping through a

243

door that was too tight for you, or one of those corridors that feature in popular nightmares, where it keeps on going and going, getting smaller, until you crouch down on all fours and squeeze through a tiny hole.

The three stepped off the dais in the second reality. Amalthea's cottage, similar to Prometheus's but in better repair, sat nearby, but Amalthea apparently was off somewhere.

The three walked lazily along until they came to a sun-drenched glen, with bright green grass, scented with the smell of pine and meadow grasses. Akea sighed. Amanda shone almost as brightly as the sun. The two lovers transformed to dragons and took off. Up in the air, Akea literally felt the magic, like the high energy of a thunderstorm. Though he could not remember being here, it felt good to be home.

Prometheus sat on the soft grass and enjoyed the warm sun. He watched Akea and Argonath chase each other over the mountains and valleys like a low-flying supersonic stunt team; well, more like an aerial version of kiss chase. After half an hour, when they came back for a pass over Prometheus, he called out, "Please come in and land. I need to talk to you."

Akea wanted to show off. He came in hard and fast, and at the last second he clapped his wings and almost hovered before he landed. Argonath outdid him by landing as gracefully and regally as possible.

"I know this is a very private matter. No human except you, old bean, has ever seen this rite. I will say my piece and go. Listen up, Akea, I've been thinking about this. Perhaps a human's will is not as strong as a dragon's will, or perhaps neither of you was ready. How do you get around this? Akea, I want you to concentrate on being with Argonath. The whole of your massive mind should be bent on one thought.

Nothing else matters, not even death. Then say the words that Argonath gives you to say. When you have completed the rite, Argonath will say, '*Ego mos non intereo vigoratus vigorous.*' This is an ancient spell and should not be used unless it is absolutely necessary; both your souls will enter the physically stronger being. I guess this will be Argonath. You will be one dragon, and since your minds are one, you will be undefeatable. You will have all Akea's power and Argonath's strength. But there is a price. You can't survive long; nowhere in the universe should two souls occupy the same space. If you stay that way, you will die. You must switch back while you still have the strength to do so."

Akea said, "Thanks, old bean."

Prometheus wandered off as the two took off. They climbed and climbed. The air was getting thin, and the acids fought through their muscles. Ice was started to form on their wing-tips. Argonath stopped and hovered as best as she could, and Akea stopped a few feet in front of her.

"I love you Akea, I miss you."

"And I you."

Akea concentrated on Argonath. His mind was bent on her as though she were the only object in the world. A dazzling, bright blue aura glowed from his whole body.

"Say after me, 'Ut unus iam quod pro infiniti' — and say it in my tongue as well: 'Thi dwosghat enurhf.' We will open up completely. This is the true meaning of love; to be in love with someone's mind is so much more than to love someone's body," Argonath thought.

Argonath spoke the words aloud, and Akea solemnly repeated them.

There were no walls, barriers, hidden feelings to overcome. Their minds met somewhere in the air between them, danced around together like mayflies. Then, like an ink drop dripped in water, their minds became one. Akea glowed bright blue. Argonath glowed the same colour blue, and just as bright.

They weaved together and shot toward the ground. They landed and sat next to each other. Argonath leaned over Akea and spoke the ancient spell: *"Ego mos non intereo vigoratus vigorous."*

An explosion ripped through time, space and magic. The meadow filled with blue and orange lights that danced on the trees, as Akea's life force entered into Argonath's soul and his body merged with hers. Cells merged and then broke apart. Argonath's body began to ripple and roil as it changed colour and size. A silent boom sliced through time and space.

Diligo stood more than thirty feet high and sixty-five feet long. Its—no, *their* head was blue, with a long snout, and four great horns stood proudly on their head like a crown. The head was supported by a long and slender but massive neck. Armour plates ran the length of their flank, and on the end of the long tail stood, like a crown, six horns spread at ninety-degree angles. The colours of the creature were hypnotic, melding from blue to burnt orange to dark red. They took off into the sky; there was no confusion, no need to confer. Akea and Argonath were one in the truest sense of the form.

Aware of Prometheus's warning they landed and split apart. They spent the rest of the day hunting and courting. By the time they arrived back at the gate, the evening sun had sunk low behind the trees. Then they stepped on the dais and in more ways than one they were brought back to another reality.

*

"We must wait and see how the Watchmen will react," Juween said. He thumped the table in frustration. The Watchmen were not supposed to die; the risk of repercussions from random killings was too high. Yesterday had been the second incident since they'd returned to the city that had resulted in the death of Watchmen. But there had been no other way. Nellis and he had spent the late afternoon trying to work out a plan to complete Prometheus's task, lubricating the discussion with wine. Akea, Amanda and Prometheus walked in on the heated debate.

"The Watchmen will not be as compassionate as you. They will meet consideration with death. This may work for us, if we can show we were trying to help and not kill unless others were going to get hurt. Do not feel so downhearted. This is a victory," the captain said. "We must come up with a plan to stop the Watchmen in one fell swoop. If only we could get into their headquarters, we could put them in their own cells and get some rebels to 'look after them.'" The captain made inverted comma signs with his fingers.

"Yeah, right." Juween was clearly pissed at this silly notion. This was the first time he had disagreed with the captain. "Even if we could get to within three miles of their HQ without being noticed, then we'd still have to get inside unseen, disable the communications—oh yeah, and shoot our way through dozens of guards who are in the station eating doughnuts and torturing people." The sarcasm was very unlike Juween.

"What would happen if one of us got arrested? That person would be inside, all subdued, and then when all of us were in place that person could tackle

247

the Watchmen inside the building and let us in," mused the captain.

Akea looked at the captain. "You mean me, don't you?"

Captain Nellis nodded. "We also need to find a hacker who can beam footage of our exploits around the world; the Internet is a powerful ally."

Chance squeezed into the now very crowded kitchenette. Right behind her came Life and Death, squabbling as usual. She spotted Fate leaning up against a wall and sidled up next to her husband and kissed him.

"He was mine," Life said to Death.

"No. It said in the book he was mine," retorted Death in his leaden, gravelly voice.

"Oh, hi, Mum, Dad," said Life, in a summery voice.

"Mother, Father," intoned Death.

"So this is the bastion of freedom, our hope. This is what we have been working for, is it? Five sorry-looking souls, two of whom do not even belong here." Death looked at the five collaborators as he spoke to the room in general.

Akea looked up. He sensed something, but he couldn't tell what it was. He felt both cold and warm.

Chapter 18: Truth, Lies and All Those in

Between

The Watchmen's headquarters on Threadneedle Street had a squalid look about them. The offices were upstairs, their rooms soundproofed. The kitchen was next to the offices. The dungeons were located under the buildings. The Patrician had offered them funds to clean the place up, but their leader had declined, retorting, "Thank you, your grace, but I don't see my men wanting flowers and wallpaper and stuff; it gives off the wrong atmosphere. Perhaps a new kettle and a better torture chamber, but not cheap pine furniture. We are mean men."

Morguhis loved his job. The woman on the steel surgeon's slab had been raped by five of his favourite men. Perks of the job, he thought to himself. The cell was warm, and the blood-smeared walls told the whole story. Next to the implements of pain, a large CD player sat on a small table near the main table. Bright, dazzling lights hung from the high ceiling. Morguhis got a knife and cut a line from the woman's sternum to her hip line, then across at the top and bottom to form two flaps. The woman screamed herself hoarse. He grabbed the exposed internal organs and squeezed and pulled. The woman screamed and screamed. Morguhis turned on the CD player and played his favourite piece of classical music as he tugged and squeezed the organs in time with the music, in a symphony of screams. She died before the first movement was over.

Morguhis showed no signs of remorse over the death of the woman—perhaps a little disappointment that she hadn't lasted longer. He cleaned himself off and went to his office.

The only light in the dim office came from the PC. Morguhis poured himself a cup of coffee and then leaned over the computer and printed out the report explaining why "three group" had not returned. He had sent a scout party to find those lazy dogs, thinking they were probably eating doughnuts. He sat down at his desk and switched on a lamp. As he read the report, he spat out his coffee. The crumpled remains of Higgins could only just be identified; Billinger had been shot in the head, Jones and Macanese mutilated, and a decent van destroyed. On the plus side, three adults and four children had lost their lives in the struggle.

Morguhis laid the report down on his desk and looked up as a tall figure in a shabby travelling cloak entered the office. The figure stepped up to the desk and lowered the hood of his cloak. It was the Patrician. This was very unusual; the Patrician would never normally be seen here. Perhaps that explained why he was dressed incognito instead of in his usual grand regalia.

"Ah, Morguhis, I see that you have met our friend Akea."

The Patrician read the night's report upside down as he sat down in the chair opposite Morguhis. The screams from the dungeons below lightly permeated the air, accented by the smell of blood.

"I see that they kicked your—what's the word? Oh yes, your arse—again. How many times were you going to let this happen before coming to me? Ninety-seven families over the last three months have gone missing, if my sources are correct. You and your damned pride. It is a predicament, and that is why I am here. Do you think I would let you run around the city unchecked? Give me some credit. You are supposed to be the most evil and sadistic man alive, yet it seems that this Akea is making you look like you couldn't fart your way out of a paper bag."

Morguhis recovered quickly, considering. "Sir, what do you suggest?" He thought to himself, I got your cards marked, arsehole. You are going down.

The Patrician continued as though he had not read Morguhis's thoughts. "We are going on a trip. Pack an assortment of weapons—pistols, semiautomatics, machine-guns, rocket-propelled grenades. We have a bit of training to deliver." He handed Morguhis a blue travelling cloak. "Please put this on."

Morguhis donned the cloak, and they walked out of the office. Outside they went to the supply store at the rear of the building and picked up two crates of supplies and requisitioned a nondescript van. With the Patrician at the wheel, they headed to the border post. A keen guard recognised the Patrician but gave no sign as he inspected the false ID and waved them through. After hours of driving through the countryside, the Patrician turned left down a dirt track with the forest growing on either side, a scratch in the rage of greenery. When the van could go no further down the rutted lane, they got out. The Patrician went to the back of the van and pulled a semiautomatic pistol.

"Morguhis, we have some unfinished business to take care of."

"What the fuck are you talking about?" said Morguhis, looking a bit perturbed. He surreptitiously undid the safety catch of his revolver.

"My dear man, you are an imbecile at times. If I wanted you dead, it would have happened in the middle of the night, or maybe I would have had someone slip poison in your night-time hot chocolate." The Patrician tucked the semiautomatic into his waistband. "Help me with these crates. We are going to see a man about a gate."

The Patrician picked up one crate and started to walk. Morguhis picked up the other and followed. Half an hour later, they reached a run-down hovel. Dishevelled curtains hung in the dirty windows, and the odd tile had slipped from the roof. Outside the front of the hut was a large, flat dais centred in a stone circle. The door of the cottage creaked open, and Morguhis saw a man who looked to be ninety years old come tottering out. He was bent double over a thin walking stick, and his long white beard touched his ankles. The Patrician pulled his semiautomatic from its hiding place, but Morguhis beat him to it. The old man fell on the floor, a single bullet hole in his forehead.

"Welcome to your new headquarters," the Patrician said to Morguhis. "From this place, we will travel between the realities."

The Watchmen leader looked utterly bemused. This meant that the Patrician, the leader of the city that had outlawed magic, was a magician. The Patrician stepped forward into the stone circle and placed his crate on the dais. He beckoned Morguhis to join him. The Patrician spoke the words *patefacio mihi* to the stones. *Patefacio mihi*. The stones shuddered and moved slightly, and a soft, light blue aura formed around the flat dais.

Stepping from one reality to another was not a pleasant experience. Morguhis felt like he was in one of his nightmares, the one with the everlasting corridor that got smaller and smaller. He squeezed his eyes shut. When he opened them again, he and the Patrician still stood on the dais, but everything seemed somehow different.

For one thing, the air was fresh and clean. Morguhis coughed; he was not used to it. The grass was a brilliant green; the sun warmed the air.

"Come on," urged the Patrician. "We must meet a person five miles from here; we do not have much time."

They marched in total silence. The Watchman was overwhelmed by the beauty of this place; it did not sit well with him at all. Morguhis missed the screams, the blood and the pain. It was hell in paradise.

They endured an hour and a half of serenity and tranquillity. It was easy going, because the Patrician had levitated their crates so they bobbed along in the air after the two men. They came to a glen, where a gentleman sat on a small chair near a fire, enjoying himself. He got up as he saw the travellers approach.

"Ah, Vaxihimler. How good to see you, and on time. Oh, you brought some presents." He turned to Morguhis. "Where are my manners? My name is Vandavor." His appearance was similar to that of the Patrician, except for his smile. His smile was cruel, very cruel.

"This is the watch leader, the one I told you about," said Vaxihimler to Vandavor.

"Would you like some coffee?"

"If it is all the same to you, we would prefer to get this over with. We do not have much time."

"Always straight to business; oh, well," said Vandavor.

They wandered through to a secluded valley, and there in the middle distance stood the most disgusting things the Watchman had ever seen. Daisies! Daisies and pansies. I mean—bloody daisies, he thought. He thanked the lords of three hells they were being crushed by a horde of mean-looking creatures.

Vaxihimler took in a sharp breath when he saw the beauty of the dark elves and dwarfs, the men and the trolls. "Vandavor, you have done well, well indeed."

Vandavor gave a wicked smile, which was not becoming to his courteous face, but showed his true character.

Vaxihimler turned to the Watchman. "This army, Morguhis, will win back the city. Like you, they will be under my control. You will no longer have free reign. Get used to it."

As they walked forward the horde became an army of thousands, column after column of soldiers, lieutenants, captains and generals. It was quite a sight, with the different colours and insignia of each band of creatures. Each band had their own terrible weapons, horses, war hogs, elephants, siege weapons, big guns and sharp pointy things that hurt a lot. The camp smelled of hunger, the lust for war.

Amalthea sat in a big tree; he tried to conceal himself as best he could. His horse was tied up somewhere nearby, but hidden. He had been reconnoitring the enemy's forces and activities. Vandavor had met with the leaders of each species and settled the terms of engagement.

The leader of the elves was one Nessa, a mean female with long blonde hair and erotic take-me-to-bed eyes. She had a tall—almost six feet—lean figure and cold, cunning, long, slender fingers that were deftly quick with the arrow. She was more at home with psychological warfare, and backdoor rather than front-door attacks; she would snuggle up to you, kiss you on the cheek and poison your beer.

Gosuxm was the leader of the trolls because he was the biggest and meanest. He was nine feet tall and almost as wide; skulls of defeated enemies hung across his bulky chest like a gruesome sash. His favourite weapons were a blunt sword and a crossbow fashioned from the remains of a ballista.

The leader of the men, Jroed, was a big burly

brute. Tribal tattoos covered his arms and most of his upper body, but even his six-foot-seven-inch frame looked puny against the mass of the troll. He had an anatomically correct figure, which would not be shamed in a body-building contest. His mean, green eyes looked this way and that. Like Gosuxm, Jroed was also at home with a crossbow and quivers of arrows.

The dwarfs and their leader Tmedar in particular preferred the quiet of their tunnels and mines. They seldom came out to play in such events, but the promise of riches and new mining rights had seduced them out of the darkness.

This band of evil had taken Vandavor, under Vaxihimler's sponsorship, months to bring together. Nothing was going to stop them now. Vaxihimler had offered new weapons, better ones from the other reality. He'd had to use some caution: Magic and technology do not mix well. Imagine a troll negotiating the fine controls of a Sherman tank through the winding streets of Upper City. However; they had been supplied with and taught how to use guns, rifles and such.

Unseen, Amalthea counted their numbers from his tree. As he climbed down, a twig cracked, and the lookouts turned their heads and started to investigate. Amalthea slipped away and climbed onto his horse with as much stealth as he could manage, but the lookouts spotted him. Shouts rang out. Arrows shot overhead and just missed him; he bent low on the horse and whispered to the animal, "Fly with all your might."

He put his hands into its mane, said some choice words, and the horse reared and leapt like a speeding rocket, heading for the gate Vaxihimler and Morguhis had left just a few hours before. The little brown equine streaked through the forest near the glen. A band of mounted men raced after him. They were catching up. "Come on, faster," Amalthea cried to the horse. "We've got to get to the gate." The creature leaped forward, its muscles straining with the effort. The pursuers slowed as Amalthea reached the gate and climbed off the horse. There was no time to feel pain, no time to feel anxieties, no time for fear. The horse collapsed and breathed its last breath; saving Amalthea had cost the brave creature its life.

Tears were rolling down Amalthea's eyes as he spoke to the stone circle. As he stepped through the gate and was sucked through to the other side, he hardly noticed the discomfort. The stones shuddered and moved into place, and a soft light hung around the flat dais.

On the other side, he spirited around the stones, calling the ancient rites passed down from generation to generation. The gate was sealed for a generation.

Vaxihimler arrived at the gate a full two minutes later.

He shouted the incantation, *"Patefacio mihi."* Nothing happened. *"Patefacio mihi,"* he screamed again at the top of his voice as he pounded and kicked at the stones. The gateway would not budge, and it was miles to the next gate.

Returning to the camp, Vaxihimler called the leaders of the troops to him. The four leaders swaggered up to him. They stood around him in a circle, hands ready on their weapons.

Vaxihimler fumed at Jroed for lack of competence failure to take the situation seriously, for allowing the spy to escape. "Where were your guards, your lookouts? You were in charge of security. You will pay for your mistakes."

Jroed laughed. "I doubt that a man of your stature

can hurt me."

As the words fell from his mouth, Jroed fell on the floor screaming, crying like a baby. The Nessa, Tmedar and Gosuxm looked at each other and then moved forward to rush Vaxihimler. Instantly all of them were rolling on the floor in pain.

It was terrible pain, indescribable. It was as though someone had injected a large syringe full of molten metal into their arms. The fiery agony coursed through their bodies. Then they were trapped in a box, with millions of tiny, unseen, antlike creatures eating them alive. Only Nessa was not affected as the others, she had screamed as the molten lead poured through her veins but did not have the hallucination of the ants. Tmedar and Gosuxm frantically scratched at themselves, ripping deep scratches in their faces and bodies. Vaxihimler leaned over them as they writhed on the ground. He placed a knife in the hand of Gosuxm and a piece of glass in that of Tmedar and watched as the two clawed terrifying wounds into their bodies, trying escape the ants. Soon they were covered with wounds of self-mutilation. Then all of a sudden, the nightmare was over.

Vaxihimler sat on the floor for a good minute, enjoying the screams and moans and groans. Morguhis had a tear in his eye; he had missed this. Vaxihimler ordered the leaders to tend to their wounds. They had one hour to break camp and be on the march. Vaxihimler said to Vandavor, "We have a five-day march, and hardly any rations."

Chapter 19: Those Who Watch the

Watchmen

It was Nellis's turn to cook. He prepared some curry and rice, a recipe he had picked up on his travels. Later, Akea sat with Amanda, Nellis, Prometheus and Juween and enjoyed the after-dinner lull. The evening weather was cool but not chilly, and the company was comfortable.

Amanda tapped the table, contemplating thoughts. She got up from the table and went over to Juween and Prometheus, "I need some fresh air, I need to talk to you both."

"What, yeah, why not," Juween stretched and got up.

"Coming," Amanda thought to Akea.

Akea got and followed them outside and sat next to Prometheus. "Any idea what's going on old bean?"

"Yes, but I am not telling you", Akea said as he watched Amanda walk up and down the little bit of yard.

"Come on out with it, I left a beer in there it getting warm", said Juween.

"I am pregnant, we are not sure how it will work," Amanda said slowly.

"Hey Prometheus your going to be a granddad, sure your not too young, old bean," said Juween with a big grin on his face, "Congratulations you two, wow, this is good news."

Prometheus just sat there looking in to the middle distance; Fate walked into the yard and stood in front Prometheus. "They cannot hear, nor see me, keep your expression blank, try not to look you are talking to someone, say nothing." Prometheus gave gossamer of a wink of comprehension.

"This of course is a unique event. But if argonath give birth in the second reality, she will have a clutch, if she gives birth here, she will have a still born abomination," Prometheus winked again.

"They are dragons, do you understand?" with Prometheus's wink, Fate was gone.

"You alright, Prometheus, you ok, Prometheus," Juween said looking Prometheus.

"Yes of course, congratulations my girl, I can see you are worried, not to worry, not to worry".

"What, of course I worried, what are going to be like? Can I keep changing? Are they human or dragon, how long will it take to come to term?"

"I'll get drinks, is it ok to tell Nellis, he is practically part of the family," said Juween. Akea nodded.

Up till now Akea didn't say much, of course he knew, the same thoughts had been going through his mind too.

"Argonath my dearest, I know that the unborn are under your protection therefore under your spell, so to speak," said Prometheus still a little bit dazed by Fate's little conference.

"You have to trust me, I can't tell you why but-"

"What did I miss," said Nellis coming though the door.

"I am pregnant, I just wanted some advice."

"Well done congratulations, ah I see Juween's got the right idea," said Nellis as walked over to Juween and helping himself to some of the wine, Juween had brought out.

"Don't any of you get it, am I dragon, Akea is human, what the hell is going happen?"

"Ah, that's the oddest part isn't it, if give you birth, in your home reality, they will be dragons, if it happens here, well don't give birth, ok. I can't pretend

259

to understand, but I just know, the magic in the second reality is strong enough to develop the eggs."

"How do you know?" said Akea.

"I can't tell you, but I know it will be ok, just trust me old bean," said Prometheus, as he said this he thought to himself, one day Akea is going to work it out that Fate is on his side, then the crap is going to hit the windmill.

"Argonath my lady," Nellis bowed slightly, " if Prometheus said its going to be ok, then its going be alright", said Nellis, who up till now tried to keep out of their affairs, but over the last few weeks, he had gotten really close to them.

Amanda seemed to calm down a bit, these human feeling are really started to get to me, she thought.

"If we make through the war, we will all go to second reality and settle there," said Juween, he looked at Akea, Akea was weeping.

"What's the matter, son?"

"Home, families, children, settling down, who would of thought it, us."

"This war has to end some day," said Juween.

"Come on mate, this is a happy time, you are not alone. You got us to do the baby sitting and such. Lest you won't have to change the nappies," said Juween.

Akea sighed, "Can I have some wine."

Amanda laughed the tension draining from her.

"Akea I want to go for a hunt."

"We better check on our friends, on the way" Akea finally said.

"Spoiling for a fight will not redeem our cause," Juween reminded Akea. "Fight the good fight. Guerrilla warfare may not win any course."

"Be daring, be vigilant. Coward!"

Juween smiled. "Akea, you are my son, take my wisdom: Don't fight every fight."

"Okay, Father." Saying it, it felt weird to Akea. As far as he could remember, he'd never had a father.

They sat still for a while longer.

This time Amanda broke the silence. "Are you okay, Akea?"

"Yeah, sorry. Look, I'm not spoiling for a fight, but we do need to make a stand."

"Do you want to come with me to the forest while I do some hunting? I have itchy claws. I need some air," said Amanda.

For some reason, the mention of this gorgeous woman hunting food like a bird of prey gave Nellis the shivers.

*

Mary was a fine girl in her mid-twenties. She never really got into trouble and always went to church. She was walking home from a prayer group before curfew in the cool night air, when four hooded men in dirty jeans started walking quickly in her direction. This normally would not be a problem. After all, who owned the streets? But Mary smelled something, something wrong. Before she could get her can of pepper spray out she was cornered.

"Your father couldn't pay, so, um, he promised us, well, um, you," said the eldest looking of the youths.

Argonath had been flying with Akea on her back, to the forest. They were flying under the cover of night, gliding quietly just below the clouds, when Argonath noticed a single woman being followed by four hooded persons. Akea saw it through her eyes.

"*Let's go and help!*"

"*Spoiling for a fight? I know your thoughts, Akea.*"

"*I want to strike fear into the hearts of those who want to abuse the innocent*."

With a soft thud, the pair landed, near an alley not more than fifty feet behind the four men. Akea climbed down off the back of Argonath, and she took off again. Akea stood in the mouth of the alley, under the dull yellow glow of a nearby streetlamp. A slight wind ruffled his black cloak. Moving silently further down the alley, he watched the four men approach the woman. The hooded figures rushed Mary. When Mary tried to scream, a hand quickly covered her mouth. The men pulled her back towards the alley and into it. Holding her arms and avoiding her knees, the four lads taunted her and described in detail what they were going to do to her.

"Your father owes the Watchmen money. They sent us as a reminder," said the leader.

Akea had heard enough. He glided like a ghost from the shadows and stood behind the youths, facing Mary. The sight of Akea's orange eyes scared the life out of Mary, and she wriggled more and more, wild fear in her eyes. She knew that she was going to die here, now, tonight. One of the gang turned his head to see what Mary was looking at. He saw something, a figure coming out of the dark; it was hard to see him. The youth pulled out a knife and turned to face the foe head on. The others by now had realised what was going on. They forgot the girl and faced Akea, staring at his eyes. "Oh great, we're going to have to kill him too," muttered the leader. Akea and he were of similar size, although Akea was slightly shorter. The boys circled Akea, like hyenas circling their prey. Mary started to run, but a hand grabbed her, whipping her round.

Using the girl as a shield, the leader spoke. "Can't you see we're busy?" He peered more closely at Akea.

"What's wrong with your eyes?" Then a look of recognition crossed his face. "Oh crap, you're the one from the border, aren't you?"

"Jove, we better leave," said the second in command, who stood just behind the first boy's shoulder.

"Yeah, right, Cail. We can take him—he's unarmed," the leader retorted.

"You haven't seen the footage, have you?" said Cail. His face had taken on an ashen pallor.

"So what? You some sort of coward?"

On the last syllable, Jove shoved Mary into the third youth's arms and rushed Akea with his knife.

Suddenly the knife glowed red-hot. It fell to the ground and landed in a puddle, smouldering and hissing. Jove dropped to his knees screaming, holding his knife hand with the other.

The third youth pulled a gun and held it shakily in Mary's face.

Akea spoke to the weapon. "Amitto of vestri vires, commodo curvo."

The weapon acknowledged the request and curved out of the way. The barrel melted as if it were made of lard; black metal dripped on the floor. The owner dropped it, and the gun made a clang as it landed on the ground and then went back to its original shape. The youth picked it up again, but as soon as he touched it, the gun started to melt.

"What did you do to the gun?" queried the startled youngster.

"I asked it not to take part in this." Akea spoke in a calm voice, almost bored.

"What do you want?"

Akea pointed his index finger at the youth's knee, which was just visible behind the girl. *"Lux lucis telum,"* he whispered.

263

A silver-coloured arrow shot from Akea's finger. It zinged straight through the knee, smashed the kneecap, took out the inner ligaments, and scored the bottom and top of the femur and tibia respectively, leaving fragments of bone in the exit wound.

The boy was in agony, pain—real pain. His knee was on fire. He screamed and fell prostrate on the floor, near his fallen gang member. The other two looked at each other and then at Akea, and bolted, running as fast as they could. Akea didn't bother to try and catch them. For the first time he turned to Mary. He asked her if she was okay, but she just stared at him in shock. Her eyes were wide open, and she had scratches and cuts over her face and arms. She stumbled backwards until she hit the side of the building and then slid down the wall and started to weep. Akea turned to the two youths. He looked at their wounds and spoke soft healing words. The wounds stopped bleeding.

Akea asked them who had sent them.

Cail explained that he had broken into the Watchmen's server and searched their hit list, looking for a target.

Akea asked for the IP address and codes. "Or would you rather I just handed you over to the Watchmen?" The boys agreed shakily, and Akea touched the medallion around his neck.

In the hideout, Juween felt the warmth on his chest and turned to Nellis.

"Get on the phone to the rebel base, they will have visitors," said Juween.

Akea used torn strips from the youths' coats to bind and gag them. Argonath had been circling the area looking for Watchmen. Sensing that the fight was over, she landed softly near the alley. Akea helped the girl onto Argonath's back. Argonath was not too

264

pleased about this; she was not a taxi service. He looked around to check if the coast was clear. Then a blue light illuminated the alley, and Akea the dragon grabbed the young men in his front claws and took off. He flew high over the city towards the rebel base and landed at the base entrance, right behind Argonath.

Akea dropped the youths roughly on the floor, and Argonath gently slid Mary off her back onto the floor. They transformed quickly to human form and walked towards the door. Akea touched the keypad near the door and looked into the video camera.

"Ah, Akea; we've been expecting you," said a tinny voice.

The huge door cracked open slowly. The rebel guards came out.

"Please take these two into custody." He pointed to the man-boys. He then turned to Mary. "Please be careful with her. She has had a traumatic time. We would like to see the elders."

The group marched through the tunnels towards the council chambers, the fluorescent lights marking off their progress. They had arrived outside the chambers and Akea was about to knock on the door, when Nalik, accompanied by fifteen guards, approached from the opposite end of the tunnel corridor and surrounded the group.

"What's the meaning of this? Oh, it's you. I thought I could smell a stench," said Nalik. His face displayed utter repulsion.

"Oh, my chest, my chest—Mummy, Mummy, that dragon ripped a hole in my chest. Now go away and play with your delusions of grandeur," said Amanda. She rather enjoyed her perception of human sarcasm.

Akea spoke to the guards and tried his best to ignore Nalik, who fumed quietly as Akea commandeered the guards and gave them instructions.

"These two were a group of four, but two got away. They tried to rape the girl. They know how to get into the Watchmen's server. Interrogate them and find out how they did it. The girl's father is in trouble with the Watchmen. We need to know who and where he is.".

"You will not ignore me!" bellowed Nalik. Amanda moved towards Nalik with murder in her eyes.

The door to the elder's chamber opened, and Iral stepped out.

"Ah, Akea and the lovely Amanda. How can we be of assistance?" the councillor asked, trying to defuse the situation.

"They came uninvited and dropped off some prisoners, undermining my authority," said Nalik indignantly.

"Nalik, please, if you don't mind, I was not addressing you," the elder rebuked Nalik.

Nalik continued to fume silently.

Akea addressed Iral. "Sir, Amanda and I saw that this woman was in trouble. We saved her from four youths, two of whom got away. However, these two did not. We would like to interrogate them."

"My dear, where do you live?" the councillor asked Mary. "We need to tell your father where you are."

Mary answered, 'Sir, err, we live above the grocer's store on Alborn Road."

"Akea, would you go and get him?"

Nalik knew better than to argue with a member of the council. He turned abruptly and stomped away. The guards took the prisoners to the cells. Akea asked Mary to accompany him and Amanda and show them where she lived.

For the second time in one night, and in fact in her life, Mary climbed on the back of a large dragon. They landed quietly in her front yard. Mary dismounted and watched in fascination as the two dragons transformed into their human forms. As they approached the door, it opened instantly, and the anxious face of Mary's father Rowan looked out. He had been beside himself with worry. Mary had never been late coming home.

"Mary, where the hell have you been?" said Rowan, his emotion cascading out of him in a torrent.

"Dad, its okay, I'm all right," Mary said as she pushed herself into the strong arms of her father.

Amanda addressed Rowan. "Sir, may we come in? We do not wish to linger on the doorway—it will raise suspicion."

The grocer's store was the brightest shop in a row of innumerable dirty shop fronts on the quiet, unobtrusive street. Rowan looked Akea and Amanda up and down, obviously wondering if he could trust these strangers. After a slight hesitation, he let them in. Whether or not he could trust them, he had to. The neighbours would phone the police to rat on anyone, just for the money. They entered the hallway and climbed the flight of stairs to the flat above the shop. It was a small room, homely, with soft, cheap lighting, and it smelled of home cooking. Rowan would not let go of Mary. He eyed the strangers, and stepped back in surprise when he got a close look at their eyes.

"Four youths attacked your daughter. They suggested that you are in trouble with the Watchmen. We stopped them; we caught two, and the other two escaped. More importantly we are here to escort you and your family out of the city tonight. We do not have much time. You must trust us. I know this is a lot to take in. But we must hurry," said Amanda.

"I don't believe you. You come here and say that Mary has been attacked. How do I know that you are not from the Watchmen?" said Rowan.

Mary tried to interject, but Akea cut across her.

"Do you have a computer with Internet access?"

"Yes, of course, doesn't everyone? Why?"

"May we show you something?"

"If you must, but I don't know how that is going to help."

Rowan showed them the computer in the spare room. It was a cheap computer, old but looked after. It was the way of this part of town. They saved up to buy what they could afford second-hand, but pride never got in the way. Akea turned it on, hacked into the Watchmen's server, and showed them the list. As clear as daylight, the name *Rowan Harking* was there.

"I still don't believe you!" said Rowan defiantly.

Akea then broke into the CCTV server and showed Rowan the video footage of the attack on Mary. It showed Akea defending Mary and stopping two of the youths. This was enough for Rowan.

"Mary, huh . . ." Rowan sighed. "You better, err, you better get some clothes."

"You won't need much, just enough for a couple of days. Leave everything else. You have five minutes," said Amanda.

"We will be outside on guard duty. Please hurry," said Akea.

Amanda and Akea went out on to the street. A wind blew up, and Argonath took off and circled from a safe distance.

Five minutes later Rowan and Mary came out of the house. Akea noticed they had been sensible about packing, unlike some of the people they tried to rescue, who wanted to take everything. Akea chuckled as he remembered one bloke who wanted to bring a large flat-screen TV and another, a woman who wanted to bring five suitcases. Argonath had just growled at them, and they had quickly realised the folly of their ways.

"How exactly are we going to get out of here? Where's the woman?" said Rowan.

Mary interjected, "Oh, Daddy, you're going to love this."

"*My love, they are ready. Once more we risk all for the unknown few,*" thought Akea.

"*You romantic fool,*" thought Argonath as she landed in the road just in front of the shop.

Rowan jumped out of his skin when he saw a twenty-foot-long, blue grey, two-tonne dragon land lightly in front of him, but he quickly recovered his composure. "My lady, you are magnificent," said Rowan and bowed. "Shall we?"

"Do you mind, that's my wife!" said Akea.

"*Don't be too upset, it's the nicest thing, a non magical person has said to me. I love it,*" thought Argonath to Akea.

They heard the screech of wheels and the high revs of at least two cars.

"We better go. Mary, please climb on Argonath. Rowan, you can fly with me," said Akea.

"What?" said Rowan as he helped his daughter climb on Argonath.

The wind picked up, and a light blue light hung in the street, fighting with the yellow of the street lighting.

"Oh!" Rowan said as he watched Akea turn into a thirty-foot-long, red and orange dragon. He gingerly climbed on and closed his eyes.

Alerted by the neighbours, the Watchmen arrived

at the house just after Akea and Amanda had taken off. Akea and Argonath circled high up, and their passengers looked down as the Watchmen broke down the door and ransacked the flat. Up in the sky Rowan watched his beloved business and home burn to the ground. Akea did not linger, but flew straight to the rebel base.

*

The counselling office was nicely decorated, magnolia in colour, its walls hung with uplifting pictures of peace and tranquillity and lakes and mountains of far-off places. Obegetho was counselling a young man. This man had been coming for weeks, trying to reconcile why his wife had left him. Obegetho spoke soul-ripping, empty words, which did not heal.

"You must consider that you should become celibate." Obegetho loved this; he was enjoying abusing this poor, hapless, meaningless spit of a soul.

Fate consulted his book and watched as the fate of the young man changed. He had been destined to be a moderately successful software analyst, with a wife, three children, a dog and a cat, but now the words blurred and changed. He would be shunned by the religion and by those he thought were his friends. He would turn to drink and end up in the streets. He would die in his own effluence four years from tonight. Such is the fine balance of fate.

Obegetho spoke with his sickly sweet voice. The young man looked up; he had been sitting in the oversized chair crying into his knees.

"What? I thought the book of law stated that you're allowed to remarry if your spouse leaves you. I am only twenty-seven. How can you sit there and tell me I should be celibate? That is a fate worse than

270

death."

"Yes," Obegetho countered, "but you have ruined one marriage. What makes you think you will do better the second time round? You must be seen as righteous; you must wait for your wife to divorce you. You should give all that she asks for; after all, you don't want her to starve on the streets. "

The young man replied, "But she committed adultery. I am innocent. If I wait for her to divorce me, I will end up lying in front of a judge. I would be committing perjury. She is now living with another man in a nice house across town. And you want me to give up everything for her?"

Obegetho felt impatient. He began to show his true colours. "If you do not do as I say, I will go to each female member of the religion and tell them that you are a lonely, desperate man who is married and should not be trusted. You will be shunned from the religion and taken by the Watchmen for not going to the temple. You will hang for heresy."

"I've had enough. You can keep your jumped-up religion. I will take my chances with the Watchmen."

The young man walked out. And Fate made sure that he walked straight into Juween. Words in the book blurred again. . . .

"Oh, I am sorry," said the young man. Tears streamed down his face.

Juween looked at him. Fate nudged him. "Erm, this may be a surprise, but I was sent here to wait for you. I am a stranger. If you want to talk, I have a keen ear."

The young man looked at the old man. Oh great, now I'm being hit on by a pervert, he thought.

But Fate nudged him, too. the man looked at Juween's scarred features "Wait—I know your face. I've seen you somewhere."

Juween looked slightly embarrassed. "I have a

271

common face."

"No, wait, now I remember. You were at the border fight. Yes, yes—I remember now. You and that other guy took on loads of guards and stuff."

"Look, let's get out of here. There is a café over at Harbour Street. I will tell my story, if you will tell yours."

Ten minutes later, they sat in the coffee house, talking quietly.

"My name is Edward—Edward Erwin," said the young man.

"That's a strange name."

"Yes; my family were from another country. They moved here before the revolution. You should hear my grandfather go on about it."

They continued discussing things, the injustice of the religion, that now well-trodden story of the fight at the border. Juween spoke of the escape to the mountains, Akea and the fight for freedom.

There was lull in the conversation; then Edward spoke from his heart.

"I would like to join your fight, but I have no skills, except software programming." He looked disheartened.

Juween's eyes lit up. "We need more than fighters, young man; we need people like you, who can help with setting up the new system."

Juween explained to Edward that if he were willing he would be taken to a training camp, far from here, where he could start a new life. This was how the system was set up. The rebels found disheartened, frightened people, who would help in setting up the new order; they were screened and then sent to the rebel camp. Juween told Edward to go to Harpers Hardware first thing tomorrow morning and ask for a list of items, which Juween wrote down and handed to

272

him. "When the store clerk rings up the price he will ask, 'How is your mother's breast cancer? Is she still in hospital?' You say, 'Yes, she's in St. Anne's.'"

The training was hard; the rebel trainees had to endure many hardships. They were cut off from the rest of the world. Accountants, solicitors, editors, street kids, tax collectors, families like Rowan and Mary, housewives, blue collar workers, white collar workers, mechanics—it didn't matter what walk of life they stepped away from, they all came to this place. They were free, in a sense. They were here because they wanted freedom and had chosen exile. They trained in combat, surviving off the land, crowd control and communications. This was not just an army; this was the new way of things.

A small, wiry man with watery eyes, Enamyah was not malicious, nor particularly evil; however; he was greedy. He was an informer for the Watchmen. Not only did they pay well for information, but also he was allowed certain licence with imported items of a questionable nature. Enamyah was enjoying a cup of coffee when he noticed Juween and Edward come in. He could just overhear them. He listened intently to their conversation and waited until the pair left, then made his way to his own home and placed a call.

A growling voice answered the phone. "Macdense. What do you want?"

"It's err, err, Enamyah." Enamyah sounded a bit nervous.

"Yes, Enamyah," said the voice in a slightly sweeter tone.

"I have some information for you. If you bring money—and I mean lots of money—to our usual spot, I can tell you where to find one of Akea's followers."

"I'll bring a couple of friends."

The store had just opened when Edward Erwin

walked into the shop. Juween had given Pablo a rough description of Edward, and Pablo could see this man was clearly apprehensive. He carried an old and overfilled backpack.

Pablo went up to the man. "Can I help you? I am the storeowner."

This eased Edward a bit. "Err, I have to do up a friend's house. You might know him, he has nasty scars on his face."

Pablo leant in as though to pick up something from one of the numerous crowded shelves. He muttered, "Be a good lad and stick to the script, you are safe here."

Edward looked dismayed, as though he thought that he had just blown it. "Uh . . . I need the items on this list." He hastily handed Pablo the list.

"Ah, yes, I got these items, but you have to come to the back yard for the copper pipes, I am afraid. Pay up first, and we will get the things you want."

At the counter, Edward had to wait for what seemed an age. The customers in front wanted to chat or pay with change which kept dropping on the floor. The crying children two customers in front grated on Edward's nerves.

Finally he reached the head of the line.

"Ah, is that all?" asked Pablo.

Edward nodded nervously.

"How is your mother's breast cancer?" asked Pablo. "Is she still in hospital?"

Edward put on a sad expression. "Yes, she's in St. Anne's."

"That is a shame. If you would like to come with me, we will get the copper piping."

They went out the back, and Pablo led him to another door. He knocked, and a few minutes later Juween opened it.

"Good morning, Edward. Please come in."

Edward stepped through the door and followed Juween down the steps into the kitchenette. Edward noticed how bright it was down here. The tastefully done light blues and greens and the smell of coffee eased his hyper-tense nerves

Juween said, "Sorry for all the stuff we had to put you through, but we needed to see if you were watched. If you spent ten minutes in the hardware store we could see if there were any Watchmen about. Anyway, this is Akea." He pointed to Akea, who was sitting at the table with his head down. Akea lifted his head and looked into Edward's eyes and nodded. Edward had to take a step back when he noticed Akea's eyes. "I am afraid Amanda is out at the moment, but she will be back soon. This is Captain Nellis. Prometheus is asleep."

Nellis put his hand out and said, "Would you like a drink—tea, coffee, or something a little stronger?"

"I think a drop of whisky and a large coffee, if you don't mind. How safe am I here? I have been living on nervous energy since last night. What happens next?"

"That's it, lad, there is no bloody harm in a drop of whisky. I think I might join you. We are safe. Do you believe in magic, son?"

"No, not really. I know about the anti-magic law, but I thought it was foolish and antiquated law, just like so many of the others," replied Edward.

"We are a small group of magicians who live to set the city free. We are protected by magic. Only those who are invited can find us," said Juween. "Today you will fly out on the back—"

"Of a dragon. But Juween, I am not doing it again, I'm sick of it." Amanda had just walked in.

"It's okay, I will take him. We need to get Edward to a safe place, but first we need to find out how much

275

of a programmer you are. We have a special assignment for the person who can hack well and not be traced," said Akea.

"What the fuck are you talking about? What do you mean, fly me out on the back of a dragon?" said Edward.

"I am a dragon, so watch your mouth," warned Amanda.

"What's the matter?" said Akea to Amanda.

"I am sick of humans talking to me as though I am human, with no respect."

"I understand, it's just they can't see the two-tonne, majestic, fire-breathing, arse-ripping, sharp-tongued, beautiful, graceful bitch—I mean, lady of the sky."

"You smooth-talking bastard."

"Edward, believe it or not, she is a dragon, and it's best refer to Amanda as 'my lady'," said Akea.

"Look, Edward, I apologise. I am very unused to humans, and I am having trouble with their lack of respect," said Amanda.

"Yes . . . my lady. I am not sure of any of this. I find myself in a whole new underworld, and it's just culture shock. About this hacking business, how can I prove that I am your guy?"

Akea sat there for a while, thinking. "Let's see if Dr Drake is awake."

Edward raised his eyebrows.

Akea continued, "I will ask if he could monitor us. Then Edward, if you could hack into the Solberg bank and take a small donation, and then hack into the Watchmen's server and erase your details, I think that should do it. We will of course give you the tools and IP addresses. The rest is up to you."

Akea showed Edward to the living room and sat him at the computer desk. Akea turned on the video console and hooked up to the Internet.

Juween followed them in. "I thought you said that we should not hack from here again."

"Can I ask what happened?" said Edward. Now that he was facing a computer, he was feeling a little more comfortable. Hacking, now that was something he could understand.

"No offence but we don't know anything about you. We have taken a great risk in bringing you here," said Amanda.

"I don't need to know the details, but I might be able to help."

"I bounced this console off seventy servers, and they nearly completed a trace. We of course had IP maskers, and some top of the range counter intrusion programs, but they found us," said Akea.

"I suppose you weren't stupid enough to drop a logic bomb in the main server, causing DoS," said Edward.

"Err. In fact, yes we did," said Akea.

"I suppose Lars told you to do that. Look, I don't trust you yet, and you don't trust me, but you have to trust me. So let's cut the bullshit. I will hack into Solberg Savings and Loan and the Watchmen's servers. I will get whatever you want. If I fail then you can hand me over to the Watchmen."

"All of a sudden you're pretty cocksure of yourself," observed Juween.

"Who is Lars?" said Akea.

"Lars is Dr Drake, he is the leader of the Solberg chapter of the Elite. I am the second-in-command of the Ordeanian chapter. My handle is Silent Knight. I sat and monitored this store owner's communications while he was talking to Dr Drake."

Edward sat in the chair, went to a Web site, and downloaded a couple of small applications. "These are

277

better than IP maskers. This one will remove your MAC address completely, and this one will show the server its own address. Do you mind if I install them?"

"Go for it," said Akea.

Edward laughed when he saw the hacking programs that Dr Drake had provided. He deleted them all. He didn't bother to ask for permission. If they were serious about him then they are going to have to trust him.

He went to at least fifteen different sites, some commercial, some public and some private, and picked up fragments of applications and data. He then went to the site of a small utility company and picked a programme that would glue the fragments together. He installed the lot, leant back and cracked his fingers, and asked for more coffee with a dash of whisky while the console rebooted.

Akea sat next to Edward. He was frankly amazed. Edward booted the application that he had just installed, and Akea gave him the list of IP addresses. Edward laughed and screwed up the piece of paper and threw it over his shoulder.

"Look, can I be frank? Lars—Dr Drake—was playing you. I was watching him. He thinks he is good, but I beat him at a hacking fest, three times. He would love to get someone in Ordeania locked up as payback," said Edward. He shook his head, almost ashamed to be associated with Dr Drake.

Juween gave Edward some coffee. "Okay, motor mouth, put your arse online."

"*Are all geeks this arrogant?*" asked Amanda.

"*Yes, I am afraid so. Remind you of anyone?*"

"Shut your mouth," said Amanda, forgetting they were communicating silently.

"What?" said Edward.

278

"Nothing, I was talking to Akea. It's a dragon thing."

Edward decided to ignore what he couldn't understand. He nodded at the computer screen. "This is a backdoor. I know the person who made it, and he never told anyone."

He broke into the Solberg bank and created four new accounts. Then he wrote a small piece of code that collected the day's interest from two hundred large corporations. Akea had never seen so much money. Edward put the funds into a few new numbered accounts, and then moved it about. He went on to fudge the balance sheets. By the time he had finished, about 70 percent of the embezzled funds sat in a new account, amounting to about five years' salary for a high-powered lawyer or surgeon. Then Edward went to the Watchmen's server through another backdoor. He was particularly looking forward to this part of the task. He went in and hacked his way to the main database of all the population of Ordeania and found his name. He noticed that there was a link on it. He followed the link and found that he was due for execution in two days' time. He deleted the entire database, he deleted all the server logs, and then he deleted the system files. This caused the servers to crash. Then he went into the fire-control system and set off the sprinkler system of the building. As a final act he went to each of the servers that he had bounced off and changed the IP address of the logs to Lars's own personal Web site. That's payback, you bastard, for trying to set me up, he thought. He had figured out that Lars had given Pablo his own IP addresses.

"What the hell did you do?" said Amanda, who was sitting across the room but watching through Akea's eyes.

"What do you mean, what did I do?" said Edward.

"I watched you; you destroyed the Watchmen's server."

"How could you see that? You are, like, what—ten feet from here. I destroyed the server so that all the people who were on that list would be safe for a while. I got a list, if you want it. You know, do your thing."

"I have seen enough. We will take you to the rebel base; ask for whatever you need. I must warn you that if we find out that you have abused your privileged position for your own needs, Amanda here will want to know why," said Akea.

"Fine," said Edward.

Akea had noticed Juween had more than the normal amount of whisky. *"He's becoming an alcoholic,"* he thought to Amanda.

"You have just noticed? We've got to finish this before he runs out of liver."

"I guess he wants freedom, like the rest of us. He wants to talk to the trees again, poor bastard."

"Where exactly will that money go?" Akea asked Edward.

"Here and there. Look into your account in two days' time."

"But you don't know our numbered account," said Juween.

"I don't need to," Edward replied rather smugly.

Akea just shook his head. He couldn't believe this stroke of luck.

"Smug git. Well, thanks, anyway," said Juween.

"Honey," Akea said to Amanda, "you take a rest. I'll handle the transport this time." He turned to Edward. "Grab your gear and come with me."

Akea took Edward for a walk. They walked for

about thirty minutes, and while they were walking, Akea brought Edward up to date on the movement.

"We are going to end this in the few days. The city is finally ready to fight back," said Akea.

"How do you mean?"

"When we first started this, no one would come out and help. Now when we turn up the whole street comes out with weapons, ready to lend a hand. This of course makes our job a lot harder. We can't protect everyone."

"How do you protect them?"

"By magic, we can put a shield around the person or object we want to protect."

"How does that work?"

"We ask the air to become impenetrable; the people can breathe but no object bigger than gas can pass."

"Oh, I see. Can people move about? I mean, does the shield follow them?"

"It's harder to protect a person, because they are moving about. I can protect about ten people, but because of the power, control and concentration it takes, I can't fight effectively."

After a few minutes Akea spoke again. "I am going to be arrested tomorrow; I am hoping the minister is stupid enough to call the Watchmen. I want you to monitor the temple and send out all the CCTV footage around the world. The rebels will give you what you need."

They walked down a back alley, Akea looked around, and a gust of wind came up and a blue light hung in the air.

Akea the dragon knelt in front of Edward. "Climb on."

Edward was completely amazed; he stood and stared at Akea. Then he grabbed his wits and his fear and climbed on. They took to the skies.

*

Pablo had a busy afternoon. He was looking forward to closing up. Suddenly everyone in the shop looked up at the sound of tyres screeching into the parking lot. A van stopped; the heavy armoured door slammed open, and four burly men armed to the teeth with guns, knives and meanness burst through the hardware door. They ordered everyone to get out of the hardware store. Out in the parking lot, the fifty or so customers stood and stared as the kind old man was taken away in the van.

Akea had just gotten back from the rebel base. He, Juween, Amanda, Nellis and Prometheus listened to the commotion above. *"Os ultra os,"* Prometheus said, and at once a small, gossamer window appeared in the thin air. The image of the hardware store appeared on it like a TV screen. They were horrified to see Pablo arrested and roughly hauled away. To Juween's surprise, Akea did not try to save him.

In the van, Pablo knew what was going to happen; he checked the secret hiding place in his shoe — luckily they hadn't checked there when they searched him inside the shop. The truth was about to die with him. It was suicide or hours, maybe days, of endless torture. The guards tried to taunt him, to get him to bring them to Akea. Pablo endured cursing, swearing, beating and being urinated on. No one was watching Pablo the moment he put the pill in his mouth. Fate made sure of it. Pablo bit hard on the pill; two hours later he would die. The beating was horrific, and Pablo fell into unconsciousness.

Back in the cellar, silent pandemonium had begun.

"I expected you to rush out and try to save Pablo," Juween said to Akea.

"There were just too many people watching. I could not protect them all and fight. Then all that we have fought for would have been lost. Pablo knows the rules and the cost," Akea replied.

"We don't have much time; we need to destroy everything and then get out of here. There are other hiding places," Prometheus cut in.

For all his power and skill, Akea could not save one of his best friends. The fact cut through him like a knife. Amanda sensed this; she moved closer and hugged him and kissed him on the cheek.

"We all feel powerless, Akea. But now is not the time to grieve. If you don't want Pablo to have died in vain, we've got to get out of here, now."

It amazed them how much stuff they had acquired in the last few months. The words *silens sanus* muffled any sound; the explosion, when it came, could be heard as a hiss. Everything was atomised; the computers along with all the books and DVDs were destroyed. They would get copies from the rebel base. They slipped through the city as silent as ghosts, invisible as the wind.

*

Pablo awoke in a small room, tied to a hardback chair. He realised he was wet through; someone had thrown a bucket of water over him. The more the torturers tried to get information out of him, the more he laughed. He was covered with burns, razor cuts and bruises; both his eyes were so swollen he could not see. His only remorse was that he would never again smell the green of grass or see the blue of sky. In this small room he fought his own war. Victory was his.

"Looks like time's up," whispered Pablo through battered lips, blood spattered everywhere.

"What was that?" the head torturer screamed. He

leant closer and slapped Pablo across the face.

"I hope the lords of the three hells show you the meaning of true pain." Pablo died with those words hanging in his mouth.

The hot, dirty torturer began to shake; he turned on his underling and started to beat, kick and punch him.

"Who frisked the prisoner? Why didn't they check everywhere?"

He used each punch to punctuate his words. Someone was going to pay for this stupidity.

They took Pablo's body and hung it in the main square to serve as a reminder to those who opposed the Watchmen.

Chapter 20: The Truth Will Out

Akea, Juween, Amanda, and Prometheus went to the main temple. It was an imposing building similar to that which Akea used to attend, some months and a lifetime ago. They walked in and sat at the back, trying to look inconspicuous. Amanda looked widely around. This was the first time she had seen the inside of a temple with her own eyes; the dragon in her could not comprehend the silliness of it all—the smells, the bells, the pompousness. It took awhile for Akea's and Amanda's eyes to adjust to the low light though their sunglasses. A large TV screen hung from the ceiling above the dais. It showed a picture of the Patrician, and then faded and was replaced by a live shot of the minister as he left his seat on the dais and stepped up to the pulpit. The sermon would later be broadcast on the government channel.

The minister faced the congregation and coughed; this was the signal for everyone in the congregation to shut up and listen.

"Good morning, ladies, gentlemen, boys and girls. For those who don't know me, I am Obegetho, the minister of this temple. Welcome. We start today with some songs of praise." He turned and resumed his seat on the dais. The cameraman stationed in the front near the pulpit turned off his camera and sat down. The image of the Patrician returned to the screen, and song lyrics began to scroll across the bottom as canned music filled the space.

The congregation sang about how good life was under this regime. Then the music ended, people settled, and the minister resumed the pulpit to share his pearls of wisdom. His image again returned to the screen.

"We have been hearing of this band—renegades, dangerous men—who are in league with dragons. Picking fights with the Watchmen, causing trouble, doing magic."

There was a sharp intake of breath from the crowd.

Obegetho continued; he knew how to work a crowd.

But people were no longer so ready to receive his message. Akea watched as a member of the congregation stood up and challenged the minister. "They saved my daughter from rape; they stopped her from being taken away."

Obegetho surreptitiously slid his hand underneath the pulpit and located the panic button he'd had installed there. The minister was not about to let this . . . this insurrection go on. "I must ask you to cease this treasonous talk. If you blaspheme again, I am sure the Patrician will hear of it and will have you taken away in the middle of the night. Do you want to go to the concentration camps?"

Akea stood up and took off his dark glasses. "Everyone, look at me. I tell you: do not listen to this liar."

The people near Akea gasped as they saw his strange eyes.

Obegetho's look of surprise was quickly masked, and his face assumed a benign expression. He slid one hand beneath the pulpit and placed his finger lightly on the panic button. "Akea de Silva, is that you? What a pleasure. It has been so long. I thought that the Watchmen had relocated you. How's your mother?"

"I am not Akea de Silva. He died. I am just Akea. Enough of the silver-tongued crap. As far as my 'mother' goes, why don't you ask her next time you visit the Watchmen?"

Obegetho had just noticed Akea's eyes. He

exclaimed, "Look at his eyes! He of the devil, he whispers lies, and he will come amongst you and devour your children."

Juween and Amanda stood turned toward the crowd. Amanda removed her sunglasses.

Amanda said, "You have heard what we have done over the last few months; do not be afraid anymore."

Another man stood up and said, "I heard he rides a dragon—is this true?"

Amanda said, "Yes, it is true that there is a dragon who counts him as a friend."

"Can we trust this—this dragon?"

Amanda's eyes flashed dangerously; Juween touched her arm.

Obegetho tried to gain control, but he had underestimated the power of curiosity. A young girl of no more than twelve stood up.

"I think there are two dragons. One's blue, that's the girl, and a boy, dark red with a burnt orange belly. They are so beautiful, why can't we see more of them, Mummy?"

The girl continued, "The dragon—I think it's the girl—well, she lifted my whole family out of the fire. The Watchmen tried to burn down our house."

The second man who had stood up interrupted, "How do we know the dragon didn't start it, or that the rape wasn't staged?"

A third man stood and said, "Phil, you're being an idiot. I saw them. The Watchmen—they started it. If it weren't for the dragon and Akea, they would be dead."

Phil sat down.

Juween said, "We're not asking you to fight; we're asking you to stand up when the time comes."

Akea left his seat and went up the aisle. He climbed the steps to the dais and walked over to

Obegetho and said to him quietly, "Why are you spreading these lies about me?"

Obegetho replied, "Because, you idiot, you are this city's best hope for freedom. You can feed these sheep anything; they will lap it up."

Akea said, "I have a message for the Watchmen."

Obegetho moved back from the pulpit and laughed. "Why don't you tell them yourself?"

Akea realised that the minister must have activated an alarm. He smiled and thought to himself, This shall be interesting. "Excuse me," he said to Obegetho, and ran back into the congregation.

"You with the video camera, please, could you place the camera to face the street outside? I want everyone to see this."

The cameraman hesitated, and then nodded and moved toward the back of the temple.

Akea then turned to Amanda and thought, *"Find me, I am yours."*

"Can you shield the building as well, or shall I get Juween or Prometheus to do it?"

"It could get tricky. I don't want anyone to be hurt. Tie up the minister and take him back to the base."

Juween shouted to the crowd, "Please step back from the windows. You can watch on the big screen. There will be loud noises, but you will not be hurt."

Akea walked through the temple with a deliberate step. He opened the door carefully and walked out into the daylight. The cameraman stepped out behind him, and Akea motioned him to remain just outside the temple doors. Akea strode out into the centre of the street and stood there, his eyes closed. He could feel the cars approaching. Twelve cars came hurtling down the road, skidding to a stop in the street and completely blocking the road. Each guard got out of his car and stood behind it. They stood transfixed for a

288

while and then opened fire on him. The shield around Akea and the building shimmered as the bullets bounced off it. Inside the building, people gathered at the windows, horror-struck as the Watchmen fired on an unarmed man. Some screamed as they watched the Watchmen fire round after round at Akea.

Juween shouted, "Please stay away from the windows. You can watch on the screen."

Most of the men had semiautomatics. Some had pistols. The captain of the Watchmen went to the back of his car and pulled out the biggest gun Akea had ever seen. Amanda's eyes widened as she saw this monster rear its head out of the boot. It looked like something out of a horror movie. Holding the high-powered rifle in his left hand, the captain leaned back into the boot and pulled out a rocket-propelled grenade launcher. He handed the grenade launcher to his second-in-command and then pointed the rifle at Akea.

"Kiss your arse good-bye!" shouted the captain.

Time slowed. Juween saw what was happening and quickly ran to Amanda.

"I'll put a shield around him. Prometheus can take the building, if Akea can capture the explosion and control it."

Amanda relayed the message not a nanosecond too soon. The captain and his right-hand man let rip. As the grenade from the launcher headed straight for Akea, the spray of bullets from the high-powered rifle bounced off him and against the building, and then off into the street. Akea moved and held out his hands as though to capture the grenade. As he grabbed it with his mind, the grenade exploded, and the pressure wave rattled and blew out windows all along the street. The car alarms had triggered on the cars that were left intact. In the middle of all this stood Akea.

In front of him was a cocoon of smoke and fire that he had formed. He made a hole at the top to allow the smoke to escape.

The captain shouted, "CEASE FIRE!"

"Akea, you are under arrest. Put your hands up," squawked someone on a megaphone.

"You have five seconds to comply. We are coming over to you. Put your hands down on the floor and spread out. You inside the building, if anyone comes out we will shoot, and then ask questions."

A rancid, noxious smell of sulphur from the guns hung in the mid-Sunday afternoon air. It took some time for the men to get to Akea—they weren't taking any chances, and the sheer volume of spent bullets meant the men were roller-skating more than walking. They eventually got to him.

Akea grinned mercilessly and said, "All you had to do was ask—I would have come quietly."

Amanda growled loudly, and left by the back door. Once outside, she transformed into a dragon. She could feel Akea's heart, wherever he was in the city.

A small girl had followed her to the back door and watched in horror as the woman turned into a dragon.

The girl ran back inside. "She . . . she is a dragon; that woman, she—she is a—"

Juween turned and spoke to the whole room. "Yes, that is correct: Amanda is a dragon. Phil, you are very lucky she did not eat you alive."

The police drove away, leaving the congregation bewildered. Was it safe to go outside? Juween tested it. He opened the front door, while Prometheus held a shield over it.

It was safe. Prometheus bound and gagged the minister, using magical binds, and took him away. Argonath circled the city, her lover's heart acting as a beacon. She felt him; he was safe.

She called to him, "*I won't leave you for long, I promise. Are you okay? A girl saw me change.*"

"*I am okay—but tired, oh dear.*"

Edward sat in the rebel base, at the video console; he had been watching the CCTV footage all day. He had stolen the video footage of Akea against the Watchmen. Now he was publishing this on a secure Web site where the world could see it.

A wily tabloid news reporter found it and raced it to his editor. It was going to make front page, the editor swore happily. "We could string this out for weeks. Find out who these people are and why the man was not hurt."

The evening news of a shrewder network picked up the story and showed the images in full. Soon, around the world, the truth about Akea was coming out, and the tide was turning. Governments convened on the subject. Never before in the history of this reality had such a small piece of footage caused so many disturbances. The world's eyes were now on a small country best known for its software and computers. Ambassadors from Solberg petitioned to see the Emperor. Fact-finding missions were conducted, countries who considered themselves world peacekeepers tried to get in on it. But no one who stood outside the borders of Ordeania was allowed in.

*

Amalthea screamed and rubbed his chest; he thought that his heart was going to explode out of his ribcage. He sat on the grass, in Juween's reality, and steadied his breathing, concentrating on peace. The previous five minutes had been just too much for a man enjoying his twilight years.

He grabbed his medallion and spoke the word *bellum*. The medallion glowed bright red.

The sister medallion glowed just as red and just as brightly. Outside of the temple, Prometheus grabbed the hot pendant and looked at it with a curious expression. Then he remembered: Hadn't Amalthea warned that Vaxihimler had been moving between the realities? This could mean only one thing: Vaxihimler has gotten reinforcements.

His thoughts were swimming; he needed to get a message to the rebels and then Amalthea.

Argonath came rocketing out of the sky, as if she had sensed that very request. She landed in front of Prometheus. Hundreds of onlookers gathered to gawk at the beautiful dragon.

"Ah, Argonath, my dear, you must send word to the rebels that war is upon us. We need help, and I fear we may not have much time. Then go and find Amalthea. He will be near the gateway. Sorry, my dear, but could you take this piece of scum with you?" Prometheus nodded to the now bound and gagged Obegetho.

"My love is in a cell in the Watchmen's headquarters, on Threadneedle Street. I fear that he may try and take on the lot."

Prometheus urged Argonath on. "Find Amalthea and take him to the rebel base!"

With that, she grabbed Obegetho in her front claws—she wasn't particularly gracious or kind to him—and flew off. Great swirls of dust rose as her immense wings flapped for lift. She circled once, and with a loud growl she was off.

Prometheus turned to Juween. "I think I have upset her. I know she is worried about Akea, but she has a job to do."

292

Juween nodded in agreement. "We must phone Nellis and tell him the news. Then we better get to Threadneedle Street before Akea does something stupid."

A nearby pensioner overheard the conversation. "Threadneedle Street, that's four miles from here—you can borrow my car."

Prometheus turned to the gracious man and smiled. "Thank you, sir."

They jumped into the saloon and drove off. Juween grabbed the mobile and called Captain Nellis. There was an eerie silence as they waited for the captain to answer. The silver family car drove steadily down Rosemead Drive and onto the main thoroughfare.

"Hello, captain—captain, are you there?"

"Yes," squawked the reply.

"We had a spot of trouble, and Akea has been taken to Threadneedle Street. Bring some men—we may need you. We will meet on Alabaster Way—you know where that is. And warn the rebels that Vaxihimler has reinforcements—we don't know how many or where they are. Argonath is on her way to the rebel camp."

"Oh, right, okay, I'll be there as soon as I can."

Chapter 21: Threadneedle Street

Juween and Prometheus sat in the borrowed car on Alabaster Street, waiting, waiting for ages. The sun shone high in the cloudless sky. The warm air hung in the car. Prometheus had rolled down a window. A Watchman patrol car pulled up. The Watchmen looked at them.

Prometheus said to Juween, "Move off slowly. I think we have been compromised."

The Watchmen followed along behind them. Juween accelerated, and the Watchmen gave chase. Juween drove this way and that, trying to shake them off.

Prometheus said to Juween, "Find an alley; we will have to deal with these two."

Juween turned right into a small back alley. The two got out of the car and started to run into the blind alley. It was darker here, and the temperature was a lot lower. The Watchmen got out of their car and gave chase. In seconds the Watchmen had the two cornered. They smiled with merciless grins.

"Run out of places to hide, have you? Where is that pathetic dragon of yours?" sneered one of the men. "Oh, I am going to enjoy killing you. I am going to gouge to out your heart and eat it while you take your last breath. Juween spoke in a clear and unafraid voice. "You will not hurt us; in fact, we are going to kill you."

The Watchmen were huge men with nasty glints in their eyes. They were covered in dirty clothes. The edges of their blackened, unsheathed, hunting knives glimmered in the half-light. Goaded on by Juween, the Watchmen turned to each other and smiled.

In a bizarre pirouette, all four men moved around, each trying to get an angle on his counterpart. Eager to inflict pain, the Watchmen moved first. Both Juween and Prometheus moved out of the away with lightning speed, and with pinpoint accuracy they launched their hands into the sides of their foes, punching their kidneys and rupturing them. The Watchmen faltered; the pain was unbearable. They could hardly stand. They all turned to face one another again. The Watchmen were dying from internal bleeding; even now their bodies were failing, shutting down. With their last breath, they lunged again at the old men. Prometheus saw it before Juween and jumped out of the way. Juween was a bit slower; a knife landed in Juween's ribs and broke off. He and the two Watchmen fell to the ground.

Prometheus went to his fallen partner. He closed his eyes and with his mind felt the blade in Juween's soft tissue. He tried to pull it out with his mind, careful not to do more damage. The knife slid out, and blood poured from the wound. Prometheus spoke the incantation *vigoratus,* but it was too late. Juween had lost too much blood. Covered in most of it, Prometheus staggered out of the alley. Passers-by stared at him, and there were a few screams. One onlooker cautiously approached the alley and peered down it. When he shouted, "Dead Watchmen!" a sort of cheer went out and the onlookers began to run away.

Prometheus got into the car and sat in the driver's seat; he closed his eyes for a brief moment and then called Captain Nellis.

Nellis answered the phone, "Yes Juween, I'm on my way."

"No. This is Prometheus. I am afraid that Juween has just died. I think we need to get him out of the alley and safe for a proper burial."

"Where, which alley?"

Prometheus explained what had happened, and where to find them.

"Stay where you are, we will come to you," said the captain, in a pseudo-calm voice.

Within minutes the captain and two of his men were with Prometheus, who for the first time looked extremely old. The blue fire had gone from his eyes. The captain took charge and ordered the men to find the body of Juween and transport it out of the city.

Prometheus stopped him. "No, no, I will put a freeze charm around him. When Argonath or Akea gets back they will take him away."

Two of Nellis's men carefully put Juween into a car and drove off. Tears rolled down the face of Prometheus as he watched them drive off.

Not too far away, Akea stirred. He felt the death of Juween, and rage boiled inside him. Argonath's flight path faltered as she felt Akea's anger. Recovering, she flew faster and harder. She landed on the ground near Amalthea and dumped Obegetho roughly on the ground, Amalthea had had the good sense to wait for her near the gateway. She told Amalthea that she had felt Akea's anger; they must fly to the rebel base at once. Amalthea climbed unsteadily onto Argonath's back; sharp movements made him sick. Argonath picked up to the squirming worm that was Obegetho. When the dragon took flight, Amalthea felt even worse.

In his office Nalik sat and surveyed the reports and drank some coffee. From the reports that had come in, it appeared that the tide of random beatings had changed. Perhaps my plans are working, he thought. He allowed himself a little grin. The office was warm, pleasant, and dim; Nalik didn't like strong lights. As he leant back in his chair, a voice on the intercom woke him from his stupor.

"General Nalik to the radar room. We have incoming," called the PA system.

Nalik got up from his chair and walked out of his office and into the main command room, a few steps away. "What is it, lieutenant?"

Bip, bip, bip sounded the radar. Nalik looked at the screen and saw a small object moving closer and closer.

"Sir, we have incoming, it's moving about 160 mph. Too slow for a jet. Maybe a propeller plane. There are no transmissions."

Nalik smiled to himself. Well, well, where are you off to in such a hurry? he thought quietly to himself. "It could not be a missile or rocket—it's too slow. It could be a bomber—yes, yes—it's a bomber." He felt an insane glee.

"Lieutenant, hail it. If it does not answer, shoot it down as an enemy bomber. That's an order."

Out in the sky, Argonath was flying hard. Obegetho was getting heavier. He would not stop wriggling, and she nearly dropped him twice—not that she cared particularly. As she approached the rebel base, a white streak came to meet them. She dodged it with a quick turn, but the heat-seeking missile circled back and gave chase. She swerved through the sky, and then slowed a bit, turned her head and let out a roar. A burst of flame engulfed the missile, and it exploded close to Argonath's tail. Another missile was right behind. It was too late to dodge the thing, and it slammed into Argonath. She rolled up into a ball, enclosing Amalthea safely, but dropping Obegetho, and plummeted the fifty feet to the ground. She landed hard and broke her left wing. Amalthea had fallen off her when they hit the ground. Obegetho lay under her, crushed. Amalthea stood up, dazed but uninjured. Rebel troops, which had emerged from the compound to watch the missiles, rushed to their aid.

In the radar room Nalik's heart lightened. He had taught them a lesson.

Don't piss on my parade, he was thinking to himself, when several of the council stormed into the radar room.

"What is the meaning of this?" shouted one of the councilmen. He grabbed Nalik, shaking him. "You've just shot down our greatest ally. We may now lose the war because of your incompetence and impetuousness. Guards, take this idiot away."

Nalik tried to protest, but the councillor cut across him. "Save it for your court martial."

"Will you please find out if Argonath is okay, and if any passengers were hurt? And bring Commander Bavlin," said the councillor to his personal aide.

The aide went away and within a minute was back. "Argonath is alive, but suffered from a broken wing. Amalthea was dazed but uninjured, and I saw what looked like a temple minister had been crushed in the crater. Amalthea said that Vaxihimler has an army and is moving. We may have eight days at the most."

Bavlin had arrived and stood next to the aide, bewilderment on his face.

"Ah, Bavlin, I am afraid the Nalik is no longer in command of this facility. I now give you the commission of commander in chief of operations. Please prepare for war. Oh, and congratulations, General Bavlin," said the council leader.

*

Far away, in the cells of the Watchmen, a man sat on his cot crying his eyes out. Akea had seen the

298

events through Argonath's eyes. He had felt the pain of Argonath's wing being broken. Slowly, an unfathomable rage gripped Akea; the walls wanted to step out of the way as he stood up. It was time. What he really needed now was control. He had to maintain control. He must not let go. The dimly lit room was filled with a brilliant blue. The door seemed to sense that Akea was going to leave, and the door was not going to stop him.

Akea stood in front of the door and opened it with his mind. With a loud, cracking explosion the door flew across the hallway, landing in a heap of molten, twisted metal. There was a pause, and then shouts, and the steps of Watchmen could be heard running down the passage. Akea walked calmly through the dark tunnel, passing small doors on either side. Screams and cries came at him from all around. He felt inside the cells, sensing the people in them. Then he stopped abruptly at a door. He felt a presence, a familiar feeling, a long lost memory. Cassandra was here, in that cell. He opened the door. The smell was beyond endurance. A normal person's guts would be heaving. Even the rats avoided this cell. On the opposite wall, the battered, beaten frame of a woman hung from chains. Barely alive, Cassandra lifted her head slightly to see who had come in.

"Akea," she said in a slow, deathly whisper.

Her head dropped, and she exhaled a long-drawn breath, her last. Full of sorrow and rage, Akea could control himself no longer. He pulled the bindings from Cassandra and held her in his arms. He tried desperately to hold on.

Akea felt the approaching Watchmen. He gently lowered Cassandra's lifeless body to the ground and turned to face the doorway as the first Watchman spotted him and dashed into the room, followed quickly by several others. Silver arrows shot from Akea's hands. The watchmen did not see what hit them. It was not hard to disintegrate them.

As he walked slowly up the passages, the cries of the prisoners within pleaded for freedom. But Akea knew that the safest place right now was in the cells.

So this is what it feels like, this is where madness begins, logic dies and truth is no longer a welcome guest. Only pain has dominion here. Hell is not a place; it is a state of mind. The depths to which one can plunge are not measured in feet and inches, but in miles and light-years. Here was insanity, a self-imposed, godlike feeling of megalomania; Akea had reached the soul-destroying point where life did not matter. But here in the midst of it all stood a young man. Shot at, fired upon, he held his own. Death walked with him, held his hand. To Akea it was surreal. He felt like a punch-drunk boxer winning the championship belt, the only soldier alive after napalm bombing, a mother watching her child dying.

Down the hallway and through the offices, enraged Watchmen charged at Akea, but they were just a blur. He felt them and destroyed them. Finally he got to the front door and opened the security door from the inside. As he stepped out, he was brought to his senses by a distant voice calling his name, and he came around as though from a trance.

Nellis and his men stood facing the building. Nellis ordered his men to move forward, but they would not move. Nellis moved in front of the men and stood by Akea's side. At this Nellis's men moved in and set point in the lobby. No one was getting out this way. Nellis, Akea and the small squad started their sweep of the building, moving from room to room. Gunshots came from every direction. Akea breathed slowly, and the world seemed to breathe with him.

He needed Argonath so badly it ached. It burned. He felt like he was dying.

He looked at Nellis. "Is it true that Juween is dead?"

Nellis was taken aback. "How the hell did you know? Yes, he is. He died fighting a Watchman."

Akea nodded. "And Argonath how is she?"

Nellis looked at him, perplexed. Then he got on the phone. "Alpha, this is Random Child. Have we had any visitors today?"

The reply was just as coded. "Confirm, Random Child, we have had a visitor, they fell, but okay, home goal, Code 49. 34."

Nellis looked at Akea apologetically. "It looks like we shot down your wife, but they are okay."

Akea roared; blue hung in the air. "And you expect me to help you, after you try and kill me?"

"All I can say is I am sorry that this has happened. I had no part in this. I hope that you will help me. Up until a few moments ago we were friends."

Akea mused at this. "Fine. I will help you, but know this: when this is over I will have my vengeance."

"No doubt."

Akea finally noticed the battle going on in the building. "Right!" he said. "One building coming up."

He calmly walked through the building and into the offices. He was looking for trouble, and he found it. Pockets of Watchmen tried to pick a fight, but lost. It was like watching a mad chicken taking on a wolf. The chicken knows that he is right, and the stronger—right up to the point where the wolf rips its head off. The Watchmen fell like lemmings to the slaughter. Akea laughed a mad cackle; this was fun. The darkness behind Akea's eyes rose up like a whale through the ocean of logic and wisdom and onto the surface. What was left of the inner walls was covered in bullet holes, blood and burn marks. The building had proved to be about as secure as Troy was, right before they hauled in a wooden horse. Akea left Captain Nellis to clean up the mess and make good.

Thanks to Edward, the CCTV, and a few passwords the word was out that a small force had taken down the Watchmen. Reporters, helicopters, and TV cameras swarmed the buildings. Captain Nellis had to do something. He arranged for a press conference for the late afternoon. He stepped out into the sunlight to face an array of cameras. The country might be closed off to the world, but journalism fought for its own freedom everyday. Reporters were sick of having their work cut and chopped in the name of censorship, and now was the time to fight back. Captain Nellis stepped up to the hastily constructed dais and cleared his throat. Akea stood a few steps behind him. Nellis began to speak.

"My fellow Ordeanians, allow me to introduce myself. I am Captain Nellis. I am in charge of the small rebel force which has taken over the Watchmen. We have no demands, nor do we hold anyone to ransom. We are here to stop the cruelty of the Watchmen. We want to see our noble country free from tyranny. Every one of you standing here today or watching at home knows of someone who has disappeared in the middle of the night, an aunt, uncle, mother, father, brother, sister. We have watched beatings in the street and been too afraid to help, thanking any god that will listen that it was not us. With our heads bowed, we walked past traitor's row. But now it has come to an end."

The reporters started to ask questions. One of the more belligerent of the reporters noticed Akea's eyes and called out, "What's wrong with his eyes?"

Another cried, "Will there be a war?"

"What will happen?"

"Was there magic involved?"

At the word *magic*, there was a gasp from the crowd. Akea stepped forward and tapped Nellis on the shoulder. Nellis moved back, and Akea took the mike. Before he could speak, someone in the crowd shouted, "He's that guy from the border fight years ago."

"Silence!" Akea bellowed.

The crowd hushed, frightened by the blue hue that had begun to become visible around him, but some of the reporters continued to shout questions. Akea pointed a finger at them and said, *"Silens sanus."* The reporters kept talking, but no sound came out. The crowd gasped again.

"You want to know about the fight at the border; yes, I was there. I'll show you if you like," said Akea. He was enjoying his moment in the sun. He pointed a finger in the air above him and said, *"Os ultra os."*

An image shrouded in mist came into view. At first the people did not realise what was going on, but soon the horrific scene became clearer. It showed from Akea's point of view the fight scene—two men standing all alone, with no weapons, being shot at by a small army. People cried out as Juween fall to the ground. Some of the crowd became physically sick when they saw Cruz's head. Everyone took a step back as they watched the silent death roll over the Watchmen.

Nellis tapped Akea on the shoulder and said, "That's enough."

The image faded and Akea again addressed the crowd. "To answer your question, I am more than a magician, I am an Ordeanian. I do not take rude questions kindly. We do not know where the Patrician is, or what he is up to. I suggest that you get ready for the worst; I will deal with rioters and looters myself. We have come here to save the city, and we will not have it ripped from us by greedy idiots."

Seizing the moment, Nellis grabbed the mike. "There are more men coming. This city is now under martial law. If we catch rioters and looters—well, you heard the man, and you've seen what he can do. There will be no more questions."

Nellis went back into the building and called the rebel base. Edward Erwin shone again, publishing the CCTV of the events on the Web site and then sending the address to the international community of online geeks and news services. The world held its breath.

Two men walked resolutely through the throng and stepped up and spoke to one of the rebel guards. Then the captain of the palace guards and the chief of police approached the first point set up in the entrance of the building with caution. At the door they held up a white flag, calling for a cease-fire. Captain Nellis allowed them entry to the first point. Akea delved their feelings and found no malice; whatever they wanted, it was honourable.

Captain Nellis spoke first. "What can I do for you?"

The captain of the palace guard was normally a pompous man, full of himself and obnoxious, but now he was quiet, almost timid. He looked nervously at Akea, who stood in the room, looking broodingly at him.

"Sir, we wish to join forces, become allies. It seems that the Patrician has betrayed us all. We want to fight alongside you—start afresh, as it were. Between us we command seven thousand troops."

Nellis had to sit down to gather his thoughts. He had never reckoned on this, and he had always assumed that he would have to fight these people.

He gathered his breath. "Sirs, please go with Akea; he will take you to the rebel base. There you will find orders and provisions."

The chief put out his hand to offer a handshake. "Sir, my name is Wellings, Chief Wellings."

Nellis took his hand and shook it. "Nellis, Captain Nellis."

"We will not need anything. In fact, we can provide weapons and stores, and we can also provide safe shelter for those who get stuck in the city."

Nellis smiled. "We have seven maybe eight days — that's all. Please go with Akea. He will not harm you, and in fact you might enjoy it."

Akea looked really pissed off at this notion. He thought, now I'm a taxi.

The three stepped back out the main door and pushed through the reporters and other onlookers camped outside the building. Akea led the two men to a small, clear area. He said the incantation *extraho vir*, and a light blue wind whirled around him. The captain and the chief stood motionless, shocked into silence by the thirty-foot dragon that now stood where a man had just moments before. For the first time in their lives, the reporters were utterly speechless.

"So the rumours are true," Wellings whispered to himself. Akea kneeled down, and they gingerly climbed on his back and clung to the armour plates, nearly ripping a couple off in their fear and nervousness. Akea felt the tugging on his plates, but he ignored it. He stood and flapped his wings, and soon he was soaring on the wind like a graceful eagle. How he loved this feeling.

His heart pounded as he raced for the mountains and the rebel base. Soon the base was in sight. At the entrance stood the council of elders. They had been warned about Akea's arrival and were awaiting him.

As Akea landed and moved toward them, he could see they looked sad and ashamed, but exhilarated. Akea stopped in front of the elders, and the captain and the chief climbed off, shaking, glad to touch terra firma.

"Where is she?" Akea roared. "Where is she?"

"She, err, she is in the forest clearing not far from here — and being attended to," Iral reassured him.

Akea roared again and flew off towards the forest.

Iral broke the ice. "Gents, I take it you want to help, and that you have met Nellis."

The captain and the chief looked at each other, utterly perplexed.

"I'll explain. The only way that you are here is because you have met with Nellis, and the fact that you came with Akea indicates you want a truce. Please come in. We have lots to talk about," said Iral. Then, as an afterthought, "Ah, my name is Iral, and this is Athel, Samond, Jisi and Hans."

Chapter 22: The United States of Mind

Evening was approaching. Akea circled the forest once and spotted a deer. He grabbed it and killed it. Then he went straight to Argonath. He landed and growled at the attendants to leave. Argonath was lying down on her side, her great lungs gently moving up and down. Her eyes were closed. Akea could feel her; she was only dozing.

"My dearest, I am sorry that I took so long."

Argonath opened one eye. *"Shhh, you had a job to do. Mmm, it seems that you are in more of a state than I am. You are in the wrong; it is not your place to seek revenge on my behalf. You should not allow grief to grip you. You must control yourself. Akea, how many lives have you taken today?"*

Akea had to think. *"I don't know; it's all a bit of a blur."*

"I tried to help, but you were too far away. All I could feel was pain, and insanity. Look: Akea, I love you, but you have so very far to go. Heal my wing, and I will take your burden."

Akea looked in her eyes. *"I love you."*

Then he wrapped his wings over her body and turned his face to look straight into her eyes. *"Capiam vestri poena, planto vos universus, capiam vestri poena, planto vos universus."* Bright blue took over the half-light of dusk, chased it out of the clearing and changed the locks. *Crack, crack, click,* and Argonath's bones moved into place. Akea screamed with pain. It was a struggle to endure the pain of Argonath's healing, but he continued to heal the broken bones. They lay there together as one.

"Right, let's see if my wing has truly healed." Argonath got up, stumbling a bit as though trying to stand up after a general anaesthetic. She growled at

307

her weakness. They took a few steps. Argonath flexed both wings. The injured wing ached, but it was healed.

"*After this battle, I want to go home, and not come back. I hate this place,*" thought Argonath.

"*We have to go back; you must give birth in our own reality,*" Akea thought back.

"*Yes, but we shall not linger.*"

Suddenly they shot into the sky. Free, they climbed and climbed—two miles, three miles, four, six, seven miles up. The air was thin, almost unbreathable; the coldness took what was left. "*Spiritus aer,*" Akea said, and Argonath gasped gratefully as life-giving air filled her lungs. She breathed flames over her body, freeing herself of the ice that had begun to form on her scales. Akea did the same.

"*Akea, give me your negative feelings, and I will take your burden.*"

Akea transferred it all. Argonath fell with the weight; it was like being shot. She plunged hundreds of feet before she recovered; the loss of Juween, the torment of Nalik, the pain of Argonath's wing, the hopelessness, the godlike feeling of slaughtering the Watchmen. It was huge. The blackness felt synonymous with singularity, infinitesimally small but with the density of planets. The roar echoed for eternity and then exploded. The rage, the insanity, the anger, the shame, the pity—the fire came out of her as if she could light the world. Akea flew down to her, and they flew together in ever-smaller circles, clinging together as they spiralled downward, their minds melded, an elongated teardrop rocketing to the ground like some obscure comet. Close to the ground, they broke apart, a firework of blue, orange, and red. They landed, converted to human form and hiked back to the rebel base.

*

Outside the main doors a patrol guard had been stationed there awaiting Akea in case he decided to turn up. The guards escorted him and Amanda to the elders' chambers, knocked on the door and left. It was not long before the door opened. They entered the room. The picture-lined walls were brightly lit, the air was warm and stuffy, and the room had been rearranged to accommodate extra chairs. The five elders at sat in their favourite chairs. To their left sat Amalthea, enjoying a nice cup of tea. In front of them sat the captain of the guard and the chief of police, who looked like they were attending a job interview.

"Ah, here they are, here they are; come in, please take a seat," said Hans, lifting his head from a deep discussion.

Akea and Amanda threaded their way through the crowded room and sat on the two remaining chairs. The soft lights and the smell of coffee and pastries soothed some of their anxiety.

Samond nodded at Akea and Amanda. "We will just bring Akea and the lovely Amanda up to speed. Amanda, my dear, this is Wellings, the chief of police, and Nordstrom, the captain of the palace guard. We have just negotiated a truce. They are on our side now."

Amanda sniffed the air and searched their minds, trying to find an excuse not to trust them.

"Between us all, we have thirteen thousand men. We can barricade the city and get people out while they still can. The temples and the palace can be used as refuge sites. But the most important question is, How are we going to defend ourselves? Captain, chief, any ideas? You have lived in the city longer than any of us," said Iral.

The captain of the guard spoke in a rather steady voice, considering he was sitting in the same room as Akea. "Sir, every fifty feet along the city wall there is an outpost, where a lookout will stand guard. The sirens will be moved to the wall. We expect the Patrician to come from the forest; the concentration of men will be at that point. We will put guards throughout the city and blockades—we will block roads and funnel them to one area to form a bottleneck. The Patrician will be expecting this and will use a double ploy; his initial assault will be a dummy—the real attack will come from the centre, and we'll be ready for him there."

"Good plan. What about weapons?" asked Jisi. He had been scrupulously helpful since Nalik's arrest.

"We have five hundred tanks and four hundred armoured vehicles. Every guard and officer will have at least a pistol, and most will have semiautomatics and RPGs. We have a large armoury, just in case."

"How's the morale?" said Iral

"Morale, sir?" said Nordstrom

"How do the men feel about the pending battle? After all, they are going against their leader and facing magic—something to be feared!" said Iral.

The discussion continued well into the late evening, Iral ordered food. Amanda being who she was wanted to go to and hunt. She made her excuses and left, though she continued to participate via Akea, demonstrating quite considerable input and wisdom, Iral thought. The experience of the Akea and Amanda thing really unnerved Wellings; however, he did have the good sense to keep his thoughts and fears to himself.

Chapter 23: Apprehension

At the end of the meeting, Iral accompanied Captain Nordstrom and Chief Wellings to the command room. As they walked into the room General Bavlin stood and greeted them respectfully. "Sir, how may I help?"

"General Bavlin, I hope your plans are going well. We find ourselves in good fortune and good company. This is Captain Nordstrom and Chief Wellings. They have considerable resource and are now on our side," said Iral.

The general put out his hand and shook the chief of police and the captain of the palace guard's hands in turn.

"Please come in to my office, if you don't mind, sir," said Bavlin.

"A good idea. Shall we?" said Iral.

They walked to what had been Nalik's office. Bavlin motioned to the elder to sit in his chair. The elder briefed the general on what was going on, and how to proceed.

"Sir, could I phone my men and brief my second? He's trustworthy. He helped me organise the weapon stashes, after I found out the truth about the secret history," said Nordstrom.

"Excellent. Please call me Iral."

The captain of the guards phoned his second-in-command.

"Palace guards, Hopkins speaking," said the voice on the other end of the phone.

"Hopkins, this is Captain Nordstrom, code: 4563654, password: Sunshine."

"Sir, yes sir, where have you been?"

"Never mind that. I want you to listen very carefully—time is short. I want you to assemble the battalion leaders and inform them that we are now in a state of war. I want you to set up a network so that all the guards can hear the briefing. We will be there in—" Nordstrom turned to Iral. "How soon can you get me back to the palace?"

"Akea can fly you there in half an hour or so."

"We'll be there in forty-five minutes. I will be landing at the front of the palace, and I want it sealed off," instructed Nordstrom.

"What about the Patrician? No one has seen him for weeks. What do you mean—land?" asked Hopkins.

"Don't concern yourself with the Patrician. All things will become clear in the briefing. You have your orders." Nordstrom put the phone down.

Iral grabbed the microphone for the PA system and told Akea to meet them at the base entrance in five minutes. Chief Wellings phoned the police station and had a similar conversation.

At the entrance to the base Akea and Argonath, with Prometheus on her back, waited for the others to arrive. They didn't have to wait long.

"Excellent, excellent," exclaimed Iral. "My lord and lady, please, could you take these two to their respective headquarters and assist in the briefing?"

Nordstrom climbed on to Akea's back in front of Prometheus, Wellings climbed on Argonath's back, and they took off, Akea headed for the palace and Argonath for the main police station.

Akea landed in front of the palace, where the battalion leaders stood to attention as Nordstrom and Prometheus climbed off his back. Although the palace guards were a well-disciplined group, there was a general gasp as Akea returned to human form.

Nordstrom gave an aide instructions to set up the main canteen for a meeting and told the men to muster there in ten minutes. When he, Akea, and Prometheus arrived at the canteen, most of the chairs and tables had been rearranged to face the back wall. A white board stood to one side. Nordstrom told the canteen workers to make ample coffee and then leave. When the canteen staff left, Nordstrom cleared his throat.

"Gentlemen, we are now as you may have heard in a state of war. We are at war with the Patrician, who has acquired a considerable army. Our sources tell us he will be here in eight days. Now I want to tell you about Ordeania—not the official history, but the secret history." He went on to explain the how and some of the whys, about the Patrician and the Watchmen. Each person present sat there listening, wondering. No one really countered the augments. To most, perhaps the majority, it made sense.

"This is Akea. He is the main fighting force in the city. Today he took on the Watchmen and defeated them. This gentleman here is Prometheus." Nordstrom pointed to Prometheus, who stood in the corner out of the way.

"Oh, so you're the leader of the fighting force. I do apologise, your worshipfulness. Remind me to bow to you when you get home. Oh . . . where is that, exactly?" thought Argonath. She had landed her cargo at the police station and was listening in on the speech making at the palace.

"It's about time you gave me some respect, peasant," Akea thought back, and smiled.

"We are going to coordinate with the police force and the rebel army. The city is now under martial law. We have to get as many of the citizens out as possible. All able-bodied civilian men will be invited to join the effort. The hospitals and essential utilities along with their staff will have to stay under heavy guard. We will be in constant contact with the police and the

313

rebels. I will assign each of you to your post. I will see each of you in turn. Dismissed."

The men got up and milled around the canteen, drinking coffee and speaking in low tones with each other.

As Nordstrom walked away from the centre of the room, Akea pulled him to one side. "Captain, may I make a request?"

"Yeah, sure. What do you want?"

"I need to commandeer some of the palace, not much, but we need a base for Nellis's men, near the back courtyard. We'll need accommodations for thirty to forty men. I want you to assign some guards. I will need to talk to them before I leave."

"Not a problem, Akea," said Nordstrom. He turned and shouted, "Attention! Zetterberg and Fraser, front and centre."

The two men walked up to Nordstrom and saluted sharply. "Zetterberg, Fraser, find some rooms for Akea near the back courtyard, and set two groups of four guards. They are on guard duty and they are not to leave their post until they are relieved."

"Gentlemen, I want you to relay this information to your guards; my wife and I and thirty-two others are going to be staying in those rooms. There will be two dragons—yes dragons. You must have seen me change from dragon to human. It is vital that you treat them with respect, always. And I mean *always*. Call them 'my lord and my lady'. Treat them as though if you pissed them off it would be the last thing that you ever did. Do I make myself clear?" said Akea.

"Sir, with respect, which is which? I mean which is the male and which is the female?"

"Bloody humans," Argonath thought from across the city.

Nordstrom butted in. "Fraser, stop being an idiot.

314

You saw Akea arrive, did you not?"

"Yes sir," replied Fraser.

"The female is a lovely blue grey, and I change into a red and orange. If you still can't tell the difference, the female is slightly smaller, with a softer expression."

"*You bastard! That's it Akea, I am so going to get you,*" thought Argonath. "Wellings has just finished his briefing. What about Nordstrom?"

"*He has finished, my love. We better let Nellis know about where his new base is.*"

"Captain Nordstrom, I believe that the police have finished their briefing and are ready to coordinate with you. Please, could I contact the rebel base?" said Akea.

Zetterberg and Fraser looked at each other as to say, how does he know that?

"Not that it's any of your business, but it's a dragon thing," Akea answered their looks.

*

Nellis had driven a large troop carrier through the border unhindered. It felt strange, just to drive through the border and not be stopped and searched. He had picked up his men from their hiding places and taken them to the main gate of the palace. Akea met him there and showed him the way to the back courtyard. The rooms were large and grand. It made a welcome change from the lofts and basements the men had lived in over the last few months.

*

When the rebel troops had entered the city two days ago, they had tried to organise the exodus, but it could only be described as a mother of a stampede which hit the gates of the city—all except the gate facing the forest to the west, that is. Millions of people tried to leave, and a good number died in the crush. This was animal rules now; civilisation had kissed the city good-bye and run away. However, there were acts of extreme bravery and kindness. One couple jettisoned all their belongings from their estate car and picked up as many stranded people as they could pack in. People like these, ordinary people, were the real heroes. They gave up everything just for a stranger in need. Two days before the battle the place was quiet, real quiet. Those who could not get out were moved to the safest, out-of-the-way buildings. Volunteers, the reserves, the last hope, armoured themselves with what they could find and the desperate hope that things could change. Akea and Argonath could not do much; there were just too many people.

*

Akea and Argonath reconnoitred the city. From high up they could see the different troop movements. They were looking for holes in the defence or potential soft spots. Travelling now in broad daylight, without the need of the cover of night, it was the first time Akea and Argonath had seen the whole city laid out below them, with its massive surrounding wall and its four gates—north, east, south and the western forest gate. Inside the wall ran a sort of no man's land, a piece of land a mile wide where the civilisation had stopped. The forest lay on a tangent, a rough line running five miles from the forest gate to the north gate. The forest was accessible from the south gate, but the journey would take several hours by road. To the north and east inside the city wall stood the mighty financial district, a myriad of faceless, monolithic buildings, standing tall like trees, defiant against all around, imposing, obnoxious and tasteless.

The geography of the city could only be described as an economic map. The richest lived near or in the financial area. Moving across the city, the buildings and homes became gradually more modest and small until one reached the southwest corner, known locally as the "slum pit." In some parts of the city the population had ventured into the no man's land, especially in the south-western slums. In the centre of the city stood the four grand palaces and impressive parks, which served as the crossroads for the two main roads that cut through the city and dissected it into quarters. Temples dotted the city; there were at least two per district. Shopping districts and malls dotted around the bigger retail parks, which were situated near the outskirts of the city. For the most part each house had a garden or at least a backyard. Akea began to wonder how he was going to defend the whole city.

Argonath could sense Akea's feelings of helplessness. She flew in a little closer to him. "*Akea I know your thoughts, you don't have to defend it all. We have thousands of soldiers to do that. We are here to make sure that the rebels win.*" They flew back to the palace and informed the rebels of their findings and, having debriefed, took off again to find food in the forest.

There was a certain something in the air. The whole city smelt of fear, as though each person in the city perspired it. It was the day before the anticipated battle, and the city had been barricaded as best as possible. Last-minute changes were being hurriedly made. There was not much more the rebels could do except wait. Clocks everywhere ticked slowly towards the impending doom or glory.

Prometheus sat in his room with Amalthea and discussed their plans.

"We better make ourselves available where it's needed, don't you think, old bean?" said Prometheus.

"Yes, I concur, Bunny, but if we run around, going from one disaster to the next, we may be too late for everything."

"Well, then, I'll take the forest gate, if you don't mind taking the north and east gates," said Prometheus.

"I tell you what, I'll start there with you at the forest gate and then go off to the north gate. We better talk to Nellis and see if he will let us have some transport of some sort," said Amalthea.

"Between you and me, old bean, I am afraid. We have planned and plotted. But have we done enough?"

"Bunny, my brother, we have Fate on our side. We are the oldest and wisest. We have done our best. But to be honest, I am a little scared, too. What is it you told me? The right man in the right place . . ."

"Not quite. 'The right man in the wrong place can make all the difference.' That is what Fate had said to me."

*

On the way back from their hunt, Akea and Argonath noticed a large troop marching slowly through the forest. Thousands upon thousands of them, marching in bands; the two dragons could see large siege weapons and catapults, wall-breaking crossbows, war elephants, trolls. Akea flew down for a closer look. Then he noticed it, a small group of soldiers, maybe five or six hundred strong, and in the lead was a man surrounded by a big group of bodyguards. The Emperor, he's here, Akea thought in horror. The pair flew directly to the palace and went straight to Nellis. He was sitting in a meeting room with his new comrades Chief Wellings, Captain

318

Nordstrom, General Bavlin, Amalthea and Prometheus. Akea burst into the room without knocking.

"Excellent, you are all here. We were flying in the forest, and we saw them."

"Who, what—the Patrician?" asked Wellings excitedly.

"Yes, of course the bloody Patrician. It wasn't exactly a herd of deer," said Amanda.

"*Calm down.*"

"*Bloody humans; as thick as bricks, some of them.*"

"We saw thousands of them marching, about thirty miles inside the forest. They have siege weapons, trolls, elephants. The fucking lot." Akea was not his usual self. He seemed frightened.

"If the Patrician is coming from the forest, he could launch a two-pronged attack, one on the forest gate and another on the north gate," speculated Nellis.

"We think we saw the Emperor, too. He has a small force about five to six hundred strong," said Amanda.

"Ah shit, that means he has brought the special forces. This means they got something up their sleeve. Damn it!" said Nellis. "Akea, I am afraid you may have to deal with them."

"Look, it's getting late. We have done all that we can, we are well prepared.

We must get some sleep," said Prometheus.

Book Four: The Retaliation and Retribution

Chapter 24: Knock, Knock

Early morning brought warm sunshine and clear blue skies. To the west of the city, in Delwiderlen Forest, the Patrician and his army camped, ready for the first wave. One group of dwarves had already been sent through the forest to the northeast of the city. Vaxihimler and Vandavor now stood amongst the dark elves, breaking them into squads of twenty. They would try to sneak one squad of elves into the city to disrupt things from within. Next the remaining elves, the men, the dwarfs and the trolls, with their siege weapons and elephants of war, would be dispatched. They had spent the previous day chopping trees down and collecting boulders. Vaxihimler had petrified five-foot tree trunks into stone. The men greased up the trebuchets and long-range ballistae, immense crossbows that fired five-foot-long, wall-breaking bolts. Vandavor used magic to sharpen and harden the arrowheads.

Limath the Emperor entered the glen, and Vaxihimler bowed instantly, while Vandavor stood still in defiance. Vaxihimler threw a look of scorn at Vandavor.

Vandavor said, politely and with a stubborn look, "He may be your boss, but he is not mine."

Limath smiled. "I see. You can call me Limath if you like, but only for today; the next time you see me, you will call me Master. I have provided, as I promised, some of my best men. I assume you have a plan. I will send my troops with the frontal assault, but not in the first wave. I will stay here and coordinate matters. I assume that you have a decent communications centre, spies and such. Show me."

The three commanders walked to the communications hub and entered the tent. The soldiers stood to attention. Vaxihimler waved a hand and went to the large folding table in the centre. It was covered with maps and plans. The three men looked at the maps, huddled together in quiet discussion.

"My lord, we will send a small troop of elves silently into the centre of the city, and attack the front at the same time," said Vaxihimler.

"How exactly are you going to do that?" said the Emperor.

"Now that the border is open, I shall send a squad of twenty elves via the south gate. They can fight their way in if they have to, but I hope to get them in undetected," replied Vaxihimler.

"Really, Vaxihimler, you are an idiot. I have a better plan. You have the *Nacrotave*, I assume?"

"No sir, I gave it to Vandavor," said Vaxihimler.

"Please, may I borrow it from you?" said the Emperor to Vandavor.

As Vandavor went to get the book of spells, the Emperor pulled Vaxihimler to one side. "Why did you give that book away? For god's sake, Vaxihimler, have you lost your mind? I have serious doubts about you; you seem to be more moronic than ever."

"Yes, my lord—I mean, no, my lord."

"Well, explain yourself."

"I wanted Vandavor to be on our side; it seemed to me that he craved power. So I gave him the book as an enticement. That doesn't mean that he's going to keep it. I will deal with him in my own time. And there is more than one copy. We will not be unevenly matched."

As Vandavor re-entered the tent with the *Nacrotave* the Emperor and Vaxihimler looked up and abruptly stopped talking. Vandavor smelt treachery.

"Ah, yes, Vandavor. Please, could you put the book on the table, and open it to page 594?" said the Emperor.

Vandavor placed the heavy tome on the table and carefully opened it. Limath leaned over the open book. His lips moved slightly as he studied the text. Then he turned to Vaxihimler and instructed him to muster the first squad of elves.

Vaxihimler assembled the elves, and the Emperor walked out and stood in front of them. He drew an oblong in the air with his first finger, calling out the chant that he had found in the *Nacrotave*. *"Cuspis ut cuspis via foris."* Blue light followed his finger, and light blue smoke emanated from the light, forming a smoky oval that stretched from ground level to shoulder height. Limath called out a set of geographical coordinates, and the smoke simmered and faded to reveal the image of a dark alley not far from the power distribution centre inside Ordinea City.

Vaxihimler ordered the squad through the magical entryway, and the twenty elves stepped through. The doorway closed behind them, first the long sides and then the top and bottom, with a slight pop.

The twenty dark elves would spread out and strike, hitting critical points throughout the city. The surprise assault was the spearhead of a larger attack. Just inside the forest to the west of the city, trolls, dwarfs, human infantry and the remaining elves were poised, ready to follow. The capture of the west end of the city would open an avenue of attack straight through. Vaxihimler expected the unmotivated, poorly led city guards who were defending the city just to melt away.

Captain Seadak, the burly, six-foot-seven rebel commander of the city guards, had trained in all forms of war and combat, though he had not seen battle. He had been waiting for this day all his life. The guards wore heavy grey armour. Cumbersome and hot, the armour would protect them from medium-sized artillery. The guards had been given the best weapons. Men strong enough to wield medium-sized machine guns and mortar cannons stood on the four outpost turrets guarding the west gate, two on each side gate. The gate was thirty feet high and five feet thick and was made of oak and heavily studded with spikes. The arch stood another twenty feet above the gate. Along the perimeter of the twenty-foot-thick wall, some thirty feet in front of it, large tanks had been positioned. Their cannons were primed, and their engines roared.

Captain Seadak walked the fifty yards between the turrets and steadied his men. He knew the brunt of the attack should be here. His clear green eyes scanned the horizon. He scratched his beard and looked at his men. Each one he had served with; each one he knew well; each one didn't want to be here; each one hated this post; yet each one stood his ground, burying his fear.

Seadak put his radio to his mouth and selected a channel.

"This is not about us. This is about our children having a home, knowing freedom. We stand here and fight for freedom. If we die, we die for what we believe in. That is our glory. This is our time. If they're going to kill us, let's give them bloody hell first. I want all of you to fight like animals, and fearlessly as dragons. And tomorrow our children will be free."

The men stood and saluted him. The guards of the forest-facing towers hated their post. Nonetheless they stood their ground. They watched the forest for any sign, the slightest sign of anything. The sun rose slowly into the sky. The clouds wandered along.

The calm before the storm is the worst time for a soldier. This time was spent in solitude for most, as they sorted out their thoughts. Some tried to talk to each other. But the conversation was short. Someone brought breakfast, and most of it was eaten. The younger soldiers tried to keep to themselves. Soon the early-morning sun shone brightly over the dark cloud of gloom.

The eight-foot-tall trolls, with livery of skulls and large clubs that dragged on the ground, stood in the glen, their dark hides shimmering in the sunlight. Next to them, about half their size, stood the burly dwarfs, covered in chain mail and long beards. Their helmets were made of wrought iron, finely decorated, and each held in one hand a semiautomatic gun adapted to fit his stubby fingers and in the other the traditional battle-axe. Contests and arguments started as the eagerness of war heightened.

About half a mile away the men of Vaxihimler and Limath stood silently. Limath's men were dressed in fine, light brown shirts and trousers with black body armour. Each man carried four grenades, a large automatic weapon and a vest full of pockets filled with the small items of war. These men prided themselves on having the best of everything and not wanting for anything. Vandavor's men wore green and grey. Coming from the second reality, they were hard to see except in broad daylight. They had body armour and large automatic weapons. Each carried a small pistol attached to his belt, and a piece of strong fabric was taped to the top of each boot bearing the blood type of the soldier who wore them plus two symbols, showing if they were allergic to the common painkillers or if their organs could be donated if they fell.

The captain of Limath's men moved forward and approached the captain of Vandavor's.

"I am Dorus, captain of the high guard of the Emperor Limath," said the first.

"My name is Thalis. I am captain of this rabble from the second reality," said the second.

"Might I enquire about the fabric tape on your boots?" asked Dorus.

"Whenever a man gets shot, the medic can deal with him, without asking dumb questions," replied Thalis.

"You seem ill equipped; we could give you more provisions," said Dorus.

"Thanks, but no. We have what we want," said Thalis. "I think it's gonna be awhile before we are sent off. I am going to relax my men. If you please, would you let them mingle?"

The men relaxed a bit and chatted to each other in the early-morning dawn. In the command tent, Vaxihimler got the signal that the elves were in place and ready. Vaxihimler called on the radio to the trolls and heavy weapons, and the charge signal went out. He turned to Vandavor and announced that battle had commenced at 6:30 a.m. as planned.

By 6:35 a.m., Vaxihimler had launched his trebuchet and ballistae at the forest gate, and targets inside and outside the city had been hit. Vaxihimler's men attacked along multiple axes. One group of trolls and dwarfs and elves advanced along three of the four routes to penetrate the city and seize key objectives, including the palace, the city section headquarters, the artillery unit compound and the city prison. The

325

second group, made up of dwarfs, struck from the northeast through the small village of Butruis, to ambush and prevent anticipated rebel reinforcements from interfering.

Just outside the city wall, Captain Nellis ordered the tanks to take aim and fire. *Boom, boom, boom!* Depleted uranium shells hurled through the air towards the elephants and blasted them apart. Vaxihimler's army were startled, but remained in rank. *Boom, boom!* More shells came hurtling towards them and blew the men apart. One shell took off the head of a troll. Vandavor laughed.

Inside the city, the twenty dark elves destroyed communications lines and attacked critical points. They were trying to get to the main power station, but they had been stopped about a half-mile from their goal. Akea and Argonath patrolled the city, spotting elves and alerting the guards. Small skirmishes broke out, and within half an hour the twenty elves were overrun and none remained.

Prometheus had joined the guards at the forest gate just before dawn. During a brief lull in the fight he stood on the wall and looked at the sun rising slowly in the sky and noticed it was still early, maybe seven o'clock in the morning.

When Amalthea arrived at the gate shortly after seven, things had turned for the worse. Most of the top of the wall had gone. The mutilated corpses of men lay askew everywhere. Horror turned to rage, and Amalthea let loose spell after spell towards the forest. He shot down the large rocks and tree trunks that flew into the air from the forest. Then he ran to the nearest radioman, who was out of the way of the action, and ordered the man to contact the lead tank to aim for the lead three ballistae on his mark. Then he told the radioman to come with him.

Scrambling to the top of the broken wall, Amalthea held out his hands towards the ballistae; then he nodded to the radioman. The call went out. All at once fifteen depleted uranium shells hurtled towards the giant wooden structures. Amalthea concentrated hard and let loose a large fireball; it almost caught up with the shells. At once the ballistae exploded in a ball of fire, killing all the trolls and men within two hundred metres.

General Bavlin had moved four battalions of guards towards the forest gate. Vaxihimler and Vandavor stood together. As they spoke a spell, a large, red force of energy rocketed to the gates. *Boom!* The gate shattered. Most of the men behind it were killed, but a few lucky ones were only injured. The guard tanks moved to barricade the hole. They shot round after round into the ranks of the enemy army. The Patrician shouted the battle cry to charge. The tanks could not aim at the fast-moving troops as they rushed the gate and broke through.

Vaxihimler and Vandavor shouted their armour-piercing spells, and the ballistae and trebuchets threw stone logs and arrows at the tanks. The armour could not withstand the force. There were many casualties. The ruined tanks filled the sky with blooms of smoke. The dwarfs slaughtered the survivors, and the remaining trolls under the command of Limath moved forward and through the gate. The general call went out to any free rebel guards to bring aid. The guards near the western gate moved forward. Prometheus also answered the general call, running up to Amalthea's aid and bringing new strength, for Amalthea's strength was waning. Together they joined forces and blasted the enemy to pieces until the rebels were able to repulse the enemy and retake the forest gate.

Vaxihimler's units began to buckle, and their commander made a crucial decision. Instead of committing more men, he decided to withdraw. Vaxihimler saw the trolls were losing and decided to even the odds. Just outside of the forest, Vaxihimler said the incantation, and turned into a forty-foot-long black dragon, with two sets of silver-tipped spikes down his back. He'd had little experience as a dragon, but this was no time to be coy. He took flight for the first time. Circling the sky, he sought out rebels, swooped down and crushed them in his claws. Long trails of fire rained down on the rebel strongholds.

Limath had moved his men forward after the main attack. He stood in the glen smiling to himself. It was going well.

Chapter 25: The North Gate

Seadak's battle speech had come over the radio about half an hour ago. The troops on the north gate seemed worried, but not overly tense. After all, it was the smallest and perhaps the most insignificant of the four gates, easier to defend than the main forest gate. It was about seven o'clock in the morning when the lookouts first spotted the trebuchets and ballistae moving slowly towards them. In the distance they could see men, dwarfs, elves, and trolls advancing behind the heavy war machines. The city tanks fired up their engines and moved forward to meet the enemy. The trebuchets stopped and were loaded. The cannons of the tanks rang with the booms as the shells left them. Shells and rocks passed each other in the air. The enemy was still out of range for small-arms fire. The trebuchets carefully fanned out to reveal the ballistae.

A small company of city snipers hid in the turrets of the wall. They began to take out the men one by one, but there were simply too many to make a difference.

After more than an hour of heavy fighting, most of the tanks were destroyed, and the dwarfs moved forward, taking cover behind the dishevelled tanks. The fighting became fiercer as the morning wore on, neither side gaining or losing an inch. The captain of the guards called for more help. Akea and Argonath were requested to join the fray. Akea heard a screech and looked north to see a massive dragon attacking the gate.

Both Akea and Argonath took to the sky. They came round like a sky-bound locomotive. Fire shot from their mouths, burning the enemy. Akea met the black dragon head on. They clashed, claws ripping

329

into each other's underbelly. Akea got the Patrician with all four claws, leaving a long gash, himself suffering only minor scratches. They banked and faced each other again. Below they could see Argonath taking on the enemy.

Then all of a sudden, there was a breach. The dwarfs had managed to break through. Some ran straight for the towers and wall to secure them, while others stormed into the city proper.

"So this is the saviour of the city, is it?" the Patrician goaded Akea, watching the scene below with glee.

Suddenly Argonath came from nowhere, slamming into the Patrician, knocking the smile off his face.

"It's a pity you won't see the outcome," snarled Argonath.

Still reeling from the impact, the Patrician managed to sneer, "You're so cowardly, Akea, you have your woman fighting for you."

"Akea, you kill him."

"Move a little to the right."

Akea took a deep breath. *Sanus offensus,* his mind screamed. A roar of clear blue shockwaves emanated from him, knocking the Patrician over and over like a leaf in a storm. Recovering, the black dragon came right back at Akea, fierce fire escaping from his mouth. Argonath flew in the direct flight path, protecting Akea from the flame. It caught her right wing and burnt holes in the fragile membrane. With her left wing still weak, she struggled to gain height, but slowly, like sycamore seeds in the autumn breeze, swirled downwards. Smoke trailed behind her, and the smell of burned flesh hung in the air. Akea went to catch her. Like a rocket, he was there in an instant. Right behind them was the Patrician. Akea grabbed Argonath. *Contego,* he thought, and a light transparent

330

shield reverberated around them, protecting them from the searing flames.

The demons within, the darkness behind Akea's eyes, rage, anger and insanity, raised their ugly heads, foaming at the mouth like rabid dogs.

"Akea, Akea! No! Don't lose control. Give me your emotions!"

"I need them to fight."

"No you don't, you need me. Akea, don't let go!"

Akea kept a hold on Argonath as he brought his head round and looked at her wing. He spoke softy to her wing. The holes filled, Argonath flapped it, and Akea gently let go. Argonath dropped a few feet and flapped her wings. Their minds met once more. Argonath took over Akea's emotions and soothed him. She flew off and steadied herself far from the battle, but near enough to have an effect. Fire burning in his eyes and flaming from his nostrils, Akea flew up to meet the Patrician once and for all.

"You're a putrescent mass, a walking vomit. You are a spineless little worm deserving nothing but the profoundest contempt. You are a jerk, a cad and a weasel. I take that back—you are a festering pustule on a weasel's rump. Your life is a monument to stupidity. You are a stench, revulsion, a big suck on a sour lemon!" said the Patrician, hate blazing in his eyes.

"Wow, and we were getting along so well, too! The question is, why?"

"I found a prophecy written five hundred years ago by a great seer, who saw the destruction of a leader of the city by someone who did not belong there. This upstart would bring about change—a new world order, ruled by dragons. So I sought you out, tried to make you comfortable. Rebellion is not born from contentment. But something went wrong. And now it

331

is time to end this."

Akea ignored the last taunt. He banked to the left and then up, like a rocket trying to touch the sky. The Patrician followed. Akea whispered the charm to fill his lungs with air and heated the ice off his wings. The Patrician, not having had the experience, did neither, and he began to become dizzy. The ice was heavy on his wings. Miles from the ground, he suffered vertigo and started to panic.

Akea grabbed his opponent in his claws and dragged him as high as he could. Then, without warning, he swept back his wings and flew straight down. The Patrician, in sheer panic now, clawed, bit and thrashed. He could not get loose. The sonic boom could be heard throughout the city. Argonath watched with terrified glee. The mass of fighting dragons fell towards the ground. The Patrician broke loose, but he could not right himself. Akea banked up to lose some speed. As the Patrician plummeted, Fate appeared midair, his clothes fluttering in the wind. He slowed time down.

"You never should have tried to cheat me. Now my family and I have conspired against you. You could have been a great magician, but you chose your own fate. This is your reward," said Fate. "The right man in the wrong place can make all the difference. Good-bye, Vaxihimler." Fate smiled a curious smile and disappeared.

Time regained itself, and the last thing Vaxihimler saw was the ground hurtling toward him. *Boom!* He hit the ground, and a large crater appeared. Bits of body, dust and earth flew into the air.

*

Vandavor laughed as he shouted, *"Extraho vir."* A massive black and purple dragon shot into the sky, and a roar of laughter, malice and power echoed across the city. The defenders of the city stood petrified as Vandavor swooped in dragon form down on the forest gates. He grabbed soldiers in his claws, crushing the life out of them. The soldiers on the ground ran for cover as their dead comrades were flung through the air like rag dolls. Great flames leaped from Vandavor's mouth, incinerating the gates and scorching the surrounding walls and catching soldiers on both sides in the flames. The smell of burning flesh, wood and paint permeated the air. Those too close emptied their breakfasts on the ground.

Akea was just recovering from his battle with Vaxihimler when he spotted Vandavor. He went after him, a bullet through the sky. *Bang!* His wings flared out and stopped him right in front of Vandavor. Argonath stayed safely back, weaving this way and that

"Per meus vires, iuguolo," screamed Vandavor, and a shock wave rolled towards Akea. It was unstoppable, armour-piercing magic, slower than a bullet but faster than an arrow. Akea was already weak from the earlier fight, and there was no stopping it. In slow motion relative to the speed of sound, the magic ripped through Akea's shield and exploded as it entered Akea, raping him of life, stealing that most precious of things. Amalthea watched from the ground, and managed to summon enough magic from somewhere to distract Vandavor. Argonath screamed; she was not ready for Akea to die. She was at Akea's side in an instant. She grabbed her falling lover in her claws and poured all her soul into his gaping wound. The terrifying cries of the battle receded as she flew him to her cave.

Limath stood and watched the events. The rebel force defence had crushed Vaxihimler's men's attack, and he had seen Vaxihimler fall to Akea. He had known Vaxihimler was essentially weak, but this Vandavor was something different. He knew that if things went badly he, Limath, had to help Vandavor.

Having drawn Vandavor's attention away from Akea, Amalthea ran as fast as he could to avoid the dragon's flames. He leapt into a gully that was too small for Vandavor to enter. Vandavor nearly collided with the ground, and shot up into the sky, roaring with frustration. Crouched in the ditch, Amalthea clutched at his chest. Pain, terrible, crushing pain, travelled up into his neck and along his left arm. "No," he screamed. With his right hand, he rummaged through his innumerable pockets, cussing the day he brought a cloak with so many pockets. He pulled out a small phial that contained acetylsalicylic acid, commonly known as willow bark. He gulped the infusion. The pain was spreading to his jaw. Soon he would not be able to speak. *"Patefacio cruor mores,"* he whispered with laboured breath. The willow bark thinned his blood; the spell opened his arteries. Blood flowed to the heart, and the pain subsided. He was still weak, and he felt sick and dizzy. He stretched out in the gully, breathing steady, slow, deliberate breaths, and concentrated on getting his heart to slow down. He thought to himself, this war is going to kill me.

Akea and Argonath entered the cave, and Akea crashed on the floor. For the first time Argonath spoke. "Don't you die, Akea, don't you dare. I, I love you." Tears rolled down her face. She spoke the incantation fiercely: *"Vigoratus, vigoratus, vigoratus. Vigoratus!"*

Slowly Akea's eyes opened. He felt different. He was home. Numbness took over.

"Akea." Argonath leaned over him and spoke the ancient spell: *"Ego mos non intereo vigoratus vigorous."*

The cave filled with blue and orange lights that danced on the walls, as Akea's life force entered into Argonath's soul. Her body rippled and roil as it changed colour and size and she became they. A silent boom sliced through time and space, and Diligo's immense form filled the cave.

Diligo stood at the entrance to the cave and took flight back to the city; the sonic boom recoiled around the mountains. A wave of debris from trees and the forest floor was sucked in by the vortex behind Diligo. The combined consciousness of the two who were now Diligo saw Vandavor in the middle distance, and their determination was fuelled by the images of the destruction that Vandavor had caused. They went straight for Vandavor. He moved to evade the mighty beast, but Diligo's tail smashed into Vandavor under the armour plates, in the soft part of his belly, leaving a long cut that healed instantly as Vandavor spoke the Latin healing incantation.

Both sides came round for another pass. Vandavor sent flame after flame at Diligo, but Diligo's shield was too strong. Diligo flew past for another swipe with the tail. Vandavor bit down onto the dragon's tail as it flew by, and Diligo responded with an electric shock through the tail. Vandavor let go and shook his head. Vandavor and Diligo circled higher, baiting each other. Diligo roared, *"Putus odium, putus vox."* The pain, the hatred, the suffering, the losses, the guilt emitted from Diligo. Like an angel, like an apparition, this force of pure power, of pure hatred, screeched through the air like a dragon made from fire. The triple consciousness guided itself away from Vandavor, and when it was ready, it went straight for Vandavor. Vandavor had no idea what to do. He had never seen anything like this. He flew as hard and as

335

fast as he could. The thing just kept coming. It collided with Vandavor, who rolled through the air, a ball of wings and fire; plummeted into the tree line of the forest; and crashed into the ground.

Diligo circled the area looking for Vandavor. Below, in shallow, blood-dripping, human breaths, the Vandavor had spoken the incantation *velieris mihi* and blended into the foliage of the forest floor. He closed his eyes. He called on all the strength he had left and tried to heal himself, but he did not have enough power remaining to heal completely.

Meanwhile, Limath had left the battle for the city in a desperate search for Vandavor. It took some time, but eventually he saw through the camouflage Vandavor had put up. He moved closer to Vandavor. Vandavor, not quite with his senses, moved to strike. Limath put his hand up and said, "It's okay, it's okay. I am here to help. Easy, friend."

Limath tried to heal Vandavor, but to little avail, and slowly and deliberately the two walked for safety and then for the gate back to Vandavor's reality. In the quiet far away, the roar of the city battle seemed like a silent whisper in a church. The gate was still days away.

Diligo started to fall to the ground, but quickly recovered. The fire dragon had taken a lot out of Akea. Argonath had used up everything to control its form. Unsteady, they travelled back to the cave. Akea was dying; he had left his body for far too long. Diligo struggled into the cave entrance. There was a flash of orange and blue, and Akea's body heaved as the life force went back to its proper home. Blood trickled down from his eyes; he had stopped breathing.

As Argonath bent over Akea, she looked up to see Fate and Life at the mouth of the cave. Fate was draped in a black, bedraggled, long, thin, almost threadbare cloak. Life wore a light flowery dress. Argonath growled at the old man. Fate looked extremely worried.

"Please let us help," Fate said to Argonath.

"Who are you? How did you get in here?" Argonath replied.

"I am Fate, and this is my daughter Life. But we must hurry," said Fate anxiously.

"Life, dear, please do all that you can," said Fate.

As Fate paced up and down in the cave, Life poured herself into Akea. After several minutes, he suddenly gasped for air and started coughing. Life stroked his head and said ancient verses.

Argonath, exhausted as she was, crawled towards him and curled herself around him. He was still on the brink of death, and so was she.

"You should not have attempted the meld, but I am glad you did," Fate said to Argonath.

"You have saved us. Thank you."

"I have one more request; Akea is not to know that we were here. With your permission, I will wipe your memory," said Fate.

Argonath nodded in agreement. Her eyes closed and she drifted into sleep. Fate wiped her memory and he and Life disappeared.

Akea awoke to an empty cave. A small fire kept the space warm.

Soon Argonath returned with a deer. She ate its guts and then changed to human form and as Amanda organised the rest of the deer on a spit over the fire.

As Akea lay on the floor and smelled the aroma of roasting meat, he realised that it had been days since he had last eaten anything.

"Akea, my love," Amanda said, kneeling next to him and stroking his face, "We will eat, and then we will go to the gate and to the second reality. Amalthea will be there waiting for us. I have everything organised. Just eat."

"We can't, not yet. We have to finish this. Can we go to the rebel base and see what we can do?" Akea said in an exhausted voice.

"My love, I don't think they deserve our help. I will not help them. They insulted me!" Amanda said.

"Then I'll go and fight on my own," Akea replied, unperturbed.

"You can't, you will lose control. If you're determined, then I will come, but I will not fight," Amanda said. She stroked Akea's face.

Chapter 26: The City

Vaxihimler had put Morguhis in command of a group of men with orders to recapture the Watchmen's headquarters, and after the north gate had been breached they had made their way to Threadneedle Street. The rebels fought hard early on in the battle, and Morguhis felt the tide turning against his men. After two hours of fighting, the rebels still fought with ferocity and vigour. Morguhis's men could not withstand the continued onslaught, and after another hour of fighting fifteen of them had been dispatched with relative ease.

As the men retreated, Morguhis fell behind and then ran off another way, trying to escape from this new nightmare. He might be a sadist, but he did not have a death wish. Now he was on his own, in the city. The fighting carried on all around him. Morguhis promised himself that Vaxihimler was going to pay for this. Suddenly he heard a shout, and looked up to see a group of rebels pounding his way. He ran back down the street the way he had come, chased by fifteen rebels, and came to a stop a few feet from Akea, who stood in the middle of the road. Akea looked at the man in front of him. He saw a weasel of a man. His eyes darted this way and that, and he did not have the guts to stand up straight. For some reason, Akea knew this man, or at least had met him before; it was his aura or something. Akea didn't care about etiquette. He looked into the man's mind, and suddenly he saw the horrors of the torture chamber and felt the man laughing as he worked over a victim. Akea exclaimed, "You're—you're the watch leader."

Derisive smiles broke out on both men's faces. Akea took a step back. The rebels moved in like a pack of wolves watching a bleating deer. Years of the

Watchmen's torture and oppression met with the city's retribution in the form of fifteen men. They walked forward and started to take their revenge. They dropped their weapons and pulled their knives. Morguhis cowered as four men pinned him to the road. After ten minutes of vicious torture, Morguhis was blind and cut to shreds. Akea called to the mob to stop. They stepped back, and Morguhis crawled forwards, pleading and whimpering with pain.

Akea looked down at Morguhis, smiled and said, "You killed my mother." He pointed a finger to Morguhis's hands, then stopped as he noticed that Morguhis had fingers missing and his left leg had been broken. Changing his mind; he knelt down and whispered the healing words. Morguhis screamed in pain as the left leg healed and the missing fingers regenerated. Akea put a finger to Morguhis's knees; silver arrows broke through the kneecaps and blasted into the road. Morguhis desperately tried to move, but the pain was too much. He fell unconscious. Akea whispered to Morguhis, "Ah, no, you don't, I will give you life, but you will wish I had not." Then he turned to the rebels. "Gentlemen, do your worst. You have thirty minutes."

Elsewhere, the streets were alive with soldiers of the dark army. In the middle of the city a patrol of rebel guards moved through the streets house to house, looking for survivors and enemies, crouching against the walls, peering round corners. Sergeant Yansey, the leader, noticed a barricade up ahead. After three days of continuous and vicious fighting Yansey's men were tired and battle weary. A group of elves had blocked their rear.

"McGinnis, you take Zip and Para. Go back the way we came for two blocks, then turn left and then left again. You should come to the blockage from their right. When you are in place, click the radio. When I click back you will open fire; this will give a chance to move closer. When I click again, ceasefire and hide." This would cause a pincer movement.

Shortly the men were in place. A click came through on the radio. The sergeant clicked twice in response. Number two unit opened fire. The elves replied with arrows. There was a brief exchange. The rebels shot five elves, and the elves got Para in the shoulder. Then both units opened fire, wiping out the elves. Zip patched Para up, and they moved cautiously to the barrier, all the time looking for snipers.

*

Akea and Argonath flew to the rebel base. They walked through the heavily guarded entrance and down the corridors to the elders' chambers. The sense of impending doom was so tangible that Akea could almost taste it. The elders greeted them.

"We have come to help," Akea said a bit louder than usual, fighting a sense of hopelessness.

Amanda cut in, "I will make this clear so you understand. I will not help you directly. I am here to make sure the enemy—or you, for that matter—do not kill Akea. Your kind has insulted me. For that you will suffer my apathy."

"As you wish. However, there are people dying. If you wish to help indirectly, then I suggest that you take a radio. Go and find survivors. The city has destroyed itself. There are pockets of resistance still holding out. We have most of our men holed up in the ATD building. But we've got to regroup." Iral spoke crossly; Amanda was right.

*

341

Yansey's team moved on. Burnt out and bullet-ridden cars served as good hiding places. The glass from broken windows filled the streets. Para was weak from the loss of blood and his wounds. They had stopped to rest for a while, crouched behind an abandoned vehicle, when a mixed group of Tmedar's dwarfs and Jroed's men turned into the street, marching down the middle of the road as if the war was won and they owned the streets.

Unusual fighting comrades, the dwarfs and men had now been through three days of battle together and won each other's respect. They wandered through the streets ribbing each other about their respective heights. Yansey had heard them from way off. Now he chanced a look. He and his men were badly outnumbered. One of the dwarfs spotted his head peaking out from behind the derelict car, and the chatter went silent. Yansey ordered his men to split up, warning them to conserve their ammo. Zip and Para moved to another car. McGinnis got on the radio and called for help. A bullet sailed past McGinnis's head. McGinnis returned fire. One of the enemy threw a grenade at the car Zip and Para were hiding behind. The force blew the car apart, and heavy pieces of it landed on Zip. Shrapnel ripped through Para. They lay dead on the ground. McGinnis screamed on the radio for help.

*

At the rebel base Akea and Argonath were in the entrance hangar, getting ready to go look for survivors, when a young lieutenant ran in. "Stop, stop, wait," he said, panting. "There is a group pinned down. Please, can you get them out, now?"

Akea and Argonath nodded. The lieutenant handed them a slip of paper with the location, and they took to the skies.

Argonath raced Akea to the city and remained circling in the air as he landed next to Yansey and changed to human form. He arrived just ahead of Nessa and a group of elves. Nessa smiled. She noticed Yansey behind the car and felt him with her mind. She grabbed his mind and squeezed. Yansey bent over, holding his head with both hands. His screams were deafening. Akea leapt forward and shot at Nessa. She evaded his fire with lightning speed, but let go of Yansey, who now lay on the ground unconscious. Akea put out a shield around himself, Yansey and McGinnis. Nessa shot an arrow at Akea. It penetrated the shield and hit him in the shoulder. Nessa laughed; she was enjoying, finally, a worthy foe.

Akea retaliated, hundreds of small silver arrows shooting out of his fingers and glinting in the sun as they streaked silently towards the enemy, the cars in between rippling as the arrows broke through their steel hulks and shattered their windows. The dwarfs and men ducked out of the way as fast as they could, but there was nowhere to hide. The darkness behind Akea's eyes smiled as he heard the screams of the dying.

The autumn air shimmered in the heat haze. The air seemed drier here, thought Nessa. If the she had not been such an evil bitch, she would have missed the green glens of home. Akea had moved away from Yansey and now stood alone behind a wrecked car. There was a glint in his eye, an evil something; an observer would have to look twice, but it was there. In the air, Argonath was worried—extremely worried. She had felt something lurking in the back of Akea's mind; she knew she had to stop him or control him. The fury that he now released was unfathomable; he reached out with his mind and crushed all those in his path. The wave of energy rolled over the enemy like the energy from an atom bomb rolled up into a small ribbon, destroying everything in its wake, a wave of instant death. The wave atomised most of the enemy. Argonath held on for all she was worth, and her flight path wavered. The blue hue around Akea was bright as the sun and deep as the ocean. Only Nessa survived, shielded by her own sheer malice. Her badly burned body crawled on the ground. Her hair was gone, her face unrecognisable. Her body shook, and she laboured to breathe. Argonath flew down, landed on Nessa, bit off her head, and then spat it to the ground with a triumphant roar.

A light blue whirlwind formed around Akea, and a dragon stood in his place. He picked up the still unconscious Yansey softly in his claws and showed McGinnis how to climb onto Argonath. The two dragons and their human cargo took off and headed for the ATD building. Arriving, they landed on the roof. The upper floors were occupied, commandeered by the rebel army. A makeshift hospital had been established on the twentieth floor. The rebels came running to meet them and took the injured Yansey away.

It was over almost as soon as it had begun. The battle was a stalemate; both sides had lost great numbers and could fight no longer. The rebels retreated to the financial district, while the invading army moved to the southwest.

Chapter 27: The Dead Remembered

In the months that followed the rebels built a wall in the northern part of the city, running from west to east and barricading the dark army from the rest of the city. During its construction the dark army sent hunting raids and skirmishes, but the wall went up, at the cost of hundreds of men's lives. When it was completed people who had fled to other cities and countries started to return to the city and nurse the civilisation back to health.

The Patrician's palace had been taken over by the rebels, and they had declared the city as the new capital and the seat of government for Ordeania. Limath had apparently seen the writing on the wall, as he had not turned up back in Mevelin. Perhaps he waited a future chance when he could return from the second reality and re-establish his sovereignty in Ordeania, or perhaps he saw new opportunities in other realities with Vandavor at his side. One or two of the more sympathetic surrounding countries jumped to acknowledge the rebel government as legitimate, and as time went on more countries followed suit.

Today, a memorial service was being held for all those who had died. A search for Pablo's body, which had disappeared after it had been hung in the square, had ended in vain. All the people of the city stood or sat on the sloping greens of one of the palace's parks, facing the veiled memorial sculpture. Important dignitaries from other countries had been welcomed and sat at the front. Akea, Prometheus, Amalthea, Bavlin and Amanda sat in the front row as guests of honour. Akea sat on the open green, with the autumn sun on his back, crying openly as a solemn figure read out the names of those who died. A sharp spear of pain pierced them all when the names of Cruz, Juween and Pablo were read out. Prometheus sat in a chair staring into the middle distance, tears rolling down his face.

A great fanfare called out, a lament and testament to the fallen, and the veil was pulled from the statue. The bronze shone in the midday sun that streamed down from a clear blue sky and revealed a baying dragon sitting on a large marble plinth. A hammer and scroll were pinned under its left paw, while cupped openly in its right paw, in the air, sat a small bronze dove. Its eyes looked to the city as though looking for the enemy, the demons within.

One of the elders led the service. He spoke about freedom and its cost, the need for respect of every person, neighbour, country, race, creed and religion. This was a sign that the peoples of Ordinea were free to worship whatever god they pleased. The press was there commentating on the speech. The memorial service was watched by the world; in many sitting rooms of ordinary people, silent tears rolled down their captured faces. The elder went on to say that the rebel army would impose martial law for three months, until a suitable police force had been commissioned, and that the elders would hold an interim government for one year until the country was ready for democratic elections to be held. Claps and cheers erupted as the tear-stained faces of the people roared with agreement. A national day of celebration was called for.

When the service had ended, Akea got up to leave, Amanda by his side, and the others followed him. He was too sad, too stricken by grief to celebrate.

Prometheus moved close to the couple. "I understand that you two are off to another reality. With your permission, I think I would like to join you."

"Bunny, you can stay with me," said Amalthea.

"Amalthea, why do you call him Bunny?" Amanda queried.

"Because he's always hopping between realities, never in one place for more than a month. That's why he's such a devil to find."

Akea was about to say something, but Amanda cut in, "We would love you to come. I will carry you on my back if you wish."

The four wandered off to a secluded spot. To them it all seemed such a distant din, a party in another world; they felt that they did not belong.

Akea and Amanda said those precious words, and they all flew to the gate.

Chapter 28: Forest Green, Magic Plenty

Prometheus spoke the words *patefacio mihi,
patefacio mihi* to the stones. The stones shuddered and
moved into place, and a soft light hung around the flat
dais. . . .

On the other side of the gate, Akea and Argonath
took Prometheus and Amalthea to Amalthea's house.
A small cottage with large windows, it stood in a
meadow. A stream flowed behind it. The sun showed
it was three in the afternoon. Amalthea opened the
front door and sighed. Akea and Argonath changed
into human form and entered the house.

Inside, the house was cold and smelled musty as
though no one had lived there for a while. A thin layer
of dust covered everything. They put their cloaks on
the coat rack in the hallway. Amalthea motioned them
to take their boots off and join him in the sitting room.
The sitting room was large. Dustsheets covered the
furniture.

"Can we help? We will have this place done in no
time," said Akea.

"Not a bad idea. I will see what food I can find,"
replied Amalthea.

Akea started to lift the dustsheets and coughed
because of the dust. Amanda smirked and coughed
herself. Amalthea came back in with some old rags
and bee's wax.

"Bloody hell old bean, do we look like the
chambermaids," said Prometheus as he wiped the
pictures on the wall with a cleaning enchantment.

"I thought since you were cleaning you could do a
proper job," said Amalthea. Amanda grabbed the rags
and wax and set to work on the bookshelves and
coffee table. She removed the numerous books and
polished underneath. The overall design of the

wooden floor looked random, but after a while the perceptive observer could work out that it reflected the ecology of the forest outside, with groups of tree families, from the pines near the mountains, to the oaks and beeches in the dense part of the forest, down to the elms near the river Tiber. Akea used a mop to clear the dust off and helped Amanda to polish it to its former glory. Prometheus went into Amalthea's bedroom and tried up.

Finally, the work done, everyone collapsed into a chair or sofa. The walls boasted paintings and pictures, which, Amalthea explained, he had drawn for the most part. Akea was impressed by the quality of the art and said as much.

Amalthea left the room and came back in shortly with a tray of cured meats, cheeses and beer. "I am afraid all I have is cured meats and cheese and beer—got plenty of that," said Amalthea.

"Old bean, what are your plans? How long you plan to stay here?" Prometheus asked Akea.

"If it is okay with Amalthea, we wish to remain for a few days, then go and look for a new home. I must seek out my brothers and explain," Argonath said.

"Stay as long as you like," said Amalthea. "Ah, yes—your brothers. Erm . . . that could be tricky. But nevertheless, it must be done."

They sat around in the sitting room, and when evening approached lit a fire. For the most part, they sat in silence. All felt oddly uncomfortable. They had spent so much time thinking about the war and little else. They might share each other's knowledge, but they had no idea of what the others were really were like. War had bonded them together, yet in a way they were still strangers.

Amalthea ventured first.

"I know some good spots in the mountains. If you

wish, I will show them to you."

Prometheus, who was the most sullen of the group, observed, "Odd isn't it, but I don't really know you. Apart from Amalthea of course."

"Bunny is right. How do we get around this?" said Amalthea.

Akea stood, faced Amalthea and extended his hand. "My name is Akea, and this beautiful creature is Argonath or Amanda, depending on her mood."

Amanda spoke. "This is silly. Of course we know each other. We have fought with and for each other. The best way get past the post-war blues is to get very drunk, sing songs, and tell jokes. We have seen the worst of times, and now is the best of times."

Amalthea broke out the beer, and they sang old songs. Amanda sang dragon chants, teaching Akea her favourites. Amalthea and Prometheus sang a rude duet about a man who had a peculiar appendage. They created a new song about their adventures.

They toasted Juween, Pablo, Cruz and all those who had died in the fight for freedom.

"What will you do now, Prometheus?" Akea asked.

"I am going to visit some old friends and perhaps go to the city and see what I can do, old bean. What about you, Amalthea?"

"Oh, I don't know. I would like to write a book about our adventures, but I would also like to accompany you, Bunny."

"Do both, old bean," said Prometheus.

"I might just do that, Bunny, I might just do that."

Later, Akea and Argonath went outside and cuddled in a nook made by a nearby tree. The night was cool, but not cold. The stars were out. Akea sighed happily and fell asleep; his head nestled against Argonath's warm belly. They awoke to the sound of bird song announcing the new day, and the early-morning sun slowly rising in the blue sky. Dew fell lazily off the greenest of grass. The smell of stir-fried cured meats and fresh herbs and vegetables and coffee wafted through an open window. Akea went into the house for some breakfast while Argonath went hunting. After breakfast Akea and Argonath took to the sky. Amalthea joined them, sitting on Akea's back. He pointed out the mountains and the best places for a dragon's cave, but the caves were either too small or had no water, or were not regal enough or accessible by foot. Argonath knew what she was looking for.

Thus the days slowly passed. They spent weeks searching the mountains and looking in caves. But Argonath was not satisfied until they spotted a cave on a small outcrop near the top of the west mountain. There was a slight shelf at the entrance just big enough to land on. They entered. The tunnel was about thirty feet in diameter and led slightly down for about a hundred and fifty feet into a cavern. The main cavern was huge, bigger than Argonath's original cave. To one side were three smaller caves. It smelt old and musty, and slightly damp. A good fire and some magic would soon put that right. At the back was a perfectly formed small pool, fed by a spring. Sunlight drifted lazily through the air, showing the dust as twinkling gems floating in the breeze. Argonath sniffed the air. There had not been a dragon here for fifty years or more. The main cavern floor was flat and smooth. Unfortunately there was no gold in sight. If this had indeed been a dragon's cave, looters must have carted off the gold years ago.

"My love, this is the place. This is where I want my family," Argonath said.

"Yes, but it seems so sparse."

Amalthea, feeling like he was invading a private moment, began to wander back out into the daylight, when Akea called to him.

"Do you have any idea how we can get Argonath's gold back here?"

"Mmm . . . if we went to the city and found a large tent or marquee, we could put most of the gold on it. I could then make it as light as a feather, and you could carry it back. But of course we may not be able to bring all of it in one haul; we'll see."

"*I do not want to linger there. If we can't bring it back in one trip, I will divide it accordingly, perhaps give some of it to the city as a benevolent fund,*" Argonath thought. "*Akea please get Prometheus, and explain what we want to do. See if he will help.*"

"Where is Akea going?" Amalthea asked.

"Oh, sorry—he went to get Prometheus."

An hour later Akea returned with Prometheus on his back.

The old magician climbed down, looking slightly disturbed. "I don't care how many times I do it, I just can't get used to flying by dragon. Sorry, Akea," he said. He turned to the others. "I was having a nice midmorning snooze, when Akea came bombing out of the sky saying something about the perfect place and the need for gold. Sorry, I was a bit drowsy. I guess we are off to the city then."

"You can fly on me, if you like," said Argonath.

"Would you mind, my dear? Sorry, Akea, she has a gentler hand."

They flew over the lakes, mountains and forests to the gate into the first reality. Amalthea asked Prometheus to do the honours. As they stepped up to the gate, Amalthea gave a shudder; he disliked going through the gate. He could never get used to the odd sensation. Once on the other side, they flew to the city. As they passed the border, people stopped and looked. They landed outside of the palace. People gathered to see them. General Bavlin heard the news and came running out to greet them.

"Welcome, welcome. What an unexpected surprise," the general said.

They chatted for a while about the city's healing and the change of government.

Finally Prometheus asked, "Would you mind if we could have a couple of large tents or marquees?"

"Certainly. I'll go and see what I can find," said Bavlin. "In the meantime, would you like something to drink?"

He called an aide and told him to find a marquee double-quick. Then he invited them into the palace. All the stained glass had been removed and plain glass put in its place. The throne had been covered with a dustsheet. The decor had been changed to light, airy colours. All of Vaxihimler's stuff had been locked away in a vault, until a qualified magician could go through it.

"Ah, old bean, I think I can help there. I will be visiting again soon. I will look at it for you and disarm any—any booby traps," said Prometheus.

"Nalik's court martial will be held next week. I urge you to be there, but I will understand if you don't come," said Bavlin.

"We will not be there, but we will of course trust that you will give a fair trial, ending in a sudden death," said Amanda.

They were sitting in the office drinking coffee when the aide knocked on the door, entered and explained that there was a truck outside with two marquees in it. They wandered outside, and Amalthea levitated the marquees out. A crowd gathered to watch. They all gasped when Akea and Amanda went from human to dragon. Prometheus and Amalthea climbed on board. They took to the sky with the

353

marquees in their front claws.

They got to the cave and entered. Argonath felt sad; it had been her home for so many years. Akea moved towards her and gave her a comforting nudge with his muzzle. They laid one of the marquees out flat on the floor like a large blanket and started to pile the gold on it. Amalthea saw to it that it didn't weigh much. It took them several hours to fill the first marquee. When it was full, Akea tied up the four corners to form a bundle. They had managed to get two-thirds of the gold in. The remainder went into the second marquee. Argonath asked Akea to take the smaller bundle and Amalthea to Bavlin and explain that it was for the families of the fallen. It should be shared out accordingly. She would leave Prometheus at Amalthea's cottage and take the other bundle to the new cave.

In the new cave, Argonath laid the gold on the floor and tried to make a nest. She sighed; she wished she had not given away so much. She missed her lavish bed and did not enjoy the fact that she had gone from a nice large pile to a smaller one.

In the evening Akea returned from the city, having dropped Amalthea off on the way home. He explained that Bavlin had accepted the gift gracefully, but refused to take it all. After much debate, Amalthea had stepped in and said to divide it in half. Akea now unwrapped the remains and added it to the pile. Ah, that's a bit better, Argonath thought.

The two dragons curled up together. Although Akea wanted to remember what it was like to be human, he was finding that more and more he preferred his dragon form.

A few weeks had passed, and Akea and Argonath were out hunting. They were in a meadow eating a deer, when a dark cloud appeared on the horizon.

Argonath looked up and sniffed. Oh well, it was going to happen at some point, she thought.

The cloud moved closer, and soon four large, dark blue dragons could be discerned flying towards them. The creatures circled above them and then landed nearby. Akea noticed how alike they were and how similar Argonath was to them, with their bright orange eyes, long slender tails and four different shades of dark blue-grey scales shimmering in the daylight. They were much bigger than Argonath; the smallest was a good forty feet long, and the largest was sixty feet long. Each boasted two horns on his head.

She nodded and in their tongue greeted each; fortunately Argonath had been wise enough to teach Akea how to pronounce her mother tongue.

"*Dearest, please don't speak to them until I give the all clear. Dragons are noble creatures bound to etiquette and unfortunately easily offended, especially by a human,*" thought Argonath to Akea.

"So the rumours are true. You have returned, and you have found a mate. Well done," said the eldest, Adrigonidd, the lord of the dragon family.

"Yes, I have returned, and I am with eggs," Argonath replied.

"Tell me, what is your name, so I can welcome you into our family?" inquired Adrigonidd of Akea.

Luceahad, second in command, butted in, "I don't recognise your markings. Who is your clan?"

"His name is Akea. He is—he is—"

"He's not an orphan, is he? Does he have much gold?" interrupted Luceahad.

"Please, if you let me finish, I will tell you. But remember I am with eggs. So please keep your temper," said Argonath, annoyed now. "He is a human magician. Through fate and misadventure we met. I—I fell in love with his mind. There, I said it."

This declaration did not sit well with Argonath's brothers. Dragons are about as xenophobic as a fascist on a bad day. As the last words fell out of Argonath's mouth, Adrigonidd growled and went for her. Akea jumped in between them and growled back at Adrigonidd.

"Don't you dare touch her. I don't care who you are—you will not harm her," warned Akea.

As the two glared at each other a lone dragon came wandering through the meadow as though he had not seen a thing. He was long and black in colour, with bright yellow eyes. His black scales shone in the sun, and his long slender tail swished behind him as he walked. It was unusual for a dragon to walk for more than a few hundred metres; this was a sign of diplomacy and nonaggression. Stopping in front of Adrigonidd and Akea, he said politely, "Excuse me, kind sirs. Please allow me to be of assistance." Fate spoke the dragon mother tongue, Draconian, an ancient and powerful language.

"Who are you, dragon?" said Adrigonidd.

"I think you'll find the question is what, not whom," said Fate. He changed back to his usual form. His cloak gently blew in the breeze, and the sun warmed his ancient bones.

"Well, *what* are you then, damn it?"

"I am an anamorphic personification known as Fate."

"So?" said Adrigonidd.

"It was I who destined these two together. If you have an argument, then it is with me."

The dragons looked at each other, and then Adrigonidd said to Akea, "If you are truly worthy of my sister's love, then you must fight me in the sky. Not to the death—the first one to submit loses. I don't want to kill my sister by killing you."

"Am I allowed to use magic?"

"If you must, since you are human and have to resort to that kind of thing, yes, you may."

"Then I accept. Shall we?" said Akea to the eldest.

Argonath interrupted. "What are the stakes?"

"If he loses, then you are banished from this reality, and shall never return. If I lose, then you can stay, and we'll take it from there."

"Please, for my sake, no fire," said Argonath, a worried look on her face.

Adrigonidd looked stunned. He had not expected her to agree. But honour was at stake.

"Adrigonidd, I would careful be with him. He is a fantastic flier and a powerful magician," warned Fate.

The two combatants took off. Argonath closed her eyes, trying desperately to control Akea.

Troennor, the youngest of Argonath's brothers, mistaking her expression, said, "Afraid that Adrigonidd is going to hurt your human lover?"

"No, I'm afraid of what Akea is going to do," she retorted.

Akea and Adrigonidd chased each other over the woods, across the lakes and along the contours of the mountains. They came in close and scratched and clawed at each other. They latched onto each other, and Adrigonidd's long talons on his rear claws and on the elbows of his wings clawed Akea's underbelly. Long gashing wounds appeared on Akea's underbelly. Akea said the Latin for *heal*, and the gashes were gone. Adrigonidd clawed at Akea's wings, and again as soon as the gashes appeared they were gone. Adrigonidd was astonished. Down on the ground Argonath concentrated hard; she didn't want to see either of them killed. It would be devastating if Adrigonidd were killed. But death awaited her if Akea died. She needed to control him. Akea broke loose and climbed higher. Adrigonidd was right behind him, trying to bite Akea's wings and tail. Rips and tears on the wings appeared and instantly disappeared.

Adrigonidd thought to himself, No one should have that much power. He caught Akea by the tail and bit hard, and Akea sent electric shocks down his tail. Adrigonidd let go, his head ringing with the shock. Akea climbed higher and higher and then swooped down and clawed at Adrigonidd's wings. Adrigonidd rolled away and leapt onto him. Still climbing, they fought hard. Four miles from the ground, Akea started to feel the air getting thin, and his muscles ached. He said the Latin and removed the ice from his wings. Adrigonidd didn't know how to do this, but held on out of sheer spite. Then it happened: Adrigonidd breathed fire in Akea's face.

"No!" screamed Argonath.

Akea, blinded by the fire, felt with his mind's eye where his foe was. At the zenith Akea took a deep breath. *'Sanus offensus,"* he gently whispered. A roar of clear blue shock waves emanated from him in ever-increasing concentric circles, stunning Adrigonidd. Unconscious, Adrigonidd started to fall to the ground. Akea hung in the air and tried to regain his sight, but it was no use. He felt Adrigonidd falling fast and arced down toward the falling dragon in a large curve. He gained as much speed as he could, his wings swept back, his mind on the single target. *Boom!* The sonic wave reverberated over the fields and the mountains and caused a small avalanche on one mountainside. A hundred and fifty yards from the ground Akea clamped onto Adrigonidd and lifted him up, but then fell back downward. He hadn't realised how heavy Adrigonidd was. He concentrated; he had to pull up, or they were going to die. Recalling the incantation that Amalthea had used to lift the gold, he uttered it, and the other dragon became lighter. Akea heaved and circled round towards the onlookers to scrub off some speed. Ten yards from the ground he let go of Adrigonidd, who thudded onto the ground and bounced along until he stopped.

Akea miscalculated his own landing, and he hit the ground with a terrible force, *crack!* Argonath was there in an instant. He had broken his right legs and four ribs.

He breathed heavily and said, "You could have let me have some more power."

"I had to hold you back, Akea, I didn't want you to kill him," Argonath sobbed.

"Capiam vestri poena, planto vos universus, capiam vestri poena, planto vos universus," said Akea in a low, heavy voice.

"Ah!" he screamed, as the bones mended themselves.

"Please steady me, while I try to repair my sight," he said to Argonath.

"Tribuo tergum os," he whispered.

Smoke and dust rose from Akea's eyelids. He unsteadily got to his feet and shook his head. His body ached. Akea walked gingerly over to Adrigonidd, who looked badly hurt. He had long cuts on his underbelly, and his front leg stuck out at an odd angle. He was out cold.

Fate said aloud, to no one in particular, "You got to admit it, the boy's got style. The right dragon in the right place can make all the difference," and disappeared.

Akea leant over Adrigonidd and whispered phrases in Latin. The bones cracked and clicked into place, and slowly and wearily, the dragon opened his eyes. He growled and said, "Remind me not to pick a fight with you again."

Troennor excitedly recounted to Adrigonidd every detail, every humiliating detail. How Akea stunned him, shot him down and then caught him. How the air had rung when he hit the sound barrier. How he had fallen to the ground and rolled badly. How Akea had crashed into the ground and gotten up.

Adrigonidd shook his head and looked at Akea. "I am not happy about this, but since you have my sister's heart, and beat me in a fair fight, you may stay. I will take my leave of you now." Akea started to reply, but Argonath nudged him to be quiet.

Chapter 29: Home

Forests filled the horizon; the lofty, snow-capped mountains in the distance sat like a brooding hen over her chicks. Akea and Argonath raced through the sky, looking for food. In a glen they saw a deer grazing near a derelict house. Argonath swooped down and grabbed the creature. Akea landed near the house.

When Argonath landed next to him and dropped the dead animal, Akea was staring at the house like he had seen a ghost.

"What's the matter, my love?" said Argonath.

"I know this place," said Akea.

The house stood in a glen near the trees of the forest. With a slight creak, the remains of the door swung gently in the breeze. Tattered curtains in the broken windows fluttered like ghost hands waving. Akea slowly approached the house, and suddenly he fell on the ground in a faint.

Argonath growled and changed to Amanda. She knelt down, cradled his head in her lap and felt into his mind. . . .

They both were standing in front of the house, but it was different. The door had not been broken. A long trail of smoke drifted from the chimney. Voices came from the far end of the glen. A baby cried from inside the house. Akea moved to go in, but Amanda stopped him. This was a vision, she told him, and they could only observe. They stood and watched, and were startled to see a younger Vaxihimler and Cassandra wandering through the glen. The Patrician had pulled a few strings for this date; he had convinced Prometheus that he wanted to come here for a romantic interlude. Prometheus had seen no harm in it and agreed, allowing them through the gate. Cassandra giggled with delight as they wandered through the most beautiful forest and glens she had ever seen. They came across the house and heard the baby crying, but the Patrician stopped Cassandra from going in.

The Patrician ventured towards the house and opened the door. He was immediately confronted with four large, dead wolves. A groan came from one of the rooms, and the sounds of a baby crying. The Patrician went outside and called Cassandra in.

"It's not a pretty sight, I am afraid; it looks like a pack of wolves tried to attack the household. There is a severely wounded man, and I can hear a baby crying. Please attend to him. I will look for the baby."

Slowly the Patrician moved from room to room. The wolves had all but destroyed everything. A picture of horror met him as he entered the master bedroom. A mutilated woman lay on the bed. The baby's cries came from the bottom drawer of the dresser. There were claw and tooth marks on the drawer, but the wolves had not been able to open it. The Patrician opened the drawer and pulled the baby out. He called to Cassandra, "Don't come in here," but it was too late. She screamed when she saw the poor dead woman. . . .

The house slowly faded away, and Akea and Amanda were standing in the Patrician's office. It was late at night. The Patrician was reading a book. His face went white as he read. . . . The vision faded again, and they stood in the same office, but it was daylight, and Cassandra stood before the Patrician.

"My dear, how are you?" he greeted her, and kissed her on the cheek.

"I am fine, apart from the nightmares. I visited the man this morning. He says his name is Juween, but he doesn't remember much else. And the baby we named Akea is okay."

"My dear, I need you to do me a . . . favour. I know you have taken to the child. How would you like to adopt him? You will be paid handsomely, and want for nothing."

"What about Juween?" said Cassandra.

"I am afraid, dear, that his wounds have overcome him. He died late this afternoon," the Patrician lied. "Poor thing, alone in the world—he is very special, and may have magic in him. But due to our laws it would unwise for him to use them. It must remain a secret from him, to keep him safe. . . ."

The vision cut again. Akea and Amanda were now in a busy ward, with bright lights and a clean smell. A young Juween sat up in bed.

"Hi, how are you doing? Do you remember much?" the Patrician asked.

"I'm okay, but I can't remember a damn thing," said Juween.

"I am just glad we found you when we did. But I am afraid I have some bad news," said the Patrician. He gazed sympathetically at the young man. "Your wife and the baby didn't make it."

Juween cried his heart out, too involved in his grief to notice the Patrician say a few words. Suddenly he stopped crying.

"Sorry about that—I don't know why I was crying," Juween said in an embarrassed voice. He had no recollection of the last few days.

"That's okay. Let me tell you how you come to be here," said the Patrician. "A girl and I were walking through the forest and found you had been attacked by an animal. . . ."

The vision faded.

Akea opened his eyes and looked up to see Amanda looking softly down at him. She cradled him as he fought with mixed emotions, the death of

Juween and the relief and freedom of the truth. . . .

The cool, darkened room was filled with books, many books. An old man sat huddled over a large desk in his office. Across from him, Death sat in the old, red leather chair. Fate smiled a curious smile. "Now you know the truth."

*

It had been three months since the fight for honour with Adrigonidd. Akea and Argonath were happy, the happiest they had ever been. They made a nest for the impending newborn. They chased each other over the mountains and fields. Akea taught Amanda how to fish and hunted daily. He tilled a small garden in the valley below. For the most part, Akea retained his dragon form, but he missed being human sometimes, a thing Amanda understood better than anyone did.

Tonight they had both taken on human form. This night was going to be a special night, just Akea and Amanda. Akea had made a stone fire pit for spit-roasting hogs and small deer, and a small deer was gently roasting on the fire. The smell emitted made Akea's mouth water. Potatoes gently baked in the embers.

There was a sound of soft landing and a clanging noise, and the sound of general greeting used when one dragon asks permission to enter another dragon's cave. Amanda put down the vegetable that she was peeling and went into the entryway to see who it was. Adrigonidd stood in the entrance and growled.

"Who are you? Has he fallen for a human woman? Wait until I get my claws on him. I will kill him."

"Don't you dare talk about my husband in that manner! And how dare you address me in that tone. Don't you know I am with egg?"

Adrigonidd looked at Amanda intently. "Sister?"

"Yes, brother, it is me," she said mildly, and spoke the incantation, and in a few moments Argonath stood before Adrigonidd, growling gently and nudging him in the neck. Adrigonidd looked utterly bewildered.

"Akea and I take turns changing, since neither one of us can last in the other form indefinitely, and this was Akea's night to be human."

Akea came to the entrance and bowed to Adrigonidd, to show respect and no hard feelings.

"Sir, I hope that I have not offended you in any way. In hindsight, we should have warned you. But we figured you might not want to see us. However, since you are here, we have plenty of food, both cooked and uncooked. We caught two deer this very morning. Please join us for dinner," said Akea.

"I shall stay for some food," the dragon replied.

Adrigonidd entered the cave and sniffed. The cave smelled slightly human, and the smell of cooking meat was off-putting. He couldn't fathom the need to burn decent food. Amanda and Akea sat on the floor near the fire and finished cooking. When it was time to eat, Akea presented a whole clean deer to Adrigonidd. He nodded graciously. Akea broke out some wine. They sat talking about this and that for a while. Finally, Adrigonidd broke the small talk.

"As to my visit, I brought some of my gold as a present, to welcome you into our clan. You are a good fighter, but that is not the reason. I have watched you for some time now, and have come to realise that you really love her. The story of your adventures has come to my ears by way of Prometheus, whom I consider a friend. You are as honourable as a dragon, Akea. It is with a glad heart that I say, welcome, brother."

Akea smiled. A tear rolled down his face.

Adrigonidd looked concerned. "Sister, I have offended him. I am not sure with humans. What does

365

this mean?"

Akea spoke softly, with a bright smile on his face. "Sir, you have not offended me, but the opposite. Finally I am home."

*

Argonath nudged Akea. It was time.

She had been broody for weeks. Akea had been expecting this, but suddenly he did not know what to do. He brought in firewood, moved the bed around and generally fussed. He tried to make Argonath comfortable, but only succeeded in irritating her. Akea paced up and down like all first-time fathers generally do. The fire roared; the cave was immensely hot.

"Dearest, please get some food and some firewood—oh, and some hot water. I want this to be perfect."

Akea paced to the mouth of the cave and back again twice.

Argonath said, "Just go."

Akea went to the ledge, stretched out his wings and took off.

Argonath screamed and roared as she laid four blue and orange eggs, one after the other. She hurried to put the eggs near the roaring fire and then gently sat on the clutch. When Akea came back he found Argonath sitting serenely on her clutch. She tilted up slightly to show the eggs to Akea, and his heart leapt. He moved his long neck and slowly, softly put his head on Argonath's flank. Then he moved up towards her head and whispered, "I love you."

*

The trial of Nalik was not a public one; it was held in a small court set in the back of the palace. At the front of the court was a large yew dais, where the judge sat. To the right and left were two doors. The judge walked into the court and strode to his chair. Nalik and his legal representatives sat on the right, in front of the judge, and the prosecution on the left. The press and public were not allowed — not that this trial hadn't made the public gossip. The judge called the court to order and read the charge of treason. The lawyers for the accused tried to argue that Nalik had made a genuine mistake during a state of war. The prosecution argued that as the Ordineans did not, in fact, have an air force and as the location of rebel base was not public knowledge, it would have been safe to assume that any incoming flying object might have been a dragon. The accused defended, and the prosecution fought back, implying that Nalik had not liked Argonath from the start and had acted with the full intent to hurt — nay, kill — Argonath.

Heated discussions ensued. The prosecution finished its final argument, and the defence motioned that Nalik had suffered a temporary state of insanity. The judge contemplated; he could not allow Nalik to be let off completely. Justice had to be done. He passed a sentence of gross misconduct.

Nalik was led away to the cells to serve the first day of a life sentence. The cells were dark and grubby, the cold hard bars exclaiming the pride of incarceration. On the second night of Nalik's new life, the guards made sure that Nalik had eaten a full meal. He lay on his cot in a deep, drug-induced sleep. There was a slight, almost silent creak as the door opened just enough to allow a black figure to gingerly step into the cell. The figure crept up to Nalik and put a pillow over the sleeping convict. In the moonlight there was a shimmer of cold, hard steel and a muffled scream. The metal of the knife shone blood red in the dim light.

The next day Bavlin received a short communiqué:
It is done, usual fee.

A year later the free city held its first democratic elections. Mr. Edward Erwin became the first prime minister in two generations. The party lasted three weeks. Newly appointed ambassadors went to the neighbouring countries to sort out new friends, help and trade.

*

Death entered the great hall. The grand staircase dominated the centre, surrounded by numerous doors. As Death walked down the passageway, the old clock ticked vociferously, *tick-tock, tick-tock*. His sandals clicked on the old marble mosaic. With a quick rap on the door, Death entered the study. The cool, darkened room was filled with books, many books. An old man sat huddled over a large desk.

Death coughed politely.

"Oh it's you," said Fate. "Sit down, son."

Death lowered himself into an old, red leather chair.

Fate rang a little bell, and Sibson came in with a silver tray bearing two cups, a silver teapot, and some milk and sugar. Death poured two cups. He picked up one, sipped, and sat back and crossed his bony legs, relaxing a little. The taste of the Earl Grey reminded him of years past. He put his fingers together under his chin.

Fate gave his son a curious smile. "The right man in the right place can make all the difference."

www.ingramcontent.com/pod-product-compliance
Lightning Source LLC
Chambersburg PA
CBHW020638030726

47498CB00002B/272